Capture the Moments

DIANE GREENWOOD MUIR

Cover Design Photography: Maxim M. Muir

ISBN-13: 978-1539067894
ISBN-10: 1539067890

CONTENTS

ACKNOWLEDGMENTS

The Bellingwood community continues to grow. One of the best places to meet new friends who also enjoy reading about these characters is on Facebook. Come spend time with us at facebook.com/pollygiller.

When I think about the number of people who are part of my life and who help me get from book to book, my heart fills, often so much that my eyes leak.

My beta readers are more than just readers. They edit, find continuity problems, point out unnecessary words / phrases / thoughts, catch strange grammar and are such a necessary part of my process. Without them, I'd be lost.

Thank you to these amazing people: Tracy Kesterson Simpson, Linda Watson, Alice Stewart, Fran Neff, Max Muir, Edna Fleming, Linda Baker and Nancy Quist. A special thank you to Judy Tew who reads and corrects my final edited copy. She gives me confidence I didn't realize I was missing.

My cover images are gorgeous photographs shot by my husband, Max Muir. They come together with the help of Rebecca Bauman, who not only sees how color and design should come together, but describes what she sees so I can make it happen.

Whenever I wonder if Bellingwood truly exists, I sit back and think about the wonderful people I encounter every day. In little and big ways, people are terrific. It's a true pleasure to be part of this community.

CHAPTER ONE

"Polly?" Heath sounded panic-stricken on the other end of the call.

"Good morning, Heath. What's up?"

Heath and his brother, Hayden, had left the apartment early, just like they did every morning. The Bell House was in no condition for them to live there yet, but they were working toward that goal.

"There's a problem. Somebody broke in."

Polly frowned. What in the world would someone want in an empty house? "How do you know?" she asked.

"You need to see this. Whoever it was just did our work for us."

"What do you mean?"

"The kitchen walls are destroyed. Hayden says they ripped out old copper pipe. It's a mess."

"I'll be right there. I'm going to make a couple of calls first, though. Any other damage?"

"They ripped up some of the kitchen floor, too."

"Damn. Okay. I'm heading out. Thanks." Polly swiped the call closed and knocked on Rebecca's bedroom door.

"Whaaa?" Rebecca asked sleepily.

"Hey honey, I'm heading over to the house. It looks like someone broke in and ripped up walls in the kitchen."

Rebecca rolled over. "Do I need to go?"

"No. You're fine. The dogs have already been outside and had breakfast. But you'll want to get up soon. Andrew and Kayla will be here."

"Yeah. Okay." Rebecca buried her face in the pillow and moaned when Han jumped up beside her.

The three kids were inseparable. After Rebecca had been kidnapped by Kayla's father, none of them felt like wandering through town by themselves, but when they were together, the three of them went everywhere. It bothered Polly that they didn't feel completely safe in Bellingwood. She knew the fear would subside as months passed, but small towns were where you were supposed to know everyone and people kept an eye out for each other. She gave her head a quick shake. And now someone had broken into her house.

Polly ran down the back steps to her truck and climbed in, then dialed Henry.

"Good morning, doll face," he said.

"Nope. That makes me sound like a mobster's girlfriend," Polly replied with a laugh. "Heath just called. Someone broke into the house and ripped out copper pipe. Do I call the police?"

"They what?"

"That's what Heath told me. The walls are destroyed. I'm on my way over there."

"Who would do that?" Henry asked. "And yes, call the police. We might as well get it on record." He huffed a chuckle. "At least we're in the middle of demolition. Whoever did it probably saved the boys a few hours of work."

"So it's not going to be terrible?"

"It's not great. It won't make Liam's job any easier, but he was planning to pull the copper out anyway. Too bad he won't be able to see the return on it."

"We must have someone in the neighborhood looking for quick cash," Polly said.

"Maybe. Who knows. Liam was going to start on that next week. I'll let him know what's going on."

Liam Hoffman, a local plumber, was a high school buddy of Henry's. He was ready to start, even though he moaned mightily at the mess in the basement. The old house hadn't had much work done on it since it was built, and of course nothing since the Springer family moved out.

Polly parked the truck and went in through the side door to find Heath and Hayden sweeping up lath and plaster.

"You were right," she said. "They did a number on these walls."

"At least the cupboards were already gone," Hayden said. "I keep telling Heath that whoever did this actually helped us."

She nodded in agreement. The boys would have soon ripped the walls out themselves. They'd worked through the other rooms on the main level while the kitchen had been slowly taken apart. The kitchen, small bathroom, and mudroom were the last intact rooms on the main floor. Once this was finished, new pipes and new electricity would be put into place. Polly could hardly wait to see a few rooms move closer to completion.

As clean as they tried to keep it, the inside of the house looked like a bomb had gone off. Nothing was left of the ceilings or walls. She'd hoped they could save some of the original interior, but it hadn't taken long for her to realize that wasn't possible.

"I'll call the police," Polly said. "Is there something else you can work on? It might be a while."

"We'll go over to the shop," Hayden said. "Mr. Sturtz is working on the boxes for the cabinets. He can use our help."

"I left room for you to get out." Polly nodded toward the door.

She followed them through the mudroom and out the side door to the steps, then sat down after taking her phone out.

"Bellingwood Police Department, how may I help you?"

"Mindy, is that you?" Polly asked.

"Sure is. Polly?"

"Yeah. Me. I need someone to stop by the house on Beech Street. It looks like we had a thief in here last night stealing the old copper pipe."

"You don't sound too upset."

Polly chuckled. "They did us a favor in the long run. We were ripping it out anyway, but it was a little unexpected."

"Are you going to have the house open during the celebration next week? I can't wait to see what you've done there."

Polly sighed. "No. The inside of the house is in terrible shape. The yard looks great and we'll have the tunnel open to the basement room, but that's it for now."

"Too bad. Will you give me a tour when you're finished?"

"You know I will," Polly said.

"It's probably going to be the Chief who shows up." Mindy chuckled. "When he heard your name, he came out to see what was going on."

"Sounds good." Polly shook her head as she hung up the phone.

She walked through the back yard, grateful for the work that Eliseo and his cohorts, Sam Gardner and Ralph Bedford, had done. It looked so different than the day Henry had given her the gazebo. Was that only a couple of months ago? Time passed so quickly.

The next thing Henry and the boys worked on was Rebecca's studio. They'd finished the walls in the underground rooms, then put a solid roof on the back room where the kegs and bottles had been stored so they could cover it with dirt and sod. Polly wasn't opposed to having a bunker. The room she'd fallen into, however, now sported a second story with a pretty stairway leading straight to the tunnel. Rebecca hadn't yet filled it up, but she'd chosen a pale lavender color for the walls. She and Polly were taking sewing classes at the quilt shop and the first thing she'd made were curtains for all of the windows.

Sonya Biederman was one of the most patient teachers Polly had ever met and they were having a blast. With the two of them interested in sewing, fabric was creeping into the house. Henry hadn't said much other than to make a comment about building cupboards in one of the upstairs rooms at the Bell House to hold what might soon become a problem. This was the first time Polly had ever focused on a handmade craft and she wondered why it had never happened before.

Polly's first projects were for Sal's new baby, Alexander. She'd sewn up a collection of burp cloths and wash cloths and now was working on a quilt. She couldn't believe that. Sonya encouraged her every week and it was coming together.

Sal's baby. Polly had actually cried on the phone when Mark called to let them know Alexander had been born. Sal needed a little boy to begin this life. She'd been so afraid of what her mother might do if it were a girl, but Lila Kahane was just as excited to have a grandson. She hadn't come to Bellingwood yet. It was only a matter of time.

Mark and Sal flew to Las Vegas Memorial Day weekend to get married, surprising everyone. Sal thought it was the great fun. Her mother would never approve and she had just done it. Polly didn't know anyone else who had ever been married in Vegas. Now she did. Sal and Mark had a terrific time, giving themselves the long weekend to celebrate and be all by themselves before the baby was born. The hardest thing on Sal was leaving her dogs for that long. She'd hired Stephanie and Kayla to spend the weekend at the house which had worked out perfectly. Those girls moved into their new apartment just after the holiday.

Polly couldn't believe they were so far into a very busy summer. The sesquicentennial celebration was nearly here. The front porch was finished and the yard looked great. She wanted to hang plants on the porch, but otherwise, it was as ready as it was going to be. She and Eliseo hadn't come to an agreement yet on what to plant around the front of the porch. It wasn't so much a disagreement as it was that Polly couldn't make a decision. Too many things on her plate had pushed that off until later.

"Polly Giller!"

She jumped, having forgotten why she was there, then turned and ran for the front yard.

"Hello, Ken. How are you?"

He looked around, nodding approvingly. "This is very nice, Polly. You've done a lot of hard work here."

"I sleep pretty well when I finally hit the pillow," she said, rolling her shoulders. "It feels like there are three thousand things I need to do before this next week kicks off, though. Do you want to see the outside before we go in?"

"I'd love to. I haven't been down in your tunnel yet."

She tilted her head. "You haven't? Let's do that first." Polly led him past the garage to the back yard. It looked so nice now, though the fence still needed to be replaced; another project that would happen after the Sesquicentennial celebration. She'd planted two flowering pear trees behind the garage. Once the fence was replaced, they would add more trees to the back yard. Again, so many things yet to do.

"Come on in." Polly unlocked the door to Rebecca's studio and held it open for him. She flipped the lights on and followed him down the steps.

"This doesn't look much like a distillery," he said.

"Back here." Polly pushed the door open to the second room. They'd hauled everything out while Henry rebuilt the room, then brought back the kegs and the distillation vat. Bill Sturtz built a rack for the vat after Polly cleaned and polished it. They filled a set of shelves with some of the labeled bottles, just for the effect.

He ran his hand over a keg. "It's hard to believe this was here all these years and no one knew."

"I often wonder what's behind all of the walls in the homes around here," Polly said.

Ken smiled at her. "So do I. Even when I do know, I wonder what else might be hiding behind the lives they show us." He sighed. "Sometimes it's pretty rough."

"I can't imagine what you see, Ken."

"Best you don't try," he replied.

Polly flipped another switch and lights came on inside the tunnel. "Go ahead. The numbers painted on the walls count down to the main house. Henry did that for me. I'm right behind you."

Ken crouched and started down the path. Polly waited for him to get ahead of her. She still went through this tunnel pretty quickly and didn't want anyone to stop her momentum once she started. Polly's claustrophobia was something she dealt with every time she entered the small passage.

They ended up in front of the door to the basement. Polly took the key off a hook, unlocked it and pushed it open, flipping another switch to bring lights on. They'd chosen to keep the room dimly lit for now. Henry had yet to cut through the wall to the basement. Until they were living here full time, he thought it would be safer to keep this room and the tunnel closed off from the main house.

"This is so hard to believe," Ken said, walking over to the desk. "It's been here all these years." He peered at the various tally boards hanging on the wall, then stepped back and pointed at one. "That has to be my grandfather."

"M. Langer?" Polly asked.

His voice grew hushed. "It was my mother's father. I had no idea." He slowly nodded. "It makes sense, though. He would have done anything to feed his family. There were a bunch of kids. Mom was the youngest of nine."

Polly snapped pictures of it with her phone. "Do you want it?"

He took a step back. "No, it should stay here. Are you keeping this room intact?"

She nodded. "I'm not ready to become a tourist site, but we're already changing the house so much, I want to keep a little of its history."

"Then it should stay here." He pointed at another with 'Bradford' on it. "I wonder if that's Bert's granddaddy. And Whitney. That has to be Nate Whitney's granddad." Ken walked past the other boards. "That's Greg Parker's granddad. You know him. Lucy at the diner? Her husband."

"She told me that he might have stories," Polly said. "Maybe more people will tell me who those names are next week."

"That's quite a collection," he replied. "A hundred years ago, I would have had to arrest them for making whiskey. Even my own granddad." Ken shook his head. "My mama would have been awfully angry at me for that."

"Maybe you could have looked the other way," Polly said.

7

"Maybe." Ken pointed at the crates. "What's in those?"

"Looks like china from the hotel, but I don't know for sure. We haven't moved them yet. I should get the boys down here to stack them along the walls so people don't trip over things." Polly shook her head. "See. One more thing. And if I don't write myself a note, I'll completely forget."

"This is great," Ken said. "Thanks for showing me around. Let's check out the damage upstairs."

They went back the way they'd come, with Polly locking up and flipping off lights along the way.

"You know, I didn't think I'd ever see this house come back to life," Ken said as they walked up the steps to the house. "People talked about tearing it down when it finally came on the market. It was turning into a terrible eyesore. Fortunately, it was tucked back in here and most of Bellingwood never paid attention to it."

He came to a stop and drew in a breath as he surveyed the room. "I'm sorry about this, Polly."

"I just can't imagine anyone breaking in here to steal the pipes."

"It's done more often than you think." He took out his phone and snapped pictures of the damaged walls. "Looks like you were ready to work in this room."

"The timing couldn't have been better," Polly said. "I just wish I didn't have to bother you with it."

"This is the kitchen?"

"Yeah. It's hard to tell what's what right now." They walked down the hallway and stopped in front of a double set of doors. "This is the dining room."

Ken lifted the layers of tarp and plastic covering the table. "This is massive."

"I know. Henry thinks they built it inside the room. It's not coming out, so we're working around it."

"I keep hearing about your fountain. Are you keeping it?"

She laughed. "Come on. I'll show you. Liam Hoffman isn't too keen on re-plumbing the thing, but he'll do it if I ask."

Polly pulled sheets of plastic back from the fountain and waited for his response.

Ken shook his head. "People do the craziest things."

"It makes sense if this was put in when the place was a hotel. Liam's pretty sure the Springers never used it. I keep thinking that if I just keep quiet and refuse to make a decision about it, someone else will decide for me and I won't have to worry. I don't care either way."

"And Henry?"

"I don't think he cares either."

Ken stepped up to look out the front window. "That's a beautiful porch. You really are doing nice things here." He pointed up the stairs. "Are those rooms gutted too?"

"Not yet. If we can finish rooms on this level, maybe we can live here while we work on the rest. It's going to take forever, though."

He tapped his notebook. "I'll write up the report. Do you all keep this place locked up when you aren't here?"

"Absolutely."

"Have you found where the thief came in?"

Polly shook her head. "I haven't even thought to look. I should check the windows to make sure nothing is broken."

"Let's take a look at the back door first," he said. "I assume you aren't using it."

"Not since Henry ripped the porch off."

Ken laughed. "You really are going to be working on this place forever."

"No kidding. Do you have any idea who might have broken in? Have there been other instances of this in town?"

She led him to the back door and he took pictures of the door jamb. It had been forced open and then closed again.

"Henry will want to reinforce this."

Polly nodded.

As they walked back toward the side door, Ken stopped. "Have you met your neighbors yet?"

"No. We've been so busy, we just haven't taken the time. I thought that once the sesquicentennial was done, we'd have a picnic and invite people over."

"So you don't know who lives down the street?"

She frowned. "No. Who?"

"An old friend of yours."

"I don't know who you're talking about. What old friend?"

"Shawn Wesley."

Polly dropped her head and then raised it again to look at him. "You're kidding." She'd never forget her encounter with that young man. Pastor Boehm had asked her to interview him for the custodial job at Sycamore House, but he really hadn't worked out.

"He's only been out of jail this last time for a few weeks. That's probably why you haven't seen him around. But you should be aware."

"I can't believe it," Polly said. Then she put her hand out to stop him. "Do you think he could have done this?"

"Nothing would surprise me."

"I don't want to deal with him again," Polly said, shaking her head. "He really doesn't like me."

"Just tell Henry and your boys to keep an eye out and make sure to lock things up when you leave."

"Thanks for coming over," Polly said as he walked away.

That was going to make things interesting. She knew exactly which house it was, too. The homes in this neighborhood weren't in great shape. Most were run-down with yards filled with junk that hadn't moved in years, but the house Ken pointed to was worse than the others. No one needed to mow because it was all dirt. A car had been pulled up into the yard and hadn't been moved as long as they'd been here. Shawn's wife drove an old beater and it was him on that loud motorcycle. Oh joy.

CHAPTER TWO

Later that afternoon, Polly was back at Sycamore House. After grumbling because Polly confiscated their phones, Rebecca, Andrew, and Kayla went to the swimming pool. Polly sat down on the sofa with her animals and rubbed Obiwan's back. When they bought the Bell House, she hadn't given much thought to the neighborhood, even though she recognized it was in bad shape. The last thing she'd considered was who their neighbors might be. She always thought she could get along with anyone, but Shawn Wesley was a different story. Polly wondered what his wife was like. The former pastor had liked the woman well enough; maybe it would be okay.

"No moping," she said out loud, jumping up. Obiwan leaped to the floor, wagging his tail.

"Nah, not this time," Polly said. "I know you like going to the barn with me, but I'm going to shake some of this off." She headed out the front door and downstairs, stopping in the office. It had been strange the first few weeks to not have an office of her own any longer, but Stephanie was so happy with the way things had ended up, Polly couldn't hold onto the regret.

"Hi there," she said to Kristen. The girl had gone from temporary help to full-time receptionist. Once Stephanie was there to train her on the systems, Kristen had taken to the job with ease.

"Hi Polly," Kristen said. "Can I get something for you?"

Polly glanced at the two open office doors and stepped forward to glance into Jeff's office. Both were empty. "Where is everyone?"

Kristen pointed to the closed door of the conference room. "They're all in there."

"Who's they?"

"Everybody," Kristen replied. "Sylvie, Rachel, Eliseo, Stephanie and Jeff. Final planning for next week."

"Oh." Polly wasn't sure that she liked being so far out of the loop that meetings were happening with her entire staff and she wasn't aware of them. The truth was, they didn't need her.

Both she and Kristen looked up when a woman in her late thirties knocked at the door.

"Excuse me?" the woman asked. Four exhausted and crabby children surrounded her. The oldest was probably ten and the youngest around six.

"How can I help you?" Kristen asked.

Polly stepped away from the desk and smiled at the woman.

"Does Eliseo Aquila work here?" she asked.

Polly glanced at the conference room door and then back to Kristen, nodding. "Yes, he does. Can I tell him who's asking?"

The woman heaved a huge sigh, looked down at the children who were with her and said, "Tell him that his wife and children are here. He can't escape us any longer. We tracked him down and he has to finally take responsibility."

Kristen's eyes grew big and she looked at Polly, pleading for help.

"I'm sorry," Polly said. "You're his wife and these are his children?"

"He didn't tell you that we existed, did he?" the woman responded. "I'm not surprised. He's been ducking his responsibility for too long now. It's time that he face us."

"You're his family?" Polly asked again.

"Yes we are. Is he available?"

Polly moved toward the conference room door, then stopped and turned back to the woman standing in the office. "Just a moment. I'll get him. Please have a seat."

Kristen sat at the desk, her mouth still wide open.

A quick knock at the conference room door and Polly entered.

"Hello, Polly," Jeff said. "We're just going over some things for next week. You're welcome to join us."

"Uhhh, that's okay," Polly replied. She dropped into a chair next to Sylvie, who was sitting beside Eliseo. "I don't know how to say this, Eliseo, but there's a woman in the front office who says she's your wife. She has your four children with her."

Sylvie took a quick breath and Jeff snapped his head up from the tablet he was looking at.

"His what?" Jeff asked.

It was so hard to discern Eliseo's facial expressions due to scarring on his face from the burns he'd received while fighting in Desert Storm. Polly had grown used to looking at his eyes for clues about what he was feeling, but right now they told her nothing.

"I don't have a wife," he said.

Polly tilted her head. "She's pretty insistent. She called you by name and knew where you worked. And there are four little Aquila children out there who are looking for their daddy."

Eliseo turned to Sylvie. "I don't have a wife or kids. I swear."

Sylvie just shrugged. "Whatever." She grabbed up her own tablet and stood, heading for the door.

"Stop," he said, jumping up to step in front of her. He put his hands out, pleading with her to listen. "This doesn't make sense."

"All you have to do is open the door," Sylvie said.

"Right." Eliseo put his hand on the door knob, took a breath and walked into the main office.

Polly was close behind Sylvie as they followed him out.

"Daddy!" the older boy cried, running to hug Eliseo. The other three clambered around him, all crying for their father.

His back shook and Polly realized he was laughing. He released the children and caught up the woman in a hug. "Elva, you're mean," he said, finally putting her back down.

"Everyone, this is my sister, Elva. And no, these are not my children, but my very naughty nieces and nephews. They've learned all of their bad behavior from their mother." Eliseo patted the top of the older boy's head. "Why would you do that to me?"

"It was funny," the boy said. "Mama said we were going to make you laugh."

"You're right," Eliseo replied. "It was funny." He bent over and scooped up the youngest, a dark-haired boy. "Did you think it was funny, Matty?"

"Yes, Daddy," the little boy said solemnly before giving his mother an ornery grin.

Polly stepped forward and put her hand out to Eliseo's sister. "I'm Polly Giller, the owner of Sycamore House. And right now, I'm really grateful that this was a joke. I was beginning to worry that I didn't know Eliseo very well."

"You think he's a good man, don't you?" Elva asked.

Polly nodded.

Elva took her brother's arm and looked up into his face. "You're absolutely right. He's one of the best. I'm so proud of my big brother, sometimes I don't know how to express it." She grinned. "So I pick on him."

Eliseo rested his face on her head, then pulled up. "Larry?"

She gave him a quick shake of the head.

He sat down in one of the chairs and put the little boy on the seat next to him, then beckoned to the two girls. They ran to him, jumped up into his lap, laughing. "This is Gabriela and Ana," he said, pointing to one and then the other.

"I'm Gabriela," the second girl said.

"And I'm Ana."

"What is an uncle to do?" he asked. "You look exactly alike."

They didn't at all. Gabriela was slight, wore thick glasses and had long, straight hair. Ana, on the other hand, was a little bigger, with curls running loose on top of her head.

The older boy had hung back and was hovering close to his mother.

"Go on," she said, pushing him toward Eliseo.

"Come here, Samuel," Eliseo said, lifting Ana into the seat on his other side. Samuel edged closer until Eliseo could pull him into a hug. "It's good to see you. I've missed your hugs." With that, the boy lay his head on the older man's chest.

"Why are you here?" Eliseo asked Elva. "You should have called to let me know you were coming. Do you have plans to stay somewhere or will you come out to my house?"

"You have a house?" Samuel asked. "Is it very big?"

"It's big enough," Eliseo said. "Will you stay with me?"

"Daddy ran away," Matty piped up.

"He what?" Eliseo looked at Elva. She shrugged.

Polly was beginning to feel uncomfortable. "Elva," she interrupted. "You should meet the rest of Eliseo's friends here. And then he should take all of you down to the barn so you can meet the horses."

"Horses?" Ana jumped down from the chair. "I want to see the horses. Can we go now?"

"Take them," Polly said. "I'll show Elva around up here." She stepped in and put her hand on Elva's back. "Is that okay?"

"That would be great. Thanks. It's been a long few days in the car. They'll be glad to get out and run."

Eliseo gave Polly a look she couldn't interpret, but he stood, picked Matty up, and walked out with the other three kids following him.

"Thank you," Elva said, breathing a deep sigh. "I'm exhausted."

"I'll bet you are," Polly said. "Let me introduce you to the rest of the crew. First off is Kristen. She's our receptionist and smiles at everyone who comes in the front door." Elva shook Kristen's hand.

Polly made introductions around the room and when there didn't seem to be anything else to say, Jeff took Stephanie's arm. "Let's go back in and finish up. We can tell Eliseo what he needs to know later."

Sylvie glanced at Polly before following Jeff back into the conference room. There would be further conversation there.

"Would you like to freshen up or at least sit on a comfortable sofa for a few minutes?" Polly asked. "My apartment is right upstairs."

"You live here?"

"For now. But I should warn you, I have two dogs and two cats. Everyone is friendly, but some people aren't comfortable with that many animals."

"I've always been around animals," Elva said. "But I don't want to bother you."

"It's really no bother. I have nothing more important to do right now."

Elva chuckled. "I shouldn't run away from them, but a quiet place with no children begging to be entertained or wondering how much longer until we're there would be terrific. Are you sure?"

"I'm sure. I'll text Eliseo to tell him that I've kidnapped you and when you've had enough of me, we can head to the barn." Polly smiled. "It only seems fair that he has to spend a little time with his children, doesn't it?"

"That was mean of me, but we've been planning it all during the drive up here. It kept the children's minds occupied."

They walked up the steps to Polly's apartment. "Can I get you something to drink?" Polly asked. "I can make coffee or there's iced tea and lemonade in the refrigerator." She grinned. "We don't have a lot of pop around here, but I do have some."

"Just water," Elva said. "Do you have a restroom where I could wash my face? I feel like I've been in the car for weeks."

Polly showed her to the bathroom off of Henry's office and went back into the kitchen. She'd taken to keeping chocolate chip cookies in the freezer, so put several of those on a plate, along with some brownies and monster cookies she and Rebecca had baked over the weekend. It was a good thing there were plenty of people moving in and out of her house with all of the baking she did.

Elva stepped out into the media room and looked around. "I can't believe this is an old school. You've made it into something really special. Seo told me what you had here. This is more wonderful than he said."

"You'll have to ask him for a full tour," Polly said. "Come on in to the living room and relax."

The dogs had been prancing around her feet since she walked in the front door and as soon as Polly sat down, they checked her out, then moved over to sniff Elva. Without hesitation, Elva put one hand on Obiwan's head and stroked down his neck, then clicked her tongue and waited for Han to sit in front of her.

"How did you know to do that?" Polly asked in amazement.

"Old family secret," Elva said with a grin. She chuckled at Polly's confusion. "Seo and I learned from our father how to work with animals. Your big dog is quiet and respectful, but the young one looks like he might have needed some help from my brother."

"He certainly did," Polly said. She handed Elva the glass and pushed a coaster across the table. "Your brother hasn't told us much about you or your family."

Elva smiled. "I'm not surprised. He doesn't talk about his personal life. He never has. And to be honest ..." She gave a quick shake of her head. "No, it's not important. Seo never had it easy." She let out a breath. "Neither of us did. Bad decisions everywhere. But it looks like he's put it all behind him and started over again. He's happy here, you know."

"I hope so. I don't know what I'd do without him."

"Good. He needed a home. I wasn't much help to him, that's for sure."

Polly frowned. "I'm embarrassed to say I don't even know if your parents are alive."

"They aren't," Elva said. "Mama died when I was in college and Daddy died three years later. He never saw Seo fully come back to life." She took a drink of water and put the glass back down on the coaster. "Seo's wounds were more than Daddy could handle. Before the war, he'd always been so tough and strong. And then he couldn't do anything for himself and that nearly killed our father. I'm afraid Seo believes it's his fault that Daddy had that heart attack." She smiled. "Look at me, telling you about our family. That would infuriate my brother. He's so private." She chuckled. "I'm the exact opposite. I talk all the time. Tell me about you. Why did you come to Bellingwood and buy this school?"

"Eliseo hasn't told you my story?" Polly asked.

"We haven't talked much," Elva replied. "As evidenced by the fact that he didn't know I was coming to town." She patted herself and around the sofa and then picked up her purse. "Where is there a good hotel? We came up through Boone and I saw a couple down there. Do you know if any of them have a swimming pool? I promised the kids that the next hotel we stayed in would have a pool."

Polly wrinkled her forehead. "You won't stay with Eliseo at his house?"

"With those four wild things? There's no way he lives in a house big enough to hold all of us."

Elva really hadn't talked to her brother much at all if she didn't know he was living in a big house out in the country. Polly wasn't quite sure what to do. But he had already made the invitation.

"We have a nice hotel here in town. In fact, my husband and I own it, too. Let me see if there is anything available. How long are you planning to stay?"

Elva dropped her eyes. "I don't know. I hadn't thought that far ahead. All I could think was that I needed to get to my brother and he'd take care of things for me." She sighed. "He hasn't been part of my life for a long time. I don't know what I was thinking. This was really a bad decision."

"It's never a bad decision to spend time with your brother," Polly said. "Let me just do a quick check." She ran into the office she shared with Henry and opened the computer. Since she had access to the reservation system, she looked for rooms, only to find that they were completely booked for the next two weeks. There was nothing available. The rooms in the addition were also filled. Polly simply didn't have space this close to the Sesquicentennial celebration. She took a deep breath and decided to do what she was best at. Stick her nose where it didn't belong. She called Eliseo's cell phone and smiled at the raucous noise in the background when he answered.

"Hello, Polly," he said.

"It sounds like you have a lot going on."

"It's good to see them. How can I help you?"

"I'm butting in," she said. "I'll apologize right now."

"For what?"

"Elva asked about staying at a hotel and Sycamore Inn is completely booked. Do you want me to keep looking?"

"What? No. Why wouldn't she stay with me?"

"I don't know," Polly said.

"Would you please ask her to come to the barn. No, I'll bring the kids up. No, that's not fair to you." Eliseo paused. "Polly, how did this get so difficult?"

She laughed. "I'm not sure. Probably because I got myself involved when I shouldn't have."

"I don't want you to have to carry messages back and forth between me and Elva," he said. "But please tell her that I have plenty of room. Has she told you why she's here?"

"No, Eliseo, she hasn't."

"Not yet, you mean."

"Hey. That's not fair!" Polly said with a laugh. "How are you doing there with the kids? Do you need her to come rescue you?"

"Not at all. They're out in the pasture with Jason, Scar and Kent. They'll be a dirty mess, but this should wear them out."

"Okay. Thank you. I'll tell her that she doesn't need to worry, you have plenty of room."

"They can have the entire second floor," Eliseo said. "I sleep downstairs anyway. That girl. She does things without thinking sometimes. Thank you."

Polly put her phone down and jumped at Elva's squeak, then the sound of voices. Kayla, Andrew, and Rebecca must be back. She grabbed her phone and raced out to the living room.

"I'm sorry, Elva," Polly said. "I didn't even think about these three coming back. This is my daughter, Rebecca."

Rebecca put her hand out and nodded.

"Her friends, Andrew and Kayla. Guys, this is Eliseo's sister, Elva." Polly looked at Elva. "I don't think I got your last name."

"Johnson."

"Elva Johnson. Are you back from swimming for good?" Polly asked.

"It got really full over there. Lots of little kids," Andrew said. "No room to do anything."

"Okay, you go get changed then," Polly said. "We'll find something else for you to do this afternoon."

Rebecca rolled her eyes and grabbed Kayla's hand, pulling her to the bedroom door. Andrew's things were in the kids' bathroom and he headed that way.

"They surprised me," Elva said.

"Me too. I wasn't expecting them back until much later." Polly sat down across from her. "The hotel is full. We have a big sesquicentennial celebration coming up next week and people are already coming into town."

"I can drive back down to Boone."

"Or you can stay with your brother. I just got off the phone with him. I don't know if you realize his house is out in the country and is big enough for all of you."

Elva's head popped up. "It is?"

"He's been working on restoring it for the last year. There's plenty of room for you and your kids. He wanted me to let you know that he'd like you to stay out there with him."

"Thank you." Elva visibly relaxed. "I wasn't sure if he'd be happy to see us. I can see that he doesn't need me in his life, but I certainly need him."

CHAPTER THREE

After Eliseo came up with the children, the apartment devolved into utter chaos. It was more fun than Polly had had in a long time. Eliseo tried to apologize for bringing the children upstairs, but she was having none of it and packed up the rest of the cookies to send home with them.

In the few minutes he'd been upstairs, Eliseo talked Rebecca, Kayla, and Andrew into going down to the barn with the dogs. There were new toys and balls for the donkeys to play with, since Jason, Scar, and Kent had taken the horses across the creek to the other meadow, leaving the donkeys behind.

Polly's phone rang and she smiled when she saw that it was Henry.

"Hey, hot stuff," she said.

"Hey, yourself. Did you forget to tell me something?" he asked.

Polly thought back over all that had happened and wondered which part of it he was asking about. She chuckled. "Maybe? Which thing?"

"There's more than one?"

"Well, Eliseo's wife showed up in the office this afternoon."

"His wife?"

"Yep. With four kids."

"He abandoned four kids? That doesn't sound like Eliseo. What did you say?"

Polly grinned. The joke had worked one more time, even though it was lame. "It's really his sister. But she came in and told us that she was his wife with their four children. She's kind of ornery. They've already gone out to his house."

Henry breathed out. "That's good to hear. I wasn't sure how I would handle you falling apart if Eliseo turned out to be a deadbeat."

"And what other thing?" Polly asked. She'd called Henry after finding out about the pulled copper pipe.

"I thought you'd call me back after Ken was there," Henry said. "What did he say?"

"That Shawn Wesley lives just down the street."

"Shawn Wesley," Henry said to himself. "That name isn't familiar to me. Is it someone you know?"

"Remember the pothead who came to work for me because Pastor Boehm tried to get him some help?"

"No, I don't remember that."

"I had to kick him off the property because he was outside smoking every ten minutes and refused to do any work."

"Hmmm," Henry said. "Is that the same guy who told Chief Wallers they should investigate you for the other janitor's death?"

Polly nodded and smiled. "Yep. That's the one."

"And he lives down the street from our house?"

"Exciting times, yes?"

"Do you think he's the one who pulled the pipe out?"

Polly sighed. "I don't want to make any assumptions, but I wouldn't be surprised. Unless he's changed since I first met him, the guy is a total loser. And now that I know who it is, the lawn in front of that house makes more sense. It's the one without any grass at all."

"You know it is really annoying to have those crappy houses across the street from us," Henry said.

"Because the Springer House was in such great shape," Polly said, sarcasm lacing her tone. "We have to give them time to catch up, Henry."

"What if they never do?"

"Then they never do. We can't worry about it."

"I'll worry about it. If Shawn Wesley lives down the street, who's to say what else is going on in those run down houses."

"Henry Sturtz," Polly scolded. "What are you talking about? For all we know, good and decent people live there. They just can't afford expensive upkeep."

"It isn't all that expensive."

"Then maybe they don't know how to do all of the things that you can do. And they don't know who to ask."

He chuckled. "I'm not getting away with that one, am I?"

"No you're not. You've lived a privileged life. You and your dad can fix anything. You know all the right people to help with any project you have to work on."

"I should have kept my mouth shut," he said. "I can see it now. You're going to be renting me out, aren't you?"

"You know me so well."

"I'm stopping at the house before coming home tonight. I bought new locks. The boys will meet me and we'll lock the place down so no one can get in. Are we having a houseful for supper again?"

With all of the work that Sylvie and Stephanie were putting into preparations for the Sesquicentennial, Kayla and Andrew had been spending evenings with Rebecca.

"I suspect so. They're playing with the donkeys and dogs right now." Polly shuddered. "You're all going to be stinky messes by the time you get home tonight."

"And the grill is over here. What do you want to do?"

"Put peanut butter and jelly out on the counter for you all while I go to Ames and eat somewhere fancy."

He laughed. "If that's what you want ..."

"There isn't much food in the house and it looks like we're going to be feeding everyone all week. Maybe I'll go to Boone so I can fill the refrigerator and cupboards. Dinner will be at six thirty. Will that work?"

"We'll be there. I love you."

"I know," she quipped.

Polly checked the cupboards and refrigerator to get a quick idea of what she actually had in the way of food and headed for the back door. She made a quick stop at the barn to let the kids know she was leaving.

Kayla was just coming out of the feed room with a bright blue ball in her arms when Polly walked in the main doors.

"Are the other two outside?" Polly asked.

"Yeah. Andrew fell in the mud when he was playing with the dogs. He's a mess."

"The mud?" It had been really dry. "Where did he find mud?"

"Eliseo had a baby pool out for the donkeys to play in. They knocked all the water out. We filled it back up. They're funny."

Polly laughed. "I'm going to Boone for groceries. You're eating with us tonight, aren't you?"

"I guess so," Kayla said. "Stephanie's always busy. When we go home, all she wants to do is watch television and go to bed."

"It will get better after next week is over. I promise."

"I hope so. She's no fun."

"Tell Andrew and Rebecca that I'm leaving. And tell them not to make too much of a mess in the house."

"I'll make them clean it up if they do."

"Sounds good to me." Polly waved and left. Just before school let out, Kayla had been given permission - and cash - to tackle Rebecca's bedroom. After that she'd sat down with the two girls and told Rebecca that if she wanted Kayla's continued help, she had to negotiate a reasonable rate and find her own way to pay for the cleaning. But Polly expected Rebecca's room to remain clean and organized from that point forward.

For the most part, Kayla shamed Rebecca into helping do the work. Rebecca, though, had worked out a monthly cleaning schedule with Kayla that would bring things back under control when she got overwhelmed with it.

Polly drove into Boone and headed for the grocery store. Shopping for food wasn't her favorite thing. Her grocery bill had gotten bigger once Hayden moved in full-time. He enjoyed helping in the kitchen, but he and his brother never seemed to get full no matter what she made. Polly walked in the front door of the grocery store and accepted a cart from someone who was leaving. She could probably fill two, but didn't know how she'd possibly manage that.

It took more than an hour for Polly to get through the store and check out. She pushed her cart out to the truck and tried to decide whether to put everything in the bed or the cab. It would be easier to just slide things in under the topper, so she pushed the cart around the back of her truck.

Polly opened the tailgate and gave a little yelp, then slammed it shut. What in the hell? Every muscle in her body went weak and she gripped the handle of the grocery cart to stop from falling. She wanted to lean against something, but she wasn't going near her truck. Not with a young woman's body lying in there.

Polly found herself breathing too fast and tried to slow it down. This was too close. When did this happen? How long had she been driving around with this girl in her truck? She looked around the parking lot to see if anyone was watching and then bowed her head. Everyone was living their own lives. They weren't paying any attention to her at all.

She swiped a familiar number.

"Polly?" Aaron asked. "Don't tell me. Where are you?"

"I'm at the grocery store in Boone," Polly said. "You have to come help me. There's a dead body in the bed of my truck."

"There's a what? When did this happen?"

"I don't know. Just come help me. I can't think straight. I opened it to put groceries in and found her."

"When was the last time you used the bed?"

"It's been over a week. Why didn't I just put my groceries in the front seat? That's what I was going to do. Why didn't I?"

"Are you okay, Polly?"

Polly pursed her lips. "Damn it, Aaron. No I'm not. It's hot out here and I have two hundred dollars in groceries with me. You won't let me take my truck home and I don't know what to do next. Oh, and I just found a dead girl in the back of my truck." She realized that her voice had risen and took a breath. "I'm not okay. Are you coming to rescue me?"

"We're already on the way," he said. "Hang up and call Henry. If he can't come get you, I'll find someone to take you home."

She pushed the cart toward the store, then turned back, unsure of where to go next. There was no way she wanted to stand next to that truck. But Aaron said he'd be here soon. Finally, Polly pushed the cart back to the front of her truck, leaned on the fender and stuck her foot under the wheel of the cart to keep it from rolling away. She took out her phone and swiped the call to Henry.

"What's up, sweetie pie?" he asked.

"Henry, you aren't going to believe it," Polly started.

"No. You didn't. Where are you?"

"I'm still at the grocery store."

"You found a body at the grocery store?"

She supposed that, in truth, she had. "Yes, but it was in the bed of my truck."

"Your truck?" Henry yelled. "In your truck? How did it get in there?"

"I don't know. I certainly didn't put it in there."

"I'm sorry." He lowered his voice. "I didn't mean to yell, but that was unexpected. Have you called Aaron?"

"Yeah. That was my first call. He's on his way. But I need you to come get me. I have all of my groceries and they're going to take my truck away and I don't know how I'll get back home." Polly's throat closed and she choked as tears filled her eyes.

"Oh honey, you know I would. But I'm too far away. Do you mind if I call Heath and Hayden? They can be there in fifteen minutes."

"Would you?" Polly asked. "I feel like such a useless fool, but I'm stranded in the parking lot and don't know what else to do."

"Let me make a quick call and then I'll call you back."

She shook her head as she saw Aaron's SUV turn into the parking lot. "No, don't call me unless they can't come down. Aaron's here and chaos is about to erupt again."

"I love you, Polly, and I'm sorry."

"I love you too. See you later."

Polly gave Aaron a hesitant wave as he pulled in behind her truck and got out. He walked past the bed of the truck, giving it a sideways glance, and came to greet her. "Did you reach Henry?"

"He's sending Hayden and Heath to rescue me," she said. "Thanks for coming so fast. I didn't know what to do."

"You did what you do best," he said with a laugh. "You call me."

Sirens announced the approach of the rest of the emergency vehicles and Polly looked up at Aaron. "I really hate being the center of attention," she said. "The people in these cars around me are going to be mad that they can't get out because you're blocking them."

"You let us worry about that," Aaron said. "You have no idea when this could have happened?"

Polly took a deep breath. "None at all. But it had to have been pretty recent. There isn't any smell."

Aaron chuckled. "It's so sad that you even know about that."

"Now that you're here," Polly said, snugging her cart up next to the truck. "Can I see her one more time before you take her away?"

"Not a good idea," Aaron said, putting his hand out to stop her.

Polly pushed his hand down. "It's my truck. Someone wanted me to find her. Just let me take a quick look." She pushed past him and pulled up short when he put his hand on her shoulder.

"You don't want to do this, Polly."

"Why not? It's not like I haven't seen it before."

"Please trust me," Aaron said, pleading in his voice. "Don't do this."

"That makes it worse," Polly replied. "Now I have to." She shrugged his hand off.

A crowd had gathered around the outside perimeter of the activity. Some were holding their phones over their heads trying to get a glimpse of what was happening, most were quietly talking to each other, while others were yelling questions at the emergency workers. Inside the perimeter, a young female deputy was taking pictures in and around Polly's truck while another deputy snapped pictures of the surrounding cars.

Polly stopped beside the tailgate and peered in, trying to stay out of the way. She knew what she was going to see, but that didn't make it any better. The young woman was covered in similar cuts, scrapes and bruises as the two people she'd found in May. This was the same killer and he ... or she ... was back. Polly had hoped beyond hope that those two deaths were an aberration. That maybe the killer had moved on, or had somehow known those two people and killed them because of an argument.

"Sheriff?" One of the EMTs held up a piece of paper. "It's here. It's the same killer."

"What is it?" Polly asked.

Aaron stepped in front of her and opened a plastic bag for the EMT to drop the paper in. "It's nothing, Polly. It doesn't concern you."

Polly was turning toward him when she caught the look of astonishment on the EMT's face. It was quickly replaced with concern. All of it directed at Polly. She took Aaron's arm and led him away from his team.

"There's something you aren't telling me about these murders," she said. "It does concern me, doesn't it?"

Aaron shook his head and took a deep breath. "You know I won't talk about an active investigation."

"That's crap and you know better than to try to use that on me." Polly glared at him.

He took another breath and looked around, avoiding her eyes. "I'm not going to talk about this now, Polly."

"Aaron, if this has something to do with me, don't you think I should know what's going on? How am I supposed to keep my family safe if I don't know who's out there and what they're doing? Am I going to find more bodies before this is over? What's going on?"

Aaron seemed to come to a decision. "I want to keep you safe. That's all that matters to me right now. And yes, you're right. It does concern you."

"Then why won't you tell me anything?"

"Because I know how badly it is going to upset you. I had hoped, just like everyone else, that when there were no more murders after you found the young man in the parking lot at the grain elevator, it was over. This tells me it isn't and it also tells me that the murderer is determined to get your attention."

"Get my attention? What does that mean?"

He started to bring up the plastic bag with the piece of paper, but then thought better of it and dropped his hand back down to his side. "Whoever is killing these young people wants you to find their bodies, Polly. He's telling us so in the notes he leaves on their bodies."

"You've found a note on each of the bodies?"

"Yes," he said, nodding. "And we also believe he watches to make sure you find the bodies."

Polly's head shot up and she looked around the parking lot. "He's watching us right now?"

"We think so. We don't know where he is, but he wants to make sure that you discover the body."

"Whatever," Polly said. "Like anyone else in the county ever finds one."

Aaron took her hand in his. "He's testing that theory, Polly. He says this is research and he's going to expose your talent to the world."

"No," she whispered. "I didn't think anything would come from that."

"From what?" Aaron asked, his brow furrowed.

"Last October when we had all of those people in town for the hauntings at the Springer House. There was a group of them who showed up at Sycamore House asking questions about how I found bodies. One man said he was a paranormal investigator and he wanted to investigate me. I kicked him out."

"Do you remember his name?"

She shook her head. "No. But he didn't look like he had it in him to kill anyone. He looked like a professor. All brains and no sense."

"If you think of anything else, call me," Aaron said. "Now you need to give me your keys. When we're finished, I'll let you know."

Polly looked over at her truck. "I can't reject one more truck because someone used it as a receptacle for a body, can I."

"You can try. Henry probably won't like it."

"This one doesn't upset me nearly as much as..." Polly looked up as she saw Heath drive into the parking lot. "... as that damned truck. I don't know what I was thinking, letting Henry send those boys down for me. Now I'm going to have to ride back home in that thing."

"We can give you a ride," Aaron said.

She rolled her eyes. "No. I'll just suck it up and get over myself. Do you need me for anything else?"

"When you get home, would you write out a list of where you've been today and email it to me?"

"You think he put the body in the truck somewhere other than at the grocery store?" Polly asked.

Aaron gave her a dejected look. "No. I'm afraid he managed to do it right here in plain sight. But just in case, send me the list."

Polly handed him the key fob and groaned. "I can't believe I'm going to be without a vehicle. These next few weeks are busy enough without me having to figure this out."

"You can rent a car," Aaron said. "But we'll try to release it soon."

"Well, I'm not driving Heath's truck. At least I can draw the line on that," she said. Polly turned to go. "Let me know if anything else comes up. I'm going to try not to worry, but it scares me he's going to escalate. This is too close for comfort."

"I will. Go take care of your groceries. I hope you didn't buy ice cream. It's soup by now."

She grinned. "No ice cream today. Thanks a lot."

Polly wended her way through the emergency workers and

back to her grocery cart. She waved at Heath who drove over to meet her. Both he and Hayden got out to help load groceries into the back seat of the truck.

"Do you want to talk about what's going on here?" Hayden asked, once they were back in the truck.

"Not really. There's a body in the bed of my truck." Polly had jumped into the back seat, even though Hayden had tried to take it.

"It's not anyone you know, is it?" Heath asked.

"No. At least there's that."

CHAPTER FOUR

In the midst of the chaos, Polly hadn't slept well at all. She couldn't stop thinking about the fact that the murders were connected to her. Since Aaron hadn't told her what was in the notes, she'd spent most of the night dreaming up different circumstances that a murderer might be creating, but nothing made any sense. If it was related to what that man had said last fall about investigating her, that was sick and twisted. He hadn't looked like a psychopath, but then, Polly wasn't sure she knew what a psychopath looked like.

It frustrated her to be stuck without her truck. Aaron hadn't said how long they would need to keep it. Other than giving it a good cleaning before she drove it, somehow it wasn't quite as appalling to her that a poor girl had been shoved in the bed of her truck as it had been when Joey Delancy and his partner had posed the girls they kidnapped in the front of her truck. Each one of those girls looked similar to Polly and had been forced into Polly's clothes. She would never get those images out of her mind.

But that still didn't get Polly any transportation. Everyone was busy as the community prepared for next week's festivities.

Events at Sycamore House were kicking off this weekend with a dance Saturday night. A local country band was playing and Jeff had asked Mark Ogden, his sister Lisa, and the kids from her dance studio to be there to teach steps and line dances. Polly was all for that. She didn't spend enough time in bars to learn the dances. Okay, she didn't spend any time at country bars. All of a sudden she felt like an old lady. If she'd known the right people ten years ago, she would have gone all the time.

Tuesday night was a Flapper Ball. Mark's mother was spending the entire week in Bellingwood and would teach the Lindy Hop and the Charleston that evening. The carnival opened on Wednesday and the big parade was on Thursday. Friday was the biggest day, with a community dinner in the evening, followed by the band concert and a street dance downtown. Everyone would be ready to drop by the weekend.

Polly and Rebecca had been working on costumes, but they'd ordered their flapper dresses. That was still a little out of Polly's sewing skill set. She'd made bonnets for everyone and sewn up a couple of simple long skirts to wear for the parade.

Her phone buzzed with a text. When Polly looked at it, she smiled.

"Hi Polly. Eliseo told me why you don't have a truck today. If you need to go anywhere, I can take you."

Jason had gotten his driver's license this summer and took every possible opportunity to drive. He didn't have his own car yet, but his mom let him use hers until they found one that was just right for him. He'd been saving every cent he earned to pay for the car and planned to have one before school started.

"Thanks, Jason. I'll let you know. I really appreciate it," Polly texted back.

"I'm serious. Mom said I can even drive in Ames if you're with me. No big deal."

Maybe she'd have to find a reason to go to Ames today or tomorrow. She shouldn't pass up such a great offer. And it came from his heart. He really wanted to be able to do something for her.

"I know you are. Let me figure out what I need to do and I'll let you know. Thank you."

Polly glanced toward Rebecca's bedroom. The girl was still sleeping. Andrew and Kayla wouldn't be here until around one o'clock. The kids liked having their mornings to themselves, so Jason usually did a round-up and brought the two over to Sycamore House for lunch.

They'd spent most of the month of June working in the yard at the Bell House getting it ready for company. At least that part of the place was gorgeous.

She and Henry had talked about different ways they could let people see what they'd been doing and have access to the tunnel. They had no idea how many people might show up, but she had to assume there would be quite a few. After a few conversations with Jeff, they decided to close out the celebration with an ice cream social in the auditorium on Saturday afternoon, then shuttle people over to the Bell House in either a large van or a wagon pulled by Demi and Daisy.

"What are we doing today?" Rebecca asked, coming around the corner into the kitchen. She yawned and stretched, still in the t-shirt and shorts that she'd worn to bed. Obiwan stood up and wandered over to greet her. She went to the far end of the peninsula and took up her phone, swiping it open, then sat in a chair and reached for one of the blueberry muffins Hayden had made.

"Good morning, Polly," Polly said, moving the plate out of Rebecca's reach.

Rebecca looked up and smiled. "Good morning, Polly. Can I please have a muffin?"

"May I," Polly said.

"Kayla wants to know if I can go with her and Stephanie to Des Moines this afternoon. Stephanie has to pick some stuff up and we won't get back until after supper." Rebecca had gone back to her phone and tentatively reached out for the plate of muffins again.

"May I, first," Polly said.

"May I please have a muffin?"

Polly smiled and pushed the plate back in front of Rebecca.

"Is there anything to drink?" Rebecca asked.

"I have coffee," Polly said. "You can't have my mug."

Rebecca dramatically rolled her eyes. "It's going to be one of those kinds of days, isn't it?"

"What kind of day is that?"

"The kind of day where you take everything literally and force me to be exact."

"Mebbe. You know where the glasses are and I'm guessing you can figure out how to open the refrigerator door."

Rebecca stood up from her chair and muttered. "One of those days. It's gonna be one of those days." She opened the fridge and said, "You didn't tell me Hayden made breakfast muffins."

"You didn't ask."

"Can I have one of those instead?"

"May I."

"May I have one of those instead?"

"You know you can eat anything you want," Polly said.

"So, can I ..." Rebecca stopped. "May I go to Des Moines with Stephanie and Kayla?"

"Sure, but what about Andrew?"

Rebecca closed the refrigerator and put a breakfast muffin onto a plate before popping it in the microwave. "What do you mean?"

"I mean, Andrew expects to come hang out with you and Kayla today. What are you doing about that?"

She huffed. "He never checks with me if he does something with one of his friends. Why should I check with him?" Rebecca took the plate out of the microwave and put it on the peninsula before sitting back down. "Rats. I still didn't get anything to drink."

She looked at Polly, who shrugged. Rebecca climbed back off her chair and went to the refrigerator. "I'll text him. He can do whatever he wants."

Polly held her tongue. Whatever Rebecca and Andrew were spatting about now would work itself out. "In that case, you may go with Kayla. Do you need money for dinner?"

"Well..." Rebecca sidled up to Polly after filling a glass with apple juice.

"What else do you need money for?" Polly asked.

"Stephanie said we might go to some thrift stores to look for outfits for next week."

"Sure. I can swing that." Polly could hardly say no. Rebecca rarely asked for money. Mostly because she simply didn't spend it on herself. The girl could stretch ten dollars over a three-week period if necessary. One of these days, probably when they moved, Polly figured she'd find a secret box filled with cash, tucked away in a dark place in Rebecca's bedroom.

"Did you sleep much last night?" Rebecca asked.

Polly frowned at her. "Why do you ask?"

"The dogs came in to sleep with me. They only do that when you're tossing and turning. And you only do that when you're upset about something. It was finding that girl in your truck, wasn't it?"

"Yeah. I guess it was," Polly said. "Whoever is doing this wants my attention."

"That's kind of creepy."

Polly laughed. "Tell me about it."

"I'm glad I wasn't with you yesterday," she said. "It was one thing when we found that guy by the train tracks. But in your truck? That's too weird." Rebecca looked up from her plate. "Do they know who those other two people are?"

"I haven't asked," Polly said. "But if they were from around here, we should have heard about it, don't you think?"

"Probably. People talk about everything in a little town. Last week when we were at the library, these two ladies were talking about Mrs. Whitcomb's daughter and how she was moving home because her boyfriend beat her up. How do they know about that?"

Polly shook her head. "I don't even know who Mrs. Whitcomb is."

"She teaches computers down in Boone. Her husband is a pharmacist in Ogden."

"How do you know these people?"

"I don't know." Rebecca shrugged. "I just meet people."

"Apparently you pay attention better than I do," Polly said. "I never listen to people when they're talking about those kinds of things."

"Beryl says that I'm supposed to always be observing the world. But sometimes I listen when I should be watching."

"You don't miss much, do you?"

Rebecca gave her a sly grin. "Not if I can help it."

~~~

It really was too hot to be outside walking, but Polly wasn't prepared to make her friends stop what they were doing just to give her a ride. It didn't take much calculating to determine that if she was planning to walk to the Bell House, a stop at the coffee shop was on the way.

Heath and Hayden had been working at the house since early morning. They wanted to finish ripping out the rest of the walls in the kitchen and downstairs bathroom. No matter that Bellingwood was having a celebration next week, their friendly plumber was nearly ready to run pipe for the main level. They were going to have running water before she knew it. The boys' goal was to move into the house and camp there as soon as possible. They'd been working toward that end for most of the summer.

Polly had laid out a few caveats before agreeing to let them live there. They had to have water, there needed to be a working furnace by early October, and at least two of the rooms on the main floor needed to be finished so they had a place to sleep. The demolition was nearly complete, and once wiring and plumbing was in the walls, the boys would put things back together as fast as they could.

Heath had really taken to construction. He was a sponge when it came to learning the building techniques that Henry and his father taught. Hayden could do the work, but for Heath, it was as if a fire had been lit under him. When he wasn't at the Bell House or running errands for Henry's crews, he spent time with Bill Sturtz and Len Specek at the shop.

Henry hadn't said much yet, but it was obvious he was excited to have someone as passionate about the business as he was.

Polly chuckled as she opened the door to Sweet Beans. She was going to have two woodworkers in her immediate family. It didn't seem fair, but she'd suffer.

The cool air in the coffee shop was a welcome relief, even though she'd only walked three blocks. Sweat was already trickling down her back. Any work she did at the Bell House today was going to be miserable.

"Good morning, Polly." Skylar Morris beamed at her from behind the counter. "Your regular?"

"Iced today," she said. "It's beastly hot out there."

"Word has it you found another body yesterday." He lowered his voice to a whisper. "Are you going for a record this year?"

"Stop that," Polly said, laughing. "You're terrible."

"I can't believe you found her in your truck. Do they know who it was?"

"I have no idea. The sheriff thinks I shouldn't be involved in their investigation."

"You're the one who ends up solving them," Skylar said. "They should just put you on the payroll."

"He threatens, but nothing ever comes of it."

Skylar pointed at the front door and Polly turned around, just as the bell hanging from it tinkled. She put money on the counter and ran back to hug Sal Kahane. "I didn't expect to see anyone up here this morning," Polly said.

"We had to get out of the house before I climbed up the walls," Sal said. "I was feeling lonely for people." She set the baby carrier on a table and then grabbed Polly's hand and put it on the handle. "You stay here with Alexander while I get coffee." She walked away. "Strong and dark, Skylar. And tall. We had a grumpy night last night."

Polly peered down at Alexander and smiled. Wisps of dark

hair covered his head and he had the prettiest blue eyes with long lashes. He reached out with a hand, then clenched it into a fist and jammed the fist into his mouth. She bent over him and waited for him to make eye contact before saying, "Hello there, handsome."

He smiled.

"I know, I know. You're going to hear that for the rest of your life, but you really are cute. Did you make your mama crazy last night?"

"Yes he did." Sal put Polly's coffee on the table, then took a long drink of her own. "Mark had to be up early this morning, so I got the privilege of figuring what it was that the little prince needed. He was one well-fed, clean, and cuddled baby by the time he finally fell asleep."

"Did you get any sleep?"

Sal shook her head. "Not much. I nodded off in the rocking chair. Mark checked on us before he left and brought me a pillow, but I was too worn out to do anything else." She unbuckled Alexander and lifted him out and into her arms. "I'm not going to complain. Mother told me that this was the worst time of her life. I refuse to be as negative about things as she is." Sal kissed her son's head and sat down at the table. "I'm going to enjoy this, even if it kills me."

Polly laughed. "I still can't believe he's here."

Alexander had come a few days early and when Mark called, Polly rushed to the hospital with Rebecca, who didn't want to miss a thing. They'd sat in the waiting room and were right there when Sal was ready for visitors. Sal had patted the bed beside her and Polly sat down and held on to her friend. So much had happened since they'd moved into a dorm room together their freshman year of college. It was hard to believe that her Boston born and bred friend was living in Iowa, married and starting a family.

"I can't either," Sal said, resting her head on top of her son's. Her face lit up. "Kathryn is going to spend a few days in town, you know. She said that she would stay with Lisa if I didn't want her around, but Polly, she raised five children. I want her help."

"She'll love that," Polly replied. "It will be nice to have someone who knows more about babies than you do.

Sal laughed. "That's everyone. Mark's good, but his mother is terrific. I wouldn't care if she moved in for a month."

"Lila would be jealous."

"You know it." Sal rolled her eyes upward. "I promised that we would fly out to see them when he's a little older." She grinned. "Maybe when he's sixteen. That sounds about right, doesn't it?"

"You don't want her coming back to Bellingwood," Polly said.

"I'm just thankful that Kathryn is nothing like her. She's only a few hours away and if my mother were that close, I'd end up in an institution. Kathryn presumes nothing, she just helps when it looks like I need help. And she hasn't said a word about any of the decisions we've made. Nothing about eloping or anything."

"If everyone were like that, the world would be boring. Your mom makes the world not boring," Polly said with a laugh.

Sal chuckled and stroked the hair on Alexander's head, then ran her fingers down his forehead, his nose, and touched his lips. "She certainly does." She took a drink of her coffee. "Mark said you had an interesting day yesterday. Are you okay?"

"I'm fine," Polly replied.

"You really found a dead girl in the bed of your truck?"

"I really did."

"Then these murders are about you. Are you safe?"

"I guess," Polly said with a shrug. "Aaron hasn't told me that I'm not. But then he hasn't told me much."

"Speaking of Aaron, his wife came over the other day. She brought three different meals, with salads and breads and cupcakes. Mark keeps making a big deal about having real home-cooked food in the house."

Polly laughed. "I think Lydia has fed every person in Bellingwood at one time or other."

"How can you be scared of the sheriff when his wife is that fabulous?"

"And people wonder why nobody ever runs against him in the elections. It isn't about him, it's because people love his wife,"

Polly said. "Okay, he's got a lot of integrity and cares about people, but still."

"We're going to have meals for weeks. Kathryn sent Mark a grocery list of things to have on hand for when she got here. She said she was going to stock my freezer with pre-made meals. All of the instructions would be on the containers. Who are these women and why am I not one of them?" Sal asked.

Polly laughed until she snorted. "I have this image of you with five kids, slaving away in the kitchen, canning tomatoes - making salsa and spaghetti sauce, snapping peas and beans to be canned, freezing corn. Basically turning into a domestic diva."

Sal dramatically lifted the back of her hand to her forehead. "Heaven forfend. If that day ever comes, it will be quite impressive, that's for sure."

"And I'll take pictures and post them so all of your friends can see what you became."

"They'll never believe it. Heck, half of them think I'm involved in some weird cult out here in the middle of the country."

"Really?"

"Oh, it was a rumor there for a while. Why would Sal Kahane ever leave Boston for a little town in the middle of Iowa?" She smiled at Alexander in her arms. "The love of a good man and a little boy. That's why."

CHAPTER FIVE

"Now, I heard you two were out here," Sylvie said, brushing flour from her apron. She stripped off a pair of latex gloves, jammed them in a pocket and sat down beside Sal. "Will you give him up to me?"

Sal smiled and put Alexander into Sylvie's arms. "This woman has been my sanity," she said to Polly. "When I think I'm doing something wrong, she reminds me that women have been raising babies since the dawn of time and the human race continues to exist. I can't screw it up that badly."

Alexander started to fuss and Sylvie stood, then paced around the room before returning to the table where she bounced back and forth.

"He might be hungry," Sal said, digging down into her bag.

Polly glanced at it and realized it was one of the classiest diaper bags she'd ever seen. "When did you get that?"

"Mother sent it. Can you imagine? Two hundred dollars for a diaper bag?" Sal shook her head, then pulled out one of Polly's homemade burp rags and handed it up to Sylvie before giving her a bottle.

"That looks a little odd," Polly said.

"What?"

"My silly little burp rag in that expensive bag."

"He loves them. I love them." Sal swatted at Polly's hand. "And don't you dare. You made something lovely for us because you love me. Mother sent this so I would tell people how expensive it is. And look, it worked."

Sylvie grinned down at them. "I doubt she intended for you to tell us in such derogatory tones." She teased Alexander's lips with the nipple and within moments he was suckling. "I know you'd rather have been nursing, but I certainly don't mind feeding this little cutie."

Sal wrapped her arms around her chest. "Those first two weeks were hell. I hurt all the time and he was always hungry. Life is much better now." She smiled at Polly. "And I can drink coffee again. Life is good for all of us."

"So what did you think about Elva?" Sylvie bumped Polly with her butt. "You spent time with her yesterday, right?"

"She's really great," Polly said. "I'm curious, though, as to why she's in Bellingwood."

"Elva?" Sal asked.

Sylvie reached down and put the baby back into Sal's arms, moving slowly enough for Sal to adjust the bottle in transition. Sal sat back and beamed at her son, making Polly's heart swell with joy for her friend. She'd never thought to see Sal so happy.

"Eliseo's sister showed up," Sylvie said. "I'm going to get some coffee. Polly will tell you."

"Yeah," Polly said. "I'll tell her how concerned you were when you heard me say that his wife and four kids were in the office."

"Wait. What?" Sal asked. "Wife? Kids? Eliseo? Sylvie, you were upset about that?"

"I was not," Sylvie said while walking away. She stopped, turned around, and waggled her index finger at Polly. "Don't you dare start any rumors."

Polly leaned in and said in a stage whisper, "She was upset."

"His wife?" Sal asked.

"No, his sister," Polly said. "Something is going on with her husband and she brought her four kids to Bellingwood. When she introduced herself, she told me that she was Eliseo's wife and implied that he had run away from her and their four children, who were right there all looking for their daddy. It was funny for a minute. Sylvie was right behind Eliseo when he ran from the meeting in the conference room to see what was going on. She was ..."

Sylvie interrupted. "I was curious. Just like everyone else."

"So you weren't worried that he had a wife? You don't really care?" Polly taunted.

Sal frowned. "I thought you were interested in Grey out at the hotel. Haven't you two been out on a few dates? I saw you a couple of weeks ago at Davey's with him." She raised her eyebrows at Polly. "And it looked like they were having a very good time. Leaning in to whisper at each other. He touched her arm a lot. Sylvie smiled and giggled ... a lot."

"Stop it," Sylvie said. "We're just friends. I'm friends with Eliseo, too. I'm not dating anyone with the intention of it going anywhere. There's too much on my plate right now."

"Does Grey know that you're just friends?" Sal asked.

Polly chuckled. For once she wasn't the one asking all the questions. Someone else was putting Sylvie on the spot. It was nice to just watch it unfold.

"Yes he does," Sylvie said. "I've made that very clear."

"Has Eliseo ever asked you out on a date?"

Sylvie looked down at her lap. "No."

"What's that look for?" Polly asked.

"I don't think he ever will." Sylvie gave her head a quick shake. "I don't want to talk about it. This isn't a good topic of conversation."

Sal laughed, then stopped when she realized she'd jostled Alexander. He finished the bottle and she put it on the table in front of them, then tucked the burp rag around his neck and pulled another out of the bag. She threw it over her shoulder and held him against herself. "Sylvie, you and I have talked about my breasts, my nether region, and the vile things that come out of my baby's body. I think we can talk about your love life." She grinned. "I think we *should* talk about your love life. You need one, lady."

"I don't need any such thing," Sylvie protested. "I have my boys and a dog who tell me they love me. I have two jobs with way too many employees who need me to take care of them. I have all of you to talk to and be social with. Tell me why I need a love life."

"That's why," Sal said. "Because you feel the need to justify yourself."

"I'm not justifying." Sylvie threw her hands up. "Why do I bother?"

"Why won't Eliseo ask you out?" Polly asked.

Sylvie leaned in. "You know he kissed me that one time, right?"

Polly nodded yes and Sal shook her head no before Polly could make her stop. "He kissed her. That's enough."

Sal's eyes grew big. "Was it a good kiss? Did you want him to keep kissing you? Did you kiss him back?"

"Yes, yes, and yes," Sylvie said. "But we both freaked out. It was when my ex-husband was around and we were living out at Eliseo's house."

Sal turned to Polly. "She was living with him and nothing came of it?"

"I know, right?" Polly said.

"Stop it, both of you," Sylvie hissed. "My love life or lack thereof is not any of your business. I'm perfectly happy right now. I have everything that a girl could possibly want. And I don't have to put up with a man in my bed."

Polly and Sal looked at each other. "Bed's where you want them," Polly said.

Sal laughed out loud. "Well, I will in a few more weeks. Though he is good for rubbing my back in the middle of the night."

"You know what I mean," Sylvie said. "I've slept by myself now for a lot of years and it wasn't much fun when I was married to the father of my children."

Polly reached across the table and took Sylvie's hand. "You're right. I'm sorry. But you know Eliseo is nothing like what's-his-name."

"Anthony," Sylvie said. "And I know that." She leaned in again. "But girls, I've never been with anyone other than Anthony. He was terrible. I mean, really bad in bed. At least, I hope it was just him and that isn't the way it is for everyone. Because if so, I don't see what the big deal is about sex."

"It was never good?" Sal asked, astonished.

"Not ever. Not even when we were messing around before we got married," Sylvie said. "Isn't that when it's supposed to be illicit and fun? Yeah. Not us. It was always ..." She stopped and thought for a minute. "Beige, with tints of dark grey. Well, that is, until he decided he liked the looks of black and blue."

Sal handed Alexander back to Sylvie, brushing her fingers across Sylvie's cheek. Then she threw the burp rag over Sylvie's shoulder. "I can't believe you've never known what it's like to have wild, raucous sex."

Polly snorted. "Or, you know, the tender love stuff, too. Good heavens, Sal, what do your neighbors think?"

"That we're having more fun than they are. We're their inspiration. I figure if we keep it up, there will be a lot of small children in the neighborhood for Alexander to play with."

"You're kidding me, right?" Sylvie asked.

"I'll tell you the truth if you'll tell us whether you'd rather be with Grey or Eliseo," Sal said. She reached over and brushed a lock of hair on Alexander's head, then giggled when he let loose a loud belch on Sylvie's shoulder. "That's my good boy."

"Grey is a perfect gentleman and I love going out with him," Sylvie said. "We always have interesting conversations. You know, about big ideas and thoughts. He reads a lot and it's fun talking to someone who doesn't just want to gossip about people in town or talk about politics or all of the trouble in the world. He's interesting and he makes me feel like an interesting person when I'm with him." She huffed. "And after spending my days with brides and their mothers or with flour and dough up to my elbows and then dealing with two testosterone-filled sons at home, it is really wonderful to have adult conversations that feel like they mean something."

"You know he'd take the relationship further with just a little encouragement, don't you?" Polly asked.

Sylvie nodded. "Yes, but that isn't all I want from a relationship. I've been single so long, it would be really nice if there were someone around who would just take care of things for me without me having to ask. And that's Eliseo. Do you know that he and Jason fixed my garage door last week? I just noticed that it needed some work, but hadn't gotten around to calling anyone. Then all of a sudden it was fixed. And he comes over and makes the boys go out with him and trim the trees and the bushes. He pays attention to those little things and just takes care of them. It's like it's nothing to him, but it's everything to me."

Polly nodded. "Do you tell him how much that means to you?"

"I suppose." Sylvie shrugged. "I tell him thank you and that I can't believe he does those things, but I've never said it like that to him."

"You should," Sal said. "He needs to hear it from you."

"It's awkward." Sylvie tucked Alexander back into her arms. "We are so comfortable when we're with each other. But then it's like we both seize up and back off before we get intimate."

"So which man do you want?" Sal pressed.

Sylvie put her face onto Alexander's tummy and rubbed her nose back and forth, then touched his nose, making him giggle. "I don't know. I wish that Eliseo and I could just get past the whole awkward thing and go out on a real date. But neither of us can figure out how to break through." She looked up. "And now that his sister is here, we'll put it off even longer. He's going to be busy with her and her kids. With the celebration coming up and all of the meals we're preparing at Sycamore House, and I have a ton of bakery orders to get out of here during these next two weeks, there isn't going to be much time for me to think about it either."

She looked at the child in her arms. "You're such a pretty boy, you're going to have lots of girls paying attention to you. You listen to your mommy and daddy and learn how to be a smart young man when it comes to dating, though. Okay?" Sylvie sighed. "I haven't done too well with my boys, that's for sure."

"Andrew and Rebecca are doing okay," Polly said.

Sylvie laughed. "That's only because Rebecca is in charge. She tells him where to be and how to get there. It's pretty funny."

Polly nodded. "At least we don't have to worry about them getting into trouble."

"Yeah," Sylvie agreed. "Especially after you scared the bejeebers out of them. And trust me, I'm grateful. But he was never going to be the aggressor. I probably scared that out of him when he was just a very little boy. Poor Jason, he wants to have a girlfriend so badly, but he doesn't know how to make the move from being a friend to being a boyfriend."

"That girl, Mel?" Polly asked.

"She's good for him. But he'll probably let her get away, too. Then he and I will live in that house for the rest of our lives - sad and pathetic."

"You need to fix this," Sal said. "Soon. If you wait for the perfect time, you will be all alone in that house."

"Do you really have wild, raucous sex all the time?" Sylvie asked, her face brightening.

Sal shook her head. "No way. You never answered my question."

"What question?"

"Which one do you want? Grey or Eliseo?"

"I want both. How's that?"

"Not good enough. If you had to choose right now. Life or death decision. Which would you want to spend the rest of your life with in that house of yours?"

"It's always been Eliseo," Sylvie said, practically in a whisper.

Polly put her hand down on the table, startled when the slap was so loud. "I knew it. I just knew it. Why won't you do something about it, then? You and I both know that there's nobody else for him but you. He fell in love with you the day he met you. And then he fell in love with your boys."

"What am I going to do?" Sylvie asked.

Sal rapped her fingers on the table. "You're going to talk to him. You're going to put your big girl sexy panties on and take him somewhere there are no kids or horses or dogs or people and you are going to talk to him. Then you're going to freakin' kiss him right on the lips."

"I can't do that," Sylvie said.

"Yes you can and you will. You've got to break through this stupid wall that the two of you have built. It's turned into something immense when it's just not that big. Nobody is around to tell Eliseo what to do, but you have two friends right here who are going to stand behind you and push until you make it happen."

"You'd have more than that," Polly said, "if the rest of your friends had the courage to step past your 'I'm in charge' persona. You've scared me off for the last couple of years and I don't scare that easy."

"Little boy there gave me more courage than I usually have," Sal said with a laugh.

Sylvie sighed and gave Alexander her finger to play with. He wrapped his little hand around it and she smiled. "Maybe I'll find my courage one of these days." She looked up. "Okay. Now I told you what you wanted to know. It's your turn. Do you really have wild and crazy sex all the time?"

"We've been known to run around the house naked; screaming and laughing. We both like sex. I never thought I'd marry someone who liked it as much as I do," Sal said. "It's so much fun. When we're making love outside, we try to be a little quieter. We don't want the cops to show up because someone thinks I'm being murdered." She turned to Polly. "You don't show up until the body is dead, not just suspicion of murder, right?"

"In your back yard? What if someone sees you?"

"We have a fence and if they're looking into our back yard, well, that's their problem. Not mine."

"Do you guys have sex like in elevators and public places?" Sylvie asked, with a bit of a gasp.

"Sure, why not? Now that Alexander is here, it will be a little more difficult to make out in the truck. But once we find a steady babysitter, I plan to keep having fun."

Sylvie turned to Polly. "Do you and Henry do this?"

Polly slowly shook her head. "Uhhh, no. Compared to Sal and Mark, we're an old married couple. I like the comfort of my bed." She winked. "And sometimes the shower."

"See," Sal said. "You aren't that old and married. There are a lot of lakes, rivers and ponds around here. You should really try skinny dipping sometime."

Sylvie put her hands over her hears. "La la la la la. I don't want to hear this. I'm never going to be able to look at Mark the same way."

Sal laughed. "There's a park in Ames that's seen a lot of action. Then there was the night we were coming back from a meeting in Des Moines and decided we weren't going to make it, so we rented a hotel room and left after we'd been there for two hours."

"No way," Sylvie said.

Polly snorted with laughter. "She's my hero."

"Three or four kids are really going to put a dent into that sex life," Sylvie said.

Sal nodded. "I already told Mark that when we have more kids and a bigger house, we're putting heavy-duty locks on the doors and sound-proofing our room. We'll put surveillance microphones in the rest of the house so we know what's going on, but I do not need our children to be embarrassed because they heard us or even worse, walked in on us."

"Maybe you should buy a house in the country so the neighbors can't hear you," Sylvie said.

Polly laughed. "Yeah. Sal, the fertility goddess. Instead of a neighborhood filled with children, she'll have lots of baby deer, raccoons and bunnies. And the trees will be filled with birds every spring."

"You guys are sick," Sal said. "But I'm not arguing. Now back to you, Sylvie. I'm giving you a deadline. You have to talk to Eliseo before the end of the Sesquicentennial celebration. Once things get going, you'll have time. Make time."

Sylvie shook her head. "You got away with talking me into spilling my guts, but deadlines won't cut it. I'll do it in my own time."

"Your time has taken two years," Polly said. "Enough of that. Talk to the poor man."

"You two are a scary team," Sylvie said. "Here, take your son. I need to go back to work." She handed Alexander back to Sal and rolled her shoulders. "I should have known better than to come out here. All I wanted to do was get a little baby snuggle. You're dangerous when you're together."

Polly and Sal watched her walk back to the bakery.

"Do you think she'll do anything about this?" Sal asked.

"I don't know," Polly said. "I hope so. Those two need each other and they just won't admit it."

CHAPTER SIX

"Looking for someone?" Kristen asked Polly when she walked into the office. "They're all gone."

"Where'd they go?"

"Stephanie and the girls already left for Des Moines and Jeff is downtown for some lunch meeting. Rachel is at a catering job and Eliseo is in the barn." She picked up the telephone. "Sycamore House, how may I help you?"

Polly hadn't even heard it ring.

"He's out of the office right now, may I take a message?" Kristen typed out the message that was given to her and smiled up at Polly at the same time. The girl was good. "Thank you very much. He'll call you as soon as he can."

"Excuse me."

Polly stepped aside and smiled at one of the guests staying in the addition. He stood in front of Kristen's desk, waiting patiently.

"Yes, Mr. James. What can I do for you today?" Kristen asked.

"I'm expecting a package this afternoon," he replied. "If I don't return until after the office is closed, would you put it in front of my door?"

"I'd be glad to. If you'd like, I could open the door and set it on the table just inside your door," she said.

He shook his head and glanced at Polly. "No, no thank you. Just leave it outside the door. It should be perfectly safe. Nothing important. Just a few things I need for my work this week."

"I'll be happy to take care of that for you. Thanks for letting me know." Kristen beamed at the man and waited until he was out of the office before slumping her shoulders and rolling her eyes.

"Everything okay?" Polly asked.

Kristen put her finger up, telling Polly to wait, so Polly stepped into the hallway and watched the man enter the addition.

"He's gone."

"We have some strange guests over there," Kristen said.

"What do you mean?"

"It's just the two guys on the main level. The upstairs guests are normal. They have family here in town and are gone most of the time. But those two? They're weird. And they ask a lot of questions about you."

"Me?"

"Yeah. They were in here yesterday at the same time and one of them said he heard you had a reputation for finding dead bodies." Kristen shuddered a little. "The next thing I know, they wanted to see where you lived…"

Polly interrupted her. "What did you tell them?"

"I just said that you lived upstairs and it was private. Everybody knows that, right? "

Polly nodded.

"They were talking about which car you drove and who your family was and what Henry did. It just felt creepy. I get it that you own the place, but seriously, mind your own business."

"That is creepy," Polly agreed. "Was it one specific man or both? "

"It was both of them. I had to take a couple of calls, so I wasn't paying a lot of attention. And then Mr. James started bugging me about other things."

"Like what?"

"I don't know why he didn't make his reservation at the hotel, but he was insistent that he wanted to stay here. He asked why we don't have vending machines, even though the guest cooler in the kitchen is filled with fresh baked things from Sweet Beans. We keep potato chips and other snacks in there for the guests, too. Every day he comes in and asks me to do something else for him. But the weirdest thing is that he just sits on the benches in the hallway sometimes. He doesn't read or check his phone or do anything. He just sits there."

Polly laughed. "Maybe he likes all of the activity around here. He could be a people watcher."

"I suppose." Kristen shook her head.

"When did he come into town?"

"Friday afternoon. He's got the room until the Monday after Bellingwood Days."

"He's probably just taking it all in."

"We've never had the whole place full since I started working here," Kristen said. "It's kind of weird to have people around all the time. I don't know how you do it."

"We rarely use the front stairs and they don't go around back. So, Mr. James is in one of the rooms. Who's the other man?"

"It's a Mr. Nicholas," Kristen said. "He has a beard and he's kind of round. I told Jeff that he had another forty years or so before it was his turn to be Santa Claus. You know, that's how they deal with that in the North Pole, don't you?"

Polly smiled. "No, I don't think I do know."

"Santas start out as normal people. If they have the right name and the right look and the present Santa is ready to retire when they get old enough, then they turn into the next Santa Claus. The other one retires to the tropics and everybody is happy."

"I see," Polly said, nodding her head slowly up and down. "You have it all figured out."

Kristen shrugged and laughed. "I just made it up when he came in here looking like a newbie Santa. But it's a good story."

Polly shook her head. "With that, I'll head for the barn. I want to see how Eliseo did with a full house last night.

"He loved it," Kristen said. "He was telling us this morning that it was fun having his nieces and nephews playing in the house. I think he's happy that his sister is here." Kristen lowered her voice. "But why do you think she showed up? And why haven't they talked very much before? Was there some big family argument? Did her husband cheat on her? Did he hurt her?"

"I don't know," Polly said. "But I'm sure we'll find out. Just don't make up stories about her like you did with Santa Claus. She'll probably be around longer than him."

"My sister always tells me I gossip too much," Kristen said. "But then she asks me a ton of questions. She wants to know what's going on."

"Maybe you should start making crazy things up," Polly said. "Just for entertainment."

"I do all the time. She never believes me. I guess she knows me too well."

Polly put her hand on the door sill. "If you need anything, let me know. I'll be around for a while." She headed for the side door and glanced in through the glass door to the main level of the addition, just as Mr. James went into his room. That was a little weird. What had he been doing? She would have seen him if he'd been listening to her and Kristen talking, so it wasn't that.

She headed down to the barn and stood at the gate, watching Jason drive Demi and Daisy hitched to cart. Eliseo walked beside him, pointing at the horses and talking. The donkeys caught sight of her and ambled her way, then veered into the barn when Polly went through the main door.

"What are you doing here?" she asked Andrew. "Rebecca said she thought you would do something with one of your buddies."

"Everybody's busy." He looked up from a laptop. "Eliseo said I could use this. I'm writing a story."

"About what?"

"About a witch who was really powerful, but after a war, hid away in a forest for three hundred years. The world had changed when she finally came out."

"Why did she come out of the forest?" Polly asked.

"Because it was time." Andrew typed a few more words, then pushed the top of the laptop down. "Someone who knew her came back to the forest to tell her that she was needed again."

"Interesting. It sounds like a good story."

"We'll see. But it's a good thing that Rebecca went away today. Gives me more time to write. She always wants to do stuff."

"Like what stuff?"

"I don't know. Talk, play games, work on her projects. It's hard to concentrate."

"Why are you down here and not up at the apartment?"

He lifted a shoulder. "I didn't know if that was okay anymore. I'm only ever up there when Kayla and Rebecca are with me. You have a lot more people living there now."

"I suppose I do, but Andrew, you're always welcome in the apartment whether we're there or not."

"It just feels different now. Back when you first moved in, it was kinda like you needed me. But now you have Henry and Hayden and Heath. You don't need me to do anything anymore." He put his hands out. "And that's okay. I get it. But I'm glad that at least Rebecca kinda needs me every once in a while. Even if it's just to go find her sketchbook."

Polly laughed. "You have to stop letting her boss you around."

"I kinda like it," he said.

"This is not a good precedent to set with that girl. She'll run you ragged. And you'll never get any writing done."

"That's okay. I can write when I'm home. At least around there, nobody cares what I'm doing."

"What?"

"That's not what I mean. I just mean that Mom and Jason don't push me to do things. If I want to read or write, they leave me alone."

"Well I want you to tell Rebecca to leave you alone if you want to do those things when you're at my house."

Andrew grinned. "Nah. I like it this way. Maybe someday when we get bored talking to each other and doing stuff together, but not now. She's too much fun."

Two dogs, Khan and Kirk, barreled into the barn and up to Polly, then sat in front of her when Eliseo entered and clicked his teeth.

"Good boys," she said, bending down to rub their necks. "I saw you out with Jason. How's he doing?"

"He's learning. How are you today?" Eliseo asked. "I understand you had another difficult day yesterday."

Polly chuckled. "Difficult day. That's a good description for those days when I find a body. I just wish I had more information about these deaths. Aaron isn't being forthcoming with details."

"Is he ever?" Eliseo took her arm and directed her through Demi's stall to the pasture.

"I guess not. At least not until I torment him."

"You'd think the man would learn. You are generally quite successful at uncovering the murderer and motive. It seems he'd appreciate the help."

"He's always appreciative, but it goes against his grain to involve a civilian, especially one that he worries about," Polly said. "So what's up?"

"I wanted to talk to you about my sister."

She smiled up at him. "That's why I came down. To ask about last night. What was it like having a house full of kids?"

"That part was wonderful," Eliseo said. "They're very good children and they seemed to enjoy the new experience. But it's Elva I'd like to speak with you about."

"What can I do?" Polly asked.

"She needs a friend. Elva and I don't..." Eliseo took a deep breath. "We don't have an easy way with each other. In fact, I'm surprised that she came to Bellingwood." He looked at Polly, expressing pain with his eyes. "I'm eight years older than she is. I left for Iraq when she was still a little girl. When I returned, I wasn't the same brother she remembered. Right when she was growing into a young woman, I was caught in my own pain. I didn't have time or energy to deal with her silly flights of fancy." He bowed his head. "I know now that it was part of her life, but I couldn't see past the mess I was in. Then we just quit trying."

"I'm sorry," Polly said, reaching out to touch his arm. "I'm sorry you were so alone."

"It wasn't fair to expect her to become part of my drama," he said. "When I thought about it, I wanted her to grow up as normally as she could. I'm happy that she had fun in high school and college and that she was able to find a husband and have children. Since her kids were born, both of us tried to stay in touch. Her husband never really liked me." Eliseo pointed to his face. "I think this scared him. And I think it bothered him that the children *weren't* scared of me."

"Why is she here? Does it have to do with her husband?"

"As much as Elva wants you to believe that she's more outgoing and friendly, more talkative and gregarious than I am, she is as private as I've ever been. She won't tell me why they're separated. And I won't push her." Eliseo looked at her and his eyes sparkled. "But you make people talk to you."

"Hey," Polly said with a laugh. She could hardly disagree, but still. "What do you want me to do?"

"Do you mind being her friend?" Eliseo asked.

"Of course not. I'd love to. She seems like a really nice young woman."

"I'm not asking you to dig into her reason for being here. If she wants me to know, she'll tell me. She and the kids are welcome to stay with me as long as they'd like. I have plenty of room." He chuckled. "It was fun waking up this morning to the rumble of feet upstairs. And when they came tearing down the steps and into the kitchen for breakfast, it was the best."

"Having kids around certainly changes the whole house, doesn't it?" Polly asked.

"Last night I thought I would never be able to sleep because I was worried about having them there, but it was one of the best nights of sleep I've had in months."

Polly took his hand in hers. "You've been lonely."

Eliseo yanked his hand back and spun toward her. "No! I'm not lonely at all. I have the animals here and my dogs at home. Jason and his buddies bring entertainment to my days. I have friends."

He glanced south toward Ralph Bedford's home. "I have so many friends."

"But you're still lonely sometimes," she pressed.

"It's not really loneliness," he said. "Not at all. But it feels good to have noise and life and children in my home." He took her hand back. "Don't worry about me, Polly. You rescued me once. You don't have to rescue me again."

She started to chuckle quietly, her shoulders shaking.

"What's so funny?" he asked.

"You people put me in precarious positions," Polly said. "It's just not fair."

"I don't understand."

"It's not mine to say. But let me assure you that I'm not finished rescuing you. At least not if I can help it."

"You gave me a job ..." Eliseo looked up as Nat ran past, chasing Tom. "A job doing something I never thought I'd do again. You and Henry found a home for me, not once, but twice. I don't need any more rescuing."

"Whatever you say." Polly grinned.

"I'd appreciate it if you would focus your energy on my sister instead of me," Eliseo said. "I am perfectly content with my life. There is nothing more I could possibly want."

Polly slid her eyes up to peer at him. "Not even a wife?"

He laughed and shook his head, then dropped her hand and stepped away to pick up a pitch fork. Walking over to a large hay bale, he poked at it, pulling hay to the ground. "What would I do with a wife?"

"I don't know. What would you do with a wife? You could always tie her to a kitchen chair or dump her off the nearest cliff, I suppose." Polly leaned against the barn and crossed her arms in front of her.

Eliseo walked out into the pasture and waved at Jason, beckoning him to come back. He turned around. "I would be glad to watch Elva's children tonight if you would consider taking her to dinner." His eyes grinned at Polly. "I know that your family is busy and won't be around."

"How do you know these things?" she asked, furrowing her brow. "I didn't even know that."

"Henry called Jason to ask if he'd like to make some extra money. They're going to finish ripping out walls tonight and tomorrow so you can get plumbing and electricity put in on the main floor. In fact, it sounds as if you aren't going to have much family in the evenings for several days."

"Really. Funny that Henry didn't tell me."

Eliseo frowned. "Are you upset?"

"No," she said, laughing. "Not at all. Henry is working hard to get things done over there. I'd never complain." Polly pushed away from the barn and walked over to join him as they watched Jason bring the team in. "You know he's never going to be able to leave these horses behind and go away to college."

Jason brought the horses to a stop and handed the reins down to Eliseo, who waited while he climbed down.

"Did you see that, Polly? All by myself."

"You were wonderful," she said. "I was just telling Eliseo that it will be hard for you to go to college and leave them behind."

His eyes grew big. "I don't want to go away. Didn't Mom tell you? I'm applying to Iowa State. That way I can live in Bellingwood."

"Oh no you don't," Eliseo said. "You aren't living at home."

"Why not?" Jason asked.

"You're going to get at least *some* college experience. You'll live in a dormitory, meet new friends, meet girls, get in trouble, all of that," Eliseo said.

Jason looked at Polly. "Tell him. I don't want to."

She shrugged. "I went all the way to Boston. I met Sal because we were roommates in college. And I met a lot of other people, too. Part of college is learning how to live on your own."

"But Mom said I could."

"You have two years yet," Eliseo said. "Maybe you'll be tired of spending time with these horses by then. Come on, son. Let's un-hitch these beauties and rub them down. You gave them a good workout today. I'm proud of you."

They led the horses to the back of the barn and Polly called out. "I need Elva's phone number."

"It's in your email," Eliseo said over his shoulder. "Don't let her say no, and take her somewhere fun. It's on me."

She'd been dismissed. Polly went back into the barn and looked around for Andrew. She checked the stalls and the feed room, but he was long gone. Hopefully he was up in the apartment. Jason and Eliseo were talking quite loudly about college; a conversation Polly didn't want any part of. She headed back up to Sycamore House and stopped when she saw Andrew in the back with Han and Obiwan. Polly turned to go around front so the dogs wouldn't see her. Why couldn't those boys have stayed nine and twelve years old? Jason and Andrew weren't even her sons, but it was hard watching them grow up and have to figure out how to make good decisions.

Polly went inside and sat down on a bench in the main hallway, opened her phone and checked her email. Sure enough, there was Elva's phone number. She entered it into the phone app and swiped the call open.

"Hello?" Elva asked tentatively.

"Hi Elva, this is Polly Giller. Would you like to have dinner with me tonight?"

CHAPTER SEVEN

"You're wondering why I'm in Bellingwood, aren't you?" Elva had barely pulled her seatbelt on. "Did Eliseo tell you to ask me?"

"Uh, no?" Polly said. She backed out of Eliseo's drive and headed down the gravel road to the main street that would take them into Bellingwood.

Elva tapped her purse. "He's paying for dinner. The man thinks he needs to fix me, so I'll let him pay for the privilege."

Polly wasn't sure what to say. "What would you like to eat tonight? We have a few choices in Bellingwood or we can go to Boone or Ames if you'd like something else."

"Anything is fine." Elva rested her head on the back of the seat. "Other than those few minutes in your apartment yesterday, I haven't been away from my children in weeks. This is nice." She paused. "And quiet."

"So maybe not the bar," Polly replied.

"Drinking's not a bad idea," Elva said, almost hopefully. She lifted her head and looked at Polly. "It would loosen my tongue."

"That's really not the reason I asked you to dinner," Polly protested. "He just thought you might like to ..." She slowed for a cat crossing the road. It darted down into the ditch and she sped up again. "Oh hell. He said you needed a friend."

"Damn it. He is always sticking his nose where it doesn't belong."

That made Polly laugh out loud.

"What?" Elva asked.

"That doesn't sound like Eliseo at all." Polly glanced at Elva. "If you stay in town long enough to get to know me, it describes me perfectly, but not Eliseo. He doesn't bother anyone."

"He bothers me. He used to big-brother me to death." Elva wrung her hands in her lap. "Of course I was much younger. He didn't get a chance to be a brother when I was older." She sighed. "He would have been so disappointed in me. I could never measure up to wonderful Eliseo, so when I was in high school, I decided not to even try."

"He was back from Iraq by then?"

"Yeah. And out of the hospital. He was in a rehab facility. Dad asked about moving him closer so we could see him more often, but Eliseo didn't want to come. Mom went to see him a few times, but it was too hard on her. Shit," Elva spat. "We were a terrible family. I was too busy making my own trouble. Mom and Dad couldn't figure out which one of us to take care of, Eliseo was too proud to ask for our help, and we all got lost in our own little worlds."

Polly pulled up in front of the Jefferson Street Alehouse. She didn't want to break Elva's conversation, but she also had no idea what to say.

"Sammy isn't Larry's son," Elva said quietly. "I don't think even Eliseo knows that. He didn't come back to California until Ana was born and the only way Matty knows his uncle is from telephone calls. We haven't even done many of those. I want the kids to know their uncle." She shrugged. "I want to know him again, too. I can't believe he has that big house and all of that land. He said it was in your husband's family."

Polly didn't know what to say. So much information had just been dumped on her and Polly wasn't sure how to process any of it. "Yeah. Henry's grandparents lived there and then his uncle until he died. Eliseo moved in and has been renovating it."

"So it's not his house?"

"It's his house," Polly said. "But it was in pretty bad shape. He's done a lot of work."

"Is this where we're eating?" Elva asked, pointing at the Alehouse.

"That's up to you. It's just regular sports-bar food. Pretty good, nothing crazy. Davey's is out on the highway. That's nicer. We can get steaks there. Pizzazz is up the street." Polly grinned. "Pizza. And the new Mexican restaurant is okay. The diner is closed at night, but breakfast and lunch are awesome there. What do you want?"

"This is great," Elva said. "I could really use a few drinks. Since big brother is paying and you're driving, I'll just enjoy my night out."

Polly raised her eyebrows and quickly lowered them before getting out of the truck. She wasn't sure what Eliseo was doing wrong when it came to communicating with Elva. His sister had no problem talking. Before the night was over, Polly was certain she'd know Elva's entire life story, why she was in Bellingwood, and what she planned to do next.

They went inside, were seated, and when asked what they wanted to drink, Elva ordered a Jack and Coke. Polly asked for an iced tea and a mixed plate of appetizers. There was no way she was going to be out of control tonight. Not while she had Eliseo's little sister to take care of. Nothing could happen to Elva.

A young man brought their drinks and took their orders. As he walked away, Elva smiled. "He's a pretty boy. Kind of nice to look at from the back. Am I right?"

Polly chuckled. He was a good looking young man, but he was about Hayden's age and it felt really wrong to be ogling him. "I guess he is. But my son is that age."

"You have a son in college? You're not old enough," Elva said. "You and I have to be about the same age. And I know I'm not old enough. Even if I'd had a baby when I was still in high school."

"He's not really my son. Henry and I adopted his younger brother, and since their parents are dead, he's part of the package."

"That makes sense." Elva frowned. "You've adopted two kids, right?"

Polly nodded. "My daughter, Rebecca, is in junior high. Her mother died last year and the adoption was in place before she passed away. Heath's parents died several years ago. He'd been living with an aunt and uncle who didn't want him. When he got into some trouble, Henry and I stepped in and took over guardianship. His older brother, Hayden, is in college. He's an adult, but we wanted him to be part of the same family as Heath."

"That's really nice of you."

"I suppose," Polly said with a shrug. "But anybody would do it."

"Nobody else did, though. How did Seo end up working for you?"

If Eliseo hadn't told his sister the story of how he ended up at Sycamore House, Polly wasn't about to reveal his secrets. "He was just here one day when I desperately needed someone to help me with four horses that I'd rescued. He was an answer from heaven to a question I didn't know I needed to ask. He's amazing with those animals."

"Just like Dad," Elva said. "He taught us everything we know. Seo did something with it. Not me. The kids always wanted a dog, but I didn't want to have to deal with four children and dogs. That's a lot of poop and pee all at once."

"They seem like good kids," Polly said.

"They are," Elva said. "Sometimes they're a little much, but aren't all kids? Seo's good with them."

"How long are you staying in town?" Polly asked. She looked up as the waiter brought their appetizer platter to the table and put two small plates down.

Elva looked up at him. "If you see this glass is empty, bring another one. I'm on the loose tonight."

He glanced at Polly, who smiled at him, then said, "Got it. Do you need anything else right now?"

"Just keep me full," Elva said, "and there will be a good tip at the end of the night." She took a long drink and put the glass down hard on the table, then picked up a plate and put onion rings on it. She looked at Polly and laughed. "I'm filling a plate for you. It's been so long since I've been at a restaurant without the children, I don't know what I'm doing. Sorry." She handed the empty plate to Polly. "You can probably do this for yourself."

"If I need any help, I'll be sure to let you know," Polly said.

Elva put cheese nuggets and fried pepper rings on her own plate, then placed it in front of her and took another drink. "I'm going to get drunk really fast," she said. "If you have deep questions, you might want to ask those first."

"I have no deep questions," Polly said. "We're just having dinner."

"As long as he'll have me," Elva said.

"What?"

"You asked how long I was staying. I have nowhere else to go, so as long as Eliseo will put up with me, I'll stay in Bellingwood. I made the kids promise to be nice to him so he'd let us stay."

"You aren't with your husband?"

Elva's eyes grew hard and she took another drink, then put the nearly empty glass back on the table. "He'd better hurry up."

"Have some water while you wait," Polly said, pushing a glass in front of Elva.

"That's a good idea." Elva sat back, but didn't touch the water. "Larry is gone. He told me that he was tired of living with a wife and four kids. He wanted his freedom back." She shrugged. "Fine with me. Who needs that crap? He was working all the time anyway. At least I think he was working. Who knows, he probably had a couple of bimbos on the side." She leaned forward and said in a stage whisper. "We haven't had sex in nearly a year. What do you want to bet he's sleeping with someone else?"

"I won't take that bet," Polly said. "Did he ask you to move out?"

"Oh nothing that mean," Elva said. "He was really nice and generous and helpful. He moved his stuff to an apartment, then we sold the furniture that I didn't need and packed everything up into a storage unit. He's paying for that and he said that when I find a place to settle down, he'll pay to have it shipped to me." She looked up when the waiter brought another glass. "That's a very good boy," she purred. "Thank you."

Elva took a drink from the fresh glass and said, "Where was I? Oh. Yeah. Guilty much? He's paying for everything. The divorce and the whole shebang. He makes a ton of money, so he told me to get a lawyer and then his lawyer would figure out what he had to pay for child support. When I told him I was coming to Iowa, I think he was relieved. The kids miss him, but honestly, they hadn't seen much of him at all this last year. When he was home, he just sat in the living room and watched television. He never played with them or took them anywhere. And he isn't fighting for custody. He just doesn't want them."

"That doesn't sound like fun," Polly said.

"We learned to live without him. It was no big deal. Everybody does it, you know."

Polly shook her head. "I can't imagine living like that."

"Once we sold the house, I packed what was left into the car and started driving. Then we ended up here. If Eliseo doesn't want us, we'll find another place to live. But I hope Iowa is good for us. The kids need to have family."

"Your husband didn't have family?"

"Yeah. He has a big family spread all over southern California. But they aren't close. They probably won't even notice we left."

"That's too bad."

"I'll probably have to get a job. Larry's child support will be okay for a while, but we can't live on that. I don't know what I want to do. I thought about going to veterinary school, but I screwed up college really bad. Then I got pregnant with Sam and then I met Larry and then it was babies all the time.

"It sounds like you just need to settle for a while," Polly said. "Eliseo isn't going to push you out of his house. He's glad you're here. There's no need to rush into anything. Especially after all the changes you and your kids have been through lately."

"There have been a ton of them," Elva said, draining the last of her drink. "But they've been good about it. Once I told them we were coming to see their Uncle Seo, that turned things around. At least they had something to look forward to."

"How hard for you, though."

Elva shrugged. "It's actually easier now. For the longest time, I was in limbo. I knew he didn't love me and I was pretty sure he didn't care about the kids, but what was I supposed to do? Every time I tried to talk to him, he went into another room and the next day he'd go to work and not come home for days. I learned to shut up and let it be. He wasn't abusive. He wasn't hateful or mean. He never said a cross word. He just quit caring. When I asked if he wanted to talk to somebody and try to get things back on track, he acted like I wasn't there."

"That's really hard."

"After a while you just get used to it. Some of my old friends will probably live out their whole lives like that. At least Larry had the balls to move on. That let me do something different with my life too. I don't know what it's going to be, but it's going to be different."

The waiter brought their sandwiches and another drink for Elva. "Anything else?" he asked.

Polly shook her head and picked up her sandwich. She'd ordered a Reuben. Elva was right. Sometimes you just had to do something different.

"So what is there to do in a little town like Bellingwood?" Elva asked. She took a small bite of her sandwich, put it back on the plate and took another long drink.

"There's always something," Polly said. "You're here just in time for Bellingwood Days. There will be a carnival and dances and all sorts of events next week. Eliseo and the horses are going to be in the parade and then because it's our sesquicentennial, he's going to take people for rides around town in the wagon during a couple of the evenings."

"Sethqwa. Ses." Elva shook her head. "What is that?"

"Hundred and fifty years."

"Oh, so like horse and buggies. Do I have to have bonnets for the girls?" She grimaced. "Bet there weren't too many little Mexican girls traveling across the plains in covered wagons back in those days."

"Probably not," Polly said. "Especially since most of them already lived in the Southwest, don't you think?"

"Is your Sycamore House that old?"

Polly shook her head. "No. Not by a long shot. But we'll be busy once everything starts."

"Seo isn't going to have much time for us, is he?"

"He'll make time, I'm sure of that. And if he's busy and you want help with the children, I know three junior high kids that would love to do some babysitting."

"I could help with something," Elva said. "I used to ride. It's been a while, but I haven't forgotten. I can also wait tables."

"Like I said. You should relax and settle in," Polly said.

Elva pushed her plate back. She hadn't eaten anything except that first bite. "But I want to help. Tell me you'll let me help somewhere. You've been so nice to me, it's the least I can do."

"We'll talk tomorrow. I'm sure we can find something."

"Polly! Hi there."

Polly turned and looked, then stood and hugged Joss. "What are you two doing out this evening?" she asked. "No kiddos?"

"Mom and Dad are in town," Joss said. "She kicked us out of the house, said they wanted to play with the babies."

"How long are they staying?"

"Two weeks," Nate said, grumpily.

Joss elbowed him in the belly. "Don't you dare complain. We have a big house now and they aren't in the way. With them here, we get nights out like this."

Nate laughed. "Just kidding, my sweet." He looked at Elva and Polly turned to her.

"This is Eliseo's sister, Elva," Polly said. "Elva, these are my friends, Joss and Nate Mikkels."

"Please to meet'cha," Elva said, slurring her words more than a little. She made an attempt to stand up, but shook her head and

dropped back into her seat. "Wow, it's been a while since I've been this drunk. And I need to pee. Where's the bathroom?"

"This way," Polly said. She turned back to Joss. "I'll talk to you tomorrow?"

Joss gave her a questioning look.

"No problem," Polly said quietly. "We'll talk later." She looped her arm through Elva's and walked the weaving woman to the bathroom.

"Well that's embarrassing," Elva said. "I meet your friends for the first time and I'm drunk on my ass. Sorry."

"No big deal. It's your night to let loose."

"Whooeee!" Elva said from inside the stall. "I'm certainly letting loose now. Ooh, that feels better." She stumbled out and over to the sink, where she fumbled for a handle. When she couldn't find one, she looked at Polly in a panic.

Polly ran her hand in front of the faucet and water came out.

"Oh. One of those. Man, I'm too drunk to wash my hands."

They made it back to the table and Elva finished another glass. "I should probably stop now. This is going to hurt bad in the morning."

Polly put her hand up to get the waiter's attention. "Could you box this up? We're heading out pretty soon."

"I don't need another one," Elva said, leaning precariously toward him. She caught herself on the table and said, "I'm-a gonna need my purse. Seo's money's in there."

Polly bent over, picked up the purse, and put it in front of Elva.

"You do it," Elva said. "I forget how to open it."

Polly knew that if she were with anyone else, this would be absolutely hilarious, but she didn't feel comfortable enough with Elva yet to laugh at her drunken antics. She unzipped the purse and opened it so Elva could look in.

"My wallet. That ugly red thing," Elva said. "Larry bought it for me." She waved her hand at the purse. "Seo gave me a hundred bucks. Tip the boy good, would you?"

CHAPTER EIGHT

This was Polly's second pot of coffee. Another night of very little sleep did not agree with her. She'd fretted over Elva. It was strange that the first thing the girl did with a new friend was get drunk.

When she got home, Rebecca was in a mood. She'd had a tiff with Kayla. That wasn't surprising. What did surprise Polly was that it didn't happen more often. Especially with the amount of time those girls spent together. Oh, they had little spits and spats, but never anything serious. This had sounded serious and Rebecca was more upset because it had happened in front of Stephanie, who'd had to tell the girls to stop talking to each other.

When the boys got home, they were filthy, exhausted and frustrated with the work they had yet to do before the plumber could start. Henry was taking today off, so he could spend it at the Bell House with Heath and Hayden. He didn't want to talk about it. The boys didn't want to talk; they just wanted to clean up and go to bed.

Rebecca didn't want to talk about what had happened either so she'd gone into her room to read. Polly finally took the dogs out for a long walk. She'd thought about stopping in to chat with Grey, but lights were on in nearly every room of the hotel and people were milling about in the lobby. He didn't need her to unload on him.

By the time they returned, everyone had gone to their separate corners. Polly made sure the doors were locked, shut the lights off and had gone into their bedroom, only to find Henry's light off. If he wasn't fully asleep when she got there, he did a good job of faking it. The house remodel was an overwhelming project for all of them. The boys were doing great work, but deadlines were tough to meet.

Polly had slipped her clothes off, pulled an old t-shirt of Henry's on and climbed into bed, then read until her eyes couldn't see straight. Even after she turned out the light, her mind wouldn't shut off. There were so many things coming up, and throughout the night the image of that poor girl in the bed of her truck kept startling Polly back awake. She'd finally come out to the media room and curled up on the couch to watch television. Henry usually came to find her, but he'd slept through the night, not even realizing she was gone. He'd been a little surprised this morning, but his mind was on so many other things, he just headed out, telling her to send the boys when they got up.

Heath and Hayden were out the door fifteen minutes later.

When Rebecca finally woke up, she ran downstairs to apologize to Stephanie. Apparently she'd spent the night worrying. Then she called Polly from downstairs to ask if it would be okay if she went over to Kayla's so they could work it out. She just couldn't wait for Kayla to come over after lunch. They had to talk right away. And it had to be face to face.

If there was one thing that Rebecca couldn't bear, it was unresolved strife. Polly appreciated that about the girl. She might be the cause of friction, but she was also the first to try to solve it. All Rebecca needed was time to calm down. Sometimes Polly could almost see her working through the chaotic conversations in her head. Once she heard what she'd said from the someone else's perspective, Rebecca was ready to make things right.

Polly opened the refrigerator. She'd promised Henry that she would take something decent for lunch to the Bell House. There was still plenty of meat left from the chicken she'd roasted yesterday afternoon. Polly chuckled. It amused her that she was the chief cook and bottle washer these days. They passed the job around most of the time, but for the last week or so, it had been all on her. That was fine. The only problem was that it forced her to get more creative in the kitchen.

The chicken came out onto the counter, along with celery and mayonnaise, Greek yogurt, and an onion. If the world was spinning the right way, she'd have slivered almonds in the cupboard. She found a bag, put them on a cookie sheet to toast in the oven and started chopping. Mary Shore had taught Polly about adding toasted almonds to different dishes, and when Polly had lived in Boston, one of her favorite delis served a chicken salad made this way. She hadn't yet made it for Henry, but he was pretty easy to please.

Once it was all mixed up, she put it back in the refrigerator to chill and filled two thermoses with ice. One she filled with water, the other she left as just ice. They had their favorite drinks at the house already. All she needed to do was take ice and plastic cups. Polly smiled. Lydia would make a big deal about preparing lunch. For that matter, so would Henry's mother. They'd pack the food in pretty picnic baskets with cloth napkins and table cloths. The boys would be lucky if Polly actually remembered to pack napkins.

She yanked plastic grocery bags out of the container under the sink and then shoved them back in. She could do better than that. Polly laughed. Nope. Plastic bags it was. She tried to remember to take her grocery totes with her, but more often than not, she was in a mad dash to pick something up. She felt guilty every time.

Thick slices of Sylvie's sour dough bread would fill the boys' tummies. She dropped apples into the bag, took a container of chocolate chip cookies out of the freezer, pulled two half-empty bags of potato chips out of the cupboard and filled the plastic bags. Just as she headed for the back door, she chuckled and went back to the kitchen for a stack of napkins.

Polly opened the door to the garage and wilted. Her truck was still in Boone. It wasn't enough that she found dead bodies, but now murderers were making things really inconvenient. She sighed, took out her phone and swiped it open to place a call.

"What's up?" Henry asked.

"I have no truck." She waited while he thought through it.

"Okay."

"No truck. No lunch for you." There. That would fix him.

"Just a sec," he said. Polly heard him yell. "Hayden, where are your keys? Polly needs to borrow your car."

He came back to the call. "Drive his car. The keys are hanging on the hook just inside the door going upstairs. His car is out front."

"Thanks. You know how I hate driving little cars, though, don't you?" she asked with a laugh.

"It's terrible being that low to the ground. I know. See ya in a bit."

Polly went back in and grabbed the keys from a hook and went out front. Hayden had parked his Impala down near the barn. She laughed as she slid down into the seat and then pulled it forward when her feet couldn't reach the gas pedal. "I hope no one smushes me on the highway," Polly muttered and headed for the Bell House.

Henry came out to the driveway when she pulled in. After she climbed out and hugged him, he stopped her before she reached back in for the bags of food. "We need to talk, Polly." His voice sounded so grim, Polly immediately grew worried.

"What's wrong? Did someone die?"

"I'm in so much trouble. You have every right to be furious at me. I just did something and I don't know how to tell you."

"Nobody's hurt, right?" Polly asked.

He frowned at her. "No. Why would you think that?"

"Nobody we know is dead, right?"

"Well, no. Well, kind of. But that's not the point."

"You're scaring me. Do you want to tell me what's going on?"

"If you'll let me."

She swatted at him and he jumped back. "Just spit it out."

"Roy called just after you hung up."

Roy Dunston was Henry's lawyer-friend from college. He lived in Chicago and worked with inner city kids. Each summer, he brought a group of them to Bellingwood so they could better understand that life wasn't only what they saw in the city. The kids worked with farmers and their families, lived in their homes, and made lasting memories.

"What's going on?"

"You remember the Fosters, right?"

She nodded. They were one of Roy's regular families for this experience. Not much phased them.

"Her youngest sister just found out she has cancer and they need to go help with the sister's family. They can't take the two boys that were going to stay with them." He bowed his head.

"And you said they could stay with us?"

Henry slowly nodded and then looked up at her. "How much trouble am I in?"

"You're not in trouble," Polly said. She put her hand on his arm. "Of course we'll take them. I'm just sorry they won't be able to experience a farm."

"I think it's okay this time," Henry said, looking relieved. "These two are pretty young. In fact, they're younger than the kids Roy usually brings. But it sounds like they need some care. Their mother died a few months ago and they've been living with their father's mother, but she's got a house full of grandchildren that she's caring for."

"So she raised some good solid kids of her own?" Polly asked, sarcasm lacing her voice.

"Uh huh. He said she's doing better with this generation than she did with the first. But the dad is in jail for murder and this woman is overwhelmed. The two brothers are the only ones who are eligible for Roy's program." Henry shook his head. "Okay, I guess the old lady isn't doing much better with this generation than the other. The older kids don't qualify for Roy's program because they can't follow the rules."

"I guess we're hosting two boys," Polly said with a smile.

"Roy was pretty upset. He was afraid he'd have to disappoint the boys."

Polly creased her brow. "For heaven's sake, no. That would be awful." She reached back in for the food and handed Henry the two thermoses. "Have you thought about where they'll sleep?"

He smiled. "Heath and Hayden said they'd set up camp here at the house and the boys can have Heath's room."

"I'm glad you three worked this all out before I got here," Polly said with a laugh. "If Heath and Hayden want to stay here for a couple of weeks, that's fine with me." She carried the bags of food as they walked around the house. "So what are we going to do with two boys? We don't have a farm."

"We have Eliseo and the animals at the barn. We have a kitchen that will be in full swing and we have a big old house that needs attention. I think we can keep them busy." Henry waved at Hayden through the window and followed Polly to the gazebo in the back yard.

"How old are the boys?" Polly asked.

"They're pretty young. But they're so impressionable," Henry said.

She turned to him and grinned. "You're avoiding the question. How old?"

"Seven and eight."

"That's second and third grade. He never lets them travel that young."

"These two need to get away from town and this was the only way Roy could think to do it. The Fosters were looking forward to spending time with boys that age. Are you really okay with this?"

Polly nodded. "I'll have plenty of help. Rebecca and Kayla will love having them around."

Hayden and Heath came around the corner of the house, laughing and pushing at each other. Hayden put his foot out and tripped Heath, sending him to the ground. The younger brother reached up, grabbed Hayden's shirt to pull him down, and soon they were wrestling.

"What in the world?" Polly asked.

Henry chuckled. "They've been like this all morning. It's a good thing we keep them busy during the day or I'm afraid Sycamore House would be in shambles.

As soon as it began, the wrestling match was over and the boys were back to chasing each other across the lawn to the gazebo.

"What was that about?" Polly asked.

Hayden scowled at his brother. "He called me a ..." he stopped and grinned. "Nothing. We were just messing around."

She turned to Heath, who just shrugged and glanced at his brother, a wicked grin on his face.

"What are you two fighting about?" she asked.

"It's really nothing, Polly." Hayden turned to Henry.

"Got it," Henry said. "Let it go, Polly. It's just brothers being brothers."

She reached into the bag and pulled out sandwiches, then muttered, "I hate being left out."

~~~

Henry and the boys hadn't wanted to take much time for lunch, but managed to send Polly home completely empty-handed. There wasn't a speck of food left, not a potato chip, not a cookie. She'd gone inside to ooh and ahh over the destruction they'd wreaked on the house. Once Jerry Allen and his crew, which included Doug Randall and Billy Endicott, re-wired the main level, and Liam Hoffman re-plumbed it, walls could start going back in. It really was just a matter of time.

She parked Hayden's car in the garage, dropped the trash into the garbage cans and opened the door up to the apartment, setting the thermoses on the first step. Obiwan and Han were standing at the top and Polly called them down. Just as she was about shut the door, she heard her name.

"Hi there," she said, looking up at Rebecca. "What are you guys doing?"

"Just hanging out. What are you doing?"

"We're going for a walk. Wanna come?"

Rebecca rolled her eyes. "Duh. No."

"Yeah. Didn't think so. By the way, you need to put extra effort into cleaning the bathroom. We're going to have guests on Saturday. A couple of boys." Polly pushed the door shut and herded the dogs to the garage door, laughing to herself. She was barely at the outside garage door when Rebecca caught up to her.

"What guests? Where are they going to sleep? Boys? Are they brothers? What are their names? When did this happen?"

"I need to walk the dogs," Polly said, trying to hold back her laughter. "I'll tell you all about it when I come back."

Rebecca grabbed her arm. "You can't do this to me. If you leave now, you won't be back for hours and you know how my curiosity will just kill me. You don't want to be responsible for that, do you?"

"I can live with it."

"Just give me a hint."

"We're getting two of Roy Dunston's boys, but they're very young. I don't know their names, but they are seven and eight years old. The Fosters have to go out of town, so they can't take care of them. Is that enough?"

"But where are they going to sleep?"

"Heath and Hayden are camping at the Bell House."

Rebecca stepped back. "That makes sense. But why do I have to clean the bathroom?"

Polly headed for the tree line to follow the dogs.

"That's not an answer," Rebecca called after her.

"It'll have to do," Polly said to herself. She took off at a jog to catch up to the dogs as they closed in on the fence of the pasture. She didn't see anyone or any of the animals, so headed for the barn door, wondering what was up.

"Hi Polly," Elva said. She was sitting on a bench with her youngest, Matty, who was scratching Tom's head. One of the cats was in her lap, purring loudly at the attention.

Obiwan and Han bolted through Demi's stall to the pasture.

"Where is everyone?" Polly asked.

"Out for a ride. My other three wanted to ride in the wagon with the boy, Jason. Seo and one of Jason's friends are riding with them.

"Where's Huck and the dogs?"

Elva shrugged and looked around. "They're here somewhere."

Polly walked through the stall and looked out into the pasture, then saw the four dogs chasing each other. Because of the horses, the dogs had learned to be careful of where they ran, but with a wide open pasture, all four were running at top speed. She spotted Huck at the far corner, looking off to the west.

"Probably wondering where everyone went," Polly said and turned to go back in. She dropped onto a bench across the alley from Elva. "How are you feeling today?"

"I'm so embarrassed," Elva said. "I haven't had that much to drink since before I got pregnant with Samuel. I hope I didn't do anything to embarrass you in front of your friends." She shook her head. "What are they going to think of me?"

"It's okay. We were in a bar. People get drunk in bars." Polly grinned. "I like to get drunk in bars. It's really no big deal."

"Seo was pissed as hell at me when I got home. Told me that I shouldn't have done that since you were his boss." Elva gave a small laugh. "He's right. That was stupid. I really am sorry."

"Don't give it another thought," Polly said. "You needed to release stress and you were in a safe place."

"But I shouldn't have done that with you. You barely know me and there I am acting like an out of control brat. I promise I'm more responsible than that."

"It's really okay." Polly put her hands up. "You have to let it go."

"I told Seo that I should cook a big dinner for you and your family. Have you come out to the house some night this week."

Polly opened her mouth to agree, then realized Henry would hate that right now. Between his job and the Bell House, he had no extra time. "This is a bad week," she said. "My husband and sons are desperate to finish tearing out walls and ceilings in the house so we can move forward with electrical and plumbing. Next week will be busy with the celebration. But if you're sticking around for a while, once things settle down, we'd love to come out."

Tom flung his head around and took off for the back door, leaving a startled Matty in his wake.

"I'll bet he heard the horses," Polly said.

"That's good. I need to go up to the pharmacy and get some prescriptions filled. Is there a doctor in town?"

Polly nodded. "Sure. For the kids?"

"Yes," Elva said.

"Doctor Mason is a wonderful man." Polly opened her phone and scrolled through her contacts. "Do you want his information?"

"That would be great." It was as if the thought of needing a doctor for her children added strain to Elva's face. Lines appeared around her eyes and her mouth grew tight.

"Is everything okay?"

Elva sighed. "All you want is for your children to be happy and healthy."

"Yours certainly look that way."

"We just found out last year that Samuel is diabetic." Elva's eyes filled with tears. "We nearly lost him."

"He almost died," Matty said. "And now he has to give himself shots. But he isn't afraid."

"No. He's very brave." Elva patted her son's head. "Ana has asthma. But she's had that forever so we mostly know what to do with it. I'd like to get them in to see a doctor though."

"If there's anything I can do to help..." Polly said.

"No, this is enough." Elva looked up at her brother who walked in. "Did you have a good ride?"

"Jason is very confident with the wagon. He'll be ready for next week," Eliseo said. He glanced at Polly.

"It's all good," she said. "We were just talking about doctors for the kids."

He nodded. "I couldn't remember who you used."

"Doctor Mason."

"Can I leave the kids with you while I go up to the pharmacy?" Elva asked her brother.

"I suppose," he said.

She looked at him, a frown on her face. "Is it a problem?"

"I'm working here, Elva."

"Let me take the kids up to the apartment," Polly said, then promptly wished she had kept her mouth shut. She didn't need to get between these two.

Eliseo shook his head. "They'll be fine here."

"I'll take Matty with me, then," Elva said. "And I'll be back in a bit to get the others." She jumped up from the bench, put her hand down for Matty to take and went out the main door.

Polly felt a little out of place and didn't know what to do or where to go. Eliseo stalked out of the barn, leaving her to breathe a sigh of relief.

She went to the door of Demi's stall and called for Obiwan and Han, who stopped what they were doing and looked at her, as if to ask if she meant it. She called their names again and the two dogs slunk over, then followed her out and up the sidewalk to Sycamore House. By the time they were at the bottom of the steps leading to the apartment, both dogs were bouncing with joy.

CHAPTER NINE

Heath and Hayden were moving over to the Bell House and it was killing Polly. She wasn't worried about their behavior; she'd miss having them around. Even when they came in exhausted and grumpy after working all day, it was still fun. She'd spent the week shopping for them, while they packed up the essentials they would need.

Until the water lines were run at the Bell House, they planned to come back to the apartment to shower in the evenings, but otherwise they were gone.

Last night, Polly had stripped and re-made Heath's bed. She wiped down horizontal surfaces while Rebecca swept the floor. Then the two of them finished cleaning the bathroom. It was worse than Polly realized and she wasn't leaving the whole task to her daughter. There were going to be six bathrooms at the Bell House. How in the world was she ever going to manage that place?

"What are you thinking about?" Henry asked. "You have a pinched look on your face, like something scares you to death. Is it the boys showing up today?"

Polly laughed. "No. Though I'm a little worried about how I will keep two little boys busy for the next couple of weeks. I was just freaking out over all the bathrooms at the Bell House. I hate cleaning bathrooms."

"I swear, I'm going to hire someone to help you," Henry said. "And as for the boys, you did great with Andrew. He was only nine when he started spending time with you."

She pursed her lips together, then said, "All he wanted to do was read and play video games. He was easy."

"Trust me," he said. "These boys won't be much different. Just think, they've never seen anything like Bellingwood. You can show them all the sights, take them out for ice cream and pizza." He laughed out loud. "And take them to Beryl's studio. Now wouldn't that be a riot."

"I know. You're right. It's just that today is finally here and now it's going to be real. I'm nervous."

Rebecca ran into the dining room and slid to a stop in front of the dining room table. "Can I borrow your camera today, Polly?"

"Sure. Why?"

"I want to take pictures of all of the boys who come here with Henry's friend. Maybe I can draw each of them a sketch so they have something to take home."

Polly nodded. "That would be wonderful. It's in the top drawer of my dresser."

"Cool. Thanks. How long until they're here?"

"Eleven thirty," Henry said. "A quick lunch in the classroom and then they'll meet their hosts and head out."

Rebecca looked up at the clock on the wall. "Cool. I have plenty of time. Are we eating lunch with them?"

"You can," Henry said. "It's just sandwiches and chips."

"Are you?" Rebecca asked Polly.

"Probably not. I'll just go down when all the other hosts are there," Polly said.

Rebecca huffed. "Okay. I'll wait, too." Then she perked up. "Kayla is coming over early because Stephanie is helping get things ready for tonight. You're going to that, right?"

"Of course I am. I've got my boots and jeans all ready to go."

"What are you going to do about the little boys?" Rebecca asked.

Polly's shoulders fell. She hadn't even thought about it.

"They'll go with us for a while," Henry said. "I'll be ready for bed before it gets too late even if Polly's still dancing."

"I should have gotten them cowboy hats," Polly said. "I want them to feel like they belong."

He laughed at her. "I love you, sweetie. They'll be fine. Remember, you can't buy too much for them. They won't be able to safely take it back home and it would be awful to make them leave things here."

"This is getting harder and harder," she complained.

"Yeah," Rebecca said. "Polly loves buying things for people." She sidled up to Polly. "And we love it when you do."

"Stop it, you little rat," Polly said. "Quit giving me trouble or I'll never buy you another thing."

Rebecca grinned up at her. "I'm so worried." She sashayed out of the dining room. "See how worried I am?"

"See," Polly said. "I'm not ready for this. I can't buy presents for the boys, I completely forgot about all of the places I need to be this next week. How am I going to find baby-sitters at this late date? Do I even have food in the house that they'll like?"

Henry backed away and looked her up and down. "Who in the world are you? What did you do with my wife?"

"I'm serious."

"I know that. But this isn't like you. You handle everything that comes at you. These are just two little boys who are coming to Bellingwood to have some fun and see a different world."

"You know what it is," Polly said.

He huffed a chuckle. "No, what's that?"

"You should have sprung the whole thing on me this morning. I thought I had time to plan, but I missed a bunch of processes. If you'd told me this morning that I was going to have two young guests, I would have just dropped into it and bullied my way forward."

"Aha." Henry tapped his forehead. "I'll remember that for next time. Last minute is much safer than four days' notice."

"Exactly." She poured another cup of coffee and waggled the pot at him. When he shook his head no, she asked, "Have you heard from Hayden or Heath this morning? Were they okay by themselves last night?"

"They were great by themselves. I told them to take the morning off." He frowned. "I forgot. Your truck is ready."

Polly's eyes grew big and she grinned. "I get my truck back? That's awesome. When can we go get it?"

"Heath will take me to Boone this afternoon. I'll leave my truck here just in case you need to take the boys shopping." He smiled at her and Polly grimaced back. Henry took his mug to the sink and rinsed it out. "Hayden is meeting friends in Ames for lunch, but I think both boys are coming to the dance tonight. They'll be here early for showers and dinner."

"Good." Polly waved her hand around the room. "This? I don't like it. It's too quiet. I like having them around in the morning. Especially Saturday mornings."

"It's going to be worse when we have electricity and water over there. They won't need to come here for showers."

Polly lifted the corner of her upper lip. "I like that even less. But once these boys have gone back to Chicago, I want Heath and Hayden to move back home."

Henry slipped his arm around her waist. "You know that's going to be really difficult to pull off, don't you?"

"What do you mean?" She turned in his embrace to face him. "They don't want to come back here?"

"Will it kill you if they don't?"

"Yes." Polly stuck her lower lip out. "It will kill me."

"Really?"

"No. Not really. But I don't like it. I miss them."

"I know that. But they're old enough to make these decisions on their own."

She set her jaw. "You better get that place ready for me, then. Rebecca and I are moving in as soon as we can."

"I thought we weren't planning to live there until at least next year."

"Electricity. Water. Walls. Doors." Polly ticked the list off on her fingers. "That's all I need. I want my family together in the same house. If they don't come back here, I'm going there."

"What if I stay here in the comfort of this beautiful apartment?" Henry asked.

"You're not fair." She poked her lower lip back out. "You wouldn't do that to me. Would you?"

"Not with any success. Let's see how this all works out. Maybe they'll be ready to move back in after a couple of weeks without any air conditioning or creature comforts."

"Yes," she said. "Make it as miserable as possible for them."

He laughed at her. "You're the one who was out buying blow-up beds and room dividers to make it nice."

"I'm a fool. I will take it all back."

"I love you, sweet girl." Henry kissed the tip of her nose. "I'm going downstairs. Come down when you want."

~~~

Rebecca couldn't stand it and took Polly's camera down early. She was excited to meet these kids who had come from such a different world. Polly wandered through the apartment, moving things around, rearranging pillows on the sofas and getting more excited as the minutes passed. Just about the time she was ready to give in, a text came in from Henry that the hosts were beginning to arrive.

"You guys stay here and be good," she said to the dogs. The cats had given up on her after she'd tripped over Leia. They were hiding on the cat tree in the bedroom.

Polly went down the steps and said hello to a family that was heading for the classrooms.

Henry met her at the door with a grin. "They're a lot younger than I expected."

"What are their names?" she whispered to him.

"Elijah and Noah."

Polly looked up. "Really?"

"Maybe they'll save the world someday just like their namesakes," he whispered back. Then he nodded at the two boys sitting together on a sofa. The youngest was practically on top of his brother as they looked through books on the side table.

Rebecca ran up to Polly. "Have you met them yet? They're adorable. And they aren't scared of me at all."

Polly laughed. "Because you are so frightening."

"Well, I might be to them. But they let me take their picture. Here, look." Rebecca flipped through pictures on the camera and stopped. The two boys were clowning it up, holding two fingers behind each other's heads, wrestling each other into headlocks, making faces. They were clearly having fun.

"Come with me," Rebecca said. "You have to meet them."

Polly let Rebecca drag her over to the boys, who looked up guiltily.

"We're sorry. We shouldn't touch things. Mr. Roy said that," the youngest boy said.

"You're fine," Rebecca said, sitting down beside them. "Books are for everyone. Do you want to meet Polly? You're staying with us and she's my mom."

The two boys stood up and the youngest put out his hand. "Pleased to meet you, Miss Polly. My name is Elijah Jones."

Polly smiled and took his hand. "It's nice to meet you, Elijah. I look forward to having you stay with us."

"This is my brother, Noah," Elijah said and elbowed his brother in the side.

Noah put out his hand and bowed his head, mumbling something.

"It's nice to meet you, too, Noah," Polly said, taking his hand. "I hope you are ready to have fun. I can't wait for you to meet my dogs and cats and even my horses and donkeys."

The boy looked up at her. "You have horses?"

"I do. Four very big horses who love people. Would you like to meet them today?"

"Can I?"

"Of course you can. Once we're finished here, we'll go upstairs and show you where you are sleeping and when you're ready, we'll go down and see the horses."

He beamed a smile at her and Polly felt her heart jump into her throat. She wanted to lean over and pull both of them into a hug, but thought that might be something that could wait until later. Scaring the two boys wasn't first on her agenda for today.

"Did you meet my husband, Henry?" she asked.

Elijah peered around her. "Is that him? He's friends with Mr. Roy, isn't he? They went to college together. Is that why we're staying with you? Because we're little and Mr. Roy knows you?"

"That's part of it," Polly turned and beckoned to Henry.

"You're Noah, right?" Henry pointed to Elijah.

"No sir, I'm Elijah," the boy replied.

Henry touched Noah's shoulder. "That means you're Elijah."

Noah looked up at him, shock evident on his face. He turned to his brother, who then also looked at Henry.

"Look at him, Noah," Elijah said. "He's teasing us. You are teasing us, aren't you, Mister?"

"Call me Henry, and of course I'm teasing you. In the Bible, Noah lived a long time before Elijah, so that's how I know. Noah is the oldest brother." He tapped Elijah's forehead. "Unless you're teasing me and you are really Noah."

Elijah giggled. "I'm still Elijah."

"I'm glad we have that settled," Henry said and turned as Roy stood up.

"If your hosts are here, you are free to leave," Roy said. "We'll meet back here Wednesday evening for dinner. Remember, if you need anything, you have my number." He touched each of the boys as he walked past them. A brush on the shoulder, a pat on the head, a short word of encouragement.

"Thank you for taking the boys, Polly," he said. "I hope this isn't too much of an inconvenience. I know it's a busy week."

"We're looking forward to having them," Polly said. She put her arm around Rebecca's shoulders. "Aren't we?"

Rebecca nodded. "We have so many things to do. I can't wait for them to meet my friends."

Roy took Polly's arm to pull her aside.

"Rebecca," Polly said. "Take the boys upstairs, would you? Remember to tell them about the dogs."

Rebecca grinned and put her hand on Noah's back, guiding him out of the classroom. "We have two dogs, but they are really friendly. The only thing you have to worry about is being licked to death. And there are two cats, too. Have you ever heard of Star Wars?"

"They'll be fine," Henry said.

"I do appreciate you taking the boys," Roy said. "I wouldn't normally bring someone that young on this trip, but I knew the Fosters could handle it. They've taken some of the most difficult of my boys over the years."

"We're glad to," Polly said. "Are the boys difficult?"

"No, no, no," he replied. "It's just that I couldn't leave them in that home without me being in town. I've lined up another home for them, but the family is gone for the next two weeks."

"What's going on with their grandmother?" Polly asked.

Roy shook his head. "She has too many kids living in that house and can barely feed them. Several of the older kids are trouble. Noah and Elijah made things worse when they moved in, causing a lot of anger and resentment. Noah is quiet and shy and has already been beaten badly. You won't like the looks of the bruises on his side and his legs."

"Did he see a doctor?"

"One of my friends," Roy said. "He'll be fine. No broken bones, just bruises. But I won't let them go back into that if I can help it."

"Elijah looks like a happy boy," Polly said.

"Aren't their personalities something?" Roy asked. "No matter what they've been through, he continues to be resilient. I hope nothing breaks him beyond what he can come back from. His brother's beating came close. I think he could have handled taking it himself, but it was hard to watch his older brother get hurt."

"Their mother is dead?"

"Yes," Roy said. "And their father will never leave prison. The boys don't have any family left to really love them. I won't lose them. I just won't."

"We'll help them enjoy their time in Bellingwood," Henry said. He chuckled. "And you just tapped into Polly's rescue vortex. She'll make sure they're safe and protected while they're here."

Roy smiled. "Thank you." He looked up at another family coming in the door.

"We're sorry we're late," the woman said. "I couldn't find my phone."

Her husband touched her ear. "That's because she was talking to her sister on it."

"I'd better go," Roy said. "Thanks again."

Polly and Henry walked out of the classroom together, holding hands. They stopped as a couple who was staying in the addition walked past. The door to the addition opened again and the man that Kristen had identified as Mr. James strode through.

"Nice day, isn't it?" he said. "Is this your husband?"

Polly smiled. "Yes, this is Henry. How are you today?"

"Doing fine. Making plans. It's going to be a big week."

"Yes, it is," she said. "I hope you have fun."

"If not fun, at least it will be interesting," he replied.

As they hit the stairs to go up to the apartment, the door to the addition opened again and another man walked into the hallway. Polly recognized him immediately as Mr. Nicholas.

"He does look like Santa," she whispered to Henry.

Henry turned to look. "Okay?"

"I'll tell you when we get upstairs."

They ran up the steps and into the apartment.

Noah and Elijah were on the floor between the sofas, each with their arms around a dog. Han looked up at Henry and broke away, yapping a hello while Obiwan wagged his tail and licked Noah's forehead again.

"I see you met the dogs," Polly said. "Did Rebecca tell you their names?"

Elijah stood up and crossed to Han, who was now sitting

beside Henry. "Is he your dog?"

"This is Han," Henry said. "He's our dog, but I'm the one who trained him."

"Han's a weird name," Elijah said. "Is it okay if I pat him?"

"Go on, Han." Henry put his hand on Han's head and the dog shivered in happiness.

"They don't know about *Star Wars*," Rebecca said. "We need to watch the movie."

"We'll do it." Polly pointed to the front bedroom. "Did you show them where they would be sleeping?"

Rebecca shook her head. "We haven't gotten past the dogs."

"Boys, can you sleep in the same bed together?" Henry asked.

"We always have," Elijah said.

Henry ruffled the boy's head. "Grab your things and let me show you where you'll sleep when you're here."

Elijah picked up a small duffel bag. Noah stood up, brushing Obiwan's fur from his chest. They followed Henry into the front bedroom.

"This is for us?" Elijah turned around with his mouth agape.

"It sure is."

"We've never slept in a bed this big!"

Henry laughed. "Do you think you'll get lost?"

"We might. This could hold ten or twenty of us. We're just little boys. Can we sit on it?"

Polly walked over to the doorway and watched the boys clamber up on the bed. Elijah dropped the duffel at the end and scrambled up to the pillows.

"Is that all they brought with them?" she asked Henry.

"I guess." He pulled her close. "You're going shopping, aren't you?"

"As soon as I can. I'll call Sylvie and see if she has any of Andrew's old clothes, but there can't be much more than a change of clothes and some underwear for each of them in that bag."

"Don't overdo it," he warned. "Promise?"

Polly scowled at him while they watched the boys roll around on the bed.

CHAPTER TEN

Eventually, Kayla and Andrew showed up; Andrew with two large tote bags filled with clothes.

"Wow," Polly said. "Thank you."

"Mom said to tell you there might be more. This is just what she could tell me how to find." He smirked. "She has a hard time throwing things away. I think she even kept our baby clothes. Those are in a box in the attic. You don't need any, do you?" he asked, grinning up at her.

Polly swatted the back of his head. "Stop it. I'm going to see what fits them and then we'll go to the barn. Want to go along?"

Kayla bounced with excitement. She loved going down there. Whether it was because she would see Jason or the horses, Polly didn't know for sure.

"Hey boys, follow me," Polly said to Noah and Elijah. They were in the dining room with Rebecca, watching while she sketched their faces.

"She's really good," Elijah said.

Rebecca pulled the sheet out of her pad and handed it to him. "You can have that. I'll do more."

"I can keep it forever?" Elijah asked.

"Absolutely," Rebecca replied. "And I'll make more, too."

Polly led them across the living room to the front bedroom and sat down on a chair, then put the totes on the floor in front of her. "While you're here, we're going to be doing a lot of different things."

"Like seeing the horses?" Elijah asked. "When can we see the horses?"

"Like seeing the horses. But those kinds of things get you really dirty and I want you to have plenty of clean clothes to change into, because when we're done with one thing..." She smiled at them. "Like seeing the horses, you'll take a shower and get ready for the next thing. Tonight we're going to have dinner and then go to a dance downstairs. Do you know how to dance?"

Elijah threw his arms in the air and swung his hips back and forth. "I can dance. Noah's better, though. Show her, Noah."

His older brother shook his head, his eyes on the bags of clothing.

"You'll meet Andrew in a few minutes," Polly said. "But he had these clothes left from when he was your age. He's not using them anymore and his mother thought maybe you could try them on. If you like something, it's yours. You can keep it forever or just wear it while you're here. Up to you."

"We don't have very many clothes," Elijah said. "We had some at Grandma's house, but she wouldn't let us take those because somebody else might wear them."

"That makes sense," Polly said. She wasn't about to say anything negative about their grandmother. Whatever that woman had to do to take care of kids in her house was what she had to do. "It looks like there are shirts in this bag and shorts or pants in the other. Do you want to dump them out on the floor?"

Noah looked at her, his eyes big. "Not on the floor."

"Okay, how about the bed. You climb up there and I'll pull the clothes out so you can see what we've got." Polly pointed at their feet. "And this time, take your shoes off first. You don't want all of the gunk from the bottom of your shoes on the bed, right?"

Elijah kicked his shoes off and climbed up onto the bed. "What kind of gunk?"

Polly pulled out a pile of shirts and then another, stacking them on the end of the bed. "What if I were to tell you that you walk through old dog poop or sometimes a person might have vomited and the rain didn't wash all the germs away."

"Ewww," Elijah said, twisting his face up. "That's gross."

"That's why you wear shoes," she said. "To protect your feet when you're outside. But that's also why you take them off before you put your feet on a couch or a bed or even a table. We don't want that nasty stuff anywhere but on the floor."

Noah took his shoes off and set them neatly beside the bed, then rearranged Elijah's so they were just as neat, before climbing up beside his brother.

"I don't know very much about little boy sizes," Polly said. "Shall we just hold these up and see what fits?"

"Can we share these clothes? We're about the same size," Elijah said.

"I don't care what you do with them."

Each boy chose a t-shirt and a pair of pants, then sat back on the bed.

"Do you want to try the pants on to make sure they fit?" Polly asked. "I'll just step out of the room."

Noah nodded and she left the room, pulling the door nearly shut behind her. Giggling and noise came from inside the bedroom and pretty soon, the door tugged open. Elijah stood there in a pair of jeans that fit him pretty well and a Spiderman t-shirt that was a bit too big.

"That looks good on you," Polly said. "What about you, Noah? Did you find your size?"

"It's the same," he said. He was wearing a plain blue t-shirt over a pair of blue jeans. "I like these jeans," he said. "They're soft."

"Then they are yours. Now, what about the rest of these clothes. Are they all the same size?"

Noah's eyes grew big again. "We can have more?"

"Of course you can. Anything that fits, you can have."

The boys scrambled to climb back up on the bed and soon had a mess of clothing lying all over the place. Polly's heart was nearly broken. How could something so simple - hand-me-downs even - bring so much happiness. They were such little boys. It made her ache to realize that in their short lives, they had never known what it was like to have plenty of anything.

In the end, there were two t-shirts that were much too big and several pairs of shorts that were much too small. Polly picked the large t-shirts up and said, "What if you kept these to wear when you go to bed?"

"That's a good idea," Elijah agreed.

She tossed the shirts at him, and caught him in the head. He laughed out loud and Polly sighed. "Sorry, Elijah. I'm the worst when it comes to throwing things. I miss every time. Just ask Henry."

"I thought you hit him good," Noah said. "That was funny."

"Since you've been in your other clothes all day long, why don't you put them on when we go to the barn. We can wash them after you shower and change into something fresh for tonight's events. Sound good?"

"Can we go now?" Elijah asked.

Polly looked at the mess of clothes on the bed. "How about I send Rebecca and her friend, Kayla, in to help you fold those clothes and put them away in the dresser. There are two drawers that have been emptied for you. That way everything will be neat when you come back, okay?"

"Will it take very long?" he pressed.

"Not if you all work together. They'll be right in. I'm going to close the door, though, so you can change back into your other clothes. You open it when you're done. Okay?"

They bobbed their heads up and down in unison. Polly smiled and left the room. Doggone, they were cute.

"We heard," Rebecca said. "So you're going to make me help clean their room?"

Polly laughed out loud. "I figure you ought to clean someone's room. Right?"

Kayla pushed her friend's arm. "I clean your room. It's only fair."

Moments later, the door flew open and Noah beckoned for the girls to come in. When Polly looked in, Elijah was already trying to figure out how to fold his t-shirts. "You can leave the night shirts on the bed," she called out to them and went into the dining room.

Andrew looked up from a book he was reading. "Did the clothes fit?"

"Nearly everything. You've made two little boys really happy and saved my bacon today." Polly bent down to hug him where he was seated at the table. "Thank you."

"Still with the hugging," he complained. "Do they know that you hug all the time?"

She chuckled. "Not yet, but they'll learn soon enough."

"Maybe I'll warn them. Make sure they know it isn't dangerous, but that it happens a lot."

"You do that." She squeezed his shoulders again and took her phone out to text Eliseo that she was bringing her new charges down to see the horses. He replied that he'd be ready any time.

~~~

The boys stood in front of Demi with their necks craned and their mouths wide open. Eliseo had found helmets in the tack room that would fit the boys. He had a little bit of everything in there.

Noah slowly turned back to her, his eyes as wide as saucers. "He's so big!"

"Wait until you see the rest of them," she said with a smile. "Do you want to sit on his back?"

"Can I really?"

Polly nodded and smiled at Eliseo. "Mr. Aquila will help you. But you have to listen to everything he says. Deal?"

"Demi is the friendliest of them all," Eliseo said. "But they're all very good horses. In a few minutes, Jason and his friend, Scar, will

meet us outside and you can ride around the pasture with them."
He leaned toward Noah. "Are you ready?"

Noah backed up, nearly falling into Polly. She put her hand on
his shoulder to steady him.

"Me first," Elijah said.

"Demi is big enough to hold both of you at once. Would that
make you feel more comfortable, Noah?" Eliseo asked.

He nodded, but didn't move away from Polly's legs. She
reached down with her hand and he took it with his.

"Demi's my favorite," Polly said. "When I didn't know anything
about horses, he let me figure it out with him first. How about I
stand on the box here while you sit on his back."

Noah led her forward and did his best to hold on to her hand
while Eliseo lifted him up onto Demi's back.

"That's it," Eliseo said. "Swing your leg around your brother.
Just like that."

Demi shook his head and Elijah giggled. "I can feel his body
move under my legs."

"Will you let me walk him around the barn while you're up
there?" Eliseo asked.

Elijah nodded enthusiastically while Noah just looked scared.

Polly patted the boy's leg. "You'll do fine. Mr. Aquila is a great
teacher. He won't let anything happen to you."

Noah looked down at her and she smiled up at him as they
walked down the middle alley of the barn.

"Can I pat his neck?" Elijah asked.

Eliseo grinned. "Of course you can. Just like any animal, horses
appreciate it when you tell them how much you like them."

Elijah leaned forward and spread his arms out. They didn't go
very far around the big horse's neck, but he lay there long enough
that Noah got worried and grabbed his brother's waistband.

"That's what a horse smells like," Elijah said. "You should try it,
Noah.

They walked out the back of the barn into the pasture. Huck
and Tom ran over to the parade to see what was happening.

Eliseo led them around the side of the barn, pushing the

donkeys away with his free hand. They insisted on being part of the action. A large barrel stood beside the hay pile and he stopped Demi beside it. "If you're ready to get off, you can slide to the barrel. Here, take my hand."

Noah took his hand and let himself be lifted to the barrel, then sat down and jumped to the ground. "Who's that?" he asked, pointing at the donkeys.

"Tom and Huck," Polly said. "They're also very friendly and they like to play. Maybe one day this week, we can put a saddle on Huck and you can ride him."

"Really?"

"Of course."

Eliseo lifted Elijah down to the barrel, but he stood there, looking out over the pasture. "There they are," he said, pointing at the bridge from the far pasture.

Jason glanced at his friend after they crossed the bridge and the next thing anyone saw was the two boys racing across the pasture. Jason turned Nat and they slowed, then he brought Nat up to stand beside the barrel.

"Noah, you should ride with Jason," Polly said quietly to the boy.

"I don't want to," he replied, tentatively reaching out to touch Huck's shoulder.

She knelt down beside him and put her hand beside his on the donkey. "Try one trip around the pasture. That way you can say that you did it. If you hate it, you can stop. But you should at least try. That's what these two weeks are all about. Trying new things."

"But I don't want to."

"Why not?" she asked.

He shrugged and headed toward the barn. Polly rushed to stand in front of him. She put her hand out and took his, then knelt back down so they were eye to eye. "If you're scared, that's okay. But you can't let it stop you from trying things. Especially when there are good people around who tell you that it's safe. Do you think Mr. Dunston would have let you stay with me if I wasn't safe?"

Polly waited for him to respond. He'd lowered his face, so she put her finger under his chin and lifted his head so he'd look at her. "Am I safe?"

He shrugged a single shoulder.

"Is Mr. Dunston safe?"

He nodded.

"Then you have to trust him to know good people. Henry and I are good and we will keep you safe. I promise you that. I also promise that Mr. Aquila is a good person."

Noah leaned in and whispered, "Why does he look so weird?"

Polly smiled. "He was burned in a war. But that doesn't mean he's not safe to be around. Do you believe me?"

His shoulders rose as he took in a deep breath.

"Jason would like to take you around the pasture on his horse. Will you let him? If it is absolutely awful, he'll bring you back when you say. Okay?"

She took his grudging sigh as acceptance and led him back to the barrel.

"You're going to love this," Jason said. "I promise not to go fast unless you tell me to."

"Don't go fast," Eliseo said. "Got it?"

"Yes sir," Jason said. He helped as Eliseo lifted Noah in front of him and then adjusted himself with his arms around the younger boy. "Are you ready?"

Noah looked down at Polly, then slowly nodded as Jason and Nat walked away. Scar came up to the barrel and smiled at Elijah, who was bouncing with excitement.

"Do you have scars? Is that why you're called that?" Elijah asked.

"Nah. My name is Oscar, but that's like an old man's name. Somebody called me Scar when I was just about your age. What are you, eight?"

"I'm seven. Not eight until next year. I just had a birthday."

"Did you get anything fun?" Scar asked.

Elijah shook his head and his shoulders slumped. "No. Mom died and we didn't have any money."

"Oh, bummer." Scar took the reins, his arms around the young boy. "Let's make this your birthday ride. How's that? If you want, I'll even sing happy birthday to you." He walked Daisy away from the barrel and bellowed at the top of his lungs, "Happy Birthday to you. Happy Birthday to you. Happy birthday, dear Elijah. Happy birthday to you."

Polly chuckled as she walked over to Eliseo. "He's such a hoot."

"Good kid." Eliseo scratched Huck's ears before the donkey went off to chase down the horses.

Jason stopped Nat on the other side of the pasture and looked over at Polly and Eliseo, then put both hands up in an "I don't know" posture as Noah bent forward and wrapped his arms around Nat's neck. The boy must have shifted, because Jason dropped them to hold Noah's hips while the kid lay on Nat.

"I'm glad you encouraged him to try it," Eliseo said.

"I couldn't let fear take over on his first day in town," Polly replied. "That poor little boy is going to be so overwhelmed by all of the sensory input coming at him, he won't be able to handle any of it if he shuts down at the first thing he's afraid of."

"Are you taking them to the dance tonight?"

She nodded. "We wouldn't miss it. Are you coming?"

"Elva wants to. We'll bring the kids for a while and then if she wants to stay, I'll just take them home."

Polly looked up at him. "Don't you let her turn you into their babysitter."

"She needs some freedom. She's had a rough time of it."

"Rough time of it?" Polly asked. "Really?" She nearly kicked herself, but the words were already out there.

Fortunately, he laughed. "You're right. As much as I want to be angry with Larry for leaving her, he did well by the family. But I still feel bad for her. A divorce isn't an easy thing."

"No it's not," Polly agreed. "But you can't be her husband."

He harrumphed. "I've never been much of anything for her. I'll do this for now. Just until she figures out what's next."

"I love that you want to take care of her," Polly said. "You're a good brother."

"But?" he asked, smiling down at her.

"But don't lose yourself."

"Yes, ma'am. Can I count on you to catch me if I do?"

Polly spun on him and started laughing. "Fine. I'll shut up. I'll sic Sylvie on you."

"That would be quite all right," he said.

"One more thing," Polly said. "Because you know I can't help myself."

"What now?"

"For heaven's sake, ask Sylvie to dance with you tonight. We aren't serving anything but snacks and Rachel has that covered, so she won't be busy in the kitchen. Sylvie's coming to have a good time. Don't ignore her."

"We'll see." Eliseo wandered back over to the barrel and beckoned at Jason, who brought Nat up to stand beside him. "How are you doing, Noah?"

"Can we keep going? Just a little while longer?" Noah turned around to look up at Jason. "Can we?"

Jason nodded, receiving silent permission from Eliseo, and guided Nat away from the barn.

"I want to give them so many memories," Polly said. "Moments like this that they'll keep for the rest of their lives."

Eliseo called Nan over and swung himself up on her bare back, then clicked his tongue and raced off after the boys. He laughed as Nan ran past them, then turned and ran back.

"You boys can call yourselves *real* cowboys tonight," he yelled.

Polly sat down on the barrel. The boys were laughing and enjoying themselves. Noah's face had lost some of the tension he carried. She was going to have so much fun these next two weeks.

CHAPTER ELEVEN

Polly had absolutely no desire to get out of bed Monday morning. There hadn't been a single quiet moment since the boys arrived. They hadn't slept well their first two nights in her house. Between fear of a new place, the silence of Bellingwood and pure adrenaline and excitement, they'd simply not been able to put their heads down on the pillow, no matter how firm she was or how hard they tried. Last night Polly camped out in their room, trying to sleep in the wing chair.

They'd had a grand time at the dance Saturday night, and since the boys showed no sign of being tired, Polly had let them stay until she was ready to drop. She'd also been surprised at how much they could eat at that first meal. They had roasted chicken strips and sliced potatoes and those two little boys ate all they could and then snacked on the crackers and cheese, muffins, and cupcakes during the dance. She didn't know where they put it. She kept reminding herself that they were growing boys.

Yesterday had started out at an insane pace and kept up for the rest of the day. Heath and Hayden came over to make breakfast and the little boys were in awe of the big brothers who actually paid attention and played with them. While Hayden made breakfast, Heath taught them how to play video games in the media room. The whole family went to church and afterwards, Henry took all of the boys over to Nate Mikkels' place to see the Woodie he was restoring. Rebecca and Polly ran to Ames to pick up some underwear and socks for the boys. Polly bought white button down shirts with bolo ties for the men in her family for the parade. Rebecca thought she was crazy, but then told her it would be really cute. Whatever.

When they got home, Polly had hoped that maybe they could get a nap, but the boys begged to go back down to the barn. Eliseo saddled up the donkeys for the boys to ride by themselves. Since Jason was busy with his family, Polly went down to make sure Eliseo had enough help.

He had come to the dance the night before, but Polly was so busy with her charges that she hadn't thought to watch whether or not he and Sylvie spent much time together. Henry didn't have a good answer for her and Rebecca, Heath, and Hayden were just as useless. They'd all learned new dance steps and hadn't come off the dance floor very often.

Quite a few of Heath and Jason's high school friends were there. Polly did see a few that she recognized. Hayden was with a girl Polly thought she recognized, but when she asked him about it, he shrugged it off, saying she was just an old friend. Did he not know that vague answers drove her crazy?

After an hour with the donkeys yesterday, she made the boys take another shower since they were going to Bill and Marie Sturtz's house for dinner. Bill and Henry grilled hamburgers and hot dogs, Marie had made salads and then they taught the boys about homemade ice cream. It was hard to believe that she missed a Sunday night at Pizzazz with her friends, but when she had called Sal, discovered that most everyone else was busy and glad for a quiet night at home.

Quiet night. Hah.

They got home about ten o'clock and Polly wanted to collapse, but the boys wanted to talk about everything that had happened to them the last two days. They told their stories to the dogs and then to the cats, they talked to each other about their adventures and when Polly finally convinced them to go to bed, they were up and down a million times, needing a glass of water, a trip to the bathroom, a book from the bookshelf. Oh, and could she please read it to them.

She didn't want to quench their excitement, but today had to be different. She needed more sleep. And so did they. Noah had drifted off about two thirty; Elijah a few minutes later. Yet even still, they startled awake at every sound and Polly did her best to soothe them back to sleep. Elijah cried out a few times. Polly couldn't imagine what he was dreaming about. Both boys thrashed in the bed all night. This morning, Polly showed them how to tuck the sheet back in and straighten things so they'd have a nice place to return to that night.

Today had to be better. If she could just get through it on no sleep. She needed to take Rebecca over to Beryl's this morning and thought she might take the boys to the coffee shop and then over to the Bell House since they hadn't seen it yet. Beryl and Rebecca would meet them at Joe's Diner for lunch.

Polly opened her eyes when Obiwan landed on her. She'd been lying on the sofa in the living room while Rebecca and the two boys watched television in the media room. Maybe after lunch, Rebecca, Kayla, and Andrew could take the boys to the swimming pool. Then it hit her. Not only did Polly have no idea whether or not they could swim, the boys had no swim trunks. Why hadn't she thought about that yesterday?

One of the boys flitted past her into his bedroom, then darted across the living room to the bathroom. He was gone before she could register his presence enough to say something and she let herself drift off to sleep. As long as Rebecca was keeping an eye on them, everything was fine. At least it was fine enough for her to take a quick nap.

~~~

The first thing Noah and Elijah did when they got to the coffee shop was head for the bookshelves along the walls. Polly pointed them to the kids' books and they were overwhelmed.

"There are books everywhere in this town," Elijah said.

Polly chuckled. "It probably feels that way. We'll go to the library and you can look at even more books. Before you settle down here though, do you want to come with me to the counter and order something to drink?"

They'd already talked about this and she'd explained to them what smoothie flavors were available, but when they stood in front of Camille, the boys stared at the menu board in awe. Polly introduced them to Camille and gave them a few moments to process.

Noah tugged on Polly's arm and she bent over to hear what he had to say. "She's pretty."

"Camille runs this place," Polly whispered back. "She's one of my friends."

"Does frozen lemonade sound good to you boys?" Camille asked, leaning on the counter. "We have strawberry, mango, raspberry and a special one with all three flavors."

"I want all three," Elijah said.

Noah nodded. "Me too."

"It's pretty exciting," Camille replied. "Would you like me to layer the flavors or mix them all up?"

Noah scrunched up his face, trying to figure out what she meant.

"I put bright red strawberry on the bottom, orange mango in the middle and pink raspberry on top. How does that sound?"

He nodded again and beamed at her. Elijah had found his way to the baked goods display and pointed in. "Are their cookies any good?"

"Which one would you like?" Polly asked.

"That chocolate cookie."

Noah followed him and looked up. "The M&Ms one?"

Polly nodded. "You boys can watch her make the smoothies or go back over to the books. Whatever you'd like."

"Coffee for you?" Camille asked.

"It's hot outside. I want a frozen caramel macchiato today."

"They're the best." Camille started working on the boys' drinks. "What are you three up to today?"

Neither of the boys spoke, so Polly stepped in. "We're going over to the Bell House and then we'll meet Beryl and Rebecca at the diner for lunch. Boys, tell her what you did yesterday afternoon."

"We rode on the donkeys," Elijah said. "We rode the horses on Saturday, but they're so big, we had to have someone older ride with us. Mr. Aquila let us ride the donkeys all by ourselves."

"Did you like riding the donkey, Noah?" Camille asked.

He nodded.

"What about the big horses?"

Noah shook his head. "They're too big."

"I haven't had the courage to ride on them yet either," Camille said. "Maybe someday." She reached across the counter with the first drink. "Who's this for?"

Elijah pointed to his brother and she put it into Noah's hands. He took a drink, gulped, then his eyes grew big and he gasped.

"Too cold?" Polly asked with a chuckle.

Camille handed Polly a glass of water from the tap.

"This will help. Take a sip," Polly said. "Then go slow from here on out. Swirl it around in your mouth before you take a big swallow."

"Cold." He said, looking at his brother. "That hurt."

"It's called brain freeze," Polly said. "You have to be careful with these things."

Elijah jumped up to look over the counter. "I want to try it."

Polly ruffled the top of his head. "You silly boy. Keep the water ready." She took money out and put it on the counter. "While you're at it, Camille, could you make up a couple of strawberry lemonades? I'll bet Heath and Hayden would like one, too. What do you think, boys?"

Noah nodded, his mouth wrapped around the straw. He was taking it very slowly now.

"Should we take them cookies, too?" Elijah asked.

"Of course we should. Let's buy a dozen cookies and we'll leave them the extras."

After Elijah got to experience his brain freeze and made it through recovery, Polly packed them back into her truck and headed for the Bell House. She pulled in behind Heath's truck and unlocked the doors for the boys. When they didn't move, she turned around in her seat. "Are you ready to go in?"

"This is your house?" Noah asked. "A house like this for one family?"

It would seem like a lot for a boy who had lived in nothing but apartments and small inner city homes with too many other people.

"You must be really rich," Elijah said.

"Not really rich," Polly replied. "This house was very inexpensive because it was so run-down. Because Henry builds homes, we knew we could fix it. Hayden and Heath are doing a lot of work. That's their jobs for the summer.

"But you own that school and the horses, too," Elijah said.

"You're right, I do." She had no idea how to explain this. It had never really come up before. People in Bellingwood might talk about it behind her back, but those who knew her and Henry accepted them for what they had and what they did. "Sycamore House is a business. We just live in the upstairs."

"You're going to have two houses?" Noah was dumbfounded.

"No, when we move into this house, we're going to turn the apartment into business offices for Sycamore House. The downstairs will become something new and different. We just don't know what yet. Are you ready to go inside and see Heath and Hayden?"

Elijah looked at his brother and nodded. They clutched their lemonades as they climbed down out of the truck, then followed Polly up to the side door.

She opened it and went inside through the mudroom to the kitchen, half expecting to see either the plumber or electricians here this morning. No one was in the immediate vicinity.

"Hello!" she called out. "Is anyone here?" She put the drinks and cookies on a makeshift table of plywood over sawhorses. "Let's go find them."

The boys put their drinks down beside hers and followed her through the house.

"Heath? Hayden?" she called out.

"You have to fix all of these rooms?" Elijah asked.

"Yeah. It's a mess right now. That's what Heath and Hayden have been doing. They tore out all of the walls so we can put new electrical lines and new plumbing lines in."

"This is what our hallway looked like before Mom died," Noah said. "Bad people just wrecked the walls whenever they wanted to."

"We did this on purpose to make the house better," Polly assured him, then called again. "Heath? Hayden?"

"In here."

"Where's here?"

"Back corner. We'll be out in a second."

It occurred to Polly that while they were hooking up electricity, she needed to ask about an intercom system in this big house. There was potential for this to become ridiculous when she regularly lost her family.

She led the boys down the hallway until they arrived in what would someday be the library. The boys stood on two ladders, with their hands on a chandelier as they attempted to lower it safely to the floor.

"Sorry," Heath said.

Polly stood in the doorway and held the boys close to her. "No problem. I'm sorry if we startled you. We brought lemonade and cookies."

Hayden clipped an electrical cord leading into the ceiling and the boys came down, holding the heavy fixture between them. They put it on the floor and breathed a sigh of relief.

"Your hair is dusty," Elijah said, pointing to Heath's dark hair.

Heath bent at the waist and shook his head, dust flying everywhere. "Like that?"

Noah laughed.

"Would you two like to climb the ladders?" Hayden asked. "There isn't much to see, but you can at least look."

The younger boys looked up at Polly and she smiled, then pushed them forward. They crept over the mess on the floor and climbed up to the top step, stopping when Hayden told them to go no farther.

"Cool," Elijah said. "Are you going to put a new ceiling in?"

"Someday," Heath said. "And Polly said she was going to clean this chandelier so we can hang it back up, too. Won't that be pretty?"

Elijah climbed back down the ladder and ran over to a window. "What's that?" he asked.

Heath followed where his finger was pointing. "That's called a gazebo. We gave it to Polly for Mother's Day."

"Can we sit in it?"

Heath looked back at Polly.

"We have time. Let's have our lemonade and cookies outside," she said.

They arrived back in the kitchen and Hayden smiled at Polly. "Thanks for this. It's a little hot today."

"I know. Thought you could use something fun."

"How about we carry your drinks," Hayden said, "and you two run as fast as possible to the gazebo. If you beat us, run around it one time."

The boys hit the back door and were off, running and laughing. They arrived long before Polly, Heath and Hayden and started around the gazebo, only to wait impatiently for the older group to finally arrive.

"Can we run anywhere back here?" Elijah asked.

"You sure can. Don't go anywhere that you can't see me, though," Polly said.

Each boy took a drink from their lemonade, then rolled their eyes in their head as brain freeze took over again.

"I forgot," Noah said. "That hurts."

He and Elijah took off running, playing a game of tag.

"Were we ever that young?" Hayden asked his brother. "It's too hot to run around like that."

Heath looked thoughtful. "Remember that summer we went camping in Minnesota? We camped on a lake somewhere. I remember Mom telling us that if we ran and played hard all day long, we'd sleep faster that night so we could play again the next day. I never wanted to stop."

"Yeah," Hayden said. "Remember Dad had that canoe and we fished in the lake and then we tipped it over?"

"You were so mad."

"We lost my favorite fishing pole. It was your fault."

"No it wasn't. You're the one who leaned over to see where the fish was going."

"Because you wouldn't turn the canoe."

Polly laughed. "Do you two still like to fish?"

Heath shrugged. "I haven't gone fishing since Dad died. I tried once without him, but he always knew just what to do. He's the one that told me which lure to use."

"I don't even know what happened to his fishing gear," Hayden said. "It just wasn't one of the things we thought about."

Noah and Elijah ran up to the gazebo and took another drink of their lemonade. "Can I have a cookie now?" Elijah asked.

"How about you each have half a cookie. We're going to meet Rebecca for lunch in a little bit and you don't want to be too full, do you?"

"I won't be," he said. "I promise. Please?"

It didn't really matter, she surmised. Life was too short to be stingy with half a cookie. "Eat the whole cookie, then. But sit here with us while you do."

Elijah dropped into a chair beside Heath while Noah sat between Polly and Hayden.

"Is Polly your mom?" Elijah asked Heath.

"Yes and no," Heath replied.

Elijah frowned.

"My mom and dad died. I lived with my aunt and uncle, but I started getting into really bad trouble because they didn't want me," Heath said. "Polly and Henry asked if I wanted to live with them, so they're in charge of me now."

"And Rebecca isn't your real daughter either?" Elijah asked Polly.

She shook her head. "Rebecca's mother died last year. But before she did, we worked it out so Henry and I could adopt Rebecca. Now she's our real daughter."

"You didn't have any babies of your own?" Noah asked quietly.

"No. Henry and I aren't planning to have babies. We like taking care of people that show up in our lives and need a home."

He slowly nodded.

"What about you?" Elijah asked Hayden. "Who's your mom?"

Hayden smiled and took a cookie out of the box. "I'm old enough that I don't need a mom, but if I did, I guess it would be Polly. Heath's my real brother, so now his mom is my mom."

"Wow," Elijah said. "Two for the price of one."

Polly laughed. "That's a good way to look at it."

He jammed the last bit of the cookie in his mouth. "Come on, Noah. Race me to that little building again. I bet I beat you."

Noah took a slow drink of his lemonade. It was nearly gone anyway. What was left had melted. He finished his cookie and met Elijah at the bottom of the steps. Elijah turned around. "Someone count off for us."

"I'll say one-two-three-go," Hayden said. "Are you ready?"

The boys took their stances.

"One. Two. Three." Hayden stopped and looked around, gazing up to the top of the gazebo and then back down. The boys had nearly taken off, but waited for the word. When he didn't say anything, they turned to look at him, then relaxed in place. "Go!" he yelled.

"You're good with kids," Polly said.

"They're easy."

"I hope so. But wow, they haven't slept much since they got here."

"I didn't sleep much either when I moved in with you," Heath said. "I didn't know if someone was going to come into my room

111

or if I was going to wake up and find out that it was all a dream. It took a couple of nights before I finally relaxed enough. They'll be better tonight."

"I hope they'll finally be exhausted." Polly chuckled. "It's too bad that people frown on lacing their milk with a little alcohol to put them to sleep."

"Polly," Hayden scolded. Then he said, "That's funny. People really did that?"

"From what I understand, yes." She smiled. "You know, back in the olden days."

"Oh. The nineteen nineties."

CHAPTER TWELVE

Rebecca jumped up from the table at Joe's Diner and ran to meet Polly, Noah, and Elijah at the front door, taking the boys' hands and leading them to the table. "These are Polly's best friends," she said and then pointed as she spoke. "This is Lydia, Andy and Beryl. I take art lessons from Beryl. She's the crazy woman." Rebecca pointed to a seat by Beryl. "Elijah you should sit there and Noah, you sit between me and Lydia." Rebecca leaned over and loudly whispered into Noah's ear. "She'll love the stuffin' out of you." Rebecca sat down and patted the chair next to her. "That's what my mom said to me when I was a little girl. She was gonna love the stuffin' right out of me."

She leaned against Polly and looked up into her face with a smile. "I'd forgotten all about that until just right now. It's kind of cute, isn't it?"

"So are you, you nut," Polly said. "I didn't expect the rest of you to be here today."

"I saw you with the boys in church yesterday," Lydia said, "but I didn't have time to get over to say hello." She reached down into her bag and took out three wrapped packages. "I never meet new

113

people without giving them a gift. And since Rebecca is one of my favorite girls, I got one for her, too." She moved the packages around. "Now which one of you is Elijah?"

Elijah shot his hand in the air. "I am, I am."

"I put your name on this package." Lydia pushed it across the table and Polly handed it to Elijah. "This one is Rebecca's." She handed a package to Rebecca." Lydia put her arm around the back of Noah's chair and touched his shoulder. "This one has your name on it. See right there?"

"Can we?" Rebecca asked Polly.

"Absolutely. No need to wait."

The three kids ripped into the packages and Rebecca laughed as she pulled out a squirt gun and a bottle of bubbles. "This is awesome! I can't wait until we get home."

Both of the boys had similar gifts. Noah held up the bottle of bubbles to Rebecca. "What is it?"

"I'll show you when we get home. It's the best," she replied. "You blow through a little wand and make bubbles." Rebecca turned to Polly. "I suppose you're going to make us play with the squirt guns outside."

"Ya think?" Polly asked with a laugh. "I'll fill a bucket with water and you can completely soak yourselves."

"Andrew is so gonna be wet," Rebecca said. "He doesn't have one. Na, na, na-na, na."

Elijah pulled the trigger on his squirt gun and quietly smiled.

"What do you say?" Polly said quietly, leaning toward him.

His eyes grew big. "Thank you!"

Rebecca smiled at Lydia. "Thank you. This is really fun."

Noah felt all eyes on him and quickly turned into Rebecca's arm. She gave Polly a look and put her arms around him while Lydia rubbed his shoulder.

"Do you want to tell her thank you later?" Rebecca asked Noah.

He nodded.

"We'll do that when no one's paying attention, okay?" Rebecca shifted so that he was sitting on his own again when Lucy came up to the table.

"My goodness, we have a crowd today," Lucy said. "How many are having your regular?" She put her hand on Noah's shoulder. "What about you? The regular?"

He looked up at her with wide eyes.

"I'm kidding you. We'll find something fun for you to eat today. Polly? A tenderloin?"

Polly grinned. "It's so hard to say no when you put it like that. Boys, I'll bet you've never had a breaded pork tenderloin."

"I think I have," Elijah said.

Noah leaned forward to frown at him.

"Well, I think I did. When I was really little."

"These are pretty special," Lucy said. "And they're really big. I don't know if a little boy like you could eat the whole thing."

"Do you want to try one?" Polly asked. "They also have good hamburgers and hot dogs and the french fries are the best."

"I like french fries," Elijah said. "Can I have some of those?"

Lucy moved over to stand beside him. "You sure can, young man. Would you like chicken strips or a hamburger or hot dog to go with them?"

His eyes lit up. "Chicken strips. They're the best."

"Got it." Lucy took orders around the table and when she got to Noah, Polly waited. But Lucy instinctually knelt down beside him. "How about you? What would you like to eat for lunch today?"

He said something very quietly and she leaned in. "A hamburger? Do you want cheese on it?"

Noah nodded.

When Lucy stood back up, she patted his head and gently squeezed his shoulder. "We'll get you all fed in a hurry. I'm glad you boys came here to eat today."

Rebecca took her phone out of her pocket and read a text, then scowled. "Kayla isn't going to be around this afternoon. She's going to Des Moines again with Stephanie, but they couldn't wait for me because Steph has to be back." She lifted a shoulder. "Oh well. You boys are going to have to have fun with me, okay?"

Noah nodded and Elijah picked up his squirt gun again. "Whoosh, whoosh," he said. "You're wet."

"I'm melting, I'm melting," Rebecca cried out.

Both boys looked at her like she'd lost her mind.

Rebecca laughed. "That's another movie we need to introduce them to."

"Oh no you don't," Beryl said. "These sweet boys don't need to watch The Wizard of Oz. Remember? Flying monkeys?"

Andy shook her head. "They scared me the first time I saw it. I wouldn't watch it for years. Then I married Len and it's his favorite movie of all time." She giggled. "Would you believe he cries at the end? He's probably seen it as many times as Polly has seen Star Wars. So I'm over the whole flying monkeys thing. Good always wins."

"Do you like scary movies?" Beryl asked Elijah.

"I don't know," he said.

Lydia chuckled. "He's seven. How many movies could the boy have seen at this age?"

Beryl pursed her lips. "I don't know. I'm not a grandma." She turned back to Elijah. "Do I look like a grandma to you?"

He nodded his head up and down and Beryl laughed, then hugged his shoulders. "You're a sweetie."

Lucy returned with drinks and put lemonade down in front of the boys. Polly had discovered that they really didn't like milk, even when she offered to put chocolate in it. They asked for coke, but that was one thing she just couldn't bring herself to let them have at every meal. She knew she only had them for a couple of weeks, but she wasn't about to change her rules about pop for kids. She and Henry had quit drinking it at dinner once Rebecca came into the house. She was tempted to take it out of the main refrigerator completely, but Henry had told her that she couldn't have a mini fridge in their bedroom. What a mean husband.

The phone buzzing in her back pocket startled her and when she pulled it out, she murmured. "Speak of the devil."

"Who is it?" Rebecca asked.

"I was just thinking about Henry. I wonder what he wants." Polly excused herself, swiped the call open and headed for the front door. "Hey there, hot stuff," she said. "What's up?"

"I know that you are busy today, but I'm desperate and need your help."

"Sure," she said. "What can I do?"

"I'd ask Dad or Len to do it, but they're installing cabinets at the Jordan's house north of town. Jerry Allen just got to the Bell House with Doug and Billy, so I can't call Heath or Hayden away and everyone else is swamped trying to get stuff done so we can take Thursday and Friday off."

"It's okay, Henry. Tell me what you need."

"Can you drive down to Ankeny and pick up some light fixtures? They're ready. All you have to do is drive in and tell them who you are. They'll load everything in your truck."

"Of course I can. Just text me the location. Is it okay if we finish lunch?"

"That's fine," he said. "I need them first thing in the morning. But really early first thing. Are you sure about this?"

"Stop it, honey. It's easy. I'll pack all the kids and we'll go off on an adventure."

"Okay, thank you."

She thought he'd hung up, but then he said. "Wait. Don't call it an adventure. Bad things always happen when you do that."

"Got it," Polly said with a laugh. "Send the information to my phone and we'll take care of this. No worries, okay?"

"Thank you. I've got to go now. I'll be home late tonight."

"We'll be waiting with bated breath," she said. "I love you."

Polly could tell he was distracted and let the phone call end. He rarely asked her to help which meant things had to be bad. No matter what, she'd find a way to be there when he did.

She went back inside and found that the food had arrived.

Elijah pointed at her plate. "I've never seen anything that big before in my whole life."

"Do you want to taste it?" she asked him. Polly cut off a piece of the tenderloin around the outside edge and put it on his plate, then cut off another and reached across Rebecca to Noah's plate. "I like ketchup and pickles on mine, but you can eat it however you want. And if you don't like it, that's no big deal."

"What did Henry need?" Andy asked.

"Me to go to Ankeny to pick up some light fixtures." Polly glanced around the table. "Are you guys up for a ride this afternoon?"

Rebecca picked up the jar of bubbles and waggled it.

"We'll have plenty of time after we come back to Bellingwood," Polly said. "I promise. Do you want to text Andrew and ask if he'd like to ride with us? I'm sure the boys would like that."

"Yeah, yeah," Elijah said. "He's nice."

"Can we pick him up at his house?" Rebecca asked Polly.

"You bet. Tell him you'll let him know when we're on the way."

"How are things going over at the Bell House?" Andy asked. "Was that the police over there last week?"

Polly looked at Lydia and Beryl before responding. "You saw the police at our house?"

Andy shrugged and gave her a knowing smile. "We can see everything."

"You can not," Polly replied. "I can't see you."

"Thank goodness," Andy said, wiping imaginary sweat from her brow. "I'd hate for you to see what happens in my little home."

Beryl put her fingers in her ears. "La, la, la, la, la. I don't want to hear this."

"Hear what?" Rebecca asked.

Polly patted her knee. "Nothing. They're just being funny. But back to you, Andy. You saw the police at our house? How?"

Lydia laughed until she let out a snort and swatted her friend's arm. "Tell her or she's going to worry."

"If you must know, Lydia and I were talking on the phone when the call came in on her scanner," Andy said. "We never did find out what happened."

Polly's shoulders fell back into place and she smiled. "Someone tore the old copper pipe out of the walls."

"Did they do much damage?" Lydia's eyes opened wide. "How awful."

"If it had been any other house, it would have been a lot of damage," Polly said, "but it was no big deal. Heath and Hayden hadn't gotten to the kitchen yet to tear out walls, so all the thief did was give them a head start on the demolition."

"Who would do that?" Beryl glared across the table. "Who would deliberately destroy someone else's home just for a few dollars?"

"I don't know who did it." Polly shook her head. "But I did discover that Shawn Wesley lives just down the street from the house. That's gonna be a joy."

Rebecca tugged on Polly's sleeve. "Who's Shawn Wesley?"

"Yeah. Who's that?" Beryl asked.

Polly looked around and realized that everyone was paying attention to her. She was so used to saying anything she wanted to say in front of her friends, that having three sets of very interested ears was dangerous.

"He was the first custodian we had at Sycamore House. Things didn't work out very well."

"Is his house the one with the trashy yard?" Rebecca asked.

Polly gave a slight nod. She'd walked into this and had no idea how to get herself out of it.

"I'm going to have my whole family here this week," Lydia said, winking at Polly. "Everybody is coming into town. I don't know where they'll all sleep, but I can hardly wait."

"You've already started cooking for them, haven't you?" Beryl asked, quickly picking up on the change of subject.

"Just a few things. I thought I'd put some meals in the freezer so I wouldn't have to spend all of my time in the kitchen."

"How many people will that be?" Polly asked. "Marilyn and her crew are staying in Bellingwood and not going back to Dayton? It isn't that far."

"They're staying," Lydia said. "Jill and Steve are bringing their little ones, too. Jim's coming back from Atlanta and he's bringing a girlfriend."

Beryl pulled her shoulders up to her ears and rolled her eyes. "Oh good heavens, there are more Merritt babies on the way."

"I didn't tell you that Sandy is bringing a foster daughter with her."

"Where's she at?" Polly asked.

"Minneapolis. Well, Edina, but I always just say Minneapolis."

Polly pursed her lips. "Have I met her yet?"

"No," Lydia said. "She doesn't get back here very often. And neither does Daniel. But he'll be here, too."

"That gorgeous boy needs to find a girl and settle down," Beryl said. "He'd make some beautiful babies." She looked at Polly and winked.

It took Polly a couple of seconds to remember an earlier conversation they'd had about Marilyn's ugly babies. She shook her head and turned back to Lydia. "That's fourteen extra people in your house. How are you going to do that?"

"And two dogs," Lydia said. "We'll make it work. We always do. And if it's too much, I'll send some of them over to Beryl's house."

"Maybe I should move in with Andy and Len and give you my keys," Beryl said with a wink.

Andy had been stirring her fork around her empty plate and looked up. "What? What did you say? You can't move in with me. I don't have room."

Beryl laughed. "Bah. Don't have room, my ..." She looked down at Elijah. "My pretty pink, uh, nose. You have two extra bedrooms. There's room for little ole me *and* my three cats. Shall we say Wednesday at seven? No, make it six thirty. I'd like dinner, please."

"You can't do that," Andy cried out. "You aren't serious."

Lydia put her hand on Andy's arm. "She's teasing you. But yes, Beryl, if I need help with space, I'm calling you. Okay?"

Beryl threw her hand in the air. "Whatever. Like I have any say in it anyway."

"Are we up for ice cream today?" Lucy asked from behind Polly.

"Yay! Ice cream!" Elijah said loudly. "Can we? Can we?"

Polly looked at his empty plate. While they'd been talking, the boy had eaten nearly everything. She turned to see what Noah's plate held. He wasn't quite as far along as his brother, but he'd made a big dent in his meal. "I don't know how you two boys do it. You had a good breakfast, frozen lemonade and a cookie, and you've polished off your meals. Now you want ice cream?"

"Yes we do," Elijah said. "Don't we, Noah?"

Noah nodded and smiled.

"I tell you what," Polly said. "Let's wait for ice cream. We'll find someplace fun to stop on the way back from Ankeny. Does that sound fair?"

Elijah slumped back in his seat and Polly put her hand on his shoulder. "I promise we'll get ice cream and it will be even more fun because Andrew can be there, too."

That made his eyes light up. "Okay."

"How did you like the tenderloin?" Polly asked. The piece she'd given him was gone from his plate, so he hadn't hated it.

"It was good. Maybe next time I can order that."

Lydia laughed. "I'll bet you could eat the whole thing."

Elijah sat back and patted his little round tummy. Polly could have sworn that it was bigger than when they'd come through the front door. He sighed deeply and contentedly. "I can eat anything."

"I'm glad you boys enjoyed your lunch," Lucy said. "I was going to offer some takeout containers, but it looks like you cleaned your plates. How about you, Polly?"

Polly nodded. "Someone will eat the rest of it. Thank you." She pointed to the door at the back of the room. "You two boys need to go use the bathroom before we start driving. Wash your hands."

"I don't have to go," Elijah said.

Lydia busted out laughing. All three older women turned to Polly, watching to see how she would deal with this.

"Go try," Polly said. "You too, Rebecca."

"What?"

"Go to the bathroom before we hit the road. Wash your hands. All of you."

"How am I supposed to go to the bathroom when I don't have to?" Elijah asked.

Polly sighed. "Take a deep breath and think about water

running into a sink or a shower pouring water over your head. Just go try."

The boys got up and Rebecca herded them to the bathroom door.

"You're going to have to stop somewhere," Beryl said.

"Probably. If they don't go here, I'll talk about it all the way over to Sylvie's house and maybe they'll have to go by the time we pick Andrew up."

"Wait until they get old," Andy said. "Then they'll take advantage of every bathroom they pass."

"How are you doing with them?" Lydia asked. "They seem like good little boys."

Polly nodded. "They haven't slept much yet and I suspect they're still on their best behavior. Noah is dreadfully shy. His brother talks for him all the time." She smiled warmly. "But I'm having a ball. They want to try new things and they're interested in everything. They've ridden the horses and the donkeys, they didn't want to leave the dance, and they were sweethearts at Marie and Bill's house last night. Now, look at them. They're just taking it all in."

Lydia reached over and took Polly's hand. "Be careful you don't fall in love with them too hard. They're going home in a couple of weeks."

"I know," Polly said, turning her hand to squeeze Lydia's. "It's just fun having them here."

CHAPTER THIRTEEN

"Andrew, look what we got." Elijah held his new squirt gun and bottle of bubbles out for Andrew to see.

"That's cool," Andrew said. "Will Polly let you blow bubbles in the truck?"

Polly chuckled. "No she won't. But she will be glad to take all of the toys and put them in the back of the truck if anyone thinks of trying it." She gave Andrew the evil eye. "So no funny stuff, bud."

She'd hoped to put Noah between Andrew and Elijah in the back seat, but he'd managed to strap himself in behind her, leaving Elijah in the middle. There had to be some way to draw this little boy out.

Rebecca leaned over to the radio. "Can we play music on the way down?"

"Sure." Polly reached over and turned it on, then punched through until she found the station she wanted.

"This again," Andrew said. "Can't we listen to something from our lifetime?" He turned in his seat. "She always makes us listen to old music."

Polly smiled at him in the rear view mirror. "I'm glad to turn it off."

Andrew huffed. "It's fine."

"What's all that?" Elijah asked, pointing out the window.

Polly looked at Rebecca for assistance.

"All what?" Rebecca asked.

"All that. What's all that tall green and brown stuff?"

"That's corn. Iowa grows a lot of corn."

Elijah crossed his arms over his chest. "Corn comes in a can."

"Yes it does," Polly said. "But first they grow it in a field like this. Did you see a lot of these fields when you drove here with Mr. Dunston on Saturday?"

"He was asleep," Noah said quietly.

Polly glanced back as Elijah yawned broadly. "Asleep? I don't believe it. Not when he was starting out on a big trip."

"He fell asleep before we got out of Chicago and didn't wake up until we stopped for breakfast. Then he went back to sleep until we came to Bellingwood."

"Did Mr. Dunston tell you about farming and corn fields?"

Noah nodded. "He said we'd see lots of land where nobody lived. I never saw that before."

"I'll bet you haven't. How you doing there, Elijah?" Polly asked.

He yawned again. "Good."

Rebecca turned as far as the seatbelt would let her. "Have you ever been outside of the city?"

Elijah shook his head. "No. My grandma said that when we were older we might."

"Might what?" Rebecca asked.

"Go somewhere else." Elijah yawned again.

Rebecca smiled. "Go where?" She tapped Polly's arm and pointed to the back, causing Polly to glance in the rear view mirror again.

Elijah was leaning on his brother, his eyes closed and his body completely relaxed. Noah didn't move.

"He's really tired," Noah said. "We should be quiet so he can sleep. He doesn't like to sleep at night."

"Why doesn't he like to sleep at night?" she asked quietly.

"Because bad things happen at night. People break into the apartment, that's when Mom died and that's when the police came to get our dad. One time a bad man came in the middle of the night and made my mom scream. He hurt her real bad. Elijah always told me that I could sleep because he'd stay awake."

Polly gulped. "He's always done this?"

Noah nodded. "He said that if he stayed awake and kept watch, we'd be safe. And it worked. When Jenner tried to come into our room and steal ..." his voice drifted off. "Anyway, Elijah caught him and yelled at him, so Jenner left. Another time, a couple of weeks ago when Grandma was at her card game, Davon told me he was going to suffocate me with a pillow because I told on him. Elijah wouldn't let him in the room."

"Oh honey," Polly said. She glanced at Rebecca, whose face was contorted in agony for the boy. A quick look at Andrew showed he had the same response. These boys had seen too much in their short years. She was so glad that Roy Dunston had insisted they come on this trip. If he was finding them a new home, she knew the boys would be safe. Roy wouldn't have it any other way.

"I like this music," Noah said. "It reminds me of Miss Lillian. She lived down the hall when Mom was alive. She always played music like this and we'd go over to see her when Mom didn't come home. Sometimes she made us brownies and kool-aid. I don't see her anymore. Grandma said we're never going back to that hellhole."

Polly chuckled. "That's what she called your old home?"

"She uses bad words a lot. Mom said we weren't supposed to use them, even though she did. She said we couldn't use them until we were in high school and if we dropped out of school before that we were never going to be able to use them. But I like school. I never want to drop out. Davon says he's going to quit school when he turns fifteen. He says that he can get a job and who needs school anyway. School never did no good for anybody."

"That's ridiculous," Rebecca said. She whispered to Polly. "I was going to say that was stupid, but it probably isn't good to use that word around little kids, is it?"

"No it's not," Polly said. "Thank you."

Rebecca turned back to Noah. "But you don't believe that about school, do you?"

"No. I like it. My math teacher says I'm the smartest boy she's ever had. Elijah is smarter than me, though. He learns all of my math when I do my homework. He says his is boring."

"What else do you like to do in school?" Rebecca asked.

"Sometimes I like to read stories, but I like it better when the teacher reads to us. When I was in first grade, my teacher read out loud all the time. She had the best books ever. Sometimes she let me take a book home." He leaned forward and then stopped when he realized he might disturb his brother. "One time," he said in a stage whisper. "She gave me a book and said I could keep it."

"What book was that?"

"Mike Mulligan and his Steam Shovel," Noah said. "I read it a lot, but then it got stole."

"Someone took the book?" Polly asked, flabbergasted.

"They stole a bunch of stuff. It was in the kitchen on the television and they took everything."

"Do you have any other books?" Andrew asked.

Noah shook his head. "Just that one. The teachers won't let us take books home anymore because kids won't bring them back."

"How's someone supposed to learn to read without books?" Andrew asked. "That's crazy. And I have Mike Mulligan in my room. Do you want to borrow it while you're staying at Polly's?"

Noah's eyes grew big. "Could I? I'll take really good care of it. I promise."

"Sure. When Polly takes me home tonight, I'll get it for you."

Rebecca and Andrew continued to talk to Noah, asking questions about his life in Chicago until Polly pulled into the lighting company's lot. As soon as she turned the truck off, Elijah woke up.

"Are we there?" he asked.

Polly smiled. "We're here. Did you have a good nap?"

"I was just resting my eyes."

"You kids stay right here," she said. "I'll run in and find out where I have to go to pick up Henry's order."

The clerk inside sent her around to a door at the back of the building. When Polly knocked on the door, a young man opened it, pushing a long cart in front of him, laden with boxes.

"You got room in the truck for all of this?" the young man asked.

Polly looked at the number of boxes and at the bed of her truck. "With room to spare," she said. How he couldn't easily make that judgment confused her, but she let it go. She pulled back the top and opened the tailgate, then stood back so he could load the boxes. He looked at her twice as if to ask for her help. She wasn't sure where he wanted her, so she waited.

He finally walked away from the cart and whistled into the warehouse, then called someone's name. An older man trotted out and frowned at the young man. "You should have said something."

"I thought she'd help," the young man said.

The older man glanced at Polly and shook his head. "Climb up into the truck. I'll hand these to you. Make sure they're in there snug and don't fill the bed higher than the sides, okay?"

"Yes sir."

In a few minutes, the truck was full and the kid walked away with the empty cart.

"Do I need to sign something?" Polly asked.

"Don!" the older man snapped.

"What?"

"Where's her paperwork?"

"Inside."

"I can go in," Polly said.

"Kid's not long for this job," the older man said, rolling his eyes. "I'll send him out with it."

Within minutes, young Don was standing in front of Polly with a piece of paper.

"Where do I sign?"

He shrugged and then pointed to a line at the bottom of the second sheet of paper.

"Do you have a pen?" Polly asked.

He looked around and sighed.

"No? I'm sure I have one in the truck. Do you have a copy of the paperwork for me to take?"

He sighed again. "I'll be right back. Sheesh."

"Sheesh is right," Polly said, opened the door and climbed in. She dug around in the console and came up with a pen, then wiggled to find a flat place to sign and stopped herself. "I'll be back, kids. Hang tight."

She climbed up into the bed of the truck and looked at the invoice in front of her, trying to make sense of their codes and information. Finally, she counted the number of boxes and the line of items on the order. The codes soon became apparent and she checked everything to make sure they'd given her the correct order. The kid hadn't given her much confidence. But it all checked out. She jumped down from the truck and slammed the tailgate shut just as Don came back. He watched her and breathed loudly while she signed the paperwork and handed it to him. He gave her another two pieces of paper and stalked away.

"Friendly little jerk," she muttered as she pulled the top back over the bed of the truck. "Helpful, too." It was a good thing she didn't have to work with him or his boss would get an earful.

"Who wants ice cream?" Polly asked when she got her seat belt back on.

Elijah barely let her finish the question before he stuck his hand in the air and said, "I do!"

"Noah?" Polly asked.

"Yes please."

"Where are you going?" Andrew asked.

"There's a Dairy Queen close. I thought we'd run over there." Before she pulled out of the parking lot, she said, "Today we're just going to have ice cream cones." She looked at Rebecca. "Or a shake. But none of the other things they serve. Okay? We're going to make it easy."

"Chocolate or vanilla ice cream cone," Rebecca said to the little boys. "Or you can have a twist cone where they put both kinds in it. That's usually what Andrew gets."

Andrew nodded.

"I like strawberry shakes," Rebecca continued. "Those are my favorite ever."

"Can I get a chocolate shake?" Noah asked.

"Of course you can," Rebecca said before Polly could speak.

"I'm having a twist cone like Andrew," Elijah said.

Polly grinned. "Me too."

They drove through Dairy Queen. Polly was thankful they'd figured it out before getting to the speaker. "We're going back the long way. There are a lot of little towns in Iowa and you can see a few of them today."

The kids were all quiet as they worked on their ice cream. Noah let Elijah try his shake and his younger brother let him have a bite of his cone. No matter what had happened to the boys, they certainly cared for each other. She hoped nothing ever happened to change that.

Rather than taking the highway into Ames, Polly drove west on a county road before coming to a stop in Madrid.

"I have to go to the bathroom, Miss Polly," Elijah said.

She glanced at the convenience store to her left and breathed a sigh of relief. Great timing. "You're in luck," she said. "There are clean bathrooms right here. Andrew and Rebecca, will you make sure they don't get lost?" Polly took her wallet out and handed cash to Rebecca. "Buy a bottle of water for everyone. Me too. I'm going to put gas in the truck." They still had another half hour before getting back to Bellingwood, and after ice cream, she was desperately thirsty.

"Did you wash your hands?" Polly asked, once everyone was back in the car.

Elijah held his out for her to see and she squeezed the hand closest to her. It was cool and damp.

"Noah?" she asked.

He nodded and put his hands up.

"Andrew?"

"Really, Polly?" Andrew asked.

"Well?"

He held his hands up, too.

"That's good. With all of the ice cream back there, I didn't know how much of a mess you might have made."

"It's clean," Andrew said. "We were careful."

Polly drove up to Luther and turned left.

"Where are you going?" Rebecca asked.

"I thought we'd drive over to the Ledges State Park so they could see it. Maybe run around a little."

Rebecca leaned over. "You're driving on back roads. You know what happens when you do that."

Polly looked down and scowled. "You stop it. Nothing is going to happen when they're in the truck with us."

"We'll see," Rebecca said.

It had taken Polly several attempts to come back to the park without fearing that she'd find another body here. The image of that poor girl tied to a tree was still vivid in her mind. Joey Delancy's insanity was never going to let her rest. He and the serial killer, Marcus Allendar, had killed several girls who looked like Polly last year. It still made her shudder.

Now someone else was killing people and associating her name with the deaths. What was it about her? It was one thing that she found people after they'd died, but it was completely different when it had something to do with her. She had quit sleeping last year because of what Joey and Allendar had done. Nightmares had plagued her for months until both of them had finally been convicted and locked away.

Polly wished that Aaron would give her more information about the bodies she'd found. First the girl who died in her arms and then the young man she'd found at the grain elevator east of Boone. Aaron said that the young girl who'd been placed into Polly's truck bed was killed by the same person. What in the world was this about? He'd been around in May and then stopped for a while.

"What are you thinking about?" Rebecca asked.

"You know what she's thinking about," Andrew said.

"Oh."

"I'm fine. Sorry if I got distracted." Polly drove into a parking lot, the same one that the bodyguard, Tonya, had driven into when Polly saw the girl's body tied to a tree. She parked at the other end. "Why don't you kids run around and blow some of your bubbles."

They opened the car doors.

"Don't go too far. I want to be able to see you," she said and put her head on the headrest as the doors slammed shut. The kids ran out into an open space and Rebecca began directing them. Polly rolled the windows down. It was warm outside, but a breeze kept her from being too hot.

She looked at the paper cups and wrappers in the console beside her and realized there was probably just as much trash in the back seat. A quick glance around the parking lot and she spied a trash bin at the other end. Polly gathered up the waste from the front seat, got out and climbed into the back seat to get the rest. When she had it all, she walked over to the bin and pushed the metal lid aside.

"Damn it all to hell," she said under her breath. "Damn it, damn it, damn it."

Polly looked at the trash in her arms and then down at the young man who had been stuffed into the bin. "I am never coming back to this place. It's dead to me." She gave a hoarse chuckle. "I didn't mean that. I didn't mean it that way. I promise."

A quick look to where the kids were playing assured her that no one was paying attention. The boys were chasing bubbles they had blown while Rebecca and Andrew were busy with the bottle that Lydia had given Rebecca.

Polly felt like crying. She jammed everything into one of the cups and started to walk away, but realized she'd seen something. It nearly made her sick, but she went back to the bin and saw the piece of paper sticking out from the hoodie jacket the young man was wearing. Aaron would kill her. Okay, that was morbid, considering what she was looking at. But he would definitely yell at her if she disturbed anything.

On the other hand, he kept refusing to tell her what was going on with this case. If the notes were about her or for that matter, written to her, it only seemed right that she knew what was on them. Maybe if she slipped it out long enough to take a picture of it with her phone, she could slide it right back in and nobody would ever know the difference. Right?

Aaron would know. She stepped away again. He always knew. Polly stopped and walked back to the bin once more. No. This time she was just going to deal with whatever he figured out. She had to know what was written on those notes. Maybe she'd have a chance at solving the mystery, but she needed information. The only way to get that information was to see what was on that paper.

She shuddered for a quick moment and then reached in and slipped the piece of paper out, cursing as soon as she did. Now her fingerprints were on it. She couldn't wipe them off, just in case the killer's prints were also there. She'd come this far; she might as well go all the way. Polly put the paper cup on the ground beside the bin, took her phone out of her back pocket and swiped it open to the camera. She didn't really want a picture of the dead guy, but she also wasn't walking too far away with evidence. The notepaper was the size of a third of a sheet of paper and he'd written on only one side of it. She focused in as close as possible, so as to avoid any obvious body parts in her picture and took two quick pictures, not bothering to try to read it. She'd do that later in the privacy of her own house. Polly slid the paper back inside the hoodie, turned around to make sure the kids were still playing, and placed the call she dreaded making.

CHAPTER FOURTEEN

"Can we fill the squirt guns at the water spigot?" Rebecca was standing beside Polly's truck waiting for her to return.

"What water spigot?" Polly looked to where Rebecca pointed. Right beside the trash bin.

"No," Polly snapped, setting Rebecca back a step.

"Why not? We're outside."

"No water from the spigot. Just go play with your bubbles."

"We're almost out. Are you ready to go home?"

"No," Polly said in resignation. "We're not going anywhere for a while."

"Why not? Is something wrong with the truck?"

"No, the truck's fine. We're just going to stay here and wait."

"For what?" Rebecca asked.

Polly glared off into the distance. "Not for what. For who. The sheriff."

Rebecca looked at the trash bin, then back at Polly. "No way."

"Yes way. I've already called Aaron."

"What's going on?"

"What's going on with what?" Andrew asked, running up to

them. Noah and Elijah were close behind him. "We're out of bubbles. Did Rebecca ask if we can fill up the squirt guns?"

"We can't," Rebecca said.

"Why not?" Elijah asked. "I know how. You just lift that handle and water comes out."

"We just can't. Polly said so," Rebecca responded. "That's all there is to it."

Andrew gave both of them a strange look, then understanding dawned on him. He put a hand on the door handle to the back seats of the truck. "What if we used the water we bought earlier. Can we do that?"

Polly nodded. "Sure. Use whatever you want. Just don't use the spigot."

He opened the door, reached in and handed a bottle to Noah and one to Elijah. "Here, boys, go out into the field and fill these up. I'll be right there with Rebecca's. Don't use it all before I'm there."

The two little boys grabbed the bottles and squirt guns and, weaving back and forth, chased each other out to where they'd been playing.

"What's going on?" he asked.

Rebecca pointed to the trash bin. "Polly found another body. She doesn't want the little kids to know about it."

Polly chuckled and wrapped an arm around Rebecca's shoulders. "You're so funny. It wasn't very long ago that you and Andrew were the little kids. Now you sound all grown up."

"We've been through this a lot with you," Rebecca said. "We know better than to freak out. But we don't know what Noah and Elijah will do if they find out that Polly's superhero power is finding dead bodies."

"Rebecca!" Polly cried.

"Well it is, you know. None of us can figure out why you fight it."

Polly shook her head. "I don't fight it. I just don't like to talk about it. It makes me sound creepy and strange."

Andrew wiggled his fingers in front of her face and drew them back, then went in and back again. "Woooo, wooo ... you're a freak!"

She swatted his hands away and smiled. "Go play with the kids and keep them occupied. I'll wait for Aaron and try to figure out how I'm going to explain this to Noah and Elijah."

"Just tell them the truth," Rebecca said. "We always know when you're making stuff up to protect us." She followed Andrew out to where the two brothers were squirting each other, laughing and running around in circles.

"You think you're so smart," Polly muttered. "Little intuitive Miss Know-it-all." She leaned against the truck and watched the kids play. She sincerely hoped that all of this activity would wear those little boys out. How she was going to make Elijah feel safe in his room, she didn't know. Maybe tonight she'd try putting Obiwan in with them. He always made her feel safe.

She remembered the picture that was waiting for her in her phone. Thinking about it made her stomach queasy. If she hadn't wanted to know what it said, she should have left it alone. Now that it was in her hands, it was time to face whatever hellish demon had been unleashed in her world. Polly reached for the phone in her back pocket and nearly breathed out a sigh of relief when she saw Aaron's SUV drive into the parking lot, followed by what looked like every emergency vehicle in the county.

He pulled in beside her and got out of his vehicle, then gave her a quick hug. "Where is it?" he asked.

She pointed to the trash bin. "In there. He's all folded up. I took the lid off to put trash in there and found him." She pointed to the ground. "That's my trash. I forgot to pick it back up."

"We'll take care of it. Don't worry. Did you touch anything but the lid of the can?"

Polly looked up into his eyes, trying to force her brain into thinking faster. She wanted to come up with a good lie to give him. She wasn't fast enough.

"Polly? What did you touch?"

"He had a note on him. I know I have to tell you because my fingerprints are on it. I pulled it out and took a picture."

Aaron frowned.

"I had to," she said. "You wouldn't tell me what was on those notes. I feel like all of this is happening because of me and no one will tell me why or what's going on."

"It's not your fault," he said.

"I know that." Polly creased her brow at him. "I'm not feeling guilty. People make their own choices. But my name is all over this thing and I want to know why." She pushed at his arm, no simple feat. The man was as strong as an ox. "And you won't tell me."

Aaron ran his hand through his silvering hair. "You aren't an easy woman to work with."

"Name one other person in the entire county that you work with as much as me on cases like this. Just one," she said.

"I can't. You're unique."

"You got that straight."

Aaron turned to the meadow where all four kids were standing in a row, watching what was happening. Rebecca, standing between Noah and Elijah had taken their hands, holding them back from running toward Polly. "Do they know?" he asked.

She nodded. "Rebecca and Andrew do. The boys don't. I have no idea what I'm going to tell them. Or how I'm going to tell them. They haven't even been with me three full days and they're exposed to death."

"If anyone can explain this, you can," Aaron said. He took her arm and guided her over to the edge of the parking lot. "I can hold the team back from lifting the body out if you want to get them out of here first."

Polly pulled her arm back, then took his hand with hers. "I don't know what the right thing to do is. Will they believe me if they don't see it?"

"They don't need to see this," he said quietly. "Take them home. Their little imaginations will be more than enough in this situation. You don't need to give them any more reality than they've already experienced."

"You're right," Polly responded. "Thank you."

"I'm sorry this is happening to you, Polly. We'll talk later after you've had time to process on what that note says."

"I haven't read it yet. I was just going to do that when you drove in."

"Take a deep breath when you do and remember that you aren't involved with the person who is doing this awful thing."

"I certainly hope I'm not." Polly stepped over the cable that separated the parking lot from the meadow and walked over to the kids. "Let's get in the truck and go home. We'll play with squirt guns in our back yard."

"Is that the cops?" Elijah asked. "Are you in trouble?"

"Not at all, sweetie," Polly replied. "Go ahead and climb in the truck and I'll try to explain everything."

"I thought maybe it was because we were with you," Noah said.

Polly stopped and knelt down in front of him. "What do you mean because you were with me?"

"Damien says that cops hate black people and we always have to be careful around them. I thought maybe we got you in trouble."

"Oh honey, no." Polly stood up. "Aaron?" she called out. "Could you come here for a minute?"

He put his hand on the back of the young woman he'd been talking to, said something more, then crossed over to Polly and the kids.

"Aaron, I want to introduce you to Noah." She put her hand on his back. "And Elijah. They're staying at our house for two weeks and are part of the group that came to Bellingwood with Roy Dunston."

Aaron bent over and put his hand out in front of Noah. "It's nice to meet you, Noah." He side-stepped to stand in front of Elijah and did the same thing. "Are you boys having fun with Polly?"

The boys nodded tentatively.

"My wife told me that she had lunch with you today."

Noah looked up at Polly.

"His wife is Lydia. She gave you those presents."

"You have a wife?" Elijah asked.

"Yes I do. I also have five kids and ..." Aaron stopped and put his hands out, counting off on his fingers. "I have five grandchildren. But they're all younger than you two."

"Can I ask you a question, sir?" Elijah asked, stepping forward.

"Of course you can, son."

Elijah walked away from the group, then turned and waved for Aaron to follow him. The two went to the other side of Polly's truck and were gone for only a moment before they came back. Polly sent a questioning look to Aaron and he smiled and nodded.

"Okay, boys. Let's get you all loaded back into Polly's truck," Aaron said. He picked Elijah up and swung him into the back seat, then gestured to Noah, asking if he'd like some help. Noah shrugged and allowed Aaron to lift him as well, then turned and sat down, pulling the seat belt on.

Polly waited until Rebecca and Andrew were in before reaching out to touch Aaron's hand. "What was that about?"

"I'll tell you later." He smiled at the boys, patted the side of the truck and walked away while Polly climbed in and took a deep breath.

"We're out of here," she said. Polly carefully backed the truck up and did her best to avoid the area where the sheriff's deputies had cordoned off the trash bin. The four kids craned their necks and did their best to see what was happening. She wasn't sure who had been more successful.

"Why did the police show up?"

"Did somebody do something wrong?"

"That cop was nice. Why aren't all cops that nice?"

"What was in that trashcan that they were standing around?"

Questions flew out of the boys' mouths until Polly put her hand up. She drove until she found a field entrance and pulled in, then stopped the car. She unbuckled her belt and turned around in her seat to face the boys. "I need to tell you something and you have to listen very carefully and try to understand what I'm saying. Deal?"

Elijah and Noah nodded solemnly.

"Somebody was killed and stuffed in that trash bin," Polly said.

"We've seen dead people before," Noah said.

"Yeah. It's no big deal. Sometimes they smell bad if they've been there a while."

Rebecca turned around in shock. "Where have you seen dead people?"

"Well, Miz Turner died one day and nobody knew it. But then it started smelling really bad every time we went past her door, so Noah and I climbed out on the fire escape and across to her balcony and looked in. We saw her lying on the floor. We didn't have a phone to call anybody. Mom was gone, but I finally knocked on old Mister Edison's door and told him that she was dead. He called someone." Noah sat back and took a breath after spewing so many words.

"Wow," Andrew said. "Who else?"

Elijah looked down at his shoes. "Darren Tate shot Baby Joe."

"You saw a baby get shot?" Rebecca asked.

"No. His name was Baby Joe. 'Cause his mama treated him like a baby all the time. But he did something bad to Darren's girlfriend, Aisha, so Darren killed him. That was right out front of our apartment. The cops took their sweet time getting there, too. Darren got away. We never told anybody who did it. Everybody knows Darren will shoot you if you talk."

Polly turned back around. She had no idea what to say to all of that. The boys certainly didn't need to hear about her tendency to find these bodies. Not today. If they asked, she'd tell them, but today their stories were bigger than hers.

"I'm sorry you boys had to see things like that," she said.

"It's no big deal," Elijah said.

"It's kind of a big deal," Rebecca replied. "Little boys shouldn't have to watch people get shot. Nobody should."

Elijah shrugged. "I'm hungry. Are we going back to your house, Miss Polly?"

Polly had always heard that kids were resilient. "Yes we are. But how about we stop at McDonalds. You can get one thing. A

139

burger or nuggets or an order of fries. I don't want to spoil your dinner."

"You can't spoil Elijah's dinner," Rebecca said. "He eats all the time."

"I'm a growing boy," he said. "I want a big hamburger. I promise it won't spoil my dinner."

Polly drove into Boone and stopped at McDonalds, then drove back to Bellingwood while her passengers ate. Rebecca and Andrew weren't quite as interested in food, and the last thing Polly wanted to do was eat one more thing. She didn't have quite the metabolism that the kids had.

Elijah had polished off his cheeseburger and was sound asleep again by the time she pulled into the driveway at Sycamore House. Noah was yawning and nodding off, but he recognized the building when she drove in.

He nudged his brother awake. "We're back. Wake up, Elijah."

"I wasn't asleep," Elijah said with a smirk aimed at Polly in the rear view mirror. "I was just resting my eyes."

"You said that before," Polly said. "Who's told you that?"

"My grandma. Can we play outside with the squirt guns?"

Polly nodded. "I told you that you could. Andrew, I think there's a bucket on the wall of the garage. Would you put water in it so they can fill their squirt guns?"

"Okay."

"I'm going upstairs to let the dogs out," Polly continued. She put her hand on Rebecca's knee. "Can I count on you and Andrew to watch the boys and the dogs?"

"Can we go down to the barn?" Elijah asked.

"Not with the squirt guns." Polly didn't want to overload Eliseo with the boys again. He'd been inundated with children this week and she wasn't landing hers on him without being there to help. "You kids play in the back here." She squeezed Rebecca's knee. "I was serious about not going to the barn. Eliseo's busy."

"Got it," Rebecca said. "Are you calling Henry?"

Polly nodded. "I probably should. He hates it when I don't tell him."

"He worries about you."

"When did you grow up?" Polly asked.

"Mom said I was always old or something like that."

"You have an old soul."

"Yeah. That's it."

Polly leaned over and planted a kiss on Rebecca's forehead. "Thanks for watching them. Give the dogs enough time to do what they need to do and then you all can come upstairs any time. I'm not trying to keep you out."

"I know." Rebecca opened the door and stepped out onto the running board. "Come on, boys. Let's get wet."

Polly opened the back door and helped Noah and Elijah climb down, then watched while they ran to follow Andrew into the garage. She went in and opened the door at the bottom of the stairs to her apartment and called her dogs down, then let them outside. Obiwan and Han ran over to Rebecca and circled her before heading for their favorite place along the tree line. Polly watched for a minute and went upstairs. She needed to figure out what to make for dinner and she had to call Henry. There was something she was forgetting about tonight. So much had happened and she was absolutely exhausted.

She sat down at the desk she shared with Henry. And then she saw it. Her flute. Tonight was the last rehearsal. She'd completely forgotten about it in all the craziness of this weekend.

Call Henry.

She swiped the phone open and placed the call. Henry answered on the first ring. "Hey there, lovergirl."

Polly laughed out loud. "I love you, too, but that's weird."

"Someday I'll find the perfect term of endearment for you."

"And until then, I'll be entertained. Do you have a minute?"

Henry turned the radio down. "Of course I do. What's up?"

"Well, I have your lights. The kids got ice cream in Ankeny. We went to the Ledges and I found another body."

He paused. "You what? Were the kids there?"

"You heard me. And yes, the kids were there, but I don't think they saw it. They were playing with bubbles and squirt guns."

"You bought them bubbles and squirt guns?"

"No," Polly protested. "Lydia did. She gave those to them at lunch."

"I need to hear all about your whole day when things quiet down tonight, but let's go back to the body. Are you okay?"

"I haven't had time to think about it. Probably. This is four, Henry. And somehow I'm involved. I took a picture of the note that the murderer stuck in the kid's hoodie."

"What does it say?" Henry asked.

"I don't know. I haven't had time to look at it."

"That doesn't sound like you."

"Well it does when there are four kids hanging around and Aaron shows up and you have to admit that you tampered with the body and then you have to deal with those four kids and drive them back and hear about how little boys have seen dead bodies and ..." Polly sighed. "And I have to go to band rehearsal tonight. I completely forgot about it."

"Damn it," he said. "I forgot about that too. I was going to call and tell you that I'd be late. We're jammed here and I wanted to work until it got dark."

She chuckled. "Because I have your lights, right?"

"No," he said with a laugh. "Because I'll be tired by then. I can put this off, though. I'll be home before you leave."

"Stop it. I'm not asking you to leave your work because I have to go to a rehearsal. We have plenty of people around who can help us out. I'll start with Heath and Hayden. If they can't do it, I'll call your mom. If she's too busy, I'll call Sylvie. No. I can't ask her. I know she's busy. But, I'll take care of it. You keep working and I'll see you when you get home."

"Are you sure?" Henry asked.

"You know I wouldn't tell you that it's okay if it wasn't, right?"

"I forget. Most of the time you're actually sane and not manipulative."

"What?"

"Just kidding, muffin."

"No," Polly said flatly. "That one is off the table."

"Yeah. I didn't like it when I said it out loud. Let me know what you figure out for tonight. And Polly?"

"Yes?"

"I love you. Thanks for making that trip for me today and I'm sorry it ended badly for you."

"I love you too."

Polly hung up and stared at her phone. She'd run into a wall and had no more energy to make decisions. Maybe everyone would be good with pizza tonight. She dialed Hayden's phone and waited.

"Hey Polly," Hayden said. "What's up?"

"Do you have plans for tonight?"

He laughed out loud. "Uh, yeah. I'm meeting up with the Bachelorette. You know they like those hunky Iowa boys, right?"

"Okay. Whatever. Are you two available to be here at the house while I go to band rehearsal tonight?"

"Sure. We should probably shower anyway. What time do you want us there?"

"I don't care. Rehearsal is at seven. Do you want to come for dinner? I think I'm just going to order pizza. My day kind of went south on me and I don't have it in me to cook."

"Let me cook, then. We can wrap up here in fifteen minutes, then we'll run to the grocery store and I'll take care of dinner. Is that okay?"

"Can I adopt you, please?" Polly asked.

Hayden laughed again. "I love you, too. We'll be there soon. Maybe you should take a nap."

"That sounds like a great idea. Thanks, sweetie."

CHAPTER FIFTEEN

Totally exhausted, Polly headed for her bedroom and dropped down on Henry's side of the bed, burying her face in his pillow. She knew what cologne he wore. Heck, she bought it for him. She knew what shampoo he used and what shower gel he used, but knowing all of that didn't change the fact that when she breathed in his scent, her entire being relaxed.

There was something else she wanted to do, but for the life of her, she couldn't remember. As she drifted off, she heard the kids come upstairs with the dogs and thought that maybe she should help keep the little boys busy. No. Rebecca and Andrew could handle it. She just needed a few minutes with her eyes closed against the world.

"Polly?"

Polly's eyes flew open. "What? Is everything okay? What time is it? Where is everybody?"

Rebecca sat down beside her. "Everything is fine. We're all here. Hayden made dinner and it's on the table. Do you want to eat before you go to rehearsal or would you rather have another half hour of sleep?"

"What time is it?" Polly asked.

"Six-fifteen. Hayden called Henry and he's not coming home until late, so we aren't supposed to wait for him."

Polly nodded. "Yeah. I knew that." She sat up in the bed. "I think my brain is working again. Yes, I want to get up and have dinner with you. I'm sorry I left you and Andrew to watch the boys."

"They were fine. Andrew's still here. His mom is working downstairs with Rachel and a bunch of other people. I guess they have a lot of catering to do this week."

"That's cool," Polly said. She ran her hand through her hair and shook it out. "Do I need to do anything before rehearsal? Is my hair okay?"

Rebecca leaned to look around Polly on both sides, then reached up and patted the top of her head. "A couple of fly-aways. You look fine."

Polly wrapped her arms around Rebecca and hugged her tight. "Have I told you lately how much I love you?"

"I love you, too," Rebecca said. Then she laughed. "Andrew's right. You do hug a lot."

"Better to have too many hugs than not enough."

They walked through the living room to the dining room where Noah, Elijah, Andrew, and Heath were already sitting at the table. Hayden smiled at Polly when she walked in. He opened the oven and took out a platter with sliced garlic bread on it and put it on the table.

"What did you make?" Polly asked.

"We helped," Elijah said. "We made lasagna and garlic bread and I tore up the lettuce into small pieces for the salad."

Polly smiled at the bowls of salad sitting at each place. "Thank you boys. This looks wonderful." Polly sat down beside Noah. "What did you help with?"

He looked up at her and with a shy grin, said, "I'm not supposed to tell. It's a secret."

She hugged his neck and kissed his cheek. Then I can hardly wait."

Hayden handed his brother a spatula before sitting down. "You wanna serve it up?"

For dessert they'd put chocolate chip cookie dough in mini muffin tins and inserted peanut butter cups as soon as they came out of the oven. Noah was quite proud of the fact that he'd been able to help with dessert, absolutely floored at putting candy into a cookie. Once the secret had been revealed, he talked and talked about how he'd never seen anything like it.

Polly finally had to leave. She stopped at the door to Henry's office and watched the kids, all still at the table, laughing and chattering. Then she grabbed her flute and music and headed down to the truck. It was hotter than the hinges of Hades outside and she didn't want to walk in it, even if the elementary school was only a few blocks away.

When she entered the gymnasium, she realized she was still early. That never happened. So she sat in her seat and pulled out her flute, taking a few moments to polish it.

Jeanie Dykstra sat down beside her. After the events last winter with Beryl's half-brother from England, Polly and Jeanie had been much more comfortable with each other. Jeff waved when he caught her eye.

Every summer, she thought about not participating in the band since she was sure that she was too busy, but she really did enjoy herself and as Henry reminded her, it was a great way to get to know more people in town. It floored her that she was still playing her flute fifteen years after leaving high school. Her dad would be so proud.

Rehearsal went well and Jeanie agreed that they were ready for the concert Friday evening. Polly felt excitement resonate through the group as they talked about the events coming up this week. Now if she could just avoid having any more bodies show up, she'd be very happy.

That was what she'd wanted to do. She was going to look at the note that had been left in the dead man's hoodie. Polly took her phone out, realized she was in the middle of a large group of people who were discussing a short jaunt over to the Alehouse for drinks, and put it back in her pocket. They didn't need to know anything about this.

"Are you coming with us?" Jeanie asked.

Polly shook her head. "I've got too many kids at my house this evening. I need to get home."

Jeanie looked at her in confusion. "More?"

"We're hosting a couple of the boys from Chicago," Polly said.

"Oh. My parents did that a few years ago. They had a great time. I think they learned as much as the boys did."

"These are good kids," Polly said. "Is your family doing anything special for the celebration?"

Jeanie laughed. "We have a float for the parade. Beryl called and asked if we wanted to do a bank robbery and she could be the thief. Dad thought that was a bit much. But we're going to follow the State Bank's float with an old-fashioned bank. Dad's got his costume all put together and Mother and I will be his customers. We have gold chocolate coins we're tossing out to the kids." She wiped her brow. "I hope it isn't this hot or they'll be a melty mess."

"That's really fun." Polly grinned. "I think having Beryl rob you guys would be hilarious!"

"Dad said it would make her brothers angry."

Polly shook her head. "I doubt that Beryl cares whether or not they got angry at something so silly." She watched people moving toward the doors. "I'll let you go. Are you coming to any of the dances at Sycamore House?"

"I might be there tomorrow night. It's the Flapper Ball, right?"

"Yeah. It should be a hoot."

"Maybe I'll see you there."

Polly walked out to her truck and yawned as soon as she hit the heat and humidity. She took her phone back out and texted Henry. *"Are you about home?"*

"Just walked in."

"Good, it's horrible out here. Tell Hayden and Heath that they should stay with us tonight."

"When are you coming home?"

"Right now."

"I love you."
"I love you, too."

Polly dropped the phone on the console and pulled her belt on before driving off. She hoped the little boys were ready to sleep tonight. She'd give it a shot with Obiwan in their room, but otherwise, they were going to have to do something different. She needed more sleep than a couple of hours in an afternoon.

Sycamore House was lit up when she drove in. There were cars in the front parking lot, all of the rooms in the additions had their lights on, the barn's lights were still on, and Eliseo's truck was there. When she pulled into the garage, quite a few people were moving around in the kitchen. Everyone would deserve a vacation next week.

She didn't even bother to poke her head into the kitchen, but went straight up the steps to the apartment. Hayden and Heath were at the dining room table with Noah and Elijah. When she looked over to see what they were doing, she smiled at the stack of games they'd pulled out. Right now they were playing CandyLand and Operation was up next.

"Thanks, guys," she said in passing.

Rebecca was sitting on the sofa with her sketch pad in hand while Andrew sat next to her reading a book.

"Where's Henry?"

Andrew pointed over his shoulder at Polly's bedroom.

She walked in and found Henry sitting in his favorite chair beside the bed.

"Did you say anything to Hayden about staying here tonight?" she asked.

Henry looked up from his tablet. "He said they'd be fine. I told him they couldn't leave."

"There's no need for them to be miserable. We can put the little boys on the couches if Hayden and Heath want the bed," she said.

"I don't care what you do."

"You're exhausted, aren't you? Did you get some supper?"

"I'm not hungry."

"Have you taken a shower?" she asked.

"Not yet."

Polly sat down on the edge of the bed. "You'll feel better, you know."

He looked over at her and glared. "Can I just sit here and read the news? Please don't try to help."

She pursed her lips. "Okay. You know how hard that is for me, but I'll go find someone else to bother. If you decide to feel human again, come join us." Polly shook her head as she left the room.

Wandering out to the dining room, Polly realized that everyone was busy and she had nothing to do, so she went in to Henry's office and closed the door. It was finally time to focus on that note that she'd found earlier today. Because she'd waited so long, it seemed to have taken on a life of its own in her head.

She swiped her phone to the photograph and enlarged the image so she could read it.

The fourth you've found.
Do you feel that you've drowned?

How long will this last
Who's next in our cast

Oh Polly, I'll be frank
I won't let you tank.

To reach you I've been bold
Your story will be told.

Polly read it through twice and swiped the app closed. She wanted to erase the whole thing from her phone's memory, but that wouldn't do any good. The murderer's words were etched into her memory. She desperately needed to talk to someone and Henry was exhausted and grumpy.

The clock in the dining room rang nine times and Polly realized she still had time before Aaron went to bed. She chuckled at the realization that she knew when her sheriff's bedtime was. Only in small town Iowa. She swiped a call, but to Lydia, not Aaron. Polly only called his phone when it was desperate and she didn't want him to think that she used it willy nilly.

"Hello dear, is everything okay?" Lydia asked.

"It's fine and I'm sorry to call so late, but I need to speak with Aaron and didn't want to call his phone. You know. Save it for those special moments between us and all?"

Lydia laughed lightly. "He told me you might try to call him tonight. You got hold of one of those notes today. He's been desperately trying to keep you away from all of this."

"You've known?" Polly asked.

"Just in general terms," Lydia responded. "I don't know anything specific. How are your kiddos doing after all that happened today?"

Polly took a cleansing breath. There was something about talking to Lydia that brought her blood pressure back down to where it belonged. "I don't know that Elijah and Noah knew what really happened out there today. They had a few questions, but those boys have seen more than their share of the underside of life. A body in a trash bin at a park in Iowa just won't resonate."

"Did you tell them about your special power?"

"Stop it, Lydia. Not you too. No, I didn't tell them."

"Dear, when you learn to accept what you are, this will be much easier for you."

"Yeah, I suppose," Polly said. "But it's hard to accept it when I get shuffled off as soon as law enforcement shows up."

"I understand that. Aaron has a tough line to walk. He wants to protect you from the business of law enforcement as well as from those who are killing people for you to find."

"I should be nicer to him? Is that what you're telling me?" Polly asked with a laugh.

"It's never bad to be nice to your favorite sheriff, but no, that's not what I'm saying. He feels it as much as you do, though."

"Did he tell you that Elijah spoke with him before we left?"

"Yes he did," Lydia's voice grew warm and soft. "That little boy was mightily impressed with my big, burly husband."

"What did he want to know? Aaron intimated he would tell me later."

"Why don't I let the two of you talk," Lydia said. "Aaron? Honey-muffin? It's Polly. Would you like to speak with her?"

Lydia came back to the phone. "He says he really didn't want to speak with you."

"Tell him he can either talk to me on the phone or I'm driving over there and leaning on the doorbell until he answers it."

"That would annoy my wife as much as it would me," Aaron said.

"Oh. Hello there, Honey-muffin."

"Stop that. She only says those things to embarrass me."

"Does it work?"

"Not anymore." Aaron chuckled. "You didn't call my phone. I'm proud of you."

Polly laughed. "I thought I would save those calls for our special moments together."

"The ones that involve dead bodies?"

"Yeah. Those."

"Tell me what you're asking tonight?" Aaron asked.

"Well, first of all, what did Elijah say to you this afternoon?"

Aaron chuckled. "He's a cutie. He wanted to know if I had ever put a little boy in jail. When I told him that I had never done anything like that, he asked if you were in trouble. I told him that you weren't in trouble and that you were a friend to the sheriff's department. That one needed a little more explanation. Then he told me about a policeman from his old neighborhood whose name is Officer Anderson. Apparently Officer Anderson bought him and Noah a hamburger and french fries the day their mother died. That's when he told them what had happened. He really liked Officer Anderson and wishes he could see him again, but it's too far away from his grandmother's house."

"I'm glad you had a good moment with him. He's an observant little boy."

"Yes he is," Aaron said. "So are you."

"I have the note. I finally got the time, the courage and the privacy to read it. Aaron, are all of the notes you've found the same?"

He sighed. "They are all rhyming poems with eight lines in each, but they say different things."

"Can I see them?"

"Polly, you know I don't want you involved."

She growled out loud. "And you know that I can help. This is about me, Aaron. Please don't keep me away from it."

"I hate that you are embroiled in it at all."

"Have you identified the people he's killed?"

It took Aaron a few moments to respond. Polly waited silently, then looked up when the office door opened. Henry walked in and she beckoned him over, then waved at him to shut the door.

Finally, Aaron said, "It took us over a month to identify the first two victims. The girl, Lynn, is from St. Louis. No one reported her missing because she was taking a class off-campus. It was some type of archeology class. Her friends and roommates thought she was just busy. Her family didn't have much contact with her. When she didn't come back at the end of May, one of her roommates finally started asking questions.

"The young man you found over by the Elevator was homeless. He lived in Omaha. The shelter he frequented asked some questions and we finally made the connection. These are lost souls he's killing, Polly. He doesn't want us to be able to easily identify them."

"So anything on the two I found recently?"

"We're still working on it. That may take some time if he's killing people who have no connections."

"That makes me think that my family is safe," she said. "He's not going after people I know."

"That's a reasonable assumption."

Henry sat on the edge of the desk and Polly mouthed Aaron's name so he knew who she was talking to.

"Thank you," Polly said to Aaron. "Can I please see the rest of these notes?"

"Are you busy tomorrow morning?"

Polly shut her eyes, trying to think through her morning. If she could get Rebecca to stay with the boys, she could be free. "I can make time. Should I come down to your office?"

"That would be fine. I will let Anita know that it's okay for you to see the notes. Maybe you'll make more sense of them than we have. Right now it just feels like he's taunting us."

"Isn't the body taunt enough?" Polly asked.

"Yes," Aaron replied. "And you're right. Maybe you'll see something."

"Thank you for not shutting me out."

"Go enjoy your family," Aaron said.

"Give Lydia a hug for me."

She swiped the call closed and then opened the note and put the phone in front of Henry. He took it from her, read what was on the screen, and his face flushed. "What in the hell?"

"This is the note that was on the body. I'm going down to the sheriff's office in Boone tomorrow morning to see the rest of the notes."

"I don't want you to be part of this."

Polly grimaced. "I'm already part of it. If I can see something that will help end this, I should at least try. Nothing in this note threatens me, and Aaron says that he's choosing people who won't be missed for a while."

"You'd kind of hope that means you're safe."

She nodded. "Are you feeling any better?"

"Yeah. Sorry about snapping. I just needed to be quiet. It was hot and awful today and I was overloaded."

"Do you have to work this hard tomorrow?"

Henry nodded. "Tomorrow and Wednesday. I'm sorry, but I am going to miss tomorrow night's dance."

Polly's face fell. "Damn. But okay. I get it. You'll be here for dinner with the kids and Roy on Wednesday, though, right?"

"I will." Henry smiled. "So where are we going to put everyone tonight?"

"Let's ask the boys where they want to sleep."

"Which boys?"

"Elijah and Noah. Maybe we can turn the living room into a campground. That way Heath and Hayden can have the big bed in the front room."

"Let's get this started," Henry said. "I want to go to bed."

"I'll pick up another couple of air beds in Boone tomorrow. If it's going to be this hot, Hayden and Heath shouldn't sleep at the house."

Henry slid off the desk and opened the door, waiting for Polly to go through.

"Hey boys. Let's figure out where everyone is going to sleep tonight," she said.

Andrew stood up as she stepped into the doorway between the dining room and living room.

"Are you spending the night?" Polly asked with a laugh.

"I don't think so. But Mom is working late. Unless she forgot me."

Polly continued to laugh. "Give her a call. One of us will take you home if she did."

"Someone can have my bed." Rebecca put her sketchbook down on the coffee table. "I'll sleep on the couch."

"We're good with the couches," Hayden said.

"Here's what we're thinking," Polly said. "Elijah and Noah, how would you like to camp in the living room? We can push the couches together. Hayden and Heath, you can have the king-sized bed in the front room. The rest of us will have our normal rooms."

Elijah nodded. "Push the couches together and make one big couch?"

"Yeah," Polly said. "Does that sound like fun?"

"Can we make a fort?"

"We can do whatever you want."

Andrew came back into the room. "She forgot me. I told her that you'd take me home."

"I got it," Hayden said. "We'll take the dogs outside and then go."

Henry nodded and yawned. "Thanks. I'll see you in the morning."

Rebecca asked to ride with Hayden and Andrew. Polly just smiled and waved them off.

Henry and Heath moved furniture and pushed the sofas in the living room together while Polly got extra sheets and pillows. Before long, Noah and Elijah were nestled into their fort.

When the dogs dashed back upstairs, Polly patted the sofa back and Obiwan jumped up and over, landing beside Elijah. "Do you want to try to sleep with him tonight?" she asked.

Noah nodded and Elijah reached out to hug the dog.

Han followed Henry into the bedroom and Heath said goodnight before going to his own room. Polly went into the media room and looked through her bookcases, then pulled out her book of children's stories. She wasn't going to let an opportunity like this pass. Maybe she should have done it the last couple of nights, but tonight it finally hit her.

Polly sat down on a chair next to the boys' fort and opened the book. "Care if I read to you?" she asked.

They clambered across the sofa to sit next to her and she started reading aloud, "Once upon a time ..."

CHAPTER SIXTEEN

Instead of rushing the next morning, everyone except Henry was slow to move. Rebecca was thrilled to make extra money by spending time with Noah and Elijah. She promised to take them all over town. The carnival was setting up and Andrew wanted to watch that this afternoon. Sylvie texted Polly to invite the kids to play at her house today. Padme missed her boy when he was gone all the time and they had a big fenced-in yard where the boys could safely play outside.

Late last night, Polly had sent an email to Anita Banks in the sheriff's office, asking if she could come down this morning. Sure enough, bright and early, Anita replied, telling Polly that she'd be glad to meet with her.

Heath and Hayden had helped Henry load the light fixtures from Polly's truck to Henry's and then they took off for Ames to run errands for Henry. They wouldn't get to the Bell House until mid-morning.

Polly finally loaded up the kids and headed for Kayla's apartment building to pick her up. If some of the kids were going to be together, they might as well all be together. When they got to

Andrew's, he was waiting on a bench on the front porch; his dog at his side. Padme jumped up and barked in greeting.

"Everybody has dogs around here," Elijah said. "I wish I could have a dog."

"They are pretty wonderful," Polly agreed. "Are you two boys ready for today?"

Rebecca poked her head back into the truck. "We'll have fun. Don't worry. And if anything happens, I have a phone."

Polly smiled as the kids ran up to the porch and into the house. No one turned around to wave good-bye. She figured that was the way of it from now on. She backed out of the driveway and headed out, taking a swoop through the downtown area first. She was astounded at how things were transforming. Barrels of flowers had cropped up in front of businesses overnight. She looked yearningly at Sweet Beans and felt the truck turn so she could park there.

"Fine. I'll give in," she muttered and went inside.

The tables were covered in pretty gingham cloth and each had an oil lantern surrounded by greenery, a few old books, and at least one pair of old-fashioned spectacles. Polly got close enough to one table to look at the lantern and saw that instead of a wick and oil, a small LED bulb was giving off light.

"Good morning, Polly," Skylar said. He looked fantastic, dressed in a white dress shirt with a small black tie and brown pants.

"You're quite the dashing young chap," she said.

He gave her a small bow. "Your regular today?"

"Of course. I wasn't going to come in, but I couldn't help myself." She glanced over her shoulder. "In fact, the truck drove into a parking space all by itself."

"I believe you," Sky said. "It wouldn't know how to drive past us."

Camille came out from the bakery, carrying a tray of breads. She was dressed in a pretty floral dress, with a long apron and matching bonnet hanging down her neck.

"You too?" Polly asked. "You look great."

Camille put the tray down and fanned herself. "It's a little warm. We might pay extra for air conditioning this week. I can't take this. Long dresses are not my idea of summer attire."

"Why are you dressed up today?"

"Most of us agreed to be ready today. Quite a few people are in town and we want to give them a sense of things. It wasn't a big deal."

"Well, the place looks wonderful."

"Thanks. We've been gathering our goods and put it all together last night."

Skylar handed Polly her iced coffee. "Anything else?" he asked, pointing at the muffins.

"No thank you. I've had plenty of breakfast this morning."

Four couples came in the side door, chattering amongst each other and pointing at the tables. They approached the counter and Polly waved and backed away. This week could only be good for everyone's business. It was fun to see the community involved and excited.

She got to the highway and turned the radio on. Classic rock made her want to dance in her seat. Polly laughed when a farmer waved at her and she realized that she'd been waving her hand in the air to the music. Driving through Boone, she toned down her dancing and turned the music off before parking to go into the sheriff's office. She sat back in her seat and took a deep breath. As much as she wanted to know what was going on, this made her nervous.

Taking a deep breath, she steeled herself before getting out of the truck. Once inside the building, she asked for Anita and waited until the girl came to take her back to her office.

"Sheriff Merritt told me to let you see the notes," Anita said. "Maybe another set of eyes will see something we haven't seen."

Polly shook her head. "I know I'm sticking my nose into this, but ..."

Anita scowled. "I kept telling him to let you in on at least this part of it. Every time you get involved, you help us." She laughed. "Even when you drive the killer to our door."

"I wasn't even sure that citizen's arrest was a thing that day," Polly said, referring to the time when she and Beryl brought Beryl's English half-brother to Boone from Ames last January.

"It's a thing for sure," Anita said. "People just don't realize it. It's probably safer that way for everyone, don't you think?"

Polly laughed. "Safer for the ones who might be arrested by me."

"Yeah, that poor man might never get over the indignity of being tied to the seat of that car. What a great idea, though." Anita clicked through a program on her computer and brought up images of the messages that had been left with the victims.

"So there weren't any fingerprints on the bodies or the messages?" Polly asked.

"Nothing on the pieces of paper. There isn't anything on the bodies either. At least nothing that has given us any leads."

"What?" Polly asked. "No single fiber from the trunk of a car that leads you immediately to the murderer?"

Anita shrugged. "Well, yeah. Fibers from a car, but it's all pretty common."

Polly peered at the screen. "Can you print those out so I can have a copy of them?"

"I told Aaron you'd want that. He said no." Anita laughed and opened a drawer and pulled out a file folder. "They're in here."

Opening the folder, Polly spread the pieces of paper out on Anita's desk, reading through them. "These are weird," Polly said. "There's no continuity."

"That's what we saw. Unless he's just bragging, we don't see any reason for them."

Polly quietly verbalized the first note:

Poor sweet Lynn,
You'd call this a sin.

When the research is done
They'll know Polly's the one

The first, it is plain
I still need to train

You'll call me a brute,
the next one's a hoot.

Then she put the second on top of it and read it to herself.

With one quick look
The bait she took

Number two is dead
I'm off to bed.

All tidy and neat
Is there plenty to eat?

The world, it should know.
Her talent will show.

The third was similar. Polly looked up before reading it aloud.
"He really was gone for a while."
"Yeah. I wonder where he went."
Polly looked back at the paper in front of her and read:

Well look, this is new
I've a room with a view

I hear when they bark,
On a ledge, in a park

But today number three
Is just a beginning for me

Catch me if you can
I'm your number one fan.

"My number one fan? What in the world?" Polly asked.

"This is when we all told Aaron to let you get involved. You'd know better than anyone if there was undue attention coming your way. Have you received any scary fan mail?"

Polly breathed. "I haven't gotten anything weird. At least none that I've seen. Have you asked Jeff?"

Anita shook her head. "I don't think so. Let me send a message to Sheriff Merritt. He'll want to check on that. But you've seen nothing?"

Polly creased her brow as she thought. "There might have been something last year after Halloween. There were a bunch of kooks who thought they should investigate my paranormal talent. I sent them away." She shook her head. "I seem to recall getting a letter from somebody asking if I would consider allowing them to follow me around. I just threw it away. I don't even remember where it was from."

"And nothing since then?"

"Not in my personal mail. Stephanie usually gives me any envelope that's addressed to me, though." Polly spread the papers out again and scanned them, using her finger as a guide through the words. One by one, she read and re-read them several times. "This isn't helpful."

Anita shrugged. "I didn't expect much. I don't think there's anything there. He's just some psychopath trying to get your attention and the only way to let us know this was about you was to write a note and attach it to the victim."

"And you're sure it's a man?"

"We had a handwriting expert look at the notes. Even though he's taken great pains to disguise his handwriting by printing in block letters, it's quite apparent that these are written by a male." Anita chuckled. "At least it was apparent to her and I'll take her word for it."

Polly's phone rang and she pulled it out of her back pocket to see that it was a call from Hayden. "It's Hayden, do you mind if I take this?"

"Sure, go ahead."

"Hey, Hay," Polly said with a chuckle.

"Been waiting a while to use that one?" he asked.

"Maybe. What's up?"

"It happened again."

"What?" she asked.

"That person broke into the house again. This time they completely wrecked the kitchen floor. It's a real mess in here. Who should we call?"

"Damn it," Polly said, then pinched her lips closed. "Sorry. Who is doing this?"

Hayden didn't respond.

"Yeah, yeah. You don't know. I'll call the police station and have someone come over. Maybe they'll be able to figure something out. Do you want me to call Henry?"

"No, don't bother him. He's really busy. Heath and I can take care of this."

"You don't want Eliseo or Bill to come over?"

"Not unless you want them here. I'll handle it."

Polly thought for a moment. "I'm sorry. I don't mean to insult you. I know you can handle it. Would you like to call the police?"

"If you want me to."

She nodded. "Sure. Go ahead. Let me give you the number."

Anita scratched something on a piece of paper and pushed it in front of Polly, who smiled and read the number to Hayden.

"Got it. We'll deal with this. Don't worry, Polly."

"I'm not. Thank you. I'm in Boone, but when I get back to town, I'll be over."

"What was that?" Anita asked when Polly ended the call.

"Someone keeps breaking into the house we're renovating. They destroyed walls while pulling copper pipe out and now they've wrecked the kitchen floor. Maybe they were looking for more pipe."

"We get those calls all the time. It happens in abandoned buildings a lot," Anita said. "You'd think they would find an easier way to make a buck."

"I think I know who it is, too," Polly said.

"Do the police know?"

"Chief Waller suspects, but we don't have any evidence. There's a guy who lives just down the street. He's a druggie and I kicked him off of my property when we were looking for a janitor back in the early days of Sycamore House. He's a real piece of work and I wouldn't put it past him to try to make an easy buck. It would also make him happy to get back at me."

"That doesn't sound good."

"Nope. If I catch him anywhere near that house, I will have him in jail faster than you can say 'bad boy,'" Polly said. She pushed the papers into a stack and slid them back into the folder. "So I can take these with me?"

Anita smiled. "They're yours. If you see anything, call us right away."

"Absolutely." Polly stood and stepped back, but when Anita stood to show her to the door, Polly stepped back in and gave her a quick hug. "Thanks for helping me out. Are you coming up to Bellingwood for any of the events?"

"I might. You guys have a great carnival and I hear there's a street dance this weekend."

"Yeah? Who'd you hear that from?"

Anita just grinned. "If I see you, I'll say hi."

"Got it. You know, maybe you'd like to meet Hayden. He's going to be in grad school this next year. That's not too young, is it?"

"You're terrible, Polly Giller," Anita said with a laugh.

"I can hardly help myself." Polly patted the folder. "Thanks again."

Polly got back into her truck, turned it on so the air conditioning would run and took her phone back out, swiping a call open.

"Hey there, Tweetie-Bird," Henry sang.

"I tot I taw a puddy-tat," Polly said.

He laughed. "What's up?"

"You aren't supposed to do anything with this. I'm letting

Hayden handle it, but someone broke into the Bell House again last night and tore up the kitchen floor. He's calling the police."

When Henry didn't say anything, Polly coughed, then said, "Henry? Are you there?"

"I was afraid of that. Some of the old houses ran their pipe underneath the floorboards. But he could have pulled that pipe from below, not from above. This sounds like deliberate vandalism."

Polly took a breath. "I really think it's that Shawn Wesley. He saw that no one was staying there last night and took the opportunity to break in. I hate that we have to expect anyone to stay there overnight in this heat."

"We can't. If he's going to wreck the house, we'll just have to deal with it. We have locks on the doors..." Henry paused. "Wait. Did Hayden say how he got in?"

"No. I was in Anita's office. I didn't ask enough questions, but I'm heading back there after I pick up a couple of air beds. I'll find out what's going on. Hayden told me not to call you because you're so busy, so you can't call him. Got it?"

"That's not true. I *can* call him."

"But you won't, right?"

Henry laughed. "Okay. I won't. We're insured and now we can put any type of flooring you want into the kitchen."

"Radiant heat?" Polly asked.

"I suppose."

"Wouldn't that be nice in the one room where we'll spend most of our time?"

"Of course it would," Henry agreed. "Are you serious?"

"If I can get away with it, I am."

"After this week is over, I'll sit down and figure out what it will take."

"No worries," Polly said. "It was just a thought. If it's too expensive, I'll just buy lots of warm rugs for winter time."

"What did Anita have to say?"

"That we're dealing with a psychopath who is trying to get my attention. I have copies of all the notes to look through. Aaron is going to ask Jeff about any threatening letters that might have come in to me. Do you remember that weird letter I got last fall?"

"Kinda."

"Yeah. That's what I told Anita. I'm sure I threw it away. I don't even remember the name on it."

"Wouldn't Jeff have given you any mail that came in?"

Polly laughed. "Not if he thought he was protecting me."

"I knew I liked that boy." Henry pulled the phone away. "I'll be right there, Ben." He came back and said, "I have to go. Talk to you tonight?"

"You're going to be late again?"

"Yeah. Pretty late. That okay?"

"Of course it is. You do whatever you have to do. I love you."

"I love you, too, Sugar-bun."

"You're a nut," Polly said with a laugh.

"Not there yet?"

"Not even close."

CHAPTER SEVENTEEN

Calmly driving back from Boone, at least as calmly as she could, Polly kept glancing at the folder sitting on the passenger seat. What were they missing? Was this guy really just going to keep killing people and leaving obscure notes on their bodies for her to find? Surely he would run out of interesting things to say.

She looked up at the road and slammed on the brakes, skidding to a stop behind a car that was on the shoulder. Two little boys were standing beside their mother who was trying to keep them on the ditch side while she spoke into the phone. Polly got out of the truck and smiled as Elva waved to her.

"Hi, Miss Polly," Matty said. "We got a fat tire."

"You did. That's no good. Where are your sisters?"

"They went with Uncle Seo. Mama took us to get groceries and then we got a fat tire."

"I see. Why don't you come get into my truck where it's cool?" Polly bent down and beckoned to his older brother. "Samuel, why don't you come with me, too. The air conditioning is on inside my truck." She reached out her arms and Matty ran into them so she could pick him up. Elva was having a heated conversation with

166

someone Polly assumed to be Eliseo. She planted the two boys in the truck and checked her pocket for the fob. The last thing she needed was for them to lock her out.

Elva gave a big sigh and dropped her arms in frustration. "Seo can't come right now. He's got everyone out on the horses."

"Matty says you have a fat tire."

"And I don't have a spare," Elva said, shaking her head.

Polly looked at the young woman in shock that she'd driven four kids across country with no spare tire. Oh well. Not her business.

"What else did he say?" Polly asked. In all of the time she'd known Eliseo, he had never refused to help someone.

"That he'd come as soon as he could. But I don't want to sit out here on the highway and wait for him."

"Of course you don't. Let's put your groceries in my truck with the boys and we'll stop by the barn with your keys and then I'll take you out to Eliseo's. It's no big deal."

"Would you?" Elva asked. "That would be fantastic. She opened the trunk. "The least I can do is make some meals for Seo. Your little grocery store doesn't have very many items, so he told me how to get to Boone. It's a really easy drive." Elva kicked the flat tire. "As long as nothing happens to your car."

Polly helped carry bags of food and then they installed Matty's car seat into Polly's truck. When they were finished with that task, Polly was sweating and found herself cursing inside her head.

"Come on, boys," Elva said. "Climb into your seats. Miss Polly is going to take us home."

Matty held up one of the copies from the file folder. "I know this word," he said. "Train. I like trains. I have Thomas the Tank Engine pajamas."

Elva snatched the sheet out of his hand and slid it back into the folder. "You shouldn't touch other people's things. Tell her you're sorry."

"I'm sorry."

Polly nodded and climbed into the driver's seat while Elva checked her boys.

"I just want to make sure I have everything out of the car," Elva said. "I'll be right back."

"Train," Polly said to herself and picked up the folder. She re-read the first note, then took the other notes from the folder. She was still looking at them when Elva opened the passenger door.

"What are those?" Elva asked.

"A puzzle that I'm trying to understand," Polly said. "Matty might have given me a hint." She closed the folder and slid it between her seat and the console, then glanced in the rear view mirror. "Are you ready to go?"

"I helped you?" Matty asked.

Polly smiled. "We'll see." She backed away from the car, then drove out onto the highway and headed to Sycamore House.

The horses were still gone. Elva took out her keys. "I'll be right back. Thank you for helping us. This is so awesome. Whenever the car broke down at home, I called the garage and they took care of everything. I've never known people who just stop and help." She jumped down and ran into the barn. In a few moments, she was back. "I'll text him to tell him where we are."

"Does he know there isn't a spare tire?" Polly asked.

"Oh yes, he knows." Elva leaned over and whispered. "He yelled at me. I know he's right, but I didn't need to be yelled at when I was standing on the side of the road with two little boys."

"So he thinks you're still there?"

Elva gave Polly an evil grin. "Yes. After yelling at me, he deserves to worry." She typed into her phone, then put it down. "There. I told him." Her phone buzzed and she looked at it and smiled at Polly again. "He says to tell you thank you."

"No problem. I'm just glad I was in the right place. How are things going?"

"They're going." Elva let out a sigh. "I drive Seo nuts. This is why we haven't spent much time together over the years. I always forget. He's so darned serious about everything." She turned to look at the boys. "He says I don't take anything seriously enough." Elva shrugged. "Maybe that's why I..." She stopped, looked back at Matty and took a breath. "That's why we're in Iowa."

"Eliseo has been alone for a long time," Polly said. "It has to be strange for him to have a house full of people."

"That's not it," Elva said. "He loves the kids. He absolutely lights up when he comes in the door and they run to say hello. He plays outside with them and the dogs, and reads to all of them at night. You should see them in that living room. All four children trying to find a place on his lap while he reads a book. The first thing he does in the morning is check their rooms. Yesterday he brought paint colors and wallpaper samples home. Not for me, but for them. He's letting them pick out what they want for their rooms."

"So you're staying?"

"I guess so. We haven't really talked about it, but he also brought plans for a swing set, and he called someone about putting the kids in school next month."

Polly chuckled. "I guess you're staying. That's terrific. How do you feel about it?"

Elva was quiet for a while, then she looked back at her boys again and reached over the console to touch Matty's leg. "I want my kids to be happy. Seo says that Bellingwood is a good place to raise kids and he's glad to help me. To be honest, I'm still numb. Everything happened so fast and now here we are. I don't have any of my things except what I could pack into the car. I have nowhere to live that's better than Bellingwood. Seo's my family, whether we rub each other the wrong way or not. I want the kids to know about family. I think I could be happy here."

She sat up straight. "I'm going to have to find a job. Anything to keep me busy during the day. I love my babies, but it's the only way I'll ever meet adults. When I was married, I knew Larry's friends and their wives. That's the only people we ever did things with." She shrugged. "I guess I knew a few of the moms from school, but we never saw each other outside of that. Now that I'm alone here, how will I ever meet people?"

"A job is a good idea. Do you know what you want to do?"

"I'm not in a hurry, but I need to be thinking about it. Maybe when the kids go to school."

Polly turned onto the gravel road leading to Eliseo's house.

"Do you like the school here?" Elva asked.

"It's great." Polly drove into his driveway and stopped the truck. "Let me help you carry things inside."

"Matty's nearly asleep. I'd planned to get him home in time for a nap. This is perfect." Elva turned in her seat. "How are you doing, Samuel?"

"I'm good." He yawned. "I'm not tired, though."

"Of course you aren't."

Between the two of them, they got everyone and everything inside.

"Would you stay for lunch?" Elva asked. "I could make sandwiches."

Polly had one foot pointed toward the door. "I really should go. There was a break-in at the house we're renovating. I'm sure it's been handled, but I should check."

"Okay," Elva said, slumping. Then she brightened up. "Maybe your daughter and her friend could babysit some day and we could have lunch. I'd like to take you. Maybe show you that I'm not a drunken fool when I go out."

"The girls would love to do that. We'll make a date." Polly headed for the front door and stopped to pat Samuel's head on the way.

He looked up from the pile of Legos pieces in front of him. "Bye, Miss Polly."

"Bye-bye," Polly said. She got out to the car and didn't know where to go first. The kids were all still at Andrew's house as far as she knew and she hadn't heard anything more from Hayden or Heath. She dialed Rebecca first.

"Hi, Polly. Where are you?"

"I'm at Eliseo's. What are you up to?"

"Sylvie brought us lunch. We're playing games and watching TV."

"Are you good for a while?"

"Yeah. Is everything okay?"

"I need to check on the Bell House. I'll call later."

"Okay. We're fine here." Rebecca's voice changed and Polly realized she'd moved to another room and was whispering. "I have so much to tell you when we get home."

"About what?"

"About everything!"

Polly laughed. "You're killing me, kid."

"Talk to you later."

Laughing, Polly hung up and headed for the Bell House. She pulled in behind trucks and cars and headed for the side door, dreading what she was going to find in the kitchen.

"Hello?" she called as she opened the door.

"We're in here," Hayden said, standing in the door between the mud room and the kitchen.

"Who's we," Polly asked.

He stepped back into the kitchen and she groaned. Linoleum had been shredded and the wooden floor underneath pried up and tossed aside. Heath was in the doorway to the dining room. A man she didn't recognize stood up and put his hand out.

"Polly Giller?"

"Yes," she said and shook his hand.

"I'm Liam Hoffman. Henry called this morning and told me what had happened. I was planning to be here this afternoon, so I shifted things around and came over to see if I could give you good news."

"I think we'd take good news if you have it," Polly said.

"This isn't the worst thing that could have happened. I probably would have run all of the pipe from the crawl space and cellar, but with this ripped to pieces, you have options." He pointed at the back porch. "It would be easy to run water out there if you'd like to use that room for laundry."

Polly turned around and looked. It was an immense room. The convenience of it made sense. Lately, they'd been talking about putting the laundry upstairs, but this would be another option. "Let me talk to Henry. It's a good idea." She pointed at the floor. "Were they pulling pipe out of here again?"

Hoffman took a breath and looked at her. "No. There was

any piping under this floor. Either they were looking for it and couldn't find any or this was just vandalism."

"That's what Chief Wallers told us," Hayden said.

Polly frowned. "How did the person get in?"

Heath pointed back toward the north corner of the house. "There's a window broken out back there."

"Someone broke a window just so they could come in here and destroy things?" Polly was livid. She wanted nothing more than to drive over to Shawn Wesley's house, stomp up to the front door and punch him in the teeth." Frustrated, she let out a loud sigh and turned on Liam Hoffman. "Is there more copper pipe in this house that someone is trying to find?"

He nodded. "All of the piping leading up to the second floor is copper."

"So this person could wreck every room in the house," she snapped.

"We'll stay here tonight," Heath said. "Henry's going to bring a swamp cooler back with him so it isn't so hot."

"You shouldn't have to stay here just to keep someone from breaking in. That's awful."

"I tell you what I'm going to do," Liam said. "I'll start pulling pipe today and unless you want to make a few extra bucks off it, we'll leave it in the front yard. If that's what this person wants, let them have it. Maybe then they'll leave the house alone."

"Because now we're making it easy for him to be a thief." Polly stomped her foot. "Damn it, this makes me mad." She looked at the boys guiltily. "Sorry."

Hayden laughed. "You can swear about this and we won't be ⸢ended."

⸢Then, dammit, dammit, dammit," she said. "So you boys can't come to the dance tonight because you feel like you have to ⸢re? Like hell. I am not letting some jackass turn you into ⸢s."

⸢. looked a little relieved and Hayden shrugged. "He's not ⸢reak in during the dance. It's still too light out and ⸢t ⸢ake. We'll come back later."

"And I just bought two new air beds for the apartment."

"Hi Polly." Doug Randall came into the kitchen. "Nice mess you have here. Planning to just leave it this way?"

"Shut up, you," she said with a weak grin. "Are you working here today?"

"For the next couple of weeks. I love these jobs in town. You keep renovating buildings so I can work in Bellingwood and I'll be very happy."

Billy came up behind him and pushed him into the kitchen, causing Doug to stumble on a plank.

"Dude," Doug said. "Grow up." He grinned at Polly. "These boys. What can you do with them?"

"Hi Polly. This is a great house," Billy said. "I can't wait to see what you do with it." He pushed Doug's arm. "You're so slow. Come on. Jerry's waiting."

"Sorry, Polly," Doug said. "My task master won't let me rest. Not even for a minute."

The two boys picked their way across the floor and moved past Polly to the mud room and out the side door.

"I'm heading for the cellar," Liam Hoffman said. "Hopefully we'll get this put back together before your vandal takes it apart any further."

Polly nodded and smiled. "Thanks for your help. Sorry I was snippy."

He laughed. "That was nothing. My wife. Now she knows snippy." He turned back to them. "Not that I don't deserve it."

"He's a good guy," Hayden said. "Get those papers, Heath."

Heath stepped back into the dining room and came back with sheets of paper in his hand, then made his way over to Polly. "It's the police report for insurance. Chief Wallers took pictures and said he'd email them to you."

"Thanks," Polly said. "What time will I see you this evening?"

Hayden nodded his head toward the door where the plumber had gone. "We'll leave when he's done. Mr. Sturtz brought over some plywood and we covered the window that was broken, so we'll lock up again."

"At least we know the locks work," Polly said. She crossed to Hayden and gave him a hug, then turned to hug Heath. "Thanks for taking care of things this morning. It made life easier for me."

Hayden smiled. "Thanks for trusting us."

"Yeah," Heath said. "It was nice to see the cops and not be worried that I did anything wrong."

"I'll have dinner ready around five thirty. But whenever you get there will be fine. Don't hurry. I just want to feed the kids and get them ready for the party."

"Did they sleep any better last night?" Hayden asked.

Polly shook her head. "I think so. They fell asleep while I was reading to them. I don't know if it was the walls of the sofa around them, or the dog, or the fact that they were in the living room, but if they want to camp out there again tonight, it's fine with me." She checked the time on her phone. "I didn't even think about it. Do you guys want me to bring back lunch?"

"Nah," Hayden said. "We're bringing in pizzas."

She reached back into her pocket. "Let me give you some cash."

Hayden scowled at her. "Everybody's buying their own. We got this."

"Are you sure?"

"Walk away, Polly Giller," he replied. "Just walk away."

"Fine. Thanks again for taking care of things this morning." Polly spun on her heels and headed out the side door, meeting Doug and Billy who were laden with rolls of cables and cord. "You two coming to the dance tonight?"

Doug stopped and clicked his heels together. "Maybe. You never know," he said with a grin.

"What does that mean?"

"He's just messing with you, Polly," Billy said. "Come on, dude. You gave me the heavy stuff."

Polly got back into her truck and backed out. She drove slowly down the street, peering in at the Wesley house. Then she saw Shawn Wesley sitting on the back steps of the house. She couldn't help herself and parked the truck and got out before her brain caught up with her actions.

"Hey Shawn," she called out. "Remember me? Polly Giller?"

He stood up and she realized he was holding a beer. Great.

"You're that lady from Sycamore House. I remember you." He spat on the ground. Polly wasn't sure if he was spitting at her or dealing with the wad of chew in his mouth. Either way it was disgusting.

"Did you know my husband and I bought the Springer House?" she asked.

He shrugged. "I guess. What's it to me?"

"Well. We're going to be neighbors."

He swiped his hand around. "I got lotsa neighbors. One more won't make a difference."

"Well, I was kinda hoping you might help me out."

"That worked out so well the last time," he said.

Polly took a deep breath. "Somebody's been breaking into the house and pulling copper pipe out of the walls. They're vandalizing the place. Last night they broke a window."

Shawn shrugged. "What do you want me to do about it?"

"Well, I was kind of hoping you'd help me keep an eye on the place. You know. If you see anybody around over there, give me a call?" She took a business card out of her phone case. "I think there'd be a reward if we figured out who was doing this and could make it stop."

That interested him. "What kind of reward?"

"I don't know. What's fair? If we catch the thief, say two hundred and fifty bucks?"

"For keeping an eye on that old house?"

"Well, only if we catch whoever's doing this." Polly reached into her back pocket and took out the cash she was carrying, peeling off fifty dollars. "We'll call this good faith money. Kinda get you started on helping me."

The back door opened and a tired and worn-looking woman stepped out onto the stoop. "Hello?" she said.

"Mrs. Wesley? I'm Polly Giller. My husband and I bought the Springer House."

"Oh. Hi. What do you want with Shawn?"

"I was just asking him if he'd consider keeping an eye on the place. We've had some vandalism over there and since we aren't living in the house yet, maybe he could help us out."

"Shawn?" the woman said.

"Yeah, yeah." He took the money and business card that Polly was still holding out. "I'll keep an eye out. Don't know that I'll see anything. You got all those bushes and stuff."

"There's more where that came from," Polly said, pointing to the money. "But only if you help us out. Okay?"

He turned around and went inside, brushing past his wife.

"You think he did it, don't you?" the woman asked. "You think he's just a pothead and a loser."

"I didn't say anything like that," Polly replied. "I just need some help."

"Well you've asked. He can do what he wants." Mrs. Wesley stepped back and slammed the inside door shut.

Polly turned to head back to her truck, shaking her head. This wasn't going to be easy.

CHAPTER EIGHTEEN

At the same moment that Polly heard the scream of emergency sirens, her phone rang.

"Hello?"

"It's me," Rebecca said. "Noah fell out of a window and I think he broke his leg."

"He what?"

"We tried to stop them, but he and Elijah were running and playing upstairs."

"Have you called 9-1-1?" Polly interrupted.

"Of course," Rebecca said. "That's probably them now."

"Are you with him?"

"He's right here. We put a blanket over him because you always talk about shock. And we haven't let him move. But Polly, he broke something."

"I'm on my way right now."

"He wants to talk to you."

"Okay. Put the phone down for him."

"Polly?" The little voice wrenched her heart. He sounded scared and hurt.

"Yes honey, I'm almost there."

"This isn't anybody's fault. I did it. I ran and jumped at that window. Don't blame Elijah or Rebecca or anybody."

Polly smiled. "It's okay. I just want to make sure you're all fixed up and healthy. We won't worry about blame."

"You're coming now?"

"Yes I am."

"The ambulance is here. I'm going to hang up," Rebecca said.

Turning the corner onto Sylvie's street, Polly took a deep breath. She knew she needed to call Henry and Roy Dunston, but right now a little boy needed her more than adults needed information. She threw the truck into park, flew out and over to where she saw a cluster of people.

Elijah saw her coming and broke away to run and meet her. "He's scared, Miss Polly. Can I go in the ambulance with him?"

"I don't think so," Polly said. "We'll see if they'll let me go. I promise you'll be able to see him as soon as possible."

"He needs his brother."

Polly knelt down and pulled Elijah into a hug. She held him for a moment, feeling his body tremble in her embrace. "You need your brother, too, don't you?" she asked.

"We take care of each other." Then in a whisper, Elijah said. "It's all my fault."

"I'm not worried about what happened right now." She stood and held out her hand. "And sometimes things just happen. We don't have to blame anyone." She looked up and saw a wide-open window with no screen. All questions she would ask later. A broken leg wasn't the worst thing that could happen to a kid, though it was definitely going to slow him down this week. Hopefully that was all there was to this.

"Hello, Miss Giller," the EMT said.

Polly nodded and knelt so Noah could see her. "I'm here, honey." She stroked his forehead and rubbed her thumb on his cheek before looking up. "What do you think?"

"We think he broke a leg. He's responsive and not complaining of any other pain. Are you his guardian?"

Polly took a deep breath. "No. I need to contact Roy Dunston. I'm sure he has medical releases for Noah. Can you take him to the hospital without that?"

"Of course we can," the young man said. "He'll need to meet us there."

"Can Polly go with me?" Noah asked.

A young woman stepped forward and smiled down at him. "You wouldn't rather hold my hand in the ambulance? I'm a pretty good hand-holder."

"Polly's better," Elijah said, reaching down to pick up Polly's hand. "She should go."

"She'd have to ride up front," the young girl said.

"You'll be fine," Polly said, touching Noah's face again. "It's only a short ride down to Boone and then I'll be there the rest of the time with you. I promise."

"What's the movie we're playing today?" the young man asked.

His partner smiled. "You know what it is," she said. "It's your favorite. *Cars*." They shifted Noah to a board and then up and into the ambulance. "Have you ever seen that movie?"

Noah nodded, completely engrossed in the conversation as the two talked about the different characters.

Polly waved as they shut the door and the emergency vehicles drove off. "Elijah," she said. "I need you to stay with Rebecca. And kids, I'm calling Hayden to see if he'll get you home. The dogs are going to be desperate pretty soon."

Rebecca stood behind Elijah and put her arms around his front. "We'll be fine. Maybe we can come see Noah when Henry gets home."

Andrew knelt down. "I broke my arm once. It wasn't so bad. He's going to be fine."

"You're going now?" Elijah asked Polly.

"Right now and I'll call Roy to let him know what happened."

Rebecca waggled her phone.

"Yes," Polly said. "I will call you the moment I know anything."

Elijah pulled away from Rebecca and ran over to hug Polly. "You have to take care of him. Promise? He's my only brother."

"I promise." She ran back to her truck, got in, waved at the kids and drove off, then stopped again after she'd turned the corner to make a quick phone call.

"You're really missing me today, aren't you, Gumdrop?"

"Not that one either."

"Picky Polly." He laughed. "That one works."

"No it doesn't. Hey, I'm following an ambulance to Boone."

"On purpose or just out for a drive?"

"Noah broke his leg. I need to get hold of Roy and I don't have his number in my phone."

Henry sucked in air. "Noah? His leg? What happened?"

"I'm not sure of the details. The kids were all pretty upset about it. I think he flew out a window at Andrew's house. Luckily, some bushes broke his fall, but we're pretty sure the leg is broken."

He breathed deeply a few times.

"Henry?" Polly asked.

"I'm breathing through this."

"It upsets you?"

"Damned straight it upsets me."

"Elijah says it's his fault. I don't want to make him feel any worse by passing blame around. This is really just kids being kids."

"That's not it. Why do these things happen when I can't do anything? I can't be with you. I can't hold his hand. I'm stuck at work, worrying about a little boy that isn't even my son."

She smiled. "I know. But he's going to be okay. And if he isn't home tonight, he'll be home tomorrow. That's when all the fun begins anyway, right?"

"How is that poor kid going to get up and down the stairs at the apartment?"

"We'll figure it out. He isn't all that big. You or Hayden can probably swing him over your shoulders and haul him up."

Henry chuckled. "We aren't going to want to do that very often, but you're right. We'll figure it out."

"I'll teach him how to go up the back steps on his butt. One step at a time."

"Okay. You're going to Boone?"

"Yes. Roy probably needs to be there to sign medical papers."

"We'll take care of this. Whatever Noah needs, we'll make sure he has it."

"I know, Henry. Call Roy. We'll be in the emergency room."

They hung up and Polly took off again. Since she didn't have to talk to Roy, she made another quick call.

"You were just here," Hayden said. "What's up?"

"Noah broke his leg and I'm on the way to Boone."

"He what?"

"That's all I really know, but I need your help. Could you go over to the Donovan's and pick up the kids? There will be four of them. Take them back to Sycamore House and maybe feed them lunch or something." She shook her head. "Rebecca can make lunch. Just let her know that she needs to."

"I'll take care of it," he said. "There are plenty of people here to keep an eye on the house. We'll just come back to lock up when they're done."

"Thank you, Hayden."

Polly turned south to head for Boone and rolled her shoulders, forcing them to relax. If it wasn't one thing, it was another. Then she remembered the dance tonight and swiped open another call.

"Thank you for calling Sycamore House. How may I help you?"

"Kristen, this is Polly. Is Jeff available?"

"Hi Polly. He's in the auditorium. Just a minute. I'll go get him."

Polly waited There were too many things spinning around in her mind. She hadn't even had time to tell Henry about her encounter with Shawn Wesley.

She grinned at herself. She felt pretty proud of her behavior with that one. When she'd wanted to do nothing more than punch him in the face, she rose above it and engaged his help. Even if he had been responsible for the theft and vandalism, this would give him pause before he considered trying that again. And if he hadn't done it, he could make some easy cash just by watching the place. If he was smart, he'd go for the easy cash. She didn't hold out much hope. He wasn't terribly responsible.

"Polly? What's up?" Jeff's voice startled her from her reverie and she slowed for the upcoming stop.

"Hey. I probably won't be there tonight. I'm heading for the hospital in Boone. Noah broke his leg."

"Is he all right?"

"I hope so. They think it's just a break. Are you okay with this?"

Jeff let loose with a small laugh. "I have to be. Don't worry. It will be fun and we'll miss you, though. Let me know what happens."

"Thanks."

~~~

Polly sat with Roy Dunston while waiting for Noah to come awake. They'd sedated him while re-aligning the bones in his lower leg. He'd been quietly crying until the nurse came to get Polly. Roy arrived not long after and then had come the wait for an orthopedist. Polly smiled at the fact that they were actually here during the day, rather than in the middle of the night.

The break hadn't been bad and in fact, they planned to release Noah. He needed to be seen by a doctor early next week and then again when he returned to Chicago, but as long as he stayed off the leg, the splint and cast would keep things straight while the bone knit back together. Roy had called the foster mother that would be taking Noah and Elijah to alert her to the boy's new status and she assured him that they were glad to take care of him no matter what.

Polly hadn't even thought about that, but felt relief that the woman was compassionate and caring.

She'd called Henry to tell him what was happening and then Rebecca to let everyone know that Noah was fine and he'd be home later. Another call to Hayden to make sure that he would be around to carry Noah up the steps to the apartment and she finally relaxed, sitting back in the very uncomfortable chair that she'd pulled up beside Noah's bed. She had her hand on his when he started to come around.

"Mario tripped me," he said and started weeping.

Polly looked at Roy and smiled. "He's sorry," she said. "He didn't mean it.'

"Yes he did. He threw a green mushroom under my feet and made me fall down. My leg hurts really bad."

"Too many games," Roy said with a grin.

"Why does my arm have a hole in it?" Noah asked, lifting the arm where the IV was inserted.

"To make you better," Polly replied. "The doctors did that. But when you go home, it will be all gone."

"But it's a big hole. What if my bones fall out?"

"Then we'll pick them all up and put them back. I promise you will be just fine," Polly said.

He slumped back into the pillow and drifted away.

A nurse who had come in to check on him smiled as she brushed his forehead with her hand. "He'll become more lucid."

Polly nodded. "It's okay. I understand."

"Just keep telling him that he'll be fine."

"I know," Polly said.

"Little boys worry about things," the nurse continued, her tone annoyingly bossy. "All they need to hear is that they are okay and the scary things won't hurt them."

Polly shut her eyes, then opened them and said, "Got it."

"If you have any trouble keeping him from being frightened, let us know and we'll help. We don't want him to be concerned while he's coming around."

Roy came over to stand behind Polly and put his hand on her shoulder. "I think Polly is doing a fine job with him. You don't need to worry about this. Just make sure Noah is taken care of."

The woman looked at him as if she were surprised he was in the room, then nodded and turned to leave. "We're just here to help," she said as she walked away.

"She's the first person I've ever met down here who wasn't fantastic," Polly said.

Roy chuckled as he went back to his seat. "You spend a lot of time in the hospital?"

183

She rolled her eyes. "More than I'd like to admit. If it isn't one thing, it's another." That seemed to be her mantra for the day.

"I suppose there has to be one in every bunch."

~~~

Noah finally grew alert enough that he could be released. Orderlies helped Polly and Roy get him tucked into her truck and she pulled out of the hospital lot.

"Polly?" Noah asked.

"Yes, honey."

"Am I in trouble?"

"Why would you be in trouble?"

"Because we were playing upstairs when Rebecca told us not to."

"Should you be in trouble?" she asked.

"Yes. I messed up your whole day and made Mr. Dunston come to the hospital."

"Elijah thinks that he should be in trouble."

Polly watched Noah's face in the rear view mirror and smiled as he processed on that information. "It was kinda his fault, but it was mine, too."

"What were you two doing?"

When she didn't receive an answer, Polly turned to look at him. He'd nodded off to sleep again and she continued to drive home.

A few minutes passed and Noah said, "We'd been playing with squirt guns. We were in the room shooting the big kids outside, trying to see how far we could shoot the water. But then we were done. At least that's what Rebecca told us."

"You weren't ready to be done?" Polly asked.

"I left my squirt gun and went up to get it. I didn't know Elijah came with me. He started wrestling with me and I fell out of the window." Noah slowly looked around and out the window. "It's a good thing those bushes were there. I might have died."

"I don't think you would have died. But you are lucky that it was just a broken leg."

"Is Rebecca mad at me?"

Polly slowed for the stop sign. "Oh honey, no. She's worried and so is everyone else. We just want you to be okay."

"I feel pretty okay right now."

"I'll bet you do," she said with a laugh.

"Are you mad at me?"

"Noah. You aren't in trouble. And besides, don't you think a broken leg is enough punishment?"

He looked down at his leg. "Oh yeah. How am I going to walk?"

"Tomorrow we'll get crutches. Tonight, you're going to have to rely on us to carry you around."

"I'm too big."

Polly pulled into the drive and up to the garage. The front parking lot was filled with cars and it was exciting to see lights on throughout the building. "You're not too big for Henry or Hayden or Heath. We've got you covered. Now stay where you are while I call Hayden. He's going to make sure you get upstairs."

"Is he going to carry me like a baby?" Noah asked.

"Either that or a sack of potatoes over his shoulders," Polly replied.

Noah giggled. "That would be funny."

"If he does, I'll take your picture." Polly dialed Hayden's phone and waited for him to answer.

"Are you here?" Hayden asked over the sound of loud music in the background. As he spoke, he must have passed through a door since it grew quiet.

"Out back." The garage door went up and both Hayden and Heath, along with Andrew, Kayla, Rebecca, and Elijah stood inside the garage.

Elijah was the first to run over to the truck. He threw open the door and clambered up beside his brother, throwing his arms around Noah's neck. "I was so worried!"

"I'm fine," Noah said.

Hayden stood behind Elijah and let the two hang on to each other a few moments before lifting the younger boy to the ground.

"We'll take him upstairs and the two of you can talk about all of this after he's settled. Okay?"

Rebecca was all decked out in a shimmery, silver 1920s shift dress with a matching headpiece and heels. Andrew wore a pair of black pants and a gray shirt and had slicked his hair back, parting it on one side. Kayla was wearing a bright red dress and black pumps. She'd pasted her hair into curls around her face, the epitome of a flapper girl style. The kids looked wonderful.

"Are you having fun?" Polly asked.

"Doctor Ogden taught us how to jitterbug," Rebecca said. "That's really fun. Do we have to go upstairs now? I want to dance some more."

"Of course," Polly said, taken aback. "Stay as long as you want."

Rebecca waited until Hayden and Heath maneuvered Noah into a cradle in their arms before bending in to kiss the little boy on his cheek. "I'm glad you're home tonight. We were worried about you."

"You look pretty," Noah said. He leaned around her to Kayla. "So do you."

Rebecca curtsied. "Thank you. Now no more jumping out of windows, okay?"

"Okay," he said, nodding.

"Wait a minute," Polly said as the kids turned to go back in. She took several pictures of them all dressed up and then shooed them off to the dance.

"Me too?" Noah asked.

Polly took more pictures of him in the older boys' arms. "There's no way you're getting him upstairs like that."

"Will you throw me over your shoulder?" Noah asked Hayden.

Hayden laughed. "Really?"

"Yeah. Polly said she'd take a picture of it."

He turned to Polly. "Really?"

"Don't you think it will be the easiest way to get up the steps?"

"I suppose." He laughed. "It's always entertaining being part of your life. Come on, Heath. You spot us from behind."

CHAPTER NINETEEN

Landing his paws on her shoulders, Han startled Polly awake as he lapped at her face. He must have just come in from being outside.

Polly was on one of the sofas in the living room with Elijah snuggled up to her, his head in her lap. Noah slept on the other sofa, Henry's tablet on his lap. She'd turned a movie on for him to watch. Her last memory was that Elijah had been watching the movie with his brother. At some point, the younger boy had chosen to snuggle in with her.

Rebecca, Hayden and Heath came in to the room and Polly put a finger to her lips. She extricated herself from Elijah, tucking a pillow under his head, and waved the kids into the media room.

"Is the dance over?" Polly asked.

"A little while ago," Hayden said. "We stuck around and helped the band pack up."

"Was it fun?"

Rebecca pulled Polly down onto the couch with her. "It was the best." She leaned on Polly's arm. "Even Eliseo and Sylvie danced together."

"And I missed it?" Polly asked. She leaned back and craned her neck to see the clock. "What time is it?"

"Eleven thirty or so," Heath said.

Polly frowned. "Where's Henry? He should have been home by now."

She took her phone out of her pocket and realized she had several messages. All of them from Henry. "Okay, that's fine. He'll be home soon." Polly took Hayden's hand. "Are you really going to sleep at the Bell House tonight?"

He shook his head. "Henry told us not to worry about it. If the person breaks in again, we'll just deal with it. He didn't have time to get the swamp cooler back here and it's late anyway."

"Good," she said. "So tell me who you danced with. Heath?"

Heath shook his head and sat down in a chair, smiling.

"You know all the girls love him, don't you?" Rebecca asked.

Polly chuckled. "So, you had plenty to choose from?"

"Whatever." He pointed at his brother. "Hayden's the one who found a new girlfriend."

"A girlfriend?" Polly spun on Hayden, who had taken the chair next to her. "You have a girlfriend?"

Hayden rolled his eyes. "She's a girl. She's a friend. We're not dating or anything. I don't have time for that. It was just fun."

"Who is it?" she asked. "Do I know her?"

"Emily Lundberg," Heath said, jumping in. "She works at the bank."

"I do know her," Polly said. "She works the drive-through. She's sweet. When are you bringing her over for dinner so I can meet her?" She gave Hayden an evil grin. Before he could answer, she turned back to Rebecca. "Okay, so give me the scoop on Eliseo and Sylvie. I can't believe I missed this. Did they dance slow dances together or just the fast dances? Were they there together or did they come alone?" Polly shook Rebecca's arm. "Come on, girl. Mama's got needs. She needs to know."

"They came separately. But Polly, Eliseo looked awesome. He was dressed all in black, with a pin-stripe vest and white tie. He looked like a gangster. Sylvie's dress was all black and she had a feather thingie around her neck and a black hat that looked like a bell and hugged her head." Rebecca pulled her hands down her head. "It had a big flower on the side. It was like they matched their outfits.

"A boa," Polly said.

"What?"

"The feather thingie. A boa. And those are called cloche hats."

Rebecca nodded. "I guess so."

"Just trying to help," Polly said with a shrug. "Did they spend the whole evening together?"

"No, not the whole evening. Eliseo's sister was there and he danced with her a few times and then Sylvie danced with Grey too. He was really snazzy."

"Snazzy?" Polly asked with a laugh.

"Yeah. That's what Beryl called him. Snazzy. He had a white hat and this red, white and black stripey jacket and a bow tie."

"Kind of like a barbershop quartet costume," Hayden said.

"Cool. And how much time did Sylvie spend with Grey?" Polly asked.

"I don't know." Rebecca sounded frustrated now. "I wasn't paying attention to her every move. I was busy having my own fun. Ask her yourself."

"Fink," Polly said. "Okay. Tell me everything else. Who was there? What were they dressed like?"

The dogs jumped up and ran for the back door, interrupting Polly's interrogation. "Henry's home," she said, standing up. She walked into the office and laughed as she waited at the top of the steps with Han and Obiwan. "This should entertain him. We're all glad he's come home from a hard day at work."

She heard the garage door go back down and a few minutes later, Han gave a sharp yap as the door opened at the bottom of the steps.

"Hello there, Hotstuff," Polly said. "Welcome home."

"How are things here?" he asked, brushing the dogs aside as he got to the top of the steps.

"The little ones are asleep in the living room and the big ones are in the media room. They refuse to tell me all I want to know about the dance, but apparently Eliseo and Sylvie danced together. That's all I could get out of our daughter."

He kissed her cheek. "Beatings commence at six thirty in the morning," he said.

"Awesome," Polly said. "I'll have her strung from the yardarm."

"Have who strung from where?" Rebecca asked as they came into the media room.

"You. Yardarm. Look it up." Polly replied. She touched Hayden's shoulder. "Could one of you take the dogs out?"

"Sure, Polly," Hayden said. He pointed at his brother. "Your turn."

Rebecca laughed. "Just because he didn't say it fast enough."

Hayden nodded. "Yep. I'll get 'em in the morning. He can do it tonight."

Heath heaved a sigh and hauled himself out of the chair. "Fine, but don't wake me up early just because you think we have to get over to the house."

"You guys don't have to hurry over to the house tomorrow and you're taking Thursday and Friday off," Henry said. He sat down at the dining room table and put his ball cap down in front of him. "I'm so tired I don't know whether to sit here all night or crawl to the bedroom."

"Do you want something to eat?" Polly asked. "Or some water?"

"No more water. I've put more water down my gullet today than I usually drink in a week."

Polly stood in front of the refrigerator. "Juice? Milk? A beer? A Coke?"

"Milk?" Henry asked. "And cookies if you have them?" He sounded pitiful.

"You poor man. You can have anything you want."

"Did I hear cookies?"

Both Polly and Henry turned to the door to see Elijah standing there rubbing his eyes.

"Do you need a cookie, too?" Henry asked. "Do we have cookies, Polly?"

She opened the freezer. "The stock is getting a little low. I'll have to bake tomorrow, but we have plenty for tonight. Is Noah awake?"

Elijah nodded. "We both are."

"Do you both need milk with your cookies?" Polly looked over Henry's head. "Rebecca, could you give me a hand?"

Rebecca came over to the dining room and stopped in front of Henry, then spun around. "What do you think?"

"I think you look much too grown up to be my thirteen-year-old daughter," he said. "Where did you put her?"

"She'll be back tomorrow," Rebecca said. "I promise. But isn't this cool?"

"You look terrific."

Polly put a plate of cookies and some napkins on the table in front of him and went back into the kitchen. "Will the young Rebecca tell me tomorrow all about who was there at the dance tonight?"

"Maybe." Rebecca stacked cookies on napkins and handed them to Elijah. "You take these out and I'll bring the milk."

When Polly brought the milk and glasses to the table, she brushed against Rebecca's arm. "Why don't you go change into shorts and clean the makeup off your face."

"I just wanted Henry to see my outfit," Rebecca said.

Polly nodded. "I'm glad you waited so he could see it. You're gorgeous. But I'd hate for you to spill anything on the dress and with two little boys..." Her voice trailed off.

"Okay. You're right. I just don't know when I'll ever get to wear this again."

"The one thing about living in Polly's world," Henry said, "is that you never know when it will happen, but there is always a possibility. Never give up hope."

Rebecca winked at him and took two glasses of milk into the living room.

They heard her talking to the boys and then her door closed.

"She was quite the little star downstairs tonight," Hayden said. "It was like she took over your job, Polly."

191

"My job?"

"Yeah. She greeted everyone she knew and stood by Jeff at the front door at the beginning of the evening, welcoming people to Sycamore House. It was pretty cool."

Polly's eyes filled with tears. "She really did that?"

He took out his phone, swiped through a few photos and brought one up, showing exactly that. Rebecca, standing beside Jeff Lyndsay, was shaking an older man's hand as he escorted his wife into the auditorium.

"How did she even know to do that?" Polly asked Henry.

"She's just a natural." He took a deep breath and then another before finishing his cookie. "I'm glad today is over."

"What made you so late tonight?" she asked.

"I'm not working for the rest of the week. I want to enjoy this." He reached over and touched Hayden's arm. "I'll go over to the house tomorrow. I want to talk to Jerry and Liam. But we're taking it easy. I'm sleeping late in the morning and maybe we'll all go out for lunch together. Who knows? But it's going to be a good weekend." He pulled Polly over and onto his lap. "How does that sound?"

"Like I don't know who you are. First Rebecca and now you. The world turned upside down on me tonight." She kissed his cheek. "And I love it. You're really not working any more this week?"

"Nope. I'm all yours."

The dogs tore across the room to greet Henry as Heath huffed into the room. "They wanted to run so we ran."

"Come have cookies with us," Henry said. He held up his glass. "And milk."

Heath stopped at the doorway to the living room. "I should get to bed. I just know Hay is going to wake me up tomorrow morning."

Henry shook his head. "No he's not. We're sleeping late. I don't want anyone to leave this house until after nine o'clock. Deal?"

Polly laughed and hugged his neck. "Even when you're trying to relax, you're a task master."

"He's not a task master," Rebecca said, coming into the dining room. "You shouldn't say that."

Henry squeezed Polly's waist. "See. Someone's on my side."

"I'm always on your side," Rebecca said.

Polly turned to look at him. "She wants something from you."

"No I don't."

"It's okay," Henry said with a laugh. "She can have anything she wants. I'm her favorite." He pushed Polly off his lap. "I'm going to take a shower. Are you kids ready for bed?"

Hayden laughed and shook his head. "Not really. Especially since I don't have to get up at five o'clock."

"Pull out some games, then. We're on vacation. Polly, how about some popcorn?"

"On it. Boys, grab the card tables and we'll play in the living room. Elijah and Noah probably had enough of a nap so they'll be awake for a while. Rebecca, would you check on Noah and see how his leg feels? He can have another pain killer if he's hurting."

They'd never done anything like this. She had half expected Henry to come in, dragging and exhausted, as grumpy as he'd been last night.

Maybe it was the prospect of a few days off, but whatever it was, she planned to embrace it. There was no reason for the kids to go to bed early or get up early tomorrow.

"This is fun," Rebecca said when she came back into the kitchen. "Noah says it hurts a little. But I think it hurts a lot. He isn't moving around at all and his face looks like it hurts."

Polly opened the cupboard, took out the pill bottle, and handed one to Rebecca. "Tell him he doesn't have to be strong. He just needs to be comfortable. Find out if he'd like more pillows or anything, okay?"

"Is Henry really taking the next three days off?" Rebecca asked, reaching into the cupboard for a glass.

"I guess so. Should we do something crazy?"

"Like what? Go away?"

"Nah." Polly shook her head. "There's too much happening in town." She slapped her hand on the counter. "We need to rent a wheelchair for Noah. Don't let me forget that tomorrow. He'll have much more fun at the carnival."

Rebecca nodded and walked back into the living room. In moments, she was back and whispered at Polly. "Can I ask Hayden to help Noah to the bathroom?"

Polly gasped. "Of course. And hurry. That poor boy has been holding it since we got home."

Rebecca walked over to the media room where Heath and Hayden were and whispered to them. Hayden got a look of shock on his face and bolted for the living room.

"I'm the worst mom ever," Polly said to Rebecca.

"Yeah. Pretty much." Rebecca bumped Polly's butt. "So awful that we're all here tonight looking forward to hanging out with you and Henry."

"It's probably a good thing those boys are going to a real home in a couple of weeks. The poor things might not be in good shape if they stay here much longer than that."

"Now you're making me feel bad about letting him break his leg," Rebecca said.

Polly opened the brown paper bag and poured the popcorn into a bowl. She put a second bag into the microwave and pressed the button. "Don't you even start. That wasn't your fault. Noah explained what happened and there's no way you could have predicted that. I could have been there and the same thing would have happened."

Rebecca leaned against her. "I wish it *was* you. I felt guilty all day."

"It's all going to work out." Polly put her arm around Rebecca and tugged her close. "And just think. He'll always have a story to remember us by."

Rebecca smiled. "Before he leaves, he'll have more than that story to remember us by."

"So I was thinking," Polly said. "You should wear that dress again on Saturday afternoon when we show people the tunnel and the underground rooms. The Prohibition was right during the time of the flappers. It would be perfect."

"Could I?" Rebecca grinned. "I can't wait to tell Kayla. That will be a blast."

Polly nodded and took the second brown bag from the microwave. She poured it into a bowl and put a third bag into the microwave.

"Where'd you learn that trick?" Rebecca asked, pointing to the stack of lunch bags Polly had taken out of the cupboard.

"On-line. I don't know if it's better for us than microwave popcorn, but at least I can control the amount of salt and butter."

"You're always thinking. See. You're a good mom."

Polly rubbed Rebecca's back and filled another bag with popcorn kernels and a shake of salt. She rolled the top of the bag down and set it beside the microwave. "Let's use hand towels tonight instead of napkins."

Rebecca nodded and opened the drawer, then counted out seven of them. "I'll start taking popcorn out. What are we going to drink? Can I have pop?"

"Not at this hour," Polly said. "No caffeine. Water, milk, juice, lemonade. Whatever anyone wants." She reached up into the cupboard and took down two bags of M&Ms. See if people want these in their popcorn."

"Really? This is a crazy night."

Polly laughed as Rebecca walked away. It *was* a crazy night and after all that had happened these last few days, she felt light on her feet. She danced over to another cupboard and took out all the covered travel mugs she could find. There was enough for everyone except her. If they were going to have a party, she could keep things as protected as possible.

"Lemonade, milk, two waters and apple juice," Rebecca said, ticking them off on her fingers.

Heath followed her in. "Can I help?"

"Ice in the cups," Polly said, pointing at what she'd put on the peninsula. "We're almost ready.

Henry came into the dining room and smiled. "Now this is what I call a party. Shall I turn on some music?"

"Seriously?" Polly asked, laughing.

"The kids got to dance tonight, but some of us were busy with other things. I feel the need for party tunes."

Polly popped the last bag of corn, poured it in a bowl and headed for the living room, laughing at the sight in front of her. The kids had arranged Noah at one end of the sofa, propping him up on pillows so he could sit as tall as everyone else. Hayden was beside him while Heath, Rebecca and Elijah were assigned the other sofa. They'd pulled it up close to the tables and arranged chairs at both ends for Polly and Henry. A stack of games was beside Polly's chair, and on the side table beside Henry, were pencils and pads of paper. They'd turned the lights down and brought out Polly's LED candles, arranging them around the table. She stepped back into the dining room and shut off the lights as "Mr. Roboto" by Styx filled the room.

Elijah was seated next to Polly's chair, bouncing up and down. "This is the best. Do you guys do this all the time?"

Rebecca pulled him back down by his waist band. "We've never done this before. Isn't it fun?"

"That's why he's sitting over there," Hayden said. "He wanted to help his brother, but there was bouncing."

Polly gave Hayden the most loving look she could. "Thank you for your help." Her eyes filled again as she realized how much she loved this young man that wasn't even her son. "You're amazing."

He shrugged. "No big thing. We got there just in time." He reached out to pat Noah's arm. "And now we have a signal."

"I really don't know how my life could be much better," Polly said. She looked across at Henry. "Can you even believe this?"

He shook his head and reached out so he could touch both Noah and Heath. "I'm a pretty lucky man." Henry pointed at the games beside Polly. "Now which one of those can I win first?"

"Bet me," she said. "It's my turn to win."

"I want to win. I want to win," Elijah cried, bouncing up and down again.

Rebecca laughed, grabbed the waistband of his pants and pulled him back to the seat of the couch.

CHAPTER TWENTY

Polly woke up, stretched, and yawned. The bed was empty and her door was closed. Henry must have taken the dogs. Last night they'd finally closed down the party about one thirty. Noah and Elijah had just begun to struggle to stay awake.

They'd played games, laughed, sung along to the music that was playing and she and Henry even danced around the living room a couple of times.

After they'd hauled everything out to the dining room, the boys slept in their sofa fortress again, keeping Obiwan with them.

She got out of bed, peeked into the living room and saw that the boys were still asleep, so she went into the bathroom and turned on the shower. When she reached out of the shower for a towel, Polly squealed with surprise when one magically brushed across her hand.

"It's just me," Henry said. "Who else did you think it was?"

"No one. You just startled me. How long have you been in here?"

He laughed. "Only a minute or we'd be having a much different conversation."

Polly wrapped the towel around herself and brushed him away. "Is everyone else up?"

"Not yet. I took the dogs out and started the coffee. The little boys are sound asleep and I didn't want to do anything to wake them."

Polly kissed him and dropped the towel to the floor.

"You're mean," he said, laughing.

"You said that everyone was sleeping."

"I doubt it will take much to wake them up. You be good."

She pulled a comb through her hair. "What time is it, anyway?"

"Eight thirty. While I was out with the dogs, I called the pharmacy to see if they had crutches or a wheelchair we could rent for Noah. It looks like I need to drive down to Boone."

"Can we just buy crutches?" Polly asked. "He'll have to take those back to Chicago."

Henry nodded. "I need him to go with me so they can make sure everything fits and he knows how to use the crutches. I talked to Roy and he's coming over about ten thirty. We'll take both Noah and Elijah."

She put her toothbrush down, stepped back, and stared at him. "You'd do that?"

"You have no idea how guilty I felt that I couldn't help you yesterday. You spent all that time in the hospital and I was nowhere to be found."

"Roy was there with me. It was okay."

"We can do this today. It won't take long."

"That's wonderful," Polly said. She kissed him again, this time not letting him go until he made her swoon. A cold, wet nose on the back of her leg made her jump and yelp.

"What?" he asked. "I didn't bite you."

She pointed to Han, who was behind her. "No, but he sniffed me with that nose. Scared me to death."

"You. Out," Henry said, pointing to the door. "When Polly's naked, nobody sniffs her but me."

Polly laughed and pushed Henry to the door. "You. Out," she said. "I need to finish getting ready."

He stuck his lower lip out in a pout and slunk through the door to the bedroom. She shook her head and finished up in the bathroom, then got dressed. The only big thing they had to do today was dinner in the auditorium with the rest of the boys who had come to Bellingwood from Chicago. Otherwise, it was a free day.

She waved at Hayden as he emerged from his room, stretching and yawning. Elijah and Noah stirred on the sofas, so Polly bent over and rubbed Noah's shoulder. "How are you doing this morning?"

He nodded. "Okay. It kinda hurts, though."

"I'll get you a pain pill. Do you need Hayden ...?"

Hayden interrupted her. "I got this, Polly. No worries." He sat down on the back of the sofa and put his hand on Noah's arm, then looked up at her. "Seriously. We've got this."

"Oh. Okay," she said. "I'm gone, then."

"What's this?" Henry asked, holding up a file folder when she walked into the dining room.

"I don't know. What is it?" Then it hit her. The folder of notes that Anita had given her yesterday. She'd forgotten about it. "Where did you find that?"

"On the desk in the office. What is it?"

"The notes that the murderer left on the bodies."

He slid it across the table to her. "Those are awful."

"I know. They make me sick. I don't know what he's doing or why he's chosen to involve me. But please, not right now. I'm in desperate need of a cup of coffee. You're ahead of me by at least one cup."

"Two," he said with a laugh.

"That's just not right." Polly picked up her mug, poured coffee into it and held it under her nose. "Ahhh. Almost." She blew across the top of the liquid, then sipped it. "Nearly there." She put the mug down on the counter. "Shall I make pancakes?"

"Pancakes!" came a little voice as Elijah poked his head around the corner.

"Does that sound good?" Polly asked.

"I love pancakes."

Henry patted the chair next to him at the table. "Have you ever put whipped cream on them?"

"No!"

"Before you sit down," Polly said. "Why don't you go into the bedroom and put some pants on. And a fresh shirt."

Henry ducked his head. "Sorry, Elijah. She's the boss."

The little boy ran out of the room, then came back. "I think Heath is still asleep. I shouldn't wake him up, should I?"

Hayden came into the dining room, Noah slung over his shoulders, giggling like crazy. "How about we all wake Heath up." He bounced Noah, making the boy giggle again. "He won't be mad at me if you two are there."

"He is so good with those boys," Polly said.

Henry nodded and picked up the folder they'd left on the table. "Put this away."

"Yeah. I want to look at it again. Elva's little boy said something yesterday and I think there's a pattern in the notes."

"Only you would find something like that."

"Anita said that they were looking for it, too, but didn't find anything. We pored over the notes while I was there with her and they looked like random messages."

"Matty saw the pattern?" Henry asked.

She shook her head. "No, but he read a word differently than I did." She chuckled. "Not like he knew all of the words on the page, but when he saw the word 'train,' he recognized it as a locomotive. I only saw it as a word that meant to learn or practice. If the murderer intended for it to be read one way and interpreted in another way, he might have done that in the other notes, too."

"Like what?"

"Like I need to stir up the pancake batter. Would you mind opening a package of bacon and arranging it on a cooling rack?"

It really was the only way to cook an entire pound of bacon at once. Polly couldn't believe it had taken her a lifetime to learn that trick. And cooking bacon in the oven cut way down on the smell of bacon grease in the house.

Henry shoved the folder to the end of the peninsula under a pile of papers, then took a jelly roll pan and cooling rack out of the cupboard beside the oven. "Aluminum foil?" he asked.

"Yeah. Might as well," Polly replied.

"Why is there so much noise out here?" Rebecca asked, coming into the dining room. "I thought we were sleeping late today."

Polly grinned. "Your life is so rough." She opened the freezer and took out a can of frozen juice. "Here. Get a pitcher and start mixing. I'm making pancakes."

"At least there's that," Rebecca said. "It sounds like a party in the boys' room."

"Good," Henry said. "I like hearing things like that."

"Whatever. You weren't trying to sleep."

He mussed her hair and she brushed him away, then tried to pat it back down. "Morning people," she said with a growl. "You're not right in the head."

~~~

By ten thirty, the apartment was empty. Polly looked at Rebecca and said, "What should we do now?"

"I don't know. You're the mom. What should we do?"

"We should probably clean," Polly said, glancing around the dining room. Everything from last night's party had been dragged in here. Nothing had been cleaned up from breakfast, and the living room was still topsy turvy from last night's sleeping arrangements.

Rebecca scowled at her. "That doesn't sound like fun at all."

Polly laughed out loud. "You're right. Especially since Henry declared we were on vacation."

"Exactly." Rebecca said. "Maybe we should go find a body or something."

"Wait." Polly mimicked Rebecca's scowl and tone of voice. "That doesn't sound like fun at all." And then she gave Rebecca a look. "And it's probably not funny."

"I know. I'm sorry," Rebecca said, suitably chagrined.

"Maybe you can help me with this, though," Polly said, standing up. She pulled the folder out from under the stack of papers where Henry had shoved it and put it down on the table. "I think there might be a pattern."

"Like what?" Rebecca moved over to sit in the chair beside Polly and spread the papers out in front of them.

For a moment, Polly squirmed at the idea that her thirteen-year-old daughter was looking at notes written by a murderer, but then she relaxed. Rebecca had seen more than most girls her age and it wasn't like any of this was new territory for them.

Rebecca pointed at the first note. "Start with this one. What's the pattern?"

"Well. Yesterday little Matty pointed at the word train, telling me he knew what it was." Polly read it out loud again.

Poor sweet Lynn,
You'd call this a sin.

When the research is done
They'll know Polly's the one

The first, it is plain
I still need to train

You'll call me a brute,
the next one's a hoot.

"What if he means to imply the train tracks in front of the grain elevator where we found that body and then the word hoot is a train horn?" she asked.

Rebecca frowned. "That's a lot of implying."

"Okay," Polly said. "Let's look at the next note. Remember this was found on the kid at the train track and then I found the next body in my truck. I just can't figure out how he knew I was going to be in the grocery store at all. This was written more than a month earlier. She read it out loud.

With one quick look
The bait she took

Number two is dead
I'm off to bed.

All tidy and neat
Is there plenty to eat?

The world, it should know.
Her talent will show.

"So what words are there?" Rebecca asked.

"I guess we should think about different definitions of words. Bait is to lure, but that's obvious. It's also used for fishing, but I was at the grocery store."

"You feed fish bait?"

Polly shook her head. "What about bed? The body was in the bed of my truck when I was buying groceries so we'd have plenty to eat."

"Obscure," Rebecca said. "But maybe. It's making more sense, I guess. If killing someone and leaving weird notes on their bodies can ever make sense. Here I'll read the next one." She picked up the sheet of paper. "This was found on the body in your truck, right?"

Polly nodded.

"And the next body was found at Ledges, right?"

Polly nodded again.

"Okay. So ..."

Well look, this is new
I've a room with a view

I hear when they bark,
On a ledge, in a park

But today number three
Is just a beginning for me

Catch me if you can
I'm your number one fan.

"It was at a park. The Ledges," Polly said. She drew her finger down the stanzas, pointing at the last word in the second to last line. "And I guess I found the body in the trash can. So ... yeah. Am I reading too much into this?"

"You're starting to make me believe," Rebecca replied. She picked up the copy of the last note and read it quietly to herself. "This one seems obvious."

Polly read it out loud to herself.

The fourth you've found.
Do you feel that you've drowned?

How long will this last
Who's next in our cast

Oh Polly, I'll be frank
I won't let you tank.

To reach you I've been bold
Your story will be told."

You mean the words 'drowned' and 'cast'? But I don't go fishing. Ever," Polly said.

Rebecca nodded. "But what if the little boys wanted to go fishing. You'd take them, wouldn't you?"

"Of course I would." Polly grimaced. "Hayden and Heath would really like to go, too. And Aaron likes fishing out at Beryl's place in the summer. I wonder if he's taking time off this week. Maybe I should ask if he'd take us all fishing."

"So we can find a body?" Rebecca grinned.

"Yeah. That just sounds bad. But Aaron would already be there. That makes it better, right?"

"He probably wouldn't think so. But it would be a first for him, wouldn't it?"

"Okay," Polly said. "We should get out of here and do something." She looked up at the clock. "We could pick up lunch and take it over to the Bell House. Make sure things are set for Saturday afternoon's fun."

"Boring," Rebecca said. "Well, not lunch, but going over there to work sounds boring."

Polly's phone rang. She hesitated at picking it up, worried that the boys were calling to tell her they'd found more vandalism at the house, but it was Eliseo.

"Good morning," she said. "How are you?"

"Fine, thank you. I was wondering if I could speak to your daughter about baby-sitting my nieces and nephews. She could take Kayla and Andrew with her. Elva has an interview this afternoon at the Alehouse."

"She does? That's great. And Rebecca was just telling me how bored she was. I'll let you talk to her."

Polly put her hand over the microphone and said, "It's Eliseo. Wonders if you would want to babysit for Elva. She has a job interview today."

"And he doesn't want to have the kids at the barn?" Rebecca whispered back.

"I don't know. Talk to him." Polly pushed the phone at Rebecca.

"Hello? Eliseo?" Rebecca said. She listened for a while. "I'd love to. I'll call the others, but I'm sure they will. Okay. Thank you."

"So?" Polly asked when Rebecca handed the phone back to her.

"Jason can take us out instead of bringing Andrew and Kayla here. He'll pick me up first. Is that okay?"

Jason had only had his driver's license for a little over a month, but he was so responsible, Polly wasn't worried.

"Of course it is," Polly said. "Go call your friends and make sure they're willing to help."

"They will be," Rebecca replied, getting up. She pointed at the papers in front of Polly. "What are you going to do about that?"

"I don't know. Sit here and fuss, I suppose."

Polly shuffled them back together in the folder and closed it. She actually couldn't take much more of the mess, so while Rebecca talked to Andrew and Kayla, she tackled the dishes and the kitchen. At least it had the possibility of staying clean for a while since they were eating downstairs tonight. Henry and Roy planned to take the boys out for lunch in Boone.

"What time are you going out to Eliseo's?" she yelled across the apartment. Then she laughed. The kids were always in trouble when they yelled like that. Especially Rebecca. Polly was just asking for a beat down. Her phone buzzed on the table and after she put the last glass in the dishwasher, she picked it up.

"Jason's picking me up at noon," the text from Rebecca read. *"And you're not supposed to yell in the house. I'm telling."*

Polly laughed and texted back. *"I love you, too. Do you know what you're doing for lunch?"*

"Eliseo said he had pizzas ordered at Pizzazz and we should pick them up. And there's pop in the fridge." Rebecca typed a smiley face. She never got pop here at the house unless it was a special occasion. This would do for a special occasion.

"Okay. I still love you."

Rebecca sent back a heart and Polly went back to work in the kitchen. By now the bacon grease had congealed. Man, she hated that word. It was gross. She wadded up the tin foil that lined the bottom of the pan, dropped it in a used zipper bag and tossed it in the trash. Mary, the woman who had raised her after her mother died, would have had Polly's head for throwing away bacon grease. She used it for everything. But Mary was a creative cook and though Polly had learned a lot from her, over the years her cooking style had grown to be much different.

"Does this look okay?" Rebecca asked, coming into the dining room. She struck a pose, then turned around.

"Are you dressing for something special?"

"No. Just wanted to look nice. Is it okay?" She was wearing a salmon-colored, flowy sleeveless top and a pair of teal shorts. She'd gotten them in New Mexico when she was there with Beryl. Her wardrobe's color range had increased after that trip. Some things she'd gotten while she was traveling and others she'd purchased once she was back in Iowa. Beryl was not afraid of wearing lots of color and ten days spent in that woman's presence had inspired Rebecca to be bold.

It was hard watching Rebecca grow up. Some days she was a young woman, other days she was a teenager, and then there were the days she still tried to be a little girl. The wildest days were those she wanted to be all three at once.

"You look great. Even if it's just to impress Andrew."

"It is not," Rebecca said. She flattened her lips and rolled her eyes, then walked back out of the room.

"Is too," Polly whispered and dropped the pan she was holding into the sink.

CHAPTER TWENTY-ONE

Laughing as she looked around, Polly finally turned to Obiwan. "What am I supposed to do now? Today was supposed to be a family vacation and everyone has ..." She shook her head. "Vacated."

The kitchen and dining room were finally back to a semblance of normal. Before Rebecca left, they'd straightened up the living room, but nothing looked like it was ready for guests.

Obiwan woofed and nosed one of his rubber balls toward her. Polly picked it up and gave it a toss, sending both dogs on the chase. "Sorry guys. Nice try, but I need more than that."

Henry had called to tell her they were headed to Des Moines since the company in Boone didn't have a wheelchair that would fit Noah.

"This is ridiculous," Polly said. "Am I really such bad company that I can't even entertain myself?" She looked around and laughed. "I guess not." She slipped a pair of shoes on and headed for the back steps, then went downstairs and into the main kitchen. Three girls in white aprons looked up in surprise when she walked through the door.

"Is Rachel here?" she asked.

One of them pointed toward the auditorium and Polly smiled, then turned around and went back to the door off the storage room. She walked through the dark hall beside the stage and opened the door into the auditorium, then quickly stepped back and pulled the door shut. At least two hundred people were eating and she just hoped no one had seen her. Now what was she to do?

"I can't get there from here," she muttered and went outside via the garage. The truth was, she felt a little out of sorts. It was her own decision to no longer have an office downstairs and she completely trusted Jeff and Stephanie. She tried to stay involved in what was happening throughout the building, but at some point, it was just too much, what with the Bell House reconstruction. Polly scolded herself silently. This was why she'd hired good people. She didn't need to know about all of the people who were checked into Sycamore Inn. Grey managed that place quite nicely. He'd hired two additional clerks to allow him a little freedom and during these summer months when the hotel seemed to be packed every night, he'd also hired temporary cleaning staff. Their guests were happy, Grey was happy, and the place was turning a tidy profit. So why was she feeling snarky about things at Sycamore House?

Polly walked around the side of the building and shook her head at the packed parking lot. How had she missed an event this big? She went in the front door and headed for the office. Kristen was on the telephone, giving directions to someone. Polly looked into her old office, but Stephanie wasn't there. When she pointed at Jeff's closed door, Kristen shook her head and pointed at the auditorium.

"Ms. Giller," a voice said behind her.

She turned quickly and looked at the man standing there, trying her best to place him. He looked vaguely familiar and then it hit her. He looked like Santa Claus. His name wasn't Klaus or Kringle. "Mr. Nicholas?" she said.

He smiled and put out his hand. "I just wanted to tell you how much I'm enjoying my stay at Sycamore House. I am recommending this to my friends back home. If they want a beautiful location with a quaint small-town feel, Bellingwood and Sycamore House offer it all."

Polly had an image of hundreds of little elves dressed in red and green showing up after the first of the year, looking for a place to relax. They might be happier if they went to Florida in January, though. She did her best not to giggle at her own silliness. "I'm so glad you are enjoying yourself. Have you spent much time around the community?"

"Why, I was out at the winery last night for their wine-tasting and I'm afraid I spent way too much money. But the wines will make beautiful gifts this Christmas."

He laughed and Polly wondered what he had said that was funny, but she smiled and nodded.

"I'm off to take a walk downtown for some lunch at the diner and an ice cream cone at the General Store." He winked at her. "Of those three things, the only one I need is a walk, but the others are why I walk."

By the time he was out of the building, Kristen had gotten off the phone. "He's so jolly," she said. "Even if he is weird."

Polly finally let out the laughter that she'd been holding back. "That's true, he is. So what's going on in the auditorium?"

"It's a Founder's Day lunch," Kristen said. "The Chamber of Commerce invited everyone who has a connection to the beginnings of Bellingwood. I saw your friend, Beryl, go in. Jeff said that nearly everyone in town thought they should be here today, so they just opened it up."

"Why wasn't I invited?" Polly pursed her lips into a frown.

Kristen grew concerned. "We sent out the invitations last month. I know you were on the list. I just figured you were coming, so I put you down as a yes."

It was her own fault and Polly knew it. Her laptop had crashed last month and she'd not bothered to fix or replace it, trying to keep up with email and messages on her phone. She could access the Sycamore House intranet from Henry's computer, so that's how she worked on the finances. Everything else had kind of fallen away.

"Okay. My fault," Polly said. "Is there anything else I didn't respond to that I should know about?"

"You're coming to the dinner tonight for the Chicago boys, right?" Kristen asked.

Polly nodded.

"And the Bell House is having tours Saturday afternoon?"

Polly nodded again.

"Then I think you're okay. Just the regular things."

"Do me a favor," Polly said. "If I don't respond to something that I'm supposed to attend, please hunt me down." She grimaced. "That's not fair. I'm a big girl and I can be responsible for my own schedule. No. Don't do anything like that."

"We should have asked more questions," Kristen said. "It's just that things have been so nuts around here." She looked up past Polly. "Can I help you, Mr. James?"

Polly turned and smiled at the man who had just come into the office.

He put his hand out. "Ms. Giller?"

"Yes. Are you enjoying your stay?"

He gave her a strange, contented smile. "It's very nice. I look forward to the sesquicentennial events beginning tomorrow. I've been waiting for this week for such a long time."

"Are you connected to the early days of Bellingwood?" Polly asked.

"No, ma'am. I'm just a history aficionado and this town is filled with interesting moments in time." He smiled again. "Such as your Bell House that used to be called the Springer House. I will quite enjoy the short tour into your underground whiskey operation. Saturday afternoon?"

"That's right," Polly said. She nodded toward the barn. "We'll be offering wagon rides from Sycamore House that afternoon as well."

"Those are beautiful horses. It's a pleasure to wake up and see them enjoying the morning. That's one of the special treats that staying at Sycamore House offers. It's quite a view. You should put that in your brochure."

"Can I help you with something, Mr. James?" Kristen asked.

He looked flustered, as if he'd forgotten why he came into the office in the first place. "Oh," he said. "I was thinking about doing a little fishing."

Polly snapped her head to look at him again.

"Do you have any brochures of county parks or local fishing holes?" he continued. "And if I catch anything, would you be able to store it in your freezer here until I leave?"

Kristen looked at Polly.

"We can certainly keep your fish frozen," Polly said, "and if you go downtown to the hardware store, they have everything you need for a fun fishing excursion. Those boys can point you in the right direction and sell you bait. They'll also clean any fish you bring back."

"That's a wonderful piece of information," he said. "I'll head there right now. Just downtown?"

"You can't miss it. Bradford's Hardware on the south side of the main street."

"Thank you very much." He shook her hand, nodded at Kristen and left.

"It can't be," Polly said, dropping into a chair.

"What can't be?"

Polly realized she'd spoken out loud and shook her head. "Nothing." She stood back up and headed for the door. "I'll see you later." She headed for the side door and the sidewalk leading down to the barn. Why was it that when the world overwhelmed her, the safest place she knew to be was standing next to a big, black horse?

She didn't even pause to look for Eliseo or Jason when she walked into the barn, just walked through Demi's stall to the main pasture where she'd seen him grazing.

"Hey, Demi," she said quietly. He nickered, then wandered over and stood in front of Polly, looking at her as if he was waiting for the rest of the conversation.

Demi stood stock still as Polly closed the distance and leaned against his shoulder.

"Aaron is going to think I'm crazy," she said into his body. "Maybe I am. Maybe I'm reading more into those notes than there really is."

He leaned his head down and she stroked his cheek, marveling again at how soft it was. "If he really is the murderer and has been living under my roof all this time, that's creepy, don't you think? And why did he ask about fishing locations in front of me today. Is he taunting me? Or is he just a regular guy who likes to fish?"

Polly backed away when Demi picked up his foot and then stamped it in the ground.

"I don't know what you're trying to tell me," she said with a laugh.

He stamped it again and then nudged her head with his nose.

"Okay, that's it," Polly said, still laughing, but beginning to worry. "If my horse is talking to me now, I'm officially creeped out."

Eliseo came around the corner of the barn, laughing out loud. "He *is* talking to you, Polly."

She looked up in shock. "What do you mean? He is not. I can't have my horses answering my questions. That's just too weird. It's odd enough that I find bodies. I don't need talking horses."

Jason was the next one around the corner, only he was driving the skid loader with a large, round bale of hay on the front. Polly breathed an immense sigh of relief.

"He wants his hay," she said, nervous laughter and weak knees causing her to bend over and catch her breath.

Eliseo laughed so hard he snorted, and Polly glanced up at him with a scowl.

"I'm sorry," he managed to get out. "We cleaned the yard this morning and have been so busy moving things around that I hadn't gotten back here with their hay."

The rest of the horses and the two donkeys crowded around, waiting for Jason to drop the hay. Eliseo opened the bale and spread it while they greedily pushed each other out of the way.

"You'd think they were starving," Polly said.

Eliseo nodded. "It's a terrible life they lead." He'd picked up one of her phrases. They'd been around each other for too long.

She shook her head. "I feel like a fool."

"Because you were talking to Demi?"

She frowned at him. "Because I was afraid he actually understood my words and was trying to tell me something. What was I thinking?"

"What did you think he told you?" Eliseo asked.

Polly peered at him.

"You must have thought he told you something in response to your question. What was it?"

"I don't know."

"Yes you do," he said patiently. "And whatever it was you thought he told you is probably what you know is the right thing to do."

"Oh." Polly looked over at the horses. "That. I need to make a phone call." She went around the horses and walked back through Demi's stall to a bench in the barn and sat down. Pulling her phone out, she looked at it before swiping the call open. "Please don't think I'm crazy. Please don't think I'm crazy," she muttered.

""Please tell me you haven't done it again. We're awfully busy getting ready for the celebration tomorrow," Aaron said.

"No. I'm safely ensconced in my horse barn right now. But I have a thought. Are you at the office?"

"Should I be?"

"It would be easier. I need to talk to you about those notes that were on the bodies." If Aaron wasn't close to them, Polly didn't want to have to try to explain herself.

"Then I am. What's up?"

"Do you have copies nearby?"

He laughed. "With Anita on staff, we're almost technologically savvy around here. Just a second and let me bring them up on my screen."

Polly waited and tried to figure out the best way to make him understand what she saw.

"Okay. I have them here," Aaron said. "What am I looking for?"

"Aaron, I'm going to jump out on a very tiny limb here and I need you to not laugh at me. If you think that I'm grasping for something that isn't there, that's okay, but just give me a few minutes."

"Okay. I'll put on my patient-Aaron demeanor."

She chose not to respond to that and said, "Look at the first note. Do you see the word train and hoot? I think he was obliquely telling us where the next body would be found."

"Kind of a stretch," he said.

"I know, but keep going. In the second note, he mentions bed and plenty to eat. The bed of my truck, plenty to eat is grocery shopping."

"Hmmm."

"Okay, okay. Now in note three he used the words ledge, park and can. The body was found in a can at the Ledges Park."

There was silence on the phone.

"Are you still there?" she asked.

"Yes and I don't like that you're making sense. Those are really obscure references, but taken all together, it feels like you're correct."

"Exactly. In the last note he used the words drowned and cast."

"So you're thinking a body of water."

"Yes. And Aaron, this morning one of my guests just came into the office asking about fishing locations nearby. What if it's him?"

"Wanting to fish isn't enough to start an investigation into someone. What did you tell him?"

"I sent him up to Bradford's Hardware."

"That makes sense. Well, I suppose the first thing I should do is call Paul to see if the man showed up."

"Are you thinking that if he didn't go there after asking me, he might have been trying to give me a hint? I always hear that criminals want to be caught. That's why they screw up."

"That or they just aren't smart enough to stay ahead of us. I'm not ready to give him any motive for asking questions. There are a lot of good fishing spots in the county, Polly. People like to fish."

"Are you going to check on him, though? Even just a little bit? Kristen also said that he and another guest were asking questions about me and Sycamore House. More than just a guest's normal curiosity."

He chuckled. "It would be foolish not to. I'm not about to let a murderer slip through my fingers because I didn't listen to you. But do me a favor, Polly. Stay away from this. I don't like having to chase you down after the fact. Your husband and my wife get very angry when you manage to get yourself into the middle of trouble."

"I was good the last time," Polly said in protest. "I let you all go rescue Rebecca without any intervention on my part."

"Yes you did and we were all quite proud of you, but the truth is, she's not much better than you when it comes to getting Henry's hackles up. That man worries about you two." Aaron huffed. "And you give him good reason."

"Whatever," Polly said, feeling like a petulant child.

"Tell me what this man's name is," Aaron said.

"All I know is that his last name is James. Kristen would have that information. Do you want me to find her and ask? I can call you back."

"No. I'll hand this off. Have you met Tab Hudson yet?"

Polly concentrated on the name and couldn't put a face to it. "I don't know."

"She's on the team handling the murders. Tab's a smart girl. It's time you got to know her."

"Tell her to reach out if she needs anything." Polly paused. "Just to be clear. You don't think I'm crazy with what I was reading in those notes?"

"If it had only been one note, I would have told you that you were grasping at straws. Maybe even two notes, but by the time you got to the third note, you started making sense. There were too many coincidences. Can you tell me how you figured it out?"

She laughed. "A little boy read the word 'train' and his interpretation wasn't the note's original meaning. That's when I wondered if the murderer was messing with me."

"If this all works out and he helped us, tell that little boy I owe him an ice cream cone. Him and his brother."

"It wasn't the boys staying with me," she said. "It was Matty, Eliseo's nephew."

She heard the catch in his breath. "Eliseo's nephew?"

"You didn't know? I thought surely Lydia would have told you about Eliseo's sister and her four children being in town."

"I didn't even think about him having a family," Aaron said. "But poor Lydia has been chasing her tail feathers this week trying to get ready for everyone to land on us tonight."

"And you're at work?"

"I'm not a crazy man. Standing anywhere near the tornado-like woman that is my wife this week would be the absolute death of me. Sandy came in last night and Marilyn came over early this morning to help their mother. When I get home, I'm putting up a tent in the back yard for me and the boys."

"Are you kidding me?"

"It sounds like a good idea, though, doesn't it?"

"I wish Lydia would have told us how much work she had. I could have helped."

"Polly, you sweet, silly girl. Lydia is in her glory right now. Besides, you have enough going on in your world with those boys and that big old house you're trying to renovate. She'd have felt guilty tying you up."

Polly chuckled as the image of Lydia tying Polly to a chair came to mind. "I would probably have resisted," she said.

"Being tied up?" Aaron laughed. "Now you get back to whatever you were doing. I need to get Tab started on this."

"Thank you for listening."

Polly felt better after talking to him. She always did. Someday she'd quit worrying that he wouldn't believe her.

CHAPTER TWENTY-TWO

As Polly walked in the back door of Sycamore House, she swiped a call open to Hayden.

"Hey Polly," he said. "What's up?"

"Wondering if you and Heath want some lunch. I'm starving."

When he didn't respond, she chuckled. "You've already eaten."

"Yeah. But there's extra here if you want to come over. Since it's just us guys here, we ordered pizza."

"No, that's okay. No big deal. What's going on over there?"

"The electricians want to finish in the back room. You know, where you're putting your library? They said they wanted one room done before stopping for the long weekend."

"And that Hoffman guy? Is he working today?"

"Yeah," Hayden said. "He's doing something in the cellar. I don't think he's having fun, though."

"What's wrong?"

Hayden chuckled. "I'm not asking. He tends to curse a lot when he runs into a problem."

"And he's cursing a lot today?"

"Well, kinda. Is Henry still gone?"

"Yes," Polly said. "They had to go to Des Moines for a wheelchair that fits Noah. They won't be back until later."

"And no Rebecca either? You should just come over. Heath and I aren't doing that much. Maybe we could go up to the attic."

Polly heard Heath say something in the background.

"He's right," Hayden said. "It's too hot up there. But come on over. We're putting finish on a work table Heath built for Rebecca."

"You are too good to her."

"She deserves it. And besides, maybe someday she'll be a famous artist and all of those little scribbles and sketches she's made will be worth a lot of money. Come over, Polly."

"Okay. You sure you don't want anything? Coffee, muffins, cupcakes. Anything?"

"We're cool."

Now she just felt pathetic. Poor Hayden was inviting her to her own house so that she wouldn't feel lonely. Polly opened the garage door, got in her truck, backed out, and turned onto the highway. As she waited for traffic to pass, she realized someone was waving at her. She waved back and saw that it was Mr. James, crossing the street back onto the Sycamore House lane. He carried a few bags with him and she watched him cross the lawn to the parking lot and up to the front door. The man seemed innocuous enough and it wasn't as if she got a bad feeling about him. Well, not a really bad feeling. Just a little bit of a bad feeling. Maybe she was reading too much into everything. At least Aaron had the information now. He could deal with it.

She drove around the block twice, waiting for a parking space to open up anywhere near the coffee shop. This was crazy. Bellingwood Days was always busy, but the celebration this year added an entirely new dimension to the town's population. People wandered in and out of the shops, stopping to talk to each other on the sidewalks. Just when she finally felt comfortable with names and faces, all of a sudden, she didn't recognize anyone. Polly wondered if she'd been transported to a new town.

Polly parked down the street near the elementary school and

walked up to the coffee shop. When she opened the front door, she stepped back to let three people leave.

"Hey there, Polly."

She drew her eyes back to the door, having followed an exceptionally gorgeous young man's exit. "Oh," she said. "Hi, Elise."

"I saw you watching him," Elise said conspiratorially. "That was nice."

"I'm embarrassed now."

"Are you walking by or coming in?"

"Coming in. I thought I'd take something sweet over to the guys working on the house. Are you on your way out?"

Elise shrugged and gave her a contented smile. "I'm on vacation. No classes, no students, no planning, no nothing. I don't care where I'm going." She laughed. "But I think I should stop with the coffee. I've had plenty."

"Join me then," Polly said. "I'll drink coffee and buy you a glass of water." She walked inside and looked around. Most of the tables had someone sitting at them and there was a short line at the counter. "Holy mackerel. This is awesome."

"Camille is so tired at the end of the day," Elise said. "But she says she's having a blast. I think she thrives on all of this."

A trio of young girls got up from a table and looked around for a trash can before leaving the shop. "Grab that table," Polly said. "I'll go place my order."

"Polly!"

She turned toward the voice and waved at Lisa Foster and her mother, Kathryn Ogden. "Hi," she said.

"Come join us," Lisa said.

Polly looked at Elise, unsure of how to proceed. Elise had met Mark Ogden's sister and mother, but Polly didn't know if she would be comfortable spending much time with them. The young woman was better now than she'd ever been about being with people, but there was probably a limit.

Elise smiled and nodded, so Polly stepped away from the line and walked over to the table. "Lisa. Kathryn. You know Elise

Myers?" She put her hand on Elise's arm. "Lisa owns the dance studio here in town and her husband runs Pizzazz across the street. She's Sal's sister-in-law and this is her mother."

"We've met," Elise said. "And well, I love your husband's pizza."

"Sit down," Kathryn said. "You're a friend of Polly's?"

Elise dropped right into the story of how she and Polly met while Polly stood there in shock. Polly assumed it was safe to leave, so she sidled away and made it to the counter. A young woman smiled up at her and asked for her order.

"Just a large iced cold-brew," Polly said. "And I need a dozen of the cupcakes. Mix them up. It doesn't matter."

Camille smiled at her while waiting on an older woman who couldn't figure out what she wanted to drink, and Skylar nodded as he seemed to be in the midst of filling a large order. One other woman behind the counter opened a bakery box for the cupcakes and yet another person came out from the bakery carrying a tray laden with muffins and scones.

Polly paid the girl and left a tip in the jar on the counter before heading back to the table.

"You missed all the fun last night," Kathryn said. "I understand you were taking care of a little boy."

Polly nodded. "I'm so glad you had a good time. Thank you for coming down to help with all of the dancing. My daughter had fun learning the jitter-bug. She had to teach it to me this morning after everyone was gone. You're staying with Lisa and Dylan?"

"When I'm not holding little Alexander." Kathryn took a sip of her coffee. "We spent the morning with him while Sal went shopping." Her eyes grew misty. "I'd spend every day with my grandchildren if I could get away with it."

"You'd miss your students," Lisa said.

"You're right, but these moments when they're so innocent are my favorite."

Lisa laughed at her mother. "You say that about every moment. You're a tenderhearted sap, Mom."

Polly's phone buzzed and she took it out to see a text come

through from Hayden: *"You're going to want to see this. Bad things have happened and it's kind of hilarious."*

"What do you mean hilarious? No wait. What do you mean, bad?"

"This you have to see for yourself. Are you nearly here?"

She chuckled at her table mates. "I need to get over to the house. One of my boys tells me something bad has happened."

Elise cocked her head. "You're not worried?"

"After what's happened these last couple of weeks, no," Polly said. "Besides, he told me it was hilarious. I can only imagine. It was nice to see you again, Kathryn. Lisa."

"I'll walk out with you," Elise said. "It was nice to meet you." She waved at Camille and followed Polly out the door. "I've never seen anything like this in Bellingwood before."

"It's pretty crazy. I've never seen anything like it either." They turned at the sound of a small clanging bell to see a tandem bicycle carrying an elderly couple coming down the street toward them. The man wore a white dress shirt, with a small black bolo tie and black shorts. He had a straw hat on his head and a pipe in his mouth. His wife rode behind him with a puffy skirt that she'd tied around her ankles and a bonnet on her head. She smiled and waved as they rode past.

Elise laughed out loud, a musical sound Polly hadn't heard before. "Do you know them?" she asked.

"I've never seen them before."

"Well, I'm going to walk down to the general store and maybe over to the library," Elise said. "This is something I don't want to miss. I'm taking it all in this weekend." She grabbed Polly's hand. "Wanna ride on the Ferris wheel with me sometime?"

Polly beamed. "Who are you and what have you done with my Elise?"

"It's so much fun. I can't miss out just because I'm shy. Right?"

"Right! I like this and I'll encourage it all I can. Of course I will ride on the Ferris wheel with you. If you want to ride other things at the carnival, I'm sure I can talk one of the kids into joining you."

Elise turned to walk away, then stopped. "I hope that it's nothing too terrible at the house. See you later."

Polly headed for her truck and turned back to watch Elise stop to talk to a little girl who was wearing a long dress and bonnet. She patted the girl on the head and wandered on down the sidewalk before turning into the hardware store.

There was enough traffic on the street that rather than making a U-turn, Polly had to turn right and head around the block in order to drive west to Beech Street.

When she pulled in, she was surprised to find Heath and Hayden sitting on the stoop outside the side door. "What's so hilariously bad?" Polly asked, as she walked up to them.

Hayden gestured toward the inside with his head. "Go on in."

"What?" she asked.

Heath dropped his head, chuckling. "Just go in."

They moved to let her go past and she went into the kitchen and came rushing back out, gagging. "What in the hell is that?"

Liam Hoffman came around from the back of the house. "That's my fault."

Polly looked him up and down and backed away as he approached her. "What happened to you?" she asked.

Hayden started laughing out loud. "It's not funny. I know it's not funny."

Hoffman grimaced. "But you're laughing anyway. Seventy-year-old crap. That's what happened to me. You wanna know why those folks moved out? Clogged pipes that they never fixed. That's why they moved out."

"But they would have had to install those pipes. There was no indoor plumbing before the Springers moved in," Polly said.

"The only thing indoor about that plumbing was that it kept everything indoors. The drainage didn't have anywhere to go," he grumbled. "All I did was tap one pipe to see how much of it was still there and all of a sudden the thing exploded all over me. Crap, leaves, debris, all of it rotted and stinking. Seventy years!" he yelled, making Polly wince. "Seventy years. Every time it rained, more rotted debris backed up in those pipes. I don't know who did the work but they should be taken out into that cemetery behind your house, shot, and left for carrion birds to find."

"I suspect they're already there," Polly said. "What are we going to do about this? We have people coming to see the tunnel that leads to that basement room."

A fresh wave of awful smell wafted past her and she backed up another step.

"I need to bring in a team to clean out your basement," Liam Hoffman said. "I can't get them here tomorrow, but maybe Thursday and Friday. After that, it's going to take time for me to figure out exactly how I'm going to fix this." He shuddered. "I can't get into my truck smelling like this. I should have been wearing a hazmat suit. These clothes just need to be burned."

"Do you have more clothes?" Polly asked.

He nodded. "Bad things happen to plumbers. Bad things always happen to plumbers." He pointed at himself. "Especially plumbers named Liam Hoffman. It wouldn't be so awful if this was the first time I was covered in crap. It seems to be my lot in life. My wife often laments the fact that I never come home smelling like roses. If I were you, I'd open all the windows in the house. We'll try to get it cleaned out before your event on Saturday, but I can't make any guarantees."

"I understand. How can I help you?"

"You can't." He shook his head. "I don't want anybody down there. The hazards of ..." he paused, then went on. "... debris that old make it dangerous." Hoffman pointed at Heath. "Could you follow me to my truck? I don't want to touch anything, but if you get some clothes out for me, I'll wash off the worst of this at the pump on the other side of the garage."

Heath got up to follow him and Polly looked at Hayden, then whispered. "There's a pump on the other side of the garage?"

"Yes?" Hayden said, grinning up at her. "It's been there forever. Apparently, there's a well."

"Is that where they got water for the house? I feel so stupid that I didn't know this."

He grinned up at her. "I'd show you, but we should let him clean up in peace. It was probably used a long time ago, but the Springers brought city water into the house when they moved in.

From what I understand it was a big deal running the water out here this far. It was because of them that the rest of the neighborhood grew up at all. Once the utilities were out this far, it became more affordable to put houses up."

"I see. But apparently they did a terrible job bringing the sewer to the house." Polly sat down beside him and put her head in her hands. "This is going to be really expensive." She sighed. "And worse than that, it's going to add more time to us moving in. I refuse to move into a house without a toilet and a shower. Especially when I have a perfectly functional one just a few blocks away."

"It will work out," he said. "And you wouldn't want to move in and then have it all fall apart on you."

"Have you told Henry?" she asked, taking her phone out. She handed it to him.

Hayden spit out a laugh. "Are you kidding me? That's your job." He pushed her hand back toward her.

She held it back out to him. "You're the one who thought it was hilarious. You tell him."

The nasty smell assaulted Polly again and she shuddered before looking up. Liam and Heath came back from the truck; Heath walking a few feet behind the filth-ridden man. The boy looked over at Polly and his brother, and rolled his eyes skyward, holding one hand over his mouth and nose.

"It was never that bad down at the barn, even if I was late cleaning out their stalls," she said. "That's hideous."

"You should have seen us inside. We didn't know anything had happened until he let out with a blue streak that would have burned your ears right off your head," Hayden said. "Then it took a few more moments before we realized that the bad things we were smelling hadn't happened due to either one of us having a gastro-intestinal issue. It was much worse than that. By the time we got outside to the cellar door, he was barreling up the steps, pissed as hell."

Polly looked at the phone in her hand and then put an evil grin on her face. "Here's the deal. I'll call Henry, but you have to go back inside and open the windows." She laughed as she said it. "Fair?"

He shook his head back and forth. "That's so not fair." Hayden glanced toward the garage. "There's no way Heath will let me get away with making him go inside after he was elected to help Mr. Hoffman." He stamped his foot. "It's not fair at all."

"Think about it," Polly said. "Liam just created the perfect security system. Nobody will spend any time in that house trying to pull copper pipe out. If we open the windows, the smell will announce to thieves that they ought to run for their lives."

"That's one way to look at it." Hayden heaved himself up from the step and adjusted his t-shirt before putting his hand on the door knob. "All of the windows?" he asked Polly.

"As many as you can get open," she said.

Hayden pointed at her phone. "I'm not going in until you dial."

She laughed. "Fine," and swiped the phone app open, then scrolled to Henry's last call. "I'm calling. I'm calling."

"I'm waiting," he said.

"Chicken."

Hayden allowed his whole body to shudder. "Absolutely. And I'm not ashamed to admit it."

"Ready?" Polly asked, her hand poised over the little green telephone button.

He nodded.

"Set." She tapped it and put the phone up to her ear. "Go."

Hayden swung the door open and Polly gagged at the smell. She stood up and walked over to her truck as the call rang to Henry's cell phone.

"Hi there," Henry said. "Are you wondering if we're ever coming home?"

"Well..." She dragged the word out. "Sure. I could be convinced to wonder about that. Are you ever coming home?"

"We're on our way. We have crutches and a wheelchair so Noah can go to events in Bellingwood without breaking a sweat. The crutches belong to Roy and we'll return the wheelchair after the boys go back to Chicago. What's up in your world?"

"Not much. It got a little lonely around here with everyone gone. Rebecca, Kayla and Andrew are babysitting out at Eliseo's place. Elva applied for a job at the Alehouse."

"That's a great idea," he said. "So you've been bored and lonely?"

"I think I know who the murderer is." Polly watched the windows on the porch open and grinned to herself.

"You do. Who?"

"I'll tell you when you get home."

"It sounds like you've had a few things going on."

"Uh huh. A few. So, uh, there's another reason I'm calling." It nearly killed her to have to tell him. Henry sounded as happy and relaxed as he had in several days and so far, all of her phone calls to him had been bad news.

"Yeah? What's that?"

"Well, uh. Hayden made me call you."

"Polly. What aren't you telling me? Did someone break into the house again?"

"Well, uh, nobody broke into the house, but someone might have broken the house. Well, not the house, per se, but something bad happened in the cellar. And it's not my fault. It's not Hayden's or Heath's fault either. None of us did anything bad." She knew it wasn't right to giggle, but this was one of those moments that she'd never experience again. At least she never hoped to experience it again. She might as well make it memorable.

"Polly Giller, you tell me what is going on right now."

"Okay. Well, uh, Liam Hoffman broke a sewer pipe in the basement and he has to bring a hazmat team in to clean it up and Hayden is opening all the windows in the house because whatever he broke smells like an entire army had a bad case of diarrhea and did it all in our house." She rattled the words out so quickly, she had to stop and take a breath.

"He what?"

"He says that it's seventy years of crap and debris and that every time it rained for the last seventy years, it backed stuff up into the house because the sewer was put in wrong."

"It what?" Henry's voice level had gone up significantly.

"It's bad, isn't it," she said quietly.

"Polly?" Roy's voice came through on the phone.

Polly giggled. "He gave you the phone because he couldn't talk to me anymore. Right?"

"Is everything okay?"

"Well. Everybody is okay, but the house kind of had a breakdown. We have a really bad sewer problem. But tell him we have a really good man to fix it, okay? We're opening windows." She giggled again. "Well, Hayden's opening windows. They'll be in yet this week to clean it out. Everything is going to be fine at some point. Tell him all that, would you?"

"I'll try," Roy said. "Is it bad that his knuckles are white on the steering wheel?"

"It's not good, but he'll breathe through this and calm down. I'm sure of that," she said with another chuckle. "I'm glad that you and the boys are with him and not me, though. It makes it much easier. How long until you're home?"

"We're just turning onto Highway 30 now. Maybe a half hour?"

"Okay. We'll be home to help get Noah upstairs. See you later."

Polly hung up and waited by her truck for Hayden to come back out of the house. She'd been talking to Henry and Roy long enough that she was starting to get worried about him. Heath came around the corner of the garage, followed by Liam Hoffman who was carrying a garbage bag that had been closed up tight.

"This is going to be a three-shower night," Hoffman said. "I can tell right now. Have you talked to Henry?"

Polly chuckled again. "Yeah. He ran out of words."

"Tell him I'll call tomorrow. We'll let him work this out in his head tonight," Hoffman replied. "Now I get to go home and explain why I smell like the sewer again." He shrugged. "It's not like she doesn't know what I do. Sorry about the mess, but we'll clean it up."

"How you doing?" Polly asked Heath, who was standing beside her looking shell-shocked.

"He stripped right down to nothing and sprayed that cold

water all over himself," Heath said. "I didn't even get a chance to turn around."

She laughed out loud. "Oh, you poor boy. This day can't get much worse, can it?"

Hayden came running out of the house. He looked up at the two of them standing there, then ran behind the garage.

"What's wrong with him?" Heath asked.

"He had to open windows."

They listened as Hayden threw up whatever had been in his stomach. He came back around toward them, green and pale. "That was the worst thing I've ever done," he said. "No one is going back in there until it's been cleaned up." He pointed at Polly. "Did you make the call?"

"Yeah. He quit talking to me. Hopefully he'll be better when they get home."

Hayden reached into his pocket and tossed keys to Heath. "You drive. If I tell you to pull over, don't ask. Just do it."

"I'll see you boys back at the house," Polly said. "Thanks for doing that, Hayden."

"Yeah, yeah, yeah." He waved her toward her truck and blinked his eyes, trying to clear them. "That was the worst."

She climbed back in her truck and laughed until she snorted as she backed out onto the street. Her family was far from normal, but she couldn't imagine anything better.

CHAPTER TWENTY-THREE

"Nobody should ever be up at this hour," Polly said.

Henry just smiled.

They'd left the apartment bright and early to meet Henry's father at the carnival grounds. He'd called to ask Henry for help erecting the tent for the church food booth. Each church was cooking a meal and they finally rounded up a tent large enough to encompass the picnic tables. Polly looked forward to seeing the carnival without the excitement of barkers and customers. Besides, Henry promised they could stop for coffee on their way.

The dinner last night for the boys and their host families had been fun. Noah received quite a bit of attention in his wheelchair. The older boys hadn't had much time for the youngsters on the trip from Chicago, but sometimes a little distance from home brings fellow-travelers together. They all promised to push him around town if they saw him and both he and Elijah ate up all of the attention.

Sylvie had brought an armless office chair on wheels from her home and it turned out to be the perfect mode of transportation for Noah around the apartment.

The little boys slept through another night on the pushed-together sofas in the living room. Obiwan climbed up with them and sprawled across the two boys until they tossed and turned and pushed him to one end of the sofa. Even still, when Polly checked on them, she found that Elijah had turned himself until he was tucked up as close as possible to the big dog. That little boy loved to snuggle in his sleep.

Henry's phone rang as he pulled into a parking place directly in front of Sweet Beans. She gestured for Henry to stay put and ran inside.

"I've never seen you here so early," Camille said, smiling up at her from a table where she was rearranging the centerpiece.

"That's because I rarely leave the house before I've had at least two cups of coffee from my own pot," Polly said with a laugh. She smiled. "Don't hurry. I never come in when all of the bakery smells are this strong. I want to just stand here and enjoy it."

Camille walked around behind the counter and took down a large cup. "Your regular?"

Polly nodded. "And Henry's too. He's in the truck. Things were crazy busy in here yesterday."

"I'm sorry I couldn't get to you," Camille said. "Skylar and I didn't even think to tell the girls you weren't really a customer."

"Don't you even," Polly said with a laugh. "I'm in here often enough that getting a little cash out of me is a good thing. She was very nice."

"Wouldn't it be wonderful if we stayed busy enough that I needed to hire her after this week?" Camille asked. "Enough locals have been in with their friends and out of town family members that I hope they discovered we were a great place to get a little coffee." She put a cup down in front of Polly. "That's yours." When she turned back to make Henry's, she went on. "You won't believe it, but Joe came in yesterday afternoon with a whole group of people he knows."

"Joe?" Polly asked.

Camille tilted her head downtown. "From Joe's Diner. He told me he was checking us out and he liked what he saw."

Polly laughed. "I can't believe it."

"Then he asked if Sylvie would consider baking fresh items for him to sell."

"Uh." Polly stood at the counter, her mouth open. "Uh. That's amazing."

"I know!" Camille said. "We have a meeting set up with him next week when everything calms down." She put a second cup on the counter.

Polly slipped some cash into the tip jar and shook her head in disbelief. "That's really terrific. You are doing such a great job here. I'm so proud of you. Have you told Jeff yet?"

"No. I haven't had time. He's been swamped. We just need things to keep moving smoothly through the week and then we can talk about our successes and failures. But I had to tell someone. I'm glad you came in when it was quiet."

"I'm so proud of you," Polly said. She put the cups on the counter and ran around behind to give Camille a hug. "Just when you think things are going well, they get better. I hope this helps you guys kick butt today."

The front door bell jingled and Skylar walked in. "Polly Giller, are you helping us today, too?"

She laughed. "No, Sky. I'm just hugging your boss. I needed coffee to jumpstart my day. Didn't think I'd beat you in, though. What are you, late?"

He looked around for the clock and wrinkled his forehead at Camille. "Am I late?"

"No, you're early," she said. "She's just messing with you."

"I'll see you two later." Polly grabbed up her coffees and headed for the front door. "Have a great day!"

She went out, jumped into Henry's truck and put his coffee in the cup holder beside him. "Sorry that took so long. Camille had a great day yesterday and needed to tell me about it. What was the phone call? Everything okay?"

"Yeah. It was just Dad telling me where to park the truck."

Polly held her coffee under her nose, sniffing its aroma. "How do people exist without coffee?" she murmured into the cup.

"By not having an addiction to it," Henry said with a laugh. He pulled to a stop. "Not that there's anything wrong with it. Who am I to judge?"

"Right," she said. "So here?"

He nodded. "Coming in with me? Dad is waiting to open the gate."

The carnival wasn't set to open until eleven o'clock, so the grounds were empty, tents covered, and rides folded up. Polly wandered in and around everything, taking in the sense of anticipation and excitement it offered. She stopped by to see Henry, his father, and Len Specek, who were working with at least two of the local pastors in town and several other men she recognized. While they put poles together, she headed for the local community booths. The Purple Hat Ladies were hosting a kissing booth. Polly wondered who was manning that. She'd have to check back and see. The Humane Society had a petting booth set up. She'd definitely have to stop in and see what animals they brought.

Polly laughed when she saw that the Bellingwood Police were sponsoring a dunk tank. People would line up for miles to get the opportunity to put some of their favorite law enforcement officers into the water. She walked over to press the large target that released the bench they sat on and chuckled. If Chief Wallers was in the tank, she'd definitely pay money. Then she laughed again as she stood up on tip toe to look in. She never hit anything. He was safe.

"Damn it," she said, stepping back. Polly's knees wobbled and she dropped her coffee. She backed further away while pulling out her phone, then looked at the time, knowing Aaron didn't get up early in the mornings. He'd just have to suffer. She swiped the call and waited, looking around for a place to sit. There wasn't anything nearby, so she headed back to the picnic tent.

"Polly?" Lydia asked. "What's wrong? Aaron's in the shower."

"I need him to come to the carnival," Polly said. "I was wrong about the last note."

"What do you mean?"

"I just found a body in the dunk tank at the carnival. I need Aaron."

She sat down at a picnic table farthest from where the men were working and took a deep breath.

"Are you okay? Is anyone else there to take care of you?" Lydia asked.

"Yeah. I'm here with Henry. Just tell Aaron, would you? I can't think straight right now."

"Of course I will, dear. Take care of yourself."

Polly bent over to put her head between her knees. This was too many at once.

"Polly, what's wrong?" She startled when Henry touched her back. He came around in front of her and knelt down. "What happened?"

"Dunk tank. Dead body." Polly pointed to where she'd come from. "Why is this happening?"

"Oh honey." Henry gathered her into his arms and held her tight. "I'm so sorry. I shouldn't have brought you with me."

"It wouldn't have mattered what you did. I had to find her."

"It was a girl?" he asked. "I'm sorry. Was that Aaron you were talking to?"

"Lydia. Aaron's in the shower." Tears threatened and Polly rubbed her face on Henry's shoulder. It didn't do any good and soon they flowed freely down her cheeks. "I'm sorry. I usually handle it better than this. I thought I knew what he'd do next and I was going to do everything in my power to avoid going fishing."

Henry sat back on his heels. "Fishing? You've never gone fishing."

"I know," she said. "That's why I thought maybe we'd catch him before he killed someone else. No matter what, I wasn't going near a fishing pole. But I was so wrong. That probably means I was dead wrong..." she paused. "Sorry."

"That's okay. Dead wrong about what?"

"About who the killer is."

"Who did you think it was?"

"There's a guy staying at Sycamore House who keeps making it a point to talk to me or ask questions when I'm around. Mr. James. I just figured it had to be him. Yesterday he asked Kristen and me about where the best places to go fishing were. Now I don't have a clue who the killer might be." She slumped her shoulders and leaned forward until he caught her. "And there's going to be another note which means he's already got the next murder planned in his mind."

"Is everything okay over here?"

Polly looked up to see the rest of the men coming to gather around. Bill Sturtz sat down on the picnic table bench behind her. "What happened, Polly?"

She turned to Henry and he shrugged.

"You might as well know," she said. "There's been another murder. I just found a girl in the dunk tank."

"The police dunk tank?" one of the men asked. Polly turned and realized it was the Methodist pastor with a look of incredulity on his face.

"Yep," she said. "Nothing like making sure everyone will get involved. This guy is taunting us now."

Bill slowly rubbed her back. "Did you call Chief Wallers?"

"I probably should have, but I called Aaron. He's the one who has this case. He'll let Ken know."

Polly's phone buzzed on the table and Henry picked it up. "It's Aaron."

She swiped it open. "Hello, Aaron. I'm so sorry I had to bother you."

"Don't you be apologizing to me, Polly Giller. I'm sorry your day started this way. Lydia said you were pretty upset."

"Yeah. I'm sorry that I was so wrong on interpreting that note, too. He used the word tank and I didn't even consider this possibility."

"At least we know that the pattern of obscure hints is really there," Aaron said. "I haven't been to the carnival grounds yet, but I heard a rumor that the dunk tank was sponsored by the Bellingwood Police. Is that true?"

"Yes."

He laughed out loud. "I have to tell Ken in person. There's no way I want to miss the look on his face when he hears what happened in his dunk tank."

"Aaron Merritt," Polly scolded. "You're awful."

"Yes I am, and I'm sorry. My team is on the way. I have to stop at the police station before I get there. Deputy Hudson will be in charge. Did you meet her yesterday?"

"No," Polly said. "I wasn't at Sycamore House much after I called you." Polly thought back to her day yesterday and shook her head. At least by the time Henry got home with Noah and Elijah, he'd calmed down about the sewer system at the Bell House. She still wasn't sure how they might be ready for Saturday afternoon, but they'd give it their best shot.

"Don't let anyone go near the dunk tank until we arrive. Can I ask you to do that?"

"Of course," she said. "Nobody's on the grounds yet. And I think I can trust Henry's dad and the town's pastors." She looked up and smiled at the men hovering around her.

"Oh." Aaron said, sounding surprised. "That explains why you're there. You're in good hands. Ken and I will be there as soon as I pick him up off the floor." He was laughing as he ended the call.

Henry stood up and took Polly's hand. "Walk with me," he said.

She followed him away from the others. "What's up?"

"I just wanted you to have some breathing room. What did Aaron say?"

"That I'm not supposed to let anyone get near the dunk tank and he's stopping to pick Ken Wallers up. I guess there's a Deputy Hudson assigned to this case. She'll be here soon."

He nodded. "You've met her."

Polly frowned. "I did? When?"

"When Uncle Loren was killed. She was out there that night."

Polly slowly shook her head and looked at him in disbelief. "How do you remember these things? It's like names go in one ear and out the other with me."

Henry put an arm around her shoulders as they walked. "You'll meet her today, make a connection and never forget her name again. It's okay." He chuckled. "I'm just glad you remember *my* name."

"Stop it." Polly swatted at his belly and he bent to avoid it.

"Do you need me to take you home after you've talked to the police?" Henry asked.

"No. I'm okay. How long will you guys be here?"

They turned back to look at the work the men were doing. Poles were in place around the perimeter of the picnic area.

"Probably another hour or so if the tent goes up without trouble."

"Then I'll stay. Gotta make that connection with Deputy Hudson, you know." Polly smiled. "I'm glad you were here this morning."

"You're taking this one worse than others."

"It's so senseless."

"They all are."

Polly stopped walking. "I know that, but for some reason this murderer is trying to get my attention and I can't figure out why. Until I do, he's just going to keep killing people."

Henry stepped in front of her and took her face in his hands. He kissed her on the lips and then said, "You can't do this, Polly. You are no more responsible for this murderer's actions than I am for the sewer explosion at the house yesterday." He grinned as he said the last. "Though I would have given nearly anything to have seen Liam's reaction when that blew up all over him. You know he has a reputation for getting into crap no matter what. It's like you and dead bodies. If there is a mess to be found, he's the one who will find it. Every single time."

"We didn't talk about it last night, but I was really worried about you on the phone yesterday. I've never known you to stop talking to me."

He dropped his hands and took one of hers again. They headed back to the picnic area. "I was pretty shook up. That's a huge deal. I'm glad Hoffman's on it, but they're going to rip out that front yard to get to the sewer and water from the street. There is so much work ahead."

"Do you think we should stop now and call it a wash?" Polly asked. "We could probably just sell it for what the lot's worth."

He sat down beside her at a picnic table. "Our family is growing. We barely have room for us now. What would we do with ourselves?"

She lifted a shoulder. "We could either build like the Mikkels' did or look for a house that's in better shape." Even as she said the words, Polly felt her throat close up. No matter what that house had thrown at her, she was starting to fall in love with it. But if Henry thought it was no longer worth it, she'd pay attention.

"I'm not ready to make a decision like that," Henry said. He picked up her hand and rubbed his thumb across the top of it. "This just hit me hard. The thing is, I know we'll run into more problems. It's never going to be easy."

"Then we'll just take it slow." Polly gave him a sad smile. "I shouldn't have been pushing so hard this summer. I know you said it would be a year, but I was kind of hoping we might be able to land there sometime this fall. Even if we had to live on the first floor."

"This isn't the end of our progress," Henry said. "Heath and Hayden have been making great forward movement. You'll be surprised at how fast things go once the electricity and pipes are in and walls go up." He hugged her. "I wouldn't hate being in there by Christmas. You have to stay positive and excited about this when I get too practical for my own good."

Polly nodded at him and leaned against his shoulder. "This has been a strange couple of weeks."

"Are you Polly Giller?"

Polly jumped up and straightened her shirt, then realized that she did recognize Deputy Hudson from the night they'd met out at Loren Sturtz's home. "I am. You're Deputy Hudson. It's nice to meet you." She stuck her hand out and the young woman smiled as she shook it.

"Would you please show me where you found the body?"

"This way." Polly touched Henry's shoulder and walked away, toward the dunk tank. This was a heck of a way to start Bellingwood Days. She didn't know how they'd be out of here before the carnival opened today. Hopefully, they'd at least have the body moved and on its way to the morgue.

"I see it," Deputy Hudson said. "Did you touch anything that I should know about?"

"Yeah," Polly said. "I pushed on the big button target thingie there." She saw her coffee cup lying on the ground. "That's my coffee. I dropped it."

"I get that," the young woman said. "We'll take care of things from here. Aaron has your number, right?"

"Yeah. You don't need me for anything else?"

"Not right now. You'll be around today?"

"Somewhere. Call if you need me."

"Will do. Thanks." The deputy took a small camera out and snapped pictures, effectively dismissing Polly.

"I'll just be on my way," Polly said under her breath and headed back to the picnic tables. The men were stretching the tent over the poles. They'd be finished soon.

CHAPTER TWENTY-FOUR

Sounds of a wide awake and excited household greeted Polly and Henry when they returned. Elijah and Noah sat at the dining room table, watching Hayden flip a pancake at Rebecca. She moved back and forth with her plate and posed when she caught it. With a flourish, she presented the plate to Elijah and took up Noah's. They didn't realize anyone was watching, and even though the dogs had run to greet Polly, the adults managed to sneak in and watch from the doorway to the office.

At the successful catch of a second pancake, Henry clapped his hands together. "Bravo!"

Rebecca laughed. "We didn't see you there. Wasn't that great?"

"Yes it was," Polly said. "Where's Heath?"

"Right here." Heath walked in, running his fingers through his hair to move it into place. "The living room has been rearranged and we're almost ready to go. What time does everything start?"

"Things are happening all over town." Polly pulled up a schedule on her phone. "Nothing really gets started until ten o'clock, so we have plenty of time. Are any of you entering the spelling bee?"

Rebecca put her hand up. "I am. So is Andrew." She gathered up a plate filled with pancakes and put it in front of Heath at the table, then leaned over to Elijah and Noah. "Either of you want to enter? I'll take you."

The two little boys looked at each other and shook their heads. "Noah's pretty good at spelling," Elijah said, "but I stink." He stood up and put his hands behind his back. "Cat. K. A. T. Cat." He took a small bow and sat down, an ornery grin on his face.

"They have prizes," Rebecca said, lifting her eyebrows. "Are you sure?"

Noah looked at his younger brother, who shrugged and said, "If you want to, go ahead. You won't catch me doing it, though. I can't even spell cat."

"Maybe you'll do the taffy pull with me," Henry said to Elijah.

"The what?"

"Taffy pull. We make taffy candy."

At the word 'candy,' Elijah's eyes lit up. "I'll do that. What else is there?"

Polly sat down beside him. "They're having sack races, three-legged races and egg races over at the Lutheran Church and I saw them spray-painting a Twister game on the grass at the Catholic Church. Lydia says that they're doing hula hoop contests and jump rope contests at the Methodist Church today. They're even having a tug of war for all ages. Wherever you go, there will be something to do."

"Not for me," Noah said.

Henry laughed. "There will be plenty for you, too. There's a hot dog eating contest, a watermelon eating contest and even a pie eating contest. If you want to get down and dirty there will be a seed spitting contest, too."

Noah looked up at him with big, round eyes. "Spitting?"

"If they give you permission, shouldn't you do it?"

He nodded.

"I want to spit seeds," Elijah said.

"It's going on all day. You'll have plenty of opportunities to do everything you want."

Hayden brought another plate of pancakes with him as he sat down at the table. "We'd better eat up, then. It sounds like we have a big day ahead of us. What time does the carnival open?"

Polly and Henry looked at each other. Surely they would have the crime scene condensed to just the dunk tank by the time eleven o'clock rolled around. What an awful way to start the festivities.

"What?" Rebecca asked. "Did you find something there?" She watched Polly's face and glared. "You. Did. Not."

"It's not my fault," Polly said.

"At the carnival?"

Polly nodded. "The dunk tank."

Hayden started to laugh.

"What's so funny?" she asked.

"I thought about you trying to hit that huge target on a dunk tank," he said. "You might as well be aiming for the moon. But when it comes to this, you're right on target. Amazing."

"Glad I could be your morning's entertainment," Polly said.

Rebecca stood up to reach across the table for the syrup. "Did you get the note yet?"

"No," Polly said and pulled the syrup out of her reach, then handed it to Henry. "Ask for it to be passed to you. Don't reach."

She glanced at the little boys, who were happily eating pancakes doused in butter and syrup. They had no idea what the conversation was about and neither paid enough attention for it to worry Polly. If she could get these boys out of Bellingwood and back to Chicago without them discovering that her superpower was finding dead bodies, she was all for that.

"Need some coffee?" Henry asked.

Polly took a deep breath. "You have no idea. Use the big mug, please."

He went into the kitchen to pour out a couple of mugs of coffee.

Everyone jumped, including Henry, when Elijah yelped as things crashed around him. The little boy jumped out of his seat, sobbing, and ran into the living room.

"What happened?" Polly asked.

Henry had already put the mugs on the counter and was headed that way. "I've got it."

"Did you see what happened?" Polly asked again.

Everyone had been watching Henry. Heath jumped up and headed for the sink while Polly scrambled to stop more juice from flowing to the floor. She used her napkin to stop some of the flow, then put her hand up to catch the cloth Heath tossed to her.

Hayden snagged it out of the air and grinned as he passed it across the table.

"You're asking for it," she laughed.

"Just thought I'd save us a few minutes."

Polly handed him Elijah's plate, then wiped the table clean before bending over to wipe up the rest of the mess from the floor. When she was finished, she called out "Incoming," and flung the cloth back toward the kitchen.

Heath made a dramatic dive as the cloth headed for the refrigerator, nowhere near the sink. It hit the floor so he picked it up, rinsed it out and came back to the table. "Do you need it again?"

"Might as well. The floor's still sticky."

Noah watched the entire thing unfold and when Polly handed the wet cloth back to Heath, he put his hand on her arm. "Aren't you mad?"

"Mad? Why?" she asked.

"Because of the mess. Everything spilled everywhere."

Polly smiled down at him. "Do you see how I throw?"

His face showed his confusion.

"Toss me the rag again," she said to Heath.

He balled it up and gave it a gentle toss. Polly put her hand out to catch it and it landed in front of Noah's plate. "See that? I can't catch."

Noah nodded and watched as Polly gathered the rag, balled it up again and threw it. Rather than arriving in Heath's hands, the rag landed on top of the refrigerator, knocking a box of cereal on its side.

"I can't throw either," she said. "And did you see me knock over the cereal?"

He nodded again, a little smile on his lips.

"Why in the world would I be upset if someone spills something when I can't even figure out how to throw a dish cloth without knocking over a box of cereal? We all mess up and as long as we don't do it on purpose, mistakes aren't something to be punished for."

"I didn't know that," he said. "Elijah doesn't either. He thinks you're going to be really mad at him."

Polly leaned over, put her arms around his shoulders and tugged him close, the wheels on his office chair making that easy. "We don't get angry about spills and mistakes around here. There is too much fun to be had without being mad all the time." She pointed at his plate. "Do you need another pancake?"

He slowly nodded. "Does Elijah get another pancake?"

Hayden picked Noah's plate up and headed back to the stove top. "Elijah gets as many pancakes as he can eat."

Noah tugged on Polly's arm and she bent over so he could whisper in her ear. "We'd get sent to our room without dinner if we spilled anything. Elijah is clumsy sometimes when he gets excited and he was always being sent away."

She turned and whispered into his ear. "When you're visiting us, you can have all the food you want and you'll never be sent to your room without dinner."

Rebecca sighed a loud sigh. "Yeah. They don't punish you by withholding food. They make you clean the bathroom. And your room. And the other bathroom. And sometimes you have to mop the floors too."

Polly laughed out loud. "You live such a horrible life."

"I know, right?" Rebecca said, laughing. "That's what I keep telling you."

"You guys are funny," Noah said.

Henry and Elijah came back into the dining room, Henry's hand resting on Elijah's shoulder. The little boy had changed his clothes and his eyes were red from crying. Noah reached out and grabbed his brother's arm when he attempted to pass behind him to sit on the other side of Polly.

"What?" Elijah asked.

"Hayden's making more pancakes. I said I wanted one, too. And Polly says that it's okay if we spill because she can't throw or catch."

A few tears squirted from Elijah's eyes again and he tugged his arm away from his brother, only to be snagged by Polly. She pulled him into a tight hug against her chest. "I'm sorry you scared yourself," she said. "But you're safe when you are in this house. Okay?"

He nodded and clung to her, doing his best not to cry.

"One cake or two?" Hayden asked from the stove.

"I want one," Noah answered.

"How about two for Elijah," Polly said. "If he can't eat it all, I'll finish it." She tugged the little boy back so she could see his face. "Am I going to have to finish your pancake?"

"No ma'am," he said. "If I eat both of those can I have another?"

"Of course you can." She released him and he sat down beside her.

~~~

"Go, go, go" Polly yelled.

Andrew and Rebecca's inside legs were tied together and they loped toward the finish line of the three-legged race. They were nowhere near winning the thing. Andrew had pulled them down to the ground a couple of times in his desire to hurry. Rebecca was still yelling at him as they crossed the line.

"We're coming back tomorrow," Andrew declared, once they'd given their ties back and come to stand beside Polly. "And tonight we're practicing."

"Let it go," Rebecca said. "All we'd win was a couple of pencils."

"But they're Bellingwood pencils. With the Sesquicentennial thing on them."

She put her hands on the back of Noah's wheelchair. "Come on, Noah. I know where the watermelon eating contest is. Do you want to be on my team for that?"

"We can be a team?" He turned around in his seat and looked up at her.

"You and I might even win something."

Andrew ran to catch up to her. "I want to win. Give me another chance."

"Eat watermelon with us," Rebecca said.

"But I don't like it."

Rebecca stopped the wheelchair and put her hands on her hips. "You don't like watermelon? That's so un-American. Who are you, anyway?"

Andrew lifted his arms over his head, wiggled his fingers, and did his best to loom over her. He made a deep moaning sound and then said, "I'm a Kroerak from Planet Zendar."

"You're a dork." Rebecca poked him in the side, bringing his arms down as he laughed.

"I won! I won!"

Polly turned as Elijah started across the street toward them. Henry caught his shoulder and stopped him, leaned down to say something, and then both of them looked to either side, making sure it was safe. Then he ran over to Noah and put two hard candy sticks in his brother's hands.

"I won the sack race," Elijah yelled. "And they gave me candy." He looked at Polly. "Henry said I had to ask you before I ate it."

She laughed and tilted her head at Henry. "Why do I have to make that decision?"

"Because I didn't want to."

"You can eat it," Polly said, "but you can't run while you're eating. If you want to run, you have to get rid of it," Polly said. "Deal?"

"Deal!" Elijah peeled the plastic wrapping back from one of them while he watched his brother open the other.

They each took a lick and Noah said, "Wanna try mine?"

The switch happened and then, the boys switched back.

Elijah put his hand on the arm rest of Noah's wheelchair and walked alongside him. "This is the best." He pointed down the street. "What do I have to do to win one of those?" he asked.

Polly leaned out into the street to see what he was pointing at. A bright and colorful booth covered with balloon animals was set up in someone's front yard.

"I'll bet it's a clown," she muttered to Henry. She leaned up to whisper in his ear. "You know how I hate clowns."

Andrew and Rebecca ran off down the street.

"Can I go with them?" Elijah asked.

"You stay here with your candy," Henry said. "We'll get there in a minute."

The little boy nodded and said, "Oh."

The two older kids ran back and stood in front of them, puffing. "He's making the best balloon animals. They're free for kids under ten," Rebecca said. She took hold of Noah's chair. "Come on. It's fun."

Polly took Henry's hand and they followed the kids, then stood back as the clown greeted his new customers.

"What happened to you, little boy?" he asked Noah.

Noah looked up at Rebecca and she nodded, then pushed his shoulder.

"I broke it."

"A little boy in a wheelchair needs a special treat." He turned to Elijah. "Are you his brother? You look just like him."

"Yes sir," Elijah said.

"Are you good at helping him?"

Elijah shrugged. "Maybe."

"I think both of you need a special animal today. Do you like dogs and cats?"

"Yes, sir," Elijah said.

"What about monkeys and giraffes?"

The boys were enraptured as the man stretched and blew up colorful balloons, then twisted them into shapes.

"Who is that?" Polly asked Henry.

"John Franks," Henry replied. "I didn't know he could do this."

In a matter of minutes, Noah was holding what looked to be a monkey hanging onto a large yellow banana and Elijah jumped up and down with an orange and yellow giraffe. The clown kept twisting balloons and soon bowed and handed Rebecca a flower on a stem. With just a few more twists, he presented a purple and green crown to Andrew.

"Thank you," Rebecca said. "This is so sweet." She leaned over to Elijah. "Tell him thank you."

"Thank you, Mister Clown," Elijah said. "This is awesome. Best thing ever!"

"Thank you," Noah echoed, rubbing the balloon so it squeaked.

Henry waved and Polly smiled, watching her kids enjoy something so wonderfully simple.

As the kids came back, Elijah waved his giraffe up at Polly. "We're hungry," he announced.

"What are you hungry for?"

"Jerry wants popcorn," he said.

"Jerry the giraffe?"

Elijah nodded. "And Manny says he wants a hot dog."

"Manny the monkey?" Polly asked. "I'm sure that we could ask the clown to make balloon food for them. How does that sound?"

He shook his head vehemently. "They want real food and Jerry said I could share it with him."

Andrew took the crown off his head and attempted to put it onto Rebecca's. She'd been paying attention to Elijah, so had no idea what he was doing and batted his hand away.

"What?" she snapped.

He backed away. "I was just trying to give you my crown." Andrew gave her a silly grin. "Because you're my princess." As soon as the words were out of his mouth, he glanced at Henry. "Sorry. I was just being funny. I didn't mean anything. I promise."

"It's all right," Henry said. He squeezed Polly's hand. "Shall we head into the carnival? First up at the church tent is loose meat sandwiches."

All of the kids drooped at that, as did Polly.

"What?" Henry asked. "They're awesome."

"I wanted a corn dog," Polly complained.

Elijah looked up, confused.

"It's a big, long hot dog." Polly held out her hands. "This long. And it's dipped in cornbread and it is the best thing ever."

"Can I have one?"

She patted his head, ruffling what little hair he had. "I think you should. And we'll get popcorn and lemonade and cotton candy and ice cream."

"Maybe we could save some of that for tomorrow," Henry said. "Start with a corn dog today. I'm having a loose meat sandwich, though." He took cash out of his wallet and handed some to Rebecca and more to Polly.

She grinned at him. "I'm already carrying, dude."

"Oh. Sorry." He laughed. "I just wanted the kids to be able to have what they wanted."

"Can we go off on our own?" Rebecca asked. Then she stopped and put her hand on Noah's chair. "Nah. That's okay. We'll stick around."

"You go," Polly said. "We've got this. We'll have lunch and find you later." She pointed at Rebecca's back pocket. "Set your alarm. Every hour you have to text me and tell me that you're okay. If I have to look for you, it will go badly."

"Got it." Rebecca grabbed Andrew's hand.

They stopped when Henry said, "Wait!"

Andrew dropped Rebecca's hand like it was a hot potato. "Sorry," he said.

Henry laughed. "No. I just wanted to give you some more money to ride the rides."

"Mom gave me some this morning." Andrew patted his back pocket.

"First of all," Henry said. "Put that in your front pocket. This might be Bellingwood, but there are a lot of people in town today and they would be glad to steal your wallet. Secondly, you aren't responsible for Rebecca's fun today. I've got it." He handed Rebecca more cash and she held it in her hand.

"Where should I put it?" she asked.

Henry turned back to Polly, who smiled. "Tuck it in your bra."

"Polly!" Rebecca said, completely scandalized.

"Trust me. It works. Just slide it in at the top, right under your shoulder. You'll be fine."

Rebecca handed the money to Andrew. "Put that in your other front pocket. I'm not doing what Polly said." She grabbed his hand again and they ran for the entrance to the carnival.

Henry pushed Noah's chair and Polly took Elijah's hand as they entered the mayhem behind the front gates. They headed for the picnic tables and she looked down toward the dunk tank. Yellow tape still surrounded it and she shook her head. They had to catch this guy fast.

"Hey there," Heath said, coming up beside them. "We were wondering when you'd get here."

"Where's your brother?" Polly asked.

"Getting ride tickets. We're going to show Noah and Elijah the tilt-a-whirl."

Noah pointed at his leg.

"No biggie," Heath said. "Hayden will carry you in and sit with you. It's all cool. We asked."

Polly smiled at him, then impulsively stepped forward and hugged his neck, kissing his cheek. "Thank you guys."

"Maybe they should ride a couple of rides before they eat," Henry suggested. "You know. Too much grease in their tummies?"

"Hey, big man," Hayden said. "Are you ready to hit a couple of the rides?" He swung Elijah up onto his shoulders and put his hand on Noah's head. "We're your tour guides for this part of the extravaganza. Whatever you want us to do, we'll do it."

Polly watched the four of them leave. "How did we get so lucky?" she asked.

Henry held out the balloon animals that he'd taken from the boys. "I don't know, but I'm really ready for a sandwich. Won't you at least sit with me?"

"You get yours and find a seat. I'll be back with my corndogs."

CHAPTER TWENTY-FIVE

After another restless night, Polly was completely exhausted come Friday morning. Since no one but Henry was out of bed yet, she assumed the rest of the household was just as tired. Wednesday and Thursday had been nonstop. As much fun as this week was, she was ready for life to find its way back to normal and yet, they were only halfway through the celebration. This evening the carnival was closing early. But that didn't mean there would be nothing to do. The town was turning into a huge picnic ground at five thirty, each church pulling out all of the stops. Polly still didn't know where they were going to eat. At seven, she was playing in the community band concert and when that was finished, the downtown area would fill up for the street dance.

The kids had been to every event they could find at least three times and had come home with quite a haul, from tote bags and notepads, to stuffed bears, sticker books and everything in between. There was more candy in the house now than any Halloween previous. Noah and Elijah had ridden in the Bellingwood wagon during the parade yesterday, but it felt like every adult that knew Polly had gathered 'just a few pieces' of the candy that was tossed to the crowd for the boys. By the end of the evening, even Elijah announced he'd eaten too much. It had been a successful day.

Polly had answered questions all day about the murder. Everyone in town was talking about it; everyone wanted to hear about what she knew. If they weren't pestering her with questions, they stared and whispered as she walked through the grounds. Rebecca and Andrew had enjoyed bringing her the latest gossip and rumors, just to watch her roll her eyes.

They'd gone to the Memorial Hall for a historical presentation in the evening. Nate Mikkels was part of the cast portraying the early settlers who arrived in Bellingwood. Joss, Cooper, Sophie, and her parents had found Polly and her crew. Sophie and Cooper were fascinated with Elijah and Noah, especially Noah's wheelchair, and once Sophie had climbed up and sat on his lap, she wasn't prepared to be pried off. Noah beamed at the attention. Though the portrayal was interesting, it was hardly enough to hold the attention of small children. Once Nate was finished, Polly escorted her young charges out and they'd headed home.

Henry was already gone this morning. He wanted to check on the clean-up progress at the Bell House. Polly had tossed and turned through much of the night, worrying about whether it would be ready for people to tour. If things were going to fall apart on her, she wanted that information today so she could announce the change in plans. Jeff had worked hard to coordinate the tour with the Chamber of Commerce's Ice Cream Social held in the auditorium.

Noah and Elijah had fallen in love with carnival food, which surprised no one. Henry complained that they were going to eat him out of house and home. Polly reminded him that they weren't actually eating at the house or the home, and he hadn't appreciated her humor. She sat with the boys last night while they chattered through their day before finally falling asleep. They had gone on and on about all of the new foods they'd tried. Polly could hardly believe they'd never eaten corn on the cob, but yesterday, when she'd put a plate filled with ears of corn on the table in front of them, Elijah and Noah were in awe. She didn't want to take the time to explain the difference between sweet corn and field corn, so she'd let them imagine fields and fields of the wonderful treat. Next week they could go out to the Sycamore House sweet corn plot on the other side of the creek and help Eliseo. He'd already harvested a great deal of it for the sweet corn feed under the sycamore trees yesterday, but there would be more to pick.

Obiwan stirred beside her and Han jumped to a standing position, his back leg firmly planted on Polly's thigh.

"Andrew texted me," Rebecca said from the doorway. Polly nodded for her to come in. "He's sick and Kayla's hanging out with her sister again today." She dropped heavily onto Henry's side of the bed with a dramatic sigh. "What am I supposed to do now?"

"Suffer with us?" Polly asked. "And what's wrong with Andrew?"

"His mom said he might have gotten heat stroke yesterday. He just wouldn't wear that hat I bought him."

Rebecca had brought a straw hat back from New Mexico for Andrew, but for some reason, he thought it was too colorful. It had a gorgeous band around it, but other than that, it was a great hat. Rebecca had also brought back a floppy hat for Polly, who had no problem wearing it to keep the sun at bay.

"He'll feel better this afternoon," Polly said.

"Yeah, but his mom won't let him spend time in the sun." Rebecca leaned over and hugged Obiwan's neck. "Boys are so dumb."

Polly laughed. "You live in a house full of them right now. That kind of talk will just get you in trouble."

"Hayden isn't dumb and Henry isn't dumb. The little boys haven't gotten to the point where their brains turn to mush."

"What about Heath?" Polly asked.

Rebecca turned to her. "Sometimes he's dumber than everybody else. But at least I understand him. He's so worried that he'll screw up again that he won't try anything."

Polly furrowed her brow. "He won't try things? What are you talking about?"

"He's missed out on a bunch of dates and parties this summer because he's afraid they'll do stuff he doesn't want to do. That's why he's working all the time. Well that, and he wants his own car so he isn't borrowing your truck."

"How do you know this?"

"People talk when the adults aren't in the room." Rebecca frowned at her. "Surely you know that."

"I guess," Polly said with a laugh. "What kinds of parties? What dates?"

"Oh, just girls from school. There was a big party at Mary Watkins' house last night that he didn't go to. She called and invited him and everything. But her parents weren't going to be back until late and he said it was just an invitation for trouble."

"What does Hayden say when Heath refuses to go to these things?" Polly asked.

"That Heath is an idiot, but then they have a fight, because Hayden isn't dating any girls either. He says it's because grad school is going to be really intense and he doesn't want to get involved and screw up his education." Rebecca put her head on Henry's pillow and looked at Polly. "Are relationships really that difficult? Sometimes it makes me think that Andrew and I don't really have a real relationship because it's just like we've always been."

Polly turned onto her side and leaned in, then spoke quietly. "Those boys are working to overcome a lot. They want to be something more than what people expect of them. Heath still thinks that people expect him to be a screw-up and a hood. Hayden thinks that people expect him to be successful so that he can take care of everything his parents couldn't."

"But they died," Rebecca said.

"Exactly. He created some huge shoes for himself to fill and even if it's obvious to the rest of us that he doesn't need to, he can't get past it."

"Are they always going to be like this?"

"It's pretty much ingrained in them at this point," Polly said. "But that's why Henry and I are here. We can help them look at life with different eyes." She slung her arm over Rebecca and then surprised the girl by tugging her in close. "And you have to be my spy when we need to step in and redirect them."

Rebecca pushed her hair of out her face. "That's probably not in the sister-code."

"We'll keep it just between you and me."

~~~

Henry returned just as Polly and Heath finished cleaning the kitchen. Hayden was helping Noah get ready for the day and Elijah flitted from person to person, excited about another day in Bellingwood. His phrase "it's just the best" applied to nearly everything he sampled.

Polly leaned against the counter as he ran back and forth, asking questions, exclaiming over something he'd won the day before. The world would suck this innocent fun out of him soon enough. She was surprised that with all he'd lived through he was still so happy and easy-going. It was almost as if his brother had taken the weight of the world on his shoulders so Elijah could enjoy life with all the gusto he could muster.

"Whoa!" Henry said as Elijah tore across the room to greet him. He swung the little boy up into his arms, squeezed him tight, then put him back down. "Are we nearly ready to head out?" he asked.

"I need to check on Rebecca, but the rest of us are close," Polly said.

Henry reached out to take Elijah's hand. "Why don't you and I take the dogs out one last time before we leave."

"Obiwan! Han! Let's go out!" Elijah yelled, running into the living room. "Obiwan, come," he commanded, standing in the center of the room.

Obiwan obediently stood in front of the little boy, wagging his tail.

"Let's go!" Elijah had started to get impatient.

"You need to head to the back door," Henry said. "The dogs will follow you."

Polly tapped on Rebecca's door. "Are you nearly ready?"

"Come in," Rebecca said. When Polly walked in, she shook her head. No matter how often Kayla cleaned this room up, Rebecca managed to overcome order with chaos. The girl was sitting on her bed, looking at her phone. "I'm a terrible girlfriend."

"Maybe," Polly said. "Maybe not. What did you do?"

"Andrew's sick and all I could think about was that I didn't have anybody to go to the carnival with today. I should do something nice for him instead of making him feel guilty for leaving me all by myself."

The words "Drama, much?" rolled around in Polly's head, but she didn't say them out loud. Adolescence wasn't coming easy for Rebecca, and Polly was a little concerned she'd have to deal with these emotional upheavals until Rebecca had her own children.

"Did he say something to make you feel guilty?" Polly asked.

"No." Rebecca shook her head and looked up at Polly with the most pitiful face she'd seen in a while. "I texted Kayla and told her that I was upset that Andrew couldn't go with me. I told her that I felt left out because she couldn't go with me either. She told me I was being selfish."

Thank goodness for Kayla. Polly sat down beside her on the bed. "So what can you do about it?"

"Maybe I should just stay here all day. I don't want to make you all feel bad because I'm being selfish and grumpy."

"That's one option," Polly said. "Do you have any others? Now think really hard about this. Your life as you know it, depends on your answer."

Rebecca looked at the floor. Polly could see the wheels turning in the girl's head.

"I could get over myself and be a good sister to Hayden and Heath and help you with Noah and Elijah?" Rebecca smiled. "That's the right answer, isn't it? But I don't want to."

"Have you ever gone anywhere with me and Henry and not had a good time?" Polly asked.

"I don't know."

"Well, I do. You have a great time with us. So paste a smile on your face until it comes naturally, get your head out of your ..." Polly stopped. "Out of the bad place, and perk up. You have two minutes to pout and sulk and then it's over. Got it?"

"Can I have three?" Rebecca gave her a weak smile.

"You have until Henry and Elijah come back inside with the dogs. Then I expect happy Rebecca to walk around town with us today."

"I'll try."

Polly stood up, crossed her arms in front of her and said in her best Yoda voice. "Do. Or do not. There is no try."

Rebecca giggled as Polly left the room.

~~~

The entire group strolled in through the gates of the carnival at eleven thirty. Elijah tugged at Henry's sleeve, desperate to check out his favorite food vendor.

"Get two corndogs for me," Polly said as Henry allowed himself to be pulled away.

Hayden bent over Noah's chair. "What about you?"

"Hot dog, please."

"Rebecca?" Hayden asked. "What would you like?"

"A hot dog with everything," she said.

"We'll be back soon. Heath and Hayden took off with Noah, and Rebecca spun around twice. "Lemonade?"

"Sounds great." Polly led the way and they ordered drinks for everyone.

As they walked back to the picnic tables, laden with trays of lemonade and water, Rebecca stopped and nudged Polly. "That guy looks just like Santa Claus. Is he the one staying at Sycamore House?"

Polly followed Rebecca's eyes until she found the man and nodded. "Yes. That's him."

"Who's that with him? An elf?"

This time, Polly had to peer around a few people to see who Rebecca was referring to. Who would he be with here in Bellingwood? He'd come into town alone and she was pretty sure no one else was staying in his room.

Kristen would have said something. She had a tendency to want to tell Polly everything. Kristen was pretty well creeped out by both of the men staying on the first floor of the addition. Even if Mr. Nicholas looked like Santa, he'd given both Polly and Kristen a bad feeling.

A young man, probably in his early twenties or late teens, was being forcibly led through the crowd by Mr. Nicholas. He was short, probably only five-three, which was what Rebecca's comment was all about. The look on his face was of pure terror.

In a split second, Polly dumped her tray of drinks in a trash can as she pushed through the people to get closer to the two men. She managed to come to a stop right in front of them and put her hand out.

"Mr. Nicholas. Is that right?" she asked with a smile.

He squinted at her.

"I'm Polly Giller," she said. "From Sycamore House." He'd met her several times. There was no reason for him to not recognize her. Strange.

"Oh," he said. "Yes. Of course."

Polly put her hand down to her side, wiped it on her shorts and then stuck it back out again, this time toward the young man whose arm was still gripped by Mr. Nicholas. "You are?"

"Bob..."

Before he could finish his sentence, Mr. Nicholas interrupted. "I'm sorry, Miss Giller. We're in a hurry."

"What could you possibly have to do today?" she asked him. "It's a beautiful day to be at the fair, don't you think?" Polly stepped to his side and took him by the arm. "You should have lunch with my family. I'd love for you to meet my husband. Maybe we'll stop here and pick something up for you and your young friend. My treat."

"I'm not his..."

The boy stopped speaking when Mr. Nicholas wrenched his arm. "We're busy. I don't have time for lunch. Thank you very much for the invitation."

Polly looked around and smiled to herself. "Before you go, I'd like you to meet another of my friends. Just this way." She refused to let go of his arm and called out. "Bert! Officer Bradford. How are you today? Isn't it a wonderful day?"

"Hello, Ms. Giller," Bert Bradford said. "It *is* a good day. Not as hot as yesterday. I'm certainly glad of that."

"Officer Bradford, I'd like you to meet one of my guests at Sycamore House. This is Mr. Nicholas. Isn't that funny? Everyone says he looks like Santa Claus." With her free hand, she gestured to his white beard. "I'll bet you are busy every holiday season. I was just insisting that Mr. Nicholas join us for lunch. Have you eaten yet, Bert?"

He took a deep breath and looked around. "I was thinking about a piece of pie. Those Lutheran women certainly know how to make pie. Are you going back that way?"

"Why yes we are," Polly said. She turned a helpless Mr. Nicholas to the right and as they brushed past a large group of kids, the young man he'd had with him pulled away and took off.

"Oh I'm sorry," Polly said. "Your friend must have had other business."

Mr. Nicholas shook his head and stopped walking. "You ruined everything."

Polly took a step and stood in front of him, leaning in toward his face. "I did what?" she said as quietly and menacingly as possible.

"You ruined it."

"What exactly did I ruin?" she asked.

As if a veil lifted from his face, the smile returned and he straightened up. "It was nothing. I didn't mean to imply anything. It was just a business deal that we were putting together. If that doesn't work out, I can always move on to something different. Now, if you'll excuse me, I really must be going. Thank you for your luncheon invitation."

Polly smiled at him, took her phone out and snapped his picture. "My friends won't believe me when I tell them that I almost had lunch with Santa Claus."

"What was that, Ms. Giller?" Bert asked, after the man had practically run away from them.

"That was our murderer, I do believe," Polly said. "And I think he is preying on his next victim."

"Won't he go back and get that young man? I should check on him."

"That young man skedaddled," Polly said. "He's here working the carnival. He knew something bad was up with that guy and bolted as soon as he could. We won't see him again. Now I need to get this picture sent off to Aaron. Do you want it, too?"

Bert grinned. "Like I didn't already take one." He waggled his phone at her. "When you act that odd around a stranger, there's a good reason. I wasn't letting you get too far ahead of me."

"You're a smart man, Bert Bradford." Polly sent the picture to Aaron and then called him.

"Why are you calling, Polly?" he asked. "This is my day off."

"I didn't want to look for Deputy Hudson's number and I wanted to let you know that I know who the murderer is."

"Do you now," he said with a laugh.

"I may have been wrong about it being Mr. James," she said. "But I don't think I'm wrong about it being Mr. Nicholas. By the way, are you going to give me a copy of the last note?"

"You didn't get it?" Aaron sounded confused.

"No. Why?"

"You'll have it in just a few minutes," he said. "And I'll be sure to get this over to Deputy Hudson. How certain are you?"

"I saw him trying to haul a young man out of the carnival. I was certain enough to make sure that I introduced him to Bert Bradford."

"Bert's there with you?"

"Yes."

"I'm proud of you for actually involving law enforcement before you knock someone to the ground."

Polly grinned. "I would have knocked him down if I was a hundred percent sure. But I thought that might get me into trouble if he really is just an old guy who looks like Santa Claus."

"Good girl. You say he's staying at Sycamore House? They'd have his license plate?"

"He's probably on video getting in and out of his car," Polly said flatly. "But yes. Kristen would have all of that information."

"Now we're getting somewhere. I'll talk to you later."

Polly and Bert got back to the picnic tables as Rebecca and Henry returned with another tray of drinks.

"Where did you go?" Rebecca asked.

Polly slid her eyes to the little boys. "I'll tell you later."

CHAPTER TWENTY-SIX

Polly loved these street dances. By now all of the work of Bellingwood Days was nearly finished. The shopkeepers were relaxed, even though they stayed open late into the evening. Even Jeff finally wound down.

The band concert had gone well. Polly's nerves about playing in front of people were long gone. Over the last couple of years, she'd learned to just relax and enjoy herself. She and Henry had left the little ones at home for a quick nap this afternoon while they transported folding chairs to the back area of Sweet Beans so they could retrieve them later. With all of the traffic in town, the trucks were staying inside tonight.

"Hello!"

Polly looked up to see Lydia and Aaron approach with a massive group of people around them. She stood up and held Henry's hand as he stood with her. "Hello there. Is this your entire family?" Polly asked.

"We've been so spread out and crazy with all that's been going on," Lydia said, "that I haven't had a chance to introduce you to everyone. Sandy, come here. I want you to meet Polly."

Sandy Merritt looked more like Aaron than any of the other kids, though Polly thought their son, Jim, would take on his father's characteristics as he grew older. Sandy had an easy smile. Her bobbed, blond hair bounced a little as she walked. Polly bet that it was straight and long when she was in high school. It was that perfect hair that did exactly what its wearer wanted. It made Polly a little jealous. She unconsciously tucked a loose strand behind her ear before putting her hand out.

"I've heard a lot about you." Sandy took Polly's hand in a firm grip. "You're the one who keeps Dad on his toes."

Polly grinned. "I suppose I do. How long are you in town?"

"Driving home on Sunday." Sandy turned and beckoned to a girl that had to be the same age as Elijah and Noah. "This is Trinity."

Trinity stood beside her foster mother and put her little hand out. Polly shook it and waited while Henry did as well. "Mrs. Lydia says you have two boys my age. Are they here?"

Polly looked around and discovered the boys had wandered off to watch the band finish its setup. Rebecca and Andrew, who had been given permission to come out for the evening's activities, walked with them, pushing Noah. She pointed. "Those two boys right there." Polly gave Sandy a questioning look and the young woman nodded and smiled.

"Do you want to join them, Trinity?" Sandy asked.

"Yes please."

"I'll walk down with you," Polly said and put her hand out. The girl took it and waved goodbye to Sandy.

"Miss Sandy told me that there wouldn't be very many people in Bellingwood who looked like me," Trinity said.

Polly was always floored at how children just said what was on their minds. "There aren't usually," she said, "but this is a special week. And I think it's pretty wonderful you all are here. It doesn't really matter what color your skin is. Right?"

The girl shrugged and Polly realized that her comment made no sense to children who experienced racism as a matter of course. "Rebecca," Polly called out, causing everyone to turn. "Wait up."

She and Trinity hurried a little faster to catch up to the small group. "Hey guys. This is Trinity. Can she go with you?"

Rebecca reached out to take Trinity's hand from Polly. "Sure. We're just going to watch the band. Let me introduce you to Elijah and Noah. Noah's in the wheelchair because he broke his leg."

"How did he do that?" Trinity asked, allowing herself to be caught up in the movement of the group.

"Come back and find us when the band starts playing, okay?" Polly said.

"We got it," Rebecca replied.

Polly headed back down to her husband and the Merritt family. They were setting up chairs on the sidewalk and street in front of the coffee shop. She waved at Mark and Sal, who were coming out of Pizzazz across the street. Sal ran to catch up to Polly.

"Do you see this?" she asked, spinning around. "I'm all alone. Just me and my man, out for a night on the town."

"How'd you do that?"

"Kathryn, that lovely, wonderful lady, said that we should give her a chance to love on her grand-baby. Mark made me say yes before I could think about it."

"How was it?" Polly asked. "You know, leaving him again?"

Sal's face dropped. "I thought I was going to cry before Mark finally made me walk out of the door. Then I did cry for the first block we walked, but now I'm okay. In fact, it feels pretty good. Kathryn can handle anything and if something happens, I have my phone. Right?"

Polly slipped her arm around Sal's waist. "It will be just fine. You don't have to stay any longer than you want, either. When you can't take it anymore, you go home."

"That's what Mark said. But I want to enjoy this. It's such a huge party."

Henry was walking with a child and Polly realized that it was Elva's son, Samuel. She looked around for Elva and saw her walking down the street carrying Matty. Eliseo walked with the two girls on either side of him, their little hands tucked into his.

"How did you get Samuel?" Polly asked her husband.

He grinned. "Eliseo told him to come to me, so he did. I'm a magnet."

She caressed Samuel's cheek. "Yes you are. Do we have chairs for them?"

"Already taken care of." He tipped his head and Polly followed his eyes. Jason and Heath were carrying more chairs down the sidewalk from the alley behind the coffee shop.

Polly glanced down when someone slipped a hand into hers and realized it was one of Marilyn Erickson's twins. "Hello there," she said.

"Grandpa says you're nice. Are you?"

"I hope so. I think your grandpa is nice. What do you think?" Polly crouched down on her knees.

"Mama says he's a teddy bear."

"That's a good word for him," Polly said. Aaron was definitely a teddy bear, even if he was the sheriff.

"We have a black girl who is a cousin now. Trinity."

"What do you think about that?" Polly asked.

"She's pretty. And she knows how to tap dance. She said she knows how to do ballet, but I don't care about that. Mama says I get to learn how to dance. Maybe even this year."

Polly stood up as Marilyn arrived. "She's telling me all about learning to dance."

"I think it's time. Trinity certainly got her excited about it. Come on, munchkin. We have your seat all ready for you."

"I'm going to dance tonight," the little girl said. "Trinity said I could dance with her."

Polly looked around for Sal and discovered she'd gone back across the street. It felt like a circus was exploding around the coffee shop as more and more of her friends showed up. Camille and Elise came out of the coffee shop and Elise gave Polly a little wave, then slipped in and around the Merritts to an open space where they could set their chairs.

"Where's your mom?" Polly grabbed Jason's arm as he went past her a third time.

He looked to his right and then to his left. "I don't know. I haven't seen her all day."

"Brat," Polly said with a laugh. "Are you hanging out with us tonight?"

He grimaced. "Are you kidding me?"

She laughed again. "I was just asking. You know, you used to like me."

"I still like you, but everyone here is either little or they're old."

"I heard that," Beryl Watson said. She popped her hand against the back of Jason's head. "You can't beat the wisdom of a woman who's been around the sun more times than you. You might beat me in a footrace, but you'll never win a war of words."

"I wouldn't even try," he said, laughing. "I'm sorry. Old isn't a bad thing. But if you don't mind, I'm going to find my much younger friends now." He leaned so that he could see around her. "You got everything you need, Eliseo?"

"Thanks for your help," Eliseo said, rearranging one of his nieces in a chair. "I'll see you tomorrow."

Beryl turned around, moving to Polly's side. "Are these yours?" she asked Elva. "Why, they're adorable." Then all of a sudden, she grabbed Polly's hand and squeezed, making a coughing sound and wild gestures with her head.

"What?" Polly demanded.

Beryl hissed under her breath. "Look at him."

Eliseo had stood up straight and his entire demeanor changed. Polly watched as Sylvie crossed the street toward them. The man had it bad for her.

"You be good," Polly whispered back.

"When will that stupid woman figure this out?"

Sylvie stopped to greet Lydia and Aaron and was introduced around the family, then came over to Henry, Polly, and Beryl.

"Are my boys here?" Sylvie asked.

"Jason just took off. He says we're too old," Beryl grumped. "I told him, though."

"I'm sure you did," Sylvie said with a laugh. "And my other boy?"

"Eliseo's behind you," Beryl said. "If that's the other boy you're talking about."

Sylvie scowled at her. "I know where Eliseo is. I have eyes."

"He only has eyes for you. Are you going to torture him tonight or flirt with him?"

"Is Andrew with Rebecca?" Sylvie physically turned her back to Beryl.

"They're down near the stage watching the band set up," Polly said. "I told them to come back when it starts. I don't want the little ones that close to the speakers."

Sylvie nodded, then turned back to Beryl. "Are you going to harass me if I sit beside Eliseo tonight?"

Beryl leaned back, shocked. "Me? Harass you? Why would you accuse me of such a heinous thing?"

"Because you're a horrible person. What if I dance with him?"

"I will try to contain myself."

Suddenly Beryl laughed out loud. "Jason was right. Look at all of these children back here in the cheap seats."

"And old people," Polly said.

"No," Beryl said, pointing. "More children. Did you realize you had so many friends with little kids?"

Polly turned and saw Joss and Nate Mikkels walking up the middle of the street from the direction of the library. Nate was pushing a stroller and had chairs in bags slung over his shoulders, while Joss carried Cooper in her arms.

"Is this where the cowards are sitting?" Nate asked. "Little kids have effectively cancelled my loud music enjoyment."

Henry took the chairs from Nate's shoulder. "I wasn't sure I'd see you tonight." He opened the bags and unfolded chairs.

Joss smiled. "What do you mean?"

"Well, you know. That old Chevy of his always needs so much work. I was worried he'd be home tonight slaving over it before the car show tomorrow."

"Bet me," Nate said. "At least I've driven mine this summer. Your T-Bird is hiding in the garage. What? Are you worried that a bird will do something awful to it?"

Joss shook her head. "I never know quite what to think."

"You'll just hurt yourself, honey," Beryl said. "Men need to measure 'em whether they mean it or not."

Polly and Joss looked at each other, then at Beryl, and laughed.

"Where are your parents?" Polly asked Joss.

"They're coming. They'll take the kids home in an hour or so. We just wanted to all be out for a while tonight."

Kayla and Stephanie walked in with Jeff. Polly wondered if she should just close Sycamore House next week. Jeff and Stephanie looked exhausted.

"Where's Rebecca?" Kayla asked. "I haven't seen her in forever."

"She went down toward the stage," Polly replied. "But they should be back here pretty soon." She glanced at the growing crowd around them. "She's wearing her lime green top. That should help you find her."

"Bye," Kayla said, waving at her sister. Stephanie raised a weary hand in acknowledgment.

"Here. Sit." Polly pointed at two empty chairs.

"We have our chairs back by Camille and Elise," Stephanie said. "I just wanted to say hi. I don't see you much anymore."

Polly stepped forward and hugged the young girl. "I miss you, too. It's weird to not be in the office anymore."

"Did you find the murderer yet?" Jeff asked. He gave Polly a hug. "I've been worried about you."

"I think so," she said. "But I need to ask Aaron some questions. I've been so busy that I haven't had time to even think about it."

"You and me both, girlfriend."

Polly took his arm. "You look tired. Are you going to make it through the weekend? Is there anything I can do to help?"

"No. I've got it. I'll sleep all day Sunday and pop right back to normal."

"You and Stephanie will take Monday off," Polly said. "And if I don't think you've rested enough, you're taking Tuesday, too."

Jeff closed his eyes slowly and then reopened them. "I might take you up on that. There isn't much going on. We have a wedding next weekend, but anymore those things just take care of themselves." He gave her a tired grin and slapped his own face. "I jinxed next weekend, that's for sure. Whatever can go wrong, will go wrong. Why don't I ever learn?"

"It will be fine," Polly said. "Just fine. Are you staying?"

He shook his head. "I just wanted to say hello, hear the band play a few numbers and then I'm going home. Ibuprofen will take me to my happy place tonight."

"I don't want to know about your happy place," Polly said.

"Honestly, this week, it's any place that my body doesn't ache." He laughed. "You need a hot tub. But make it a big one."

"That's not the worst idea in the world," Polly said. "But first I just want to get the house habitable."

"What happened with the sewer smell?"

Polly frowned. "It's not all gone, but it's better than it was. We're still running fans. Henry's plumber friend got a good cleanup crew in, but that stuff landed on the dirt floor and tucked itself into nooks and crannies everywhere. They're coming back next week to make another run at it."

"He had to have just died when that happened to him." Jeff laughed. "What a horrible job. Who chooses to be a plumber, knowing that at any time the worst stuff that humanity creates might end up all over them?"

"Only saints and crazy people," Polly said. "I'm pretty sure Liam Hoffman is a little bit of both. He's such a good guy. I hated laughing at him, but I could hardly help myself."

"It's called schadenfreude and you're the master of it."

Polly stood tall and preened. "Yes I am." She poked him in the side. "Nice word, by the way."

"I have to keep up with you," he replied. "Are you good to go tomorrow?"

"Yeah," she said, nodding. "We'll just burn candles and get through the day. Besides, this will encourage people not to linger. Right?"

Laughter burst from him. "Now there's how you handle it. Okay, I'm going to wander around and say hello. I probably won't see you again. I'm outta here."

"Jeff?" Polly stopped him and then pulled him in for a tight hug. "Thank you. I never say that enough, but thank you."

"It's my job."

"It's more than your job, you nut. Let me tell you thank you and be okay with it."

"Okay." He pulled back, then quickly kissed her cheek. "See you later."

Dusk had settled on the town, street lights were on, and the noise of people talking to each other continued to increase. Polly looked to see if her family was returning and she saw Hayden coming up from Sycamore House. He'd met some of his friends in Ames for dinner and promised to be back in time for the dance. She waved at him and stood up on her tip toes to try to find Rebecca.

"Good evening," a voice boomed out from the stage. "Welcome to Bellingwood's Sesquicentennial celebration. We hope you've had a great time this week and it's so good to see this big crowd filling our downtown. Wouldn't it be great if it was always this busy?"

Cheers and applause rang through the streets.

"Since I have you all here..."

This time it was groans that echoed off the storefronts.

"Just kidding. Please welcome our band, 'Lenny and the Misfits' and have a great night."

The opening chords of the Rolling Stones' "Start Me Up" brought people to their feet and Polly couldn't help but join them. She dragged Henry out of his chair, then clapped her hands over her head and moved into an open space in the street. If this was how they started the evening, it was going to be fun.

Out of the corner of her eye, she caught a glimpse of Rebecca's lime green shirt moving toward the coffee shop and reached out to grab Henry's hands. He just smiled while they danced, singing the familiar lyrics at the top of their lungs.

CHAPTER TWENTY-SEVEN

Alone in the house, Polly embraced the silence. Henry had taken off to do some last minute cleaning of his T-Bird for the car show and Rebecca was with Beryl, helping as the woman judged the quilt show. Sandy Merritt had asked last night if Noah and Elijah would like to go to the carnival with Trinity for a couple of hours. The boys had been ecstatic and Polly couldn't refuse those faces. Hayden was at the Bell House. He wanted to make sure that things were in good shape for this afternoon's tours. Jason had talked to Heath last night about helping him and Eliseo get the horses ready today. Polly didn't think Heath was needed, but Jason was making an effort and Heath responded well to it.

She worked to pick up the living room. Hayden and Heath made sure to get the sofas back into place, but there were books and toys scattered everywhere. Once she finished, she headed for the dining room and kitchen. It wasn't horrible, but there hadn't been time to do any of their normal pickup around the house. When they got home each night, everyone was exhausted. Even though they stayed up to play and talk, the idea of cleaning was on no one's mind. Polly moved things back and forth to whichever room they belonged and made sure the dishwasher was filled with dirty dishes. She was wiping down the stovetop when her phone rang. She patted her back pocket and couldn't find it, looked around the room and tried to remember where she'd last had it. The ringing persisted. It was close. Polly tracked it down to the dining room table under a pile of folded towels that needed to be in the kids' bathroom. The number was a Boone phone number, but she didn't recognize it.

"Hello, this is Polly Giller."

"Ms. Giller, this is Deputy Hudson. I'm sorry it has taken me so long to get back to you."

"That's okay," Polly said. "What's up?"

"I wondered if you had any time at all today we could meet. I know you're busy with Bellingwood Days."

Polly really didn't have to be anywhere for a while. "I'm free right now. Where are you?"

"I can be in Bellingwood in fifteen minutes. Is there a good place we could meet?"

Polly laughed out loud. "I'm partial to the coffee shop. In fact, I could use more coffee. How about you?"

"I'm always up for coffee. Nine thirty?"

"That sounds great."

She'd asked Aaron last night if he knew anything more about the case. After tagging Mr. Nicholas as a possible suspect, that was the last thing Polly had heard. Deputy Hudson hadn't gotten back to her with the contents of the note that had been found on the body in the dunk tank and with all that was going on, Polly didn't have time to confront the young woman. They'd either figure it out or they wouldn't. She sincerely hoped they would figure it out ... and soon. Polly wasn't ready to find any more bodies. This was the worst she'd ever experienced and it was long past time to be finished with it.

Polly headed down the back steps to take her truck, then realized it was foolish to drive those two and a half blocks, so slipped out the garage door and walked down the lane to the garden on the corner and waited to cross the street. It took more time than usual with all the traffic in town. As exciting as it was to have so many people visiting Bellingwood, she would be glad for some of the sanity to return. When a small break in traffic arrived, she ran across the highway and headed downtown.

"Good morning, Polly!"

She turned and saw Dylan Foster get out of a van behind his pizza shop, so she crossed the street. "How are you?"

"Good. That was fun last night."

Polly nodded. "It really was. I love that Bellingwood turns out in force for these events."

He laughed out loud. "Yeah. You'd almost think we never had anything going on."

"Are you opening early today?"

Dylan pushed the back hatch up. "No. I didn't have the heart to keep my people late last night to clean up. I promised them I'd take care of it this morning." He smiled. "I can do that every once in a while. They work hard for me. Are you headed up for coffee?"

"You know me, don't you," Polly said.

"I do see you in there quite often," he agreed with a laugh. "But then I shouldn't say much. Lisa tells me that I was killing our budget with my new coffee addiction."

"You're kidding."

He chuckled. "Yep. But it's nice to have excellent coffee right across the street. And Sylvie's muffins? Those are cruel." He frowned and shook his head. "Am I an idiot?"

"I don't think so." Polly was confused.

"We've been buying our cookies from the same place we get our dairy products." He rolled his eyes. "Don't you dare tell Sal that it didn't occur to me to buy from the bakery. Will they sell to me at wholesale prices?"

Polly nodded. "They're working on a deal with Joe at the diner. Talk to Camille or Sylvie. They'll set you up." She saw the sheriff's vehicle drive by. "I need to go. I'm actually meeting someone. It's nice to talk to you."

"You too," he said.

She heard him mumbling to himself about cookies and muffins

as he headed for the back door of Pizzazz. Before Sylvie knew what was happening, she was going to be too busy to do anything but bake.

Polly crossed the street and waved at Tab Hudson as the deputy got out of her SUV. "Good morning," Polly called out.

Deputy Hudson nodded and smiled. She got to the door before Polly and held it open as they walked in. "I haven't been in here yet," the young woman said. "What's good?"

"Everything," Polly replied. "My friend, Sylvie, runs the bakery. If you want delectable sweet stuff, it's here. And they have great coffee."

"I could use some great coffee. This has been a long week."

Polly leaned over and whispered conspiratorially. "This is on me. Order what you want. You should know I'm a part owner."

"Really? Don't you own Sycamore House and the hotel out on the highway, too?"

"I do. Renovating old buildings seems to be my thing. Luckily I married a contractor who isn't afraid of a challenge."

"That has to be fun," Deputy Hudson said.

"For the most part it is," Polly agreed. They were behind several people in line. "I won't talk to you while you figure out what you want. My order is pretty standard."

"What do you get?"

"In the summer I either get an iced cold brew or if I'm feeling particularly needy, I get an iced caramel mocha."

"Needy? I might be feeling needy," Deputy Hudson said with a smile.

A booth opened against the wall after they got their orders and the two women sat across from each other. Silence fell as they took a few drinks. Deputy Hudson's eyes had lit up at the plate filled with chocolate muffins, so they each had to have one.

"What was it you needed to speak to me about, Deputy Hudson?" Polly asked.

"Call me Tab."

Polly smiled. "Okay, Tab. Is that short for Tabitha?"

The young woman laughed. "Yes. My mother had a thing for

Bewitched. Her name is Samantha and she couldn't help herself. But I made my family shorten it when I went to school."

"Not Tabby?"

"Oh no. My older brother called me Stabby Tabby. I wasn't going to put up with that from anyone else."

"It sounds like you knew what you wanted," Polly said with a small laugh.

"Mom and Dad told me I was bossy. It never sounded like a bad thing. I just knew what the right thing was and let everybody know they should fall in line." Tab Hudson smiled when she spoke, but it didn't sound like she was joking. "Anyway, I wanted to show you this." She reached into a pocket and pulled out a folded piece of paper. "I probably should have gotten it to you earlier, but ..." her words trailed off as she unfolded the note and pushed it across the table.

Polly took a deep breath and read it to herself.

It was nice to meet you
To the tale, I'll be true

You'd never have guessed
This all was a test.

Your new home, oh so grave
There are none you can save.

The research I've done
Will show you're the one.

"Do you think he's finished?" Polly asked.

"It sounds like it, but Sheriff Merritt ..." she paused and a flash of something flitted across her face. "and apparently many of the others believe that you'd have good insight into this."

Polly wrinkled her forehead as she took in Tab Hudson's attitude. "Have I done something to upset you, Deputy?"

The young woman looked at the floor first on one side and

then the other. "I guess not."

"But something is bothering you. What is it?"

"Your whole story. It's ridiculous. I hope I don't offend you, but I just have to say it. Nobody finds dead bodies like you do. Everybody acts like it's some supernatural gift that you have. They think you're infallible. You're just a person. Nobody special." She put her hands up. "I didn't mean that. I know you do a lot of good things here in Bellingwood, but this..." She waved her hand across the top of the paper. "This all doesn't make sense."

Polly sat back in the booth and smiled.

"What's that smile about?" Tab asked.

"I like you."

The girl laughed a little and gave Polly a perplexed look. "What do you mean by that?"

"It's awesome to have someone around who doesn't just believe I'm a dead body magnet. I love it," Polly said. "You haven't offended me in the least."

"Really?"

Polly took out her phone and opened it to her notes program, then swiped until she found the earlier notes the murderer had left. "This person believes that I have some strange power and was willing to murder people to prove it."

"I need to let you know that we interviewed Peter Nicholas."

"I didn't know his first name." Polly said.

"We brought him in for questioning and the young man you saw him with at the carnival was not his next victim. Would you believe me if I told you that Bob Jester is an elf?"

"Ummm." Polly laughed. "No. I mean, yes? What?"

"Those two travel together to perform as Santa and an elf. A company in Fort Dodge had hired them for a Christmas-in-July gig and Jester knew about Bellingwood Days. He has a brother who's one of the carnival workers. So Nicholas decided to stay in Iowa and come to the festival here. It was a vacation before their next event. Bob Jester, though, informed his buddy that he wasn't doing any more elf performances. He was tired of it all. When you stopped them, Nicholas was dragging his business partner away from Jester's brother and friends so they could have a ..." She raised her hands and made air quotes. "Discussion."

"Well that's embarrassing," Polly said.

"What do you mean?"

"I was just sure the murderer had to be staying at Sycamore House." She flipped to the third note and pointed at it. "Room with a view. And he mentions barking. He would have seen me out with the dogs." Polly flipped to the next note. "He says he was bold when he reached me. Mr. Nicholas went out of his way to introduce himself to me. I thought it was strange at the time, but people are often odd when they first meet someone. And now, you show me this. He knows about my new house which overlooks the cemetery. He says again that we met." Polly stopped and stared at the paper in front of her.

"What about the rest of your guests?" Tab asked.

"The two couples who are staying upstairs are related to people who live in Bellingwood. I can find out who exactly, but those reservations were made a long time ago. They arrived in the middle of June, just after school was out. One of the ladies is a teacher. They're leaving in a week or so." She sat forward. "This has to be related to last fall."

"What happened then?"

"The town was full of people who were here to see Muriel Springer's ghost." Polly nodded her head up and down. "And a group of people came to Sycamore House to ask questions about something. I don't remember why exactly, but I got trapped in the conference room with them. All of a sudden instead of talking about the ghost, they asked me about finding dead bodies. There was one guy who scared me a little bit. He looked like a professor. I tried my best to just ignore it and let it go. But I do remember feeling icky." She spat out the word. "He kept insisting that my gift was going to be exposed. He wanted to do research." Polly tapped the note in front of her. "It has to be him. But neither of the men look like that guy."

"Did he stay at Sycamore House that time?"

"No. If it wasn't Mr. Nicholas, it has to be that other guy. I knew it all along," Polly said. She realized her voice had gotten excited and she pressed herself back in the seat. "Sorry. It was Mr. James. Did you investigate him when I talked to Aaron?"

"We couldn't find much information about him just from the little bit he gave your receptionist and we haven't been able to find him yet."

"So. Weird question," Polly said. "Do you think he's killed before?"

"I'd have to say probably not. He didn't finish what he'd done to that first girl you found on the road. He was in too much of a hurry when he dumped her."

"He dumped her?" Polly asked.

Tab frowned. "You didn't know? We found where she'd climbed out of the ditch. It was just luck that you came upon her when you did."

"She knew my name. And she knew that I find dead bodies."

"I read the report," Tab said. "But you thought she was from around here, right?"

"Yes, but Anita said she was from Saint Louis. That means he must have told her about me."

"More than likely."

"Tab," Polly said. "Do you believe he killed all these people simply to find out whether or not I'd discover their bodies?"

With very precise movements, Deputy Hudson took another drink from her coffee cup, then broke the second half of her muffin into smaller pieces. She put a piece of chocolate into her mouth and chewed it slowly before taking another drink, all the while, staring at Polly. "It's beginning to look that way. Even if I have difficulty believing this to be true about you, I can't discount the fact that someone else believes it." She huffed a laugh. "The truth is, I'm probably in a small minority of people who refuses to accept it."

"If he goes public with this terrible research, my life is over," Polly said. "Even if he's caught and ends up in prison, my name will be associated with him forever. It won't be fair to my family or even the people here in Bellingwood. The last thing they need is notoriety because of me." She grimaced. "It was bad enough when I bought the school and started making big changes in town. Half the town hated me, some thought it was the greatest thing, and the rest chose to ignore me. If I bring this down on Bellingwood, it will be awful."

Tab nodded, listening thoughtfully.

"That's one of the reasons I trust Aaron like I do," Polly continued. "He is always willing to protect me. As soon as law enforcement shows up, he lets me leave and I'm not exposed."

"That won't change, Polly."

"But it will if this guy gets a chance to tell his story." Polly put her head in her hands. "We should go back to Sycamore House and ask more questions. Kristen will know if his car has been around the last couple of days. Maybe we can get into his room and you can..." She shrugged. "I don't know, dust for prints? Maybe you'll find him in some database?"

"We can do that."

"I'm sick to my stomach right now," Polly said. "I don't want to lose my life here because some crazy man wants to prove that I have a special gift. I just can't."

Tab reached across the table and took Polly's hand. "We'll do whatever we can to protect you. That won't change."

Polly felt tears threaten and took her hand back to brush them away. "I know. Thank you. I can't let this tear me apart. Not right now." She took a deep breath and sat up straight. "Let's go deal with this." She picked up trash from the table and dropped it into the waste can on the way out the door, then turned and waved to Camille and Sky. When she got outside, she swiped open a call to Henry.

"Hey there, Pol-doll," he said.

"Hey there. I just had coffee with Deputy Hudson and we're going back to Sycamore House to look for details. Do you remember me telling you about the creepy people at Halloween who wanted to study me and my gift? I think it's one of those guys. And I think it's that Mr. James. Mr. Nicholas isn't involved."

"Do you need me to come home?"

"No. I just needed to say it all out loud. I'm worried, Henry."

"That this is going to get all public and ugly?"

"Yeah. Right now I want to sell everything and run away."

"You know I'll go with you, right?"

"I love you so much. That's just what I needed to hear. Deputy Hudson isn't quite as worried as I am, but this has the potential to go really bad."

"It also could be nothing," he said. "Just breathe through it and we'll take it one step at a time. Just like we do with everything we have to face. You're the one who taught me that. Listen to yourself."

"Okay," she said with a sigh. "I'll let you know what we find out."

"Remember I love you."

"I love you too."

CHAPTER TWENTY-EIGHT

Rachel introduced Polly to several young people dressed in white aprons as she passed through the kitchen to the office. There was an Amy and a Ryan and … Even as Polly walked down the hallway to the office, she realized she hadn't paid a whit of attention. Students from the community college came through here all the time and she'd given up trying to remember all of their names.

"Is Jeff in?" Polly asked Kristen, nodding at Deputy Hudson.

"He and Stephanie are here somewhere. Maybe the auditorium. Do you want me to find them?"

"I can look," Polly said. "I'll be right back."

She headed out and stopped when she saw Jeff's curly hair inside the front door. He and Stephanie were coming in, so she waited.

"What are you doing here?" Jeff asked. "Shouldn't you be out and about chasing small children or renegade husbands?"

"I released them to the universe," Polly replied. "Do you two have a minute?"

Stephanie glanced back and forth and said, "I should really …"

281

"Deputy Hudson is here and we need to ask some questions about our guests."

Stephanie nodded. "We have time."

When they walked into the office, Deputy Hudson turned, a grim look on her face.

"What's happened now?" Polly asked.

"Miss Travis tells me that your Mr. James' car hasn't moved at all this morning. In fact, it's parked in the same place it was when she went home last night."

"You think he's in his room?"

"I believe we should check," Tab said. "I'll be right back." She strode out the door, her hand on her weapon when she realized Polly was following her.

"What are you doing?" she asked, stopping before she reached the side doors leading to the addition.

"Coming with you. If he's there and opens the door, I want to know what's going on. If he doesn't open the door," Polly waggled her phone. "I can unlock it."

Tab gave a quick shake of her head and drew her weapon, holding it in one hand as she pushed through the doors. Polly opened the inner door to the hallway of the addition and held it for the deputy to enter and then stood back as the young woman knocked and announced that she was from the sheriff's office and wanted to speak to Mr. James.

They waited a few moments before the deputy repeated the knock and command. After a third attempt, Tab nodded for Polly to open the door.

As soon as Polly stepped closer, she wrinkled her nose. "Crap," she whispered. "Don't you smell that?"

"Smell what?"

Polly beckoned the woman forward and leaned in. "That. Something is dead in there."

"Open the door," Tab said.

With two swipes, Polly heard the lock snick and pushed the door open. "I even had to be here when you were found, didn't I, Mr. James."

Deputy Hudson kept her gun out and swept through the room, pronouncing that it was clear before leaning over the man sitting in a chair.

"Please let me call him," Polly said.

"Sheriff Merritt?"

"Yes. This last one. Let me do it."

"Sure. Go ahead. I was just going to call the office."

Polly swiped the call open to Aaron and waited.

"Polly, dear girl, what are you doing? I thought you were with Deputy Hudson this morning. Tell me she's still alive."

"Oh Aaron," Polly said. "What a horrible thought. Of course she is. But I'm afraid our murderer isn't. We just found him in the addition at Sycamore House."

"We?"

"I'm with Deputy Hudson."

"Why are you calling me then? She ..." Aaron chuckled. "What am I asking? Of course you're calling me. Tell the deputy that I'll get everyone moving."

"Thanks, Aaron." Polly ended the call and watched as the young woman worked with professional detachment.

"There's no gunshot wound, no bruises, no obvious foul play," Tab said. "I can't tell what killed him."

"Smell his breath," Polly said.

Tab chuckled. "He's not actually breathing, but I get it." She bent over and sniffed, holding back a shudder. Polly was glad that he hadn't been dead all that long before they found him. That would be a horrible mess to clean up. As it was, she would replace the chair he was seated in. Maybe Eliseo would just burn it for her.

"Well?"

"Almonds. I'd call this a suicide."

Polly took a step into the room and lifted her foot again, but stopped when Tab gave her a warning look. "Is there a note on him anywhere?" Polly asked. "He likes writing notes. I can't imagine that he'd let this opportunity pass without a few last words to me."

The deputy reached into her pocket. "I have no idea some days why I carry these and then on days like today, I'm glad they're here." She slipped a glove onto her right hand and patted the man's chest. "They're usually right here."

While Tab focused on the body, Polly gingerly stepped further into the room and sidled up to the desk. "It's over here," she murmured, angling her head so she could read it without going any further. As her eyes skimmed the words he had printed, she gulped. "He's insane," Polly said. "Absolutely insane."

"What does it say?" Tab crossed to Polly's side and read quietly to herself while Polly re-read the note.

Dear Polly,

While what I did was necessary, I find that no matter how hard I try, I can't live with myself. But the research is complete and the world now has recorded evidence of your role in bringing death from darkness into light. You are a treasure and should not be hidden in this small Iowa town. Police departments around the nation will want to use your gift to help them find those who are lost. You can no longer deny the power you have over death; it is time to use it to bring release and closure for those families who are looking for their loved ones. How could you possibly refuse a task so important?

The documentation for my research will be released to news agencies and other researchers Monday morning. You can't stop this. Please accept it and allow yourself to become what it is you were meant to be. I die knowing that I have changed the world for the better.

Yours,
Nathan James

"We'll stop it," Tab said. "We have until Monday morning to stop whatever it is he's done. Don't panic." She put her hand on Polly's shoulder, then drew out her phone and placed a call.

Polly was still trying to breathe through the haze that had fallen over her. This couldn't be happening.

"Anita?" Tab said. "I need you in Bellingwood right now. We have a situation. Bring all of your best email-cracking, internet-stopping tools." She listened for a moment. "Yeah, okay. I know that isn't a thing, but you need to be the one to deal with this computer. It's about Polly." Tab chuckled while she listened again. "I know, I know. Just get up here to Sycamore House. Okay?"

"What was that?" Polly asked.

"Anita has been trying to tell me for the last two years that I didn't know you and that once I did, I'd bend over backwards to help you out."

"Thanks?" Polly said.

"She was right. I won't let this go until you're safe from whatever it is that he has done."

The phone buzzed in Polly's back pocket and she took it out and read the text that came in, then smiled. Lydia had sent a message that she and Sandy would keep the boys as long as Polly needed them to be out of the way. They'd had a wonderful time at the carnival. Brian, Marilyn, and Sandy were taking the older kids up to a park to fish. They'd feed the boys supper and bring them back later in the evening if that was okay. If Polly needed them to spend the night, Lydia could always find room.

"Do you know Aaron's wife?" Polly asked Tab.

"Not very well. She seems like a really nice person, though. She's forever sending treats and goodies with the sheriff. I've been to a few parties at their house. Mrs. Merritt is a wonderful cook and she makes everyone feel at home."

"She's always taking care of me," Polly said. "I don't understand how she seems to know when I need her the most."

"She raised five kids. Guess that comes with the territory."

They both looked up at a sharp rap at the door. "Hey Hudson, what 'cha got here?" Stu Decker stepped just inside the door. "Have you been properly Polly-fied?"

"He's been around me much too often," Polly said. "For a very long time."

Tab smiled. "He's the source of most of our stories."

"Stories?" Polly raised her eyebrows at Stu.

"You do have a lot of them," he replied and stepped back into the hallway as two people dressed in coveralls came in. They left the gurney in the hallway and after a few minutes of conversation with Tab, approached the body.

"I should probably leave," Polly said. "Get out of your way. Let me know if you need anything more."

Tab nodded. "I will. Anita will probably be here all afternoon." She smiled. "The poor girl is stuck in her office so often; I think she actually looks forward to being onsite."

"No day off for her?" Polly asked.

"Not with something like this. She'll take care of you. Don't worry."

"Thanks." Polly slipped into the hallway, past another woman dressed in coveralls.

"You okay?" Stu asked her.

"I guess. This one has been really rough. And now I find out that this guy killed all of those innocent people because he was doing research on my freakin' gift." The more Polly thought about it, the angrier she became and the faster words flew out of her mouth. "My entire life is hanging by a thread because he thinks that it's my damned responsibility to go out there and find everyone that's ever been killed." Polly reached out and gripped Stu's arm. "Is he right? Should I give up my life to this? Am I being selfish because I want to live a quiet life with my family and friends?"

They walked through to the main hallway in Sycamore House, ducking and weaving past the large numbers of emergency personnel coming in the doors. Stu stopped and turned Polly toward him, taking her upper arms in his hands. "Listen to me, Polly Giller, and listen to me good. This man was insane. Anyone who thinks that murder is an appropriate way to do research is certifiable." He released her and stepped back. "And by the way, how many bodies have you found outside this area?"

"None," she said quietly.

"Do you believe that there were other deaths and murders in the rest of Iowa? Places you've traveled to?"

"Probably."

"It doesn't work anywhere else. His research was flawed."

"Thank God," she breathed out. Then she looked up at him in fear. "Unless it wasn't. What if he killed people in other parts of the state and they just haven't been found yet?"

"Think about it, Polly. He left notes on every victim you found. And from what I understand, you discovered that each note led to the next one."

"Yes."

"He's not a scientist. He was an odd man with an idea and he came up with a twisted manner of proving that it was true."

Polly nodded. "Thanks, Stu. I try to make this not about me and then I fall apart and lose my sense of equanimity."

"You're fine. Have you talked to Henry? I saw him at the car show, looking all proud of his pretty T-Bird. When are those boys going to finish the Woodies they wanted to restore?"

"No idea," Polly said. "They believed it wouldn't take very long, but there is never enough time to get much work done. I quit asking months ago because every time I did, poor Henry winced."

"Poor Henry needs to know what's going on down here today, you know." Stu said.

Polly nodded toward the office. "So do they. The last they knew I was heading out with Deputy Hudson and she had a firm grip on her weapon."

"I'll head back into the fracas," Stu said. "Take care of yourself. We've got your back. You know that, right?"

On impulse, Polly hugged him, giggling as she tried to negotiate the belt filled with technology, weaponry, and whatever else he carried. He returned the hug and then she headed into the office.

"What in the actual hell?" Jeff asked.

Polly laughed at him. "Where did you get that phrase?"

He pulled his head back. "I read things. But what's going on?"

"Well, it's kind of my thing, you know," Polly said. "At least this time law enforcement was there."

"So. Another man died in Sycamore House," Jeff retorted. "You and I have talked about this. I don't like the aura it lends to our image."

"Oh whatever."

Her phone buzzed in her pocket again, so she reached back and pulled it out to answer a call from Hayden.

"Hello, Hayden. What's up?" She'd had to get rid of 'hey' as her opening salutation with him. It sounded too strange.

"Hey Polly. I just had a visit from your friend down the block."

"Shawn Wesley? What did he want?" Polly walked into the hallway again. People were going in and out of the addition. She wondered if the body had been taken out yet.

"He wanted you to know that he hasn't seen anybody down here."

"Well, duh. Nobody's broken in since I talked to him," she replied. "Did he say anything to you about the reward?"

"Well, he did mention that if you wanted him to keep an eye on the place, you could at least pay him something."

"I see. Well, I told him that if he found the person who broke in, I'd give him two hundred and fifty bucks."

"Oh," Hayden said. "That's why he said that."

"Said what?"

"He mumbled something about his wife getting the money."

Polly ground her foot into the floor. "Damn it. He did do it."

"Do you really think so?" Hayden asked.

"Yes," she said. "I don't know what I'm going to do with him. He's such a loser and just doesn't want to make things better. His wife yelled at me when I was over there. She implied that he hadn't done it. I can't figure out whether he's more of a drain on her or a help. I don't think he works at all and I can't see him doing any kind of work around the house, even taking care of the kids."

"He was high," Hayden said. "And he reeked."

"Okay, thanks. I'm going to stick my nose in places it shouldn't be again. I'll talk to you later. How does it smell over there?"

"It's not great, but it isn't the worst thing in the world either. I'll light the oil lamps in that room."

"Thanks." Polly had purchased scented lamp oil, so maybe that would help.

She scrolled to Rebecca's phone number and called it.

"Hey Polly, what's shakin'?" Rebecca asked.

"Are you still with Beryl?"

"Yeah, baby. I've seen more quilts than one girl should ever have to suffer through. But we're almost done."

"Good. How ready are you for this afternoon?"

"I'm so ready, you can't even believe it," Rebecca said. "All I need to do is change my clothes and then I can tell everybody all about how whiskey saved America from completely falling apart."

Polly laughed. "That's not the whole story."

"I know. I know," Rebecca said with a giggle. "But I am going to start off with that. It will make people laugh and then they will be ready to hear the rest of the story. What are you doing?"

"Well, about that. I found the murderer this morning."

"He was dead, wasn't he?" Rebecca asked, her voice flat.

"Yeah. In his room. And then, I need to go talk to someone about Shawn Wesley and his wife."

"Who's that?"

"The guy who lives down the street. He was over at the house talking to Hayden. I'm pretty sure he was the one who ripped up the kitchen."

"Who are you going to talk to?"

"I just need to figure out if his wife wants him to stay home with her or would be better off with him gone. But if I'm not at the house right away, will you be fine?"

Rebecca gave a quick laugh. "Of course I will. Who do you think you're talking to? Andrew and Kayla will be there with me and so will Hayden. It'll be great."

"Thanks sweetie. You know I'm proud of you, right?"

"You might consider putting that into some sort of monetary format," Rebecca quipped.

"Really? You're tapping me for money because I'm proud of you?"

"Would there be a better time for me to do it?"

Polly laughed and laughed as she hung up the phone. That girl was priceless ... and she was so thankful they'd found each other.

"Hi there, Polly."

She turned toward the front door and smiled at Anita Banks. "Were you doing something terribly important this morning when Deputy Hudson called?"

Anita waggled her fingers at Polly. "It was mani-pedi time. I let the girl finish my fingernails, but Tab owes me a pedicure. I had to walk away from that and my feet are highly annoyed. The worst thing is I usually get to have a couple of days to enjoy my manicures before I destroy these nails on a keyboard. It sounds like I'm about to get all dirty and ugly on some bad guy's laptop."

"How about I'll owe you a manicure," Polly said, walking with Anita toward the addition. "Let me know if I can help you."

Anita watched as two young men carried bags out to their vehicle. "I tell you what. You have a better eye for detail than anyone I know. Maybe you can give me a hand once they're gone and I'm sitting all by myself in a room where a man died."

"I'll bring coffee and muffins," Polly said. "Or donuts. Or scones. Or brownies or cookies or cake or anything you want. I'll bring you a pork tenderloin if that will help."

Anita lit up at the idea of a tenderloin.

"That's what you'd like?" Polly asked.

"Will you have lunch with me? We can dig through his computer."

"Of course I will. I need to run an errand and tell Henry what's going on. Why don't you text me a little after noon and tell me when you'll be ready for me to show up."

"Sounds great," Anita said. "Talk to you later."

CHAPTER TWENTY-NINE

The auditorium was quiet as Polly walked through to her truck. She climbed in and sat there, wondering if she should get this involved. One way or the other Shawn Wesley needed to be dealt with.

No one else needed to know what she was about to do, so she backed out and headed for the Methodist Church. There would still be quite few people around, but if she could find the pastor and take a few minutes of his time, she'd know better what to do next.

She drove into the parking lot and looked around. For the last few days, the pastor had been spending time with the younger kids and hula hoops. Sure enough, he was helping a couple of young kids try to learn how to twist their hips and waist just right. She shook her head at the sight of him with that hoop going round and round. The kids were laughing, he was laughing, and even several parents were enjoying themselves.

Taking a deep breath, she hopped out of the truck and walked toward him. He saw her coming and beckoned a teenager to take his place.

"Ms. Giller, you look as if you want to speak to me. Can I help you?"

Polly nodded and they walked away from the crowd, back into the parking lot.

"I know things have been stressful for you," he said. "Is that what you're here about? I've got a good ear."

"What?" she asked, then she realized that he'd been there the other morning when she found the last victim in the dunk tank. "Oh. No. The murderer has been found. And I'm okay with all of it, I guess. That's not why I'm here. I need to ask you about Shawn Wesley. I know that Pastor Boehm tried to help him and his wife. She was in a bible study here at the church?"

He nodded. "Yes. She still is. We don't see much of Shawn. Not nearly as much as she'd like."

Polly stopped and turned to face him. "He broke into the house we're remodeling and ripped out copper pipe for money. Not just once, but twice. Now the thing is, he actually helped us. We were going to take it out anyway and we were going to destroy those walls, but it's still vandalism."

"I see."

"No, I'm not making myself clear," Polly continued. "I need to know what to do. What would be best for his family. I know this is just plain nosy of me, but I don't want to make things worse for his wife if I don't have to and I don't know who else to ask."

"They don't have many friends in town." He shook his head. "There isn't any family around here either."

"We called Chief Wallers to come out, so there are a couple of police reports already. He's the one who told me that the Wesleys live just down the street. I had an encounter with Shawn a couple of years ago. It didn't go well. Do I ask Ken to arrest Shawn? He pretty much admitted to my adopted son this morning that he did it."

"What do you want to do?"

"Having him arrested isn't the most important thing to me," Polly said. "What I want to know is which would be easier for his wife. Is it harder on her when he's gone or not? If I thought I could help him out by giving him a job, I'd do that. But I tried it once and he simply refused to work. I asked him to keep an eye on my house because there'd been a couple of nights of vandalism. Nothing has happened since then. His wife denied that he'd done it. She was pretty angry with me. But this morning he stopped in at the house and tried to talk Hayden out of more money to keep an eye on the place."

The pastor took Polly's arm and led her away from a car that had pulled in to park. "I appreciate where your heart is, Ms. Giller, but I don't have good advice. At least not easy advice. Mrs. Wesley will not see her husband for who he is, so putting him in jail or leaving him at home will make no difference to her."

"Does he help her?" Polly asked.

"When he can."

Polly ran her hand through her hair in frustration. "Okay," she said. "Thank you. I probably just needed to hear someone tell me that I can't rescue this guy no matter what."

He smiled. "It never hurts to try. Who knows? Maybe all of the seeds that have been planted over the years will find their fruit in what you do."

"Then I'm just going to let this be for now. If something else comes up, I'll talk to Chief Wallers. I'm sorry to have bothered you. You looked like you were having fun."

He smiled again. "I'm not too old yet, but the day is soon coming. And it was no bother. If there's anything else I can do for you, please feel free to ask."

Polly shook his hand and watched him walk away. She had no better idea of what to do, but now she wanted to talk to Henry. This had been a long morning. That would teach her to wake up thinking that she had a lazy Saturday in front of her.

~~~

"Hello Polly-Dolly," Henry said. He stood up and walked across the lot to give her a hug.

"Hi. How are things going here?"

"We're wrapping up pretty soon." He tucked her hand in his arm and they walked. "So I heard a rumor."

"About a dead murderer at Sycamore House?"

"You found him?"

"In his room. Dead. Suicide. And he left me a message." Polly felt her anger seething inside again, wanting to rise to the surface. "He wants to out me, and thinks that it's my responsibility to help people all over the world find their dead loved ones. That I should be using my gift. He's releasing his research to news agencies and other researchers on Monday."

"It's not going to be that bad," Henry said after swallowing a few times. "We can get through this."

"Uh huh," she said. "Just a *few* little rumors about me brought a psychopath to town. He killed five people to test his theory that I would find their bodies. If any more of this gets out because of what he's done, if I have to be interviewed by reporters or if people in town start responding to interviews, what then? Is everyone in Bellingwood going to sell my story for a quick buck? Will Forty-Eight Hours show up to do a freakin' documentary on me?"

Henry pulled her in tight. As he wrapped his arms around her, he whispered into her ear. "That's not going to happen. You're safe here."

"No I'm not," she whimpered. "Nobody is if this gets out. The only safe thing is for us to sell everything and move."

"Are you going to move all of your friends? How will you leave Lydia and Beryl, Andy and Sylvie? What about Mark and Sal? Can you leave them? What about my family and Jessie and Jeff and Stephanie? Or Joss and Nate and their kids. Are you ready to leave them? Or Doug and Billy or Jason and Andrew and Kayla. Can you walk away from them? Will you make Hayden give up grad school and come with us?"

She hated it when he got pragmatic. "I know I'm being ridiculous, but it scares me to death. I don't want to disrupt everybody I love just because I happen to find a dead body once in a while."

"This will be okay," he said. "I'm fully confident that we'll figure it out."

"You'd better be fully confident that Anita Banks figures it out. She's at Sycamore House right now tearing into his computer to discover where he's put all of these so-called research files." She shook her head. "I just can't believe that he gave us time to look for it. Why didn't he send them before he killed himself?"

"Why did he kill himself?" Henry asked.

"Because he felt guilty for murdering those innocent people."

"Maybe deep down he knew that it was wrong to expose you."

"I suppose. It seems stupid though."

Henry chuckled. "One thing I've learned these last few years is that criminals aren't the brightest that humanity has to offer."

Polly's phone buzzed again and she took it out. "It's Anita. I'm going to pick up lunch and take it back to Sycamore House. She says I can maybe help her if things are tricky."

He nodded and Polly answered the phone.

"What did you find, Anita? Anything?"

"Oh I found everything, Polly. You can stop worrying. He had emails scheduled to go out to about seventy-five different people on Monday morning. I've been through his entire computer and found all of the files. He'd posted videos and documentation - what he called his research - in a cloud file on Amazon of all places. The emails have a link for those who want to access it."

"No other cloud location?" Polly wasn't yet prepared to claim the relief that was starting to well up inside her.

"He had a couple of other sites, but there was nothing in them that referred to you and he hadn't communicated with anyone else about what he'd done. Stu and Tab think that he wanted to make sure he was long dead before anyone got the files. That way he wouldn't be punished for what he'd done. The emails are filled with apologetic words about the manner of his research. He was feeling terribly guilty."

"So it's over? The information isn't going to be released?"

"No," Anita said. "And with him dead, there won't be a trial. We'll just close the case file. You're in the clear, honey."

Polly gripped Henry's hand as tears of relief flowed down her cheeks. "I can't believe that you and I aren't going to be stuck in a small dark room, hacking his computer right up to zero hour Monday morning. Isn't that the way it's usually done?"

"I don't make enough money for those types of shenanigans," Anita said. "Here, Tab wants to talk to you."

"Ms. Giller?"

"You can't call me Polly by now?"

"Okay. Polly. While Anita was going through his computer, we also found a journal. He *was* here in Bellingwood last fall. He writes of his encounter with you and how frustrating it was that you denied your talent. It was then that he put plans in motion to out you. He thought he was doing the world a favor. But I wanted you to know that. I think you can put this behind you now."

"Thank you, Deputy Hudson," Polly said.

"You can't call me Tab by now?" the young woman echoed.

"Okay. Tab. Thank you. I was just telling Henry that I was afraid ..." Polly stopped. "No. It's over. I'm not going to be afraid. Thank you for all your help. Are you staying in town or heading for Boone?"

"We're out of here. Thank you for coffee this morning. I'm glad you introduced me to that little shop."

"Someday I'll take you to lunch at Joe's Diner," Polly said. "Is Anita leaving, too?"

"I believe so. She needs to wrap things up at the office so she can have the rest of the weekend. We'll come have lunch with you one of these days."

Polly took a deep breath and relaxed after she put her phone away. "It's over," she said. "Just like that. It's over. Anita found the emails and the website where he kept whatever documentation he'd gathered. I don't have to think about it anymore. There won't be a trial since he killed himself. There won't be anything that points to me and my stupid gift."

Henry kissed her cheek. "It's a wonderful gift and I'm angry that he made you look at it any differently than you should. Do you want to make out in my T-Bird for a while?"

"No. It's too small. But I have my truck. We could go make out in the back seat. It's a nice back seat."

~~~

"I'm heading over to the house to make sure everything is ready," Henry said. After the car show, he and Polly had come back to the house for lunch. As much as she wanted a pork tenderloin, the restaurants in Bellingwood were all still busy. She could wait until next week.

"That's great. I'm heading downstairs to see if they need me. I'm sure Jeff has everything covered, but after the morning's excitement ..." Polly let the sentence drift away. While she made sandwiches, Henry took the dogs out. She made up a bag full of extra sandwiches for Hayden and the kids at the Bell House.

They went down the back stairs together and she walked with him to the garage. "What are we going to do when things go back to normal and it's quiet around here again?" he asked.

"You live with me," Polly said, reaching up to kiss him. "Normal is for the birds."

"I always forget. See you after a while?"

Polly nodded. "I'll ride over with Heath so I don't bring another vehicle."

She watched him drive away and went back into the kitchen. "How are things going?" she asked Rachel.

"Good. We'll be ready."

The General Store uptown had brought over containers of several flavors of their ice cream, and Rachel and her crew had been making vanilla ice cream since yesterday. Machines were still churning away and Cyrus was prepared to bring more from the store if they ran out. No one was really sure how many visitors were still in Bellingwood. The ice cream social and a quick tour of the underground tunnel and room at the Bell House were the last events on the schedule. Churches were holding their annual combined outdoor service tomorrow morning, but otherwise, the weekend was winding down.

Plates filled with pie, cake, brownies and cookies were stacked on trays and hundreds of plastic utensils were already wrapped in napkins. They were ready.

"You don't need me for anything?" Polly asked.

Rachel smiled. "I think you've had enough for today.

"I'm okay," Polly said with a shrug. "I'm just glad it's over."

"Do you ever feel like there was all of that windup and then nothing?" Rachel asked.

"What do you mean?"

Rachel moved closer to her and lowered her voice. "He killed those people and I know I was worried about who would be next. I worried about you because he was focused on you. In my head I built the killer up like some criminal mastermind and then he's just some poor, misguided murderer who wasn't even courageous enough to face what he'd done."

"Kind of like those mass killings we always read about," Polly said. "The killers are nothing more than cowards. They want to get attention, but they don't want to take responsibility for their actions so they kill themselves before they're caught. They scream and taunt and make everyone scared and then poof, it's over and they're gone." She shook her head. "The weird thing is, they want all of that attention, but for the most part, the names we remember are those who lived long enough to go to jail and trial. The victims remember the killer's name, but the rest of the world forgets them. And maybe that's as it should be." Polly sighed. "The thing is, this guy killed people who had very few connections to the world. In twenty years, nobody will remember them or him."

"You will," Rachel said.

Polly nodded. "Yes I will." She turned slowly to look at Rachel. "You just gave me an idea."

"What?"

"Another garden."

Rachel chuckled. "You don't do gardens."

"Okay," Polly said with a grin. "You got me there. But something beautiful that commemorates the lives of the people I've found."

"You could do a fountain and maybe put their names in bricks around it," Rachel said. "Or even one of those spray grounds or splash pads or whatever they're called. Where kids play in the water fountains that spurt out of the ground."

Polly grabbed her arm. "Kids? Water? Memories? Oh Rachel, that's it. What a great idea. Now where will I put it?"

"There's that vacant lot downtown. You know, where the old shoe store burned down? It's a mess right now, but if you bought it and put something like this in there, it would really clean that area up." Rachel was getting excited at the thought.

"I didn't know what had been in there," Polly said. "I didn't even know that a building burned out of there. It's been empty as long as I've lived in Bellingwood."

"It burned down before we got here," Rachel said. "Like in the seventies or something is what I heard."

Polly pulled Rachel into a hug. "You've given me the best idea ever. Thank you."

"I always wanted to do something with that lot," Rachel said. "When I was in junior high, I thought it would be fun to put a park in there. But Mom reminded me that we had a lot of parks around town. Then I wanted to get one of those food trucks and sell tacos. Put picnic tables out for people and feed them. When I got older I thought it would be great for a hot dog stand in the summer. Or maybe even a coffee stand."

"You dream about being an entrepreneur, don't you?" Polly asked.

Rachel nodded. "I guess. I like what I'm doing right now, though. Sylvie gives me a lot of freedom with the catering. She's always around to back me up. It's almost like it's my own business, but I don't have to worry about paying the bills." She gave her head a quick shake. "That's not true. I have to make sure everything works out before I give it to Kristen or Stephanie, but at least I don't fret about running out of money or going out of business."

"And that's the right thing," Polly said. "You let us worry about that and enjoy your job."

"I do. Thank you for believing in me."

Polly looked up when Jeff came into the kitchen. "Are we ready?" he asked.

Rachel nodded. "We're ready. Are you?"

"That's my girl," he said with a smile. "All I have to do is open the doors. Everything is good to go. What are you doing here, Polly?"

"Just checking to see if you needed anything. I'll ride over on one of Heath's early shuttles."

"We're at the half hour mark, girls," Jeff said. "Time to set everything out."

Rachel grinned at Polly. "We've got it, Jeff. No problem." She pushed the tall pan rack filled with plates of desserts to the front door of the kitchen where one of her helpers took it and headed into the auditorium.

A second helper pushed the second rack into place beside the serving counter and set a variety of plates out. Baskets of wrapped plastic-ware were ready to replace the two on the counter and stacks of paper bowls were set out beside trays with buckets of water and ice cream scoops.

Jeff smiled at Polly and she laughed at him. She would always be thankful for what he did."

CHAPTER THIRTY

Yawning as she came awake early Saturday morning, Polly felt a sense of dread. It took a moment to realize what it was. A full week had passed since Bellingwood Days and during these last two weeks, Noah and Elijah had become part of the family. She couldn't imagine letting them go.

Last night, the whole family stayed in. They were up late, just as they had been nearly every night this week. She didn't care. The only important thing was that they had fun together.

Rebecca wanted to play Twister, so they'd cleared a space in the living room, pushing chairs and sofas against the wall. They spun the wheel and twisted their bodies into unnatural poses, generally ending up in a heap of laughter. It didn't even matter who won, but little Elijah generally did. Noah sat with Henry, watching and laughing, spinning the wheel and yelling as loud as anyone.

When they'd had enough of that, Polly popped more popcorn and took out more bags of M&Ms while they played board games at the dining room table. There was more laughter and it was all Polly could do to not think about today.

The week had been filled with day trips and excursions. On Monday, she and Noah went to see the orthopedist and the little boy was declared fit for whatever came his way. She rented a big van on Tuesday and took Andrew, Jason, Kayla, Elijah, Noah, Heath and Hayden, along with Marie, Molly and Jessie over to the Grotto in West Bend. They'd gone to Story City Wednesday morning to ride the carousel and down to the Boone & Scenic Valley Railroad on Thursday for a train ride. Since everyone was pretty well exhausted by Friday, they'd made a short trip down to Woodward to see cows and eat ice cream at a dairy farm and creamery. She hoped that the boys would remember their two weeks in Bellingwood. Somehow Polly had managed to keep the talk of murder and death away from them, a much more difficult task earlier in the week when the rest of her family wanted to hear what she'd been through.

"You're thinking again," Henry said. He wrapped an arm around her and snuggled in close.

"I'm going to miss those little boys," Polly said.

"You know they're going to be okay, right? Roy will make sure of that."

"I know." Polly turned so she could face him. "But I'm going to miss them. It's weird to think that after all we've done together, I might never see them again. Did we make a difference in their lives by spending these two weeks with them?"

"Is that what matters?" he asked.

"Of course it does."

"You're making too much of it. We gave them these two weeks. That will always be part of their memories. For the rest of their lives they'll know there is a family in Iowa who cared for them. Even if it was a short visit. That's the only difference they need to take away from this."

"You're right. I hope Elijah can have a dog. You know, I'm sure that's who helped him sleep better. And maybe I should tell them about the walls of the sofa. I think that helped too. Would it be weird if I wrote his new family a letter telling them all that I learned about him? And about how Noah watches out for his little brother, even if he doesn't say much? And how he loves so easily? And even how once he feels safe, he completely relaxes?"

She patted Henry's chest. "And how much Elijah likes popcorn and hot dogs and that they both fell in love with corn on the cob. Good heavens, Henry, I can't believe how much of that we've had this week. The boys would eat it for every meal if I let them."

"You let them a lot," Henry said. "Not that I'm complaining, but I can be done with sweet corn for a while."

Polly chuckled. "Until next week. Doesn't it sound good? Sweet corn with butter and a bit of salt? Fresh tomatoes with a grilled hamburger and some cottage cheese? How is that not a perfect meal?"

He kissed her forehead. "Of course it is. Okay, I'm getting up. I'll take the dogs out while you get ready. What are we doing for breakfast?"

"The boys' favorite. Pancakes. And bacon and sausage and more pancakes."

"Great." He kissed her again and headed for the bathroom. Polly heard the shower turn on. Han and Obiwan came in from the living room, pushing the door open. They went into the bathroom to help Henry. The dogs had learned that when Henry got up in the morning, it wasn't long before they were taken outside so they waited as close to him as possible.

After he left, she took a quick shower and then headed for the kitchen. The boys were still sound asleep. It always surprised her that they could sleep so hard in the morning when Henry, Hayden, and Heath got up to leave the house.

"Can I help?" Hayden asked, causing Polly to jump. She managed to not drop the egg shell into the pancake batter, but egg was all over her hand.

"Good morning," she said. "Sure. Do you want to do the bacon?"

He opened the refrigerator and took out a pound of bacon, then went over to the peninsula to unwrap it and prepare it for the oven. "Those little guys are going to leave a hole."

"I know," Polly said. "I'd forgotten how much fun it is to see things through the eyes of a seven-year-old. When I first met Andrew, he was only nine. Everything fascinated him and he wasn't afraid to talk about it to anyone."

Heath came into the dining room, rubbing his eyes and looking generally disheveled. "We were up late last night," he said.

"Yeah, buddy. All that drinking and carousing." Hayden said "Heads up!" and tossed an apple at his brother.

"This is breakfast?" Heath asked.

"Yep. Everyone else gets pancakes and bacon, but since you were doing all of that carousing, you get fruit." When Polly reached up for a mug, she realized that no one had turned the coffee pot on. She moaned and flipped the switch. It would only take a few minutes. She repeated that to herself. "It will only take a few minutes."

"I'm getting you a full-fledged coffee system for Christmas," Hayden said. "You can program it the night before and never run into this."

Polly sidled up to him and smiled. "You'll have to program it for me *and* make sure it always has coffee and water in it. Otherwise, it will be as useless as this one."

"You're the one who's useless," he said with a laugh.

"Every bit of that," Henry said coming in with the dogs. He rubbed his hand down Heath's back. "You're looking a little rough this morning."

"I keep trying to tell them that you kept me up too late last night."

"Whiner." Hayden picked up another apple and tossed it at his brother.

Henry grabbed it out of the air. "Do you need extra fiber in your diet?" he asked Heath.

"I don't know why he's throwing these at me. I'm barely functioning."

Hayden leaned over Polly. "You're making Mickey Mouse pancakes?"

"It's the only thing I've got in my repertoire. And I'm just practicing right now. Can you do better?"

"I wasn't saying anything bad," he protested. "I was just making a comment."

"Uh huh. You're picking on your brother and now you're picking on me. I see how it's going to be."

He gave her a quick hug and slipped the bacon into the oven.

"Alright everybody," Henry said, loud enough to wake the dead. "It's time to get up. We're going to have a morning with these boys before they head home. Up, up, up!"

Polly looked at him in shock. "What are you doing?"

"I'm spending the morning with my family. They don't get to sleep it away. They can sleep tonight."

"You might want to knock on Rebecca's door, then. Otherwise, she'll just ignore you."

"Ignore me? Hah! There will be no ignoring me." Henry left the dining room and she heard him talking to the little boys, then a loud rapping on the door frame of Rebecca's room. "Up, up, up, little miss. If you aren't dressed and out here in ten minutes or less, I'm opening the door and using the closest squirt gun I can find."

When he came back into the dining room, he had slung Noah into his arms.

Elijah yawned as he followed Henry. "Can I have some coffee?" Elijah asked.

Polly laughed. "No, little man, you can't. But I'm sure Heath would be glad to pour you a glass of juice or milk. Right, Heath?"

He nodded, though he'd been staring at Henry since the man seemed to have lost his mind.

"Do you have grape juice?" Elijah asked.

"I don't know," Polly said. She turned to Heath. "Do we?"

He shrugged and Polly pointed to the freezer. "Time to make the juice," she said.

"You two are weird this morning," Heath said to her.

"You bet we are. Here's the deal. When you get old like us, you quit worrying about whether or not you're weird. You just accept what you've got. And oh, by the way, your kids have to accept it too. Lucky you. Now find out what Noah wants to drink."

"Noah, do you want grape juice, too?" Heath asked, pulling the frozen can out of the freezer door.

Behind him, Polly shook her head at Noah and mouthed the word 'strawberry' at him.

The little boy looked up at Hayden and asked, "What'd she say?"

Polly laughed until she snorted and said out loud, "Strawberry."

"Yeah. That's what I want," Noah said. "Strawberry."

Heath spun and took in Polly's face. "You're mean."

"I know. It's what I do." She opened the cupboard and pulled down two pitchers. "Make 'em both up. We'll drink it."

"What in the actual world?" Rebecca asked when she came into the dining room. She'd done her best to pat her hair down, but had not looked in a mirror.

"That's the second time this week I've heard that phrase," Polly said. "I like it."

"Why am I up so early?"

Henry patted at Rebecca's hair and then laughed. "Because we're having family time this morning. I don't want to miss a minute of it."

"Didn't we have enough last night? I'm tired."

"You'll live." He planted a kiss on the top of her forehead and gave her a little push toward a chair. "Sit. Heath is making juice."

"Do we have raspberry?" Rebecca asked.

Polly laughed again and opened the cupboard for a third pitcher. "Why of course we do. Heath?"

"You're kidding me," he said.

"Nope. It doesn't sound like it," Polly retorted.

"Rebecca, don't you want strawberry or grape?"

"Raspberry?" she asked again, this time with a wicked grin.

"You're having juice," he muttered. "*You're* having juice. The whole crazy place is having juice."

Polly put two plates on the peninsula, both with Mickey Mouse pancakes on them. "While you're over there, Heath, could you get out the syrup?"

He looked up at her as he ripped the top away from the raspberry juice concentrate. "I'm a little busy here."

"Oh," she said. "Busy, are you? Well, okay, then. I'll do it." She stepped in front of him, then used her elbows to push him out of the way. When he didn't move, she threw her whole body into it. "Oh, sorry. It's right there on the bottom shelf. I guess I wasn't paying attention."

"You are so weird," he said.

Polly kissed his forehead. "Yep. Always will be." She slid the jug of syrup across the countertop to Henry's waiting hands and went back to the stove top. "Hayden, since your brother is so busy, would you mind pulling plates and silverware? Rebecca, check the pantry for more napkins."

~~~

After breakfast, they helped Noah and Elijah pack their things into matching backpacks that Polly had purchased for them. She'd had their names embroidered on the front so the boys could tell them apart. They'd acquired enough things these last two weeks that she also found a couple of tote bags they could carry with them.

Polly had done her best to keep her purchases to a minimum and was proud that she'd managed to contain it to two bags. Each of the boys from Chicago had been given a Sycamore House t-shirt to wear home today, and after their showers, Noah and Elijah proudly wore theirs.

Noah was doing great with his crutches. For the last few days he'd practiced going up and down the stairs by himself.

"Miss Polly?" Elijah said. "Could you come here?"

She walked out of the kitchen and found the two boys sitting on the sofa with enough space between them for her to sit. "What's up?" she asked, taking the seat offered. She leaned back enough to put her arms around them.

"We made you something," Noah whispered.

"Well, we didn't make it, but it's from us," Elijah corrected. He put a package on her lap. The boys had wrapped it using lots of tape and folds in the paper.

Her eyes filled and she couldn't speak.

"Don't cry," Elijah said. "It's a nice present."

"Oh honey." Polly pulled him close as the tears streamed down her face. She tugged Noah closer to her. "I'm sure it is. I've fallen in love with the two of you and it's going to be hard to say good-bye. But I know you're going to a nice home with wonderful people who want to love you. And you two are so lovable." She collected herself enough to sit forward and pick up the package. "Shall I just rip it open?"

He nodded and both boys watched her every movement. Polly carefully pulled back tape, trying to extend the moment as long as possible.

"Just open it," Elijah said, reaching in to rip back a piece of the paper.

"Okay. Got it." Polly kissed his head and ripped the paper off. The frame was upside down and she turned it over and whatever she'd done to collect herself was useless. Tears streamed down and she realized that she was about to do some ugly crying. Through the sobs and choking, she hugged and kissed both of the boys again, then smiled up at Rebecca.

Polly recognized Rebecca's work. She had done a pencil sketch of Noah and Elijah hugging each other from a picture Polly took at the carnival. The two boys were waiting for the Ferris wheel to start up. It was their first time and both had been so excited they could barely contain themselves. Polly managed to get them to pose for a quick picture before the ride took them away. They had waved and shouted, then when they rose up over the tree line, their faces both turned to awe as they looked out over Bellingwood. She watched them point at Sycamore House and then crane their heads to see what else they could find. The moment had been a wonderful memory.

"Thank you," she said. "This is perfect. I can't wait to hang it up."

"Where will you put it?" Elijah asked.

"I could put it in my bedroom," she responded. "Or maybe in the dining room near the clock. What do you think?" Polly turned to Noah.

"Dining room. Then you can see our picture when you eat."

That brought more tears. When Polly finally looked up, not a person in her family was dry-eyed. "Then that's where we'll hang it. Do you want to help Henry do it right now?"

"Can we?"

"Of course. We still have time before we need to be downstairs. Go ahead."

Henry stood and swung Noah up into his arms again. "My picture hanging stuff is in the office. Let's go."

Rebecca slid into the seat beside Polly and took her hand. "Are you going to be okay?"

"I don't want them to leave," Polly said through more tears. "I'm being a ninny, but I feel like they're my boys."

"They will always know how much you love them," Hayden said. "That's more than can be said for a lot of kids."

"I know," she replied. "You're right. They're going to have a great life and tomorrow I'll wake up and start living without them here. It will be okay." She squeezed Rebecca's hand. "And besides, I have the three of you here to make me crazy, right? You'll just have to put up with all of this extra love I've built up."

"We'll suffer for the cause," Rebecca said. "Are you going to make it through this whole thing downstairs?"

"They usually just hug everybody and go away," Polly replied. "I'm so glad Roy doesn't do some kind of big ceremonial good-bye or I'd be a wreck."

"Maybe you'll get it all out right now."

"Yeah. Maybe."

Henry plopped Noah on the table in front of where he was hanging the sketch and pulled a chair out so Elijah could climb up beside him. He put his hand out and Noah handed him the molly and nail that would go in the wall. When it was ready, he took the sketch from Elijah and put it into place. "How's that?" he asked, pushing the left corner up a smidge. "Polly?"

"It's perfect." She put her arm around Rebecca's shoulder. "You make such amazing gifts. Thank you."

"It was the boys' idea. They kept you busy while I worked in secret."

"That's what that was," Polly said. "I wondered why you were gone so much."

"Yeah. We were a di-ver-sion," Elijah said, sounding out the bigger word.

"And a very good one you were." Polly saw that it was time for them to head downstairs. "We should get going."

They went down the back steps and Polly waited above while Noah negotiated his way. Through the auditorium to the main hallway, she kept an eye on him, now confident that he had this. When they opened the door, she smiled at all of the kids in their Sycamore House shirts. All different colors, all fresh and new.

Roy Dunston finally had to tell the boys to go outside and load up the van. It was packed a little tighter than it had been for the trip to Bellingwood, but everyone fit. Noah took the front seat because of his crutches and Elijah sat right behind him, bouncing on the seat in his excitement.

Polly kissed their heads one more time, doing her best to hold back tears, but felt like she was failing. "I love you," she said to each of them. "I hope you have a great year in school and remember, you can write letters to me. Mr. Dunston has my address."

"I'll write you," Noah said. "I promise."

"Tell me everything. Okay?"

He nodded and a tear dropped to his cheek. Polly brushed it away and then stepped back, closing the door. Roy shook her hand and then he and Henry hugged each other before he closed the back door of the van and walked around to the driver's seat. Within minutes the van pulled out and was gone. Polly finally stopped waving and took a deep breath.

"Well, now what?" she asked.

The other families had all gone to their cars and driven off, leaving hers standing in front of Sycamore House.

"We should go over to the other house," Hayden said, finally breaking the silence. "There's still plenty to do."

"Can you give me a ride up to Beryl's?" Rebecca asked. "She told me to come over when we were done here."

The three kids went inside and Polly looked up at Henry. "I feel like my heart just broke in half and then everything snapped back to normal."

"That's really the way of it, isn't it? What should we do?"

"I don't want to go upstairs just to sit and mope." She brightened. "Let's go for a ride. Maybe we'll find a dive along the way that serves the best pork tenderloins around."

"Do you have someplace in mind?"

"You drive and I'll look for something online. Can we take the dogs?"

"Absolutely."

Polly looked down the highway one more time, took a deep cleansing breath, and reached out to take her husband's hand as they went inside and up the stairs.

THANK YOU FOR READING!

I'm so glad you enjoy these stories about Polly Giller and her friends. There are many ways to stay in touch with Diane and the Bellingwood community.

You can find more details about Sycamore House and Bellingwood at the website: http://nammynools.com/

Join the Bellingwood Facebook page:
https://www.facebook.com/pollygiller
for news about upcoming books, conversations while I'm writing and you're reading, and a continued look at life in a small town.

Diane Greenwood Muir's Amazon Author Page is a great place to watch for new releases.

Follow Diane on Twitter at twitter.com/nammynools for regular updates and notifications.

Recipes and decorating ideas found in the books can often be found on Pinterest at: http://pinterest.com/nammynools/

And, if you are looking for Sycamore House swag, check out Polly's CafePress store: http://www.cafepress.com/sycamorehouse